Beirut
in
Shades
of Grey

Beirut in Shades of Grey

Dana Kamal Mills

Ameera Publishing
Los Angeles, California, USA

Calligraphy by Julien Breton, Nantes, France, www.kaalam.com

Book and cover design and editing services by The Man Upstairs

Publisher's Cataloging-In-Publication Data
(Prepared by The Donohue Group, Inc.)

Mills, Dana Kamal.
    Beirut in shades of grey / Dana Kamal Mills.
    p. ; cm.
    ISBN: 978-0-9715451-7-5

1. Lebanon--History--Civil War, 1975-1990--Fiction. 2. Photojournalists--Lebanon--Fiction. 3. Hostages--Lebanon--Fiction. 4. Women and war--Lebanon-Fiction. 5. War stories. 6. Love stories. I. Title.

PS3613.I566 B45 2007

813.6   2007923976

For

Dad and Mammina, who gave us life . . .
time and again

◆

Acknowledgments

My thanks go to all those ever-present in the gestation period of this work. To my husband, for his encouragement and untiring pep talks. My children who, by their constant demands and affection, remind me of my blissful reality. Thank you for being as proud of your Lebanese heritage as I am. My brothers, who make me look back on our war years together with some nostalgia. It was too brief a time that we shared as a family before events landed us on different continents.

My gratitude to The Man Upstairs for making endless corrections with good humour, and for pandering to my incessant requests. And NaSh, as always, editor extraordinaire.

Finally to loved ones who are no longer with us, each of you a perpetual flame of inspiration.

La Beauté

Chapter One
Beirut - November 1981

◆

The taxi skidded on the wet road as the driver rammed the gas pedal down to the floor. Bursts of machine-gun fire shot out like thunderclaps from the Jeep close on its tail. Its driver leaned on the horn. "He's going to hit us!" Rasha shrieked. The persistent honking and rat-tat-tat sent her heart racing. Her knuckles blanched on the door handle. She sank low in the back seat pleading with the taxi driver to get out of the Jeep's way. They were trapped in an alley. Parked cars choked it on either side. The driver saw an opening and rode the battered Mercedes over the curb. The car bucked and bounced. The exhaust pipe came loose with a rattle. The pile of books next to her flew off the seat and scattered on the floor of the car. Rasha was flung sideways, but she held on tight to the door handle. She felt her shoulder snap. A searing pain darted down her arm. The Jeep screamed past them. Wild-eyed militiamen clung to its sides, the butts of their Kalashnikovs wedged against their hips, firing, firing. Among them Rasha saw a boy, face too young to shave, standing legs apart in the back of the Jeep, machine gun blazing, smiling with all his teeth.

Even when they were in the clear, Rasha's pulse pounded, almost audibly, in her neck.

The driver looked at her in the rear-view mirror: "Are you okay, miss?"

She nodded, the words caught in her throat. Her eyes locked with his. Five minutes ago they were total strangers. Now they had shared a brush with death.

The short route home from the university was an interminable labyrinth of blind corners and stretches of ashen streets. Rasha did not move a muscle, seized by the prolonged aftermath of a chilling incident that had lasted a few minutes at the most. The ringing in her ears; the caustic smell of fear that burned her nostrils; a distorted perception that made familiar surroundings unrecognizable and hostile; all sapped her of what little resilience she had left. Rasha could've sworn she had held her breath from the second the first volley of shots rang out to the moment the taxi pulled into the parking lot of her building.

Fingers trembling, she fished out the fare from her wallet. She tipped the driver generously, in effect putting a value on her life of no more than a few liras.

"God be with you," he said, reaching over to open the door for her.

She stepped out into the twilight. Wobbly legs somehow carried her into the building and up four flights of stairs to the apartment. Trying hard to steady her hand, it took a couple of attempts before she managed to fit the key into the keyhole. Her mouth was dry as chalk but the urgency to take refuge in her room stopped her from going into the kitchen where her mother would be preparing dinner with Umm Samir the housekeeper.

She had rounded the corner to the passage and made it halfway to her bedroom when her father's voice boomed from the family lounge.

"Rasha!"

"Yes, Baba." Reluctantly, she backtracked and stood in the doorway.

"You're late." He sat in his *'abaya*, the newspaper splayed before him in the faint light of a battery lamp set on low.

"I'm sorry, I had a faculty meeting. Mama knew about it." She leaned against the doorjamb, her legs about to give way, the books digging into the crook of her arm.

Amin glanced at the grandfather clock as it chimed once. "It's five-thirty," he said flatly.

"A few teachers were running late. I couldn't phone to let you know. The lines were down because of the power failure."

He scrutinized her over the rim of half-moons. "What's the matter? You look pale."

"Just tired. I still have papers to grade so if that'll be all Baba . . ."

A brisk nod before he returned to his newspaper.

Rasha raced to her bedroom and shut the door behind her. She threw her handbag and files on the bed. Her arms were numb, as if disjointed from the rest of her body. Nausea welled up in her throat. Her legs finally buckling underneath her, she collapsed on the edge of the bed, rested her head in cupped hands and wept.

The tears eased her shock and lingering terror. But there was work to do. Harrowing, life-threatening incidents were commonplace in war-torn Beirut, too frequent to dwell on. Another deadly day in the Paris of the Middle East was coming to a close.

Depleted, she willed herself to her feet, retrieved the file of essays and made her way to the desk. She slumped in the chair, her head dead weight against a tight fist. But the letters danced on the page, and the dismal light shed by the battery lamp on the English 201 essay did nothing if not add to her despair. The pen she held in her free hand swept across the paper of its own volition, mechanically.

"It was a great trajedy." She crossed out the "j" in thick red, scribbled a "g" and the editorial symbol for "insert" in the margin—a pointless addition when she knew that its significance would be lost on Youssef, the student in question. Why she constantly engaged in such exercises in futility was beyond her. If she were to tilt her head ever so slightly, she would see it, in sharp focus, right there on her bookcase: a reminder of an ambitious project stifled at birth, physical proof of her limitations. For three years now her proposal to introduce a course on "Islam in English Literature" has been wedged, untouched and discarded, between Gibran Kahlil Gibran's The Prophet and Tolstoy's *War and Peace*.

She had researched and toiled over her idea for months. She had reviewed the objectives and curriculum to ensure the proposal was watertight. She had proofread her final draft until her eyes glazed over. So the day she was called to the dean's office—a day still vivid after three years—she had had every reason to be hopeful.

"Quite a thorough proposal you put together, Rasha." The dean intertwined his fingers over the piece of work, giving her a stiff half-smile. She waited, expressionless.

"But . . ."—*There it was, the blow*— "and despite its merits, faculty members feel that, under the circumstances, it would be unwise to start up any course with a religious content."

"What I'm proposing, sir, is an overview of Islam in a literary sense . . ."

He held out a hand, stopping her in her tracks. "The country's in flames over political and religious issues, Rasha. You cannot bring reason or hairline distinctions to bear here." He removed his glasses and pinched the bridge of his nose. "Besides, and please don't take this as a reflection on your performance so far, your bachelor's degree does not in fact qualify you to teach literature courses. University policy, I'm afraid."

"I'm aware of that, sir." Rasha shifted in her seat as if to displace the stab to her ego. "But since most of the qualified professors have left the country, I thought the university would be prepared to make an exception."

"All the more reason why we should uphold our standards. We cannot allow the war or any goings-on outside this campus to dictate how this university is run. I'm sorry."

For a brief moment, she considered pointing out that the violence and infighting that had gripped the country had in fact repeatedly infiltrated the ancient stone walls of the institution. She could cite countless incidents of student clashes and demonstrations, suspension· of classes due to skirmishes, targeted shelling that claimed the lives of faculty, staff and students. She fought back the urge to debunk his notion, sadly a pervasive one, that integrity was an impregnable bastion against artillery. For the dean's rebuff was all-too-familiar in an atmosphere of contradictions, malevolence and double standards. It was an attitude that had plagued Rasha's life on both the professional and personal levels since the outbreak of the war: the more she challenged the status quo, the more intractable it seemed to become. Those averse to taking up arms, she concluded, could only combat the upheaval in their country by clinging to their high morals in the hope that righteousness would triumph over the forces of evil. It was this belief that condemned Rasha to teaching an introductory and unchallenging course on the English language. That, and the turn of events at home that forced her to obey her father's wishes and give up her dream to pursue a master's degree.

As she leaned back in her chair, her gaze strayed to a year-old picture of Zahra on the pinboard above her desk. There stood her great-aunt between Rasha and her brother Karim at the entrance to their father's childhood home in a small village near Tripoli. Behind them, the fig tree whose purple fruit she and Karim feasted on during their occasional trips to the village. Zahra, diminutive and shrivelled up with age, the shadow of a smile on her face, stared back at her with moist eyes, pips in disappearing sockets. Four months after the picture was taken, her frail little body was found splayed out like a rag doll in a pool of blood on her front porch. Zahra became a statistic of war. The number of villagers who were massacred was too vast for newspapers to list each by name. As crimes of brutality piled on in the war of attrition, the survivors of that raid, once forgotten, were left to grapple with their ghosts unaided, haunted by the lacerating visions of that fateful day.

The muezzin's keening rose against the rumble of mortars in the distance. Rasha stroked the scar across her left eyebrow as was her habit when she got agitated or sank into contemplation. She thought of Paris. The normality of life beyond Lebanon seemed so surreal that any recollection of it filled her with unbearable sadness.

She sauntered up to the window in a trance and pushed the curtain to one side. With a pang of nostalgia, she recalled a time when her desk was strategically positioned against that wall so that, in a moment of reverie, she could let her eyes wander through an animated reel of a bustling neighbourhood across to the cyan expanse of the Mediterranean. At the time, even though she was confined to her room, the activity beyond it would rise and stream in with all its sounds and colours breathing life into her dull existence. They were visceral moments, when she imagined herself to be the young woman decked out in evening dress hailing a taxi, the child behind a low wall hoping not to be discovered in a game of hide-and-seek, one of two lovers communicating with furtive hand gestures across balconies.

Then, one summer afternoon, she had got up to answer the phone just as an ear-splitting explosion sent a spray of glass and shrapnel flying across her desk onto the blue carpet. A close call, one of many during the war, that dissolved her bones to marrow and left a metallic after-taste on her palate. Incidents of the kind underscored the bitter truth that her fate actually lay in the bloodied hands of mortals—that she, like other bystanders, clawed at the ragged edge of survival.

Now, she looked out into the sinister void as darkness eclipsed the city of Beirut. Streets shimmering with streaming headlights were a thing of the past. The pleasant calls of corn sellers and the boisterous exchanges of neighbours dim echoes in her yearning mind. The bustling, exciting capital, a fading memory. What she beheld right then was a chilling tableau of wartime: face-less shadows, thrown up by the flicker of candlelight and battery lamps, scampering in stacked apartments of shredded buildings.

She made her way to the bed and pulled out her handbag from underneath the pile of books and files. Retrieving a key-chain from the side pocket where she kept her ID document and university alumna card, she unlocked the top drawer of her desk and extracted a worn 1976 journal stuffed with loose sheets of paper.

Her first entry, April 11: My twentieth birthday today. Big deal! I'm stuck at home cramming for exams. My friends are planning a party this weekend. There's been talk of holding it in Brummana or at a friend's house in 'Aley. Baba forbids me from going. He says there are explosions and kidnappings everywhere, that it isn't safe.

I know it's just a pretext. He would never permit it, even under the best of circumstances.

30 April 1976: No one seems to know what's going on. Unsuspecting civilians are being pulled out of their cars and shot because of their sectarian denomination. The violence is indiscriminate and unjustified. Personal vendettas are being settled under the cloak of war. Somewhere, every day, there are skirmishes and shelling. We constantly hear of ongoing negotiations that will bring us out of the impasse. We're told that the following Tuesday or Wednesday or weekend will be decisive. Our lives have been turned upside down, literally. We stay up all night when the shelling is at its heaviest, and sleep during the day. It'll be over soon. I'm sure of it.

14 May 1976: I was planning on sneaking out this morning to meet _____, but there was no chance as Baba was home. Since it's become too dangerous for him to cross the Green Line to the factory in East Beirut, he rarely goes anywhere. Lately he's been in a foul mood, well, fouler than usual, and I'd be stupid to stir the pot. Not that I ever really dared. The dark circles around his eyes have gone a deep shade of purple. He barely says a word at table. I feel for him. He'd be devastated, crushed, if he were to lose the juice-bottling business his father had worked so hard to build up. It's mind-blowing that this imaginary dividing line, this Green Line, has sliced this capital in two. Baba has to rely on his Christian manager to look in on the factory and do what he can to keep it running. That is if anything is really left of it after the recent vicious battles. I can imagine how frustrated and helpless he must feel. But I can't stand the fact that he vents his anger by being unpleasant to us.

3 June 1976: The situation has gone from bad to worse. Warnings that medication and food supplies will suffer from the power failure have spread panic throughout the country and people are leaving en masse from the

port. It's the only way out, now that the airport is closed. How did all this chaos start in the first place?

A crack rang out in the street. Rasha jumped. Her heart hammered against her ribcage. A car backfiring. *Basita*, no problem, she heard herself say. *Basita*, that commonest of Arabic words. If only it were true. Trying to steady her hands, she skipped pages.

Undated: The schools have shut down. The country's dying. We have no electricity. Karim, Umm Samir and I haul plastic gallons filled with water up the stairs because the pumps can't operate without power. We've been cut off from the rest of the world since the phone lines went dead. Baba watches over us like a hawk. I feel stifled. There's no question of us leaving. Baba can't give up on the factory. He simply can't afford to.

Sometimes I wonder what shape my life, all our lives really, would've taken had there been no war. I wonder whether Baba would've grown a little more lenient with time. Whether, in the absence of all threat, he would've allowed me more freedom. Unlikely, I guess, when his mentality is steeped in tradition and an antiquated value system. Why can't he understand that I have no intention of challenging his sense of propriety, and that I would never, intentionally at least, put the family name at stake? It would be a different matter if we lived in a conservative country but this is Lebanon, for heaven's sake—a cosmopolitan and broad-minded society. Young women go out, they date, they drive cars and hold important positions in the workplace without necessarily dishonouring their families.

August 1977: Baba called me over today so I prepared myself for a talking-to, not knowing what recrimination he had dug up against me this time. It was worse, much worse. I should've guessed as much by the way Mama sat with her hands clasped between her knees, her head bowed, as she always did when things were beyond her control. In his matter-of-fact way he delivered a decision, *his* decision, that would change my future. I'll have to start teaching at the university at the beginning of the next scholastic year. No chance of me working towards a postgraduate degree. He's already spoken to the English Department and they've agreed to interview me for a post. He's so bloody proud he'll never admit that we're going through a financial crisis, and that he needs my help, as the eldest, to bring in an income. My hopes are shot to hell! I know that we're living in a time of war, and that I should be grateful we're still alive. That other people have it much worse. I cannot help this anger that eats at me. If only he'd broken the news to me with compassion, a little understanding. If he'd begun with "Habibti Rasha, I know you've had your mind set on an MA, but because of the difficulties I've been having with the factory, it won't be possible." Or something along those lines. Anything to sugar-coat a bitter pill.

28 November 1978: It's freezing cold and we have no electricity, so no heating. We wheel the propane heaters from room to room. It's a nightmare. Most of my friends have packed up and left with their families. Our building is practically empty. Baba's adamant that everyone's jumping the gun and everything will be back to normal in no time at all. No one can talk to him, not even Mama. I understand him. I do. He has no choice and probably feels helpless. He never goes out of the house, and leaves us with very little breathing space. Whenever I begin to sympathize with him, he does something that upsets me. The other day, he told me off because he'd heard that I'd been to Uncle Sam's with a classmate, (a boy, *horrors*). "You know the rules" he'd said. Me, Rasha, who's considered old and responsible enough to go out and earn a living to help out with expenses and Karim's schooling? The one who unquestioningly gave up her dreams to obey him and earn his trust. People are drop-

ping around us like flies and *he's* concerned about propriety! Talking about decency, order and sanity. We're living in a state of chaos, loose morals and criminality! Our streets and homes are being overrun by barbarians! And you speak of morals? Let me ask you this Baba, is it *morally* right, is it actually *wise*, to have your family cowering under heavy shelling day in day out? Is it reasonable to expect your daughter to put up with the danger and threat day after day, night after night while depriving her of the little harmless pleasures of life? Is that okay?

She heard the thud of her father's slippered steps outside her door, and made to put her journal away. She waited until they tapered off then turned a few pages.

5 August 1979: The world has forgotten us. We're now just another country at war. That humanity is capable of such atrocities makes me sick. My home was once my prison. Now it's my only refuge in a deadly city. The only route I dare take daily is to the university and back. Still, each time, I dread a "flying roadblock," that latest of perversions: barriers set up by bloodthirsty sociopaths to help them trap, kidnap and kill whomever they deem their enemy. Every car on the way could be booby-trapped. Every day, passers-by are killed in random explosions. On their way to the bakery. Dropping their children off at school. Leaving the mosque or the church.

There's nothing worth fighting for at home any longer. Baba got his way, as usual. I stay within these four walls, not to make him happy but because there's actually nothing worth risking my life for. I feel no joy. I'm dead inside.

September 18, 1980: Today a deep, deep sadness weighs on my heart. We made our first trip to the village since the war broke out. I barely recognized the courtyard and the village centre that were our playgrounds, now full of craters and potholes. Old deserted homes have sprouted weeds in the cracks of their stone walls. People I've known since my childhood looked as if life had been sucked out of them. They were dry with despair. Time had stood still in my mind and I'd retained a mental picture of everyone there as they had been when we last met. Then I saw Baba's uncles and aunts, their faces drawn, their bodies bent with time and lassitude, their eyes dull as charcoal. One by one, they held me tight, shedding tears of gratitude for our survival and of anguish for what we had all become, prisoners and refugees in our own country. As we sat around sipping coffee—which tasted so different, so bitter on that day—they reeled off tragedy after tragedy and horrific acts of violence. Children lost to stray bullets, people maimed by explosions, young men executed by makeshift firing squads, old friends turning against each other because of their new allegiances. I wanted to run out of the room but my body was pure lead. Yet their faith was strong and they were eternally grateful that nothing worse had touched them. When we got up to leave, they clung to us again as if we would never meet again. I cried shamelessly knowing that they could be right. This bloody, cruel, war is ripping us apart. Even if we were to escape with our lives in the end, not one of us will ever be the same.

On the drive home, my eyes steady on the back of Baba's head, I suddenly noticed how grey his hair had gone, how wrinkled his neck had turned, like leather . . . Not long ago, my smaller self had sat in the back seat of the car doing the same, watching him with young eyes. He'd made me feel so safe. One look at him and a strong sense of security would wash over me. Then I could lean my head against the car window and drift off. He was my hero, my anchor. Now, years on, he's the anchor that tugs me back and keeps me under when I so desperately want to move on, to escape the hell our lives have become. I feel my love for him slipping away and I so wish he would help me hold on to it.

She flipped through the pages, rants against her father's conservatism, her lack of freedom and the deteriorating situation in her country. A loose leaf fell to the floor. One of many written while they took cover in the stairwell from the shelling. On those occasions when they had to race for shelter without any forewarning, she would grab a piece of paper and a pen to scribble her feelings or what could very well end up being her dying thoughts. Unspoken words had become her only outlet.

Undated and barely legible: I'd do anything to let this fear let go of my body. I'm paralyzed, terrified. I sit listening for incoming mortars, waiting for them to hit, not knowing whether we'll be the next victims. There's nothing any of us can do. Baba's listening to the radio. Mama's chatting with everybody. Am I such a coward that I can't hold a pen straight? Dear God, please let this be over.

Rasha flinched as a wave of collective cheer roared through the neighbourhood and her room was flooded with a sudden glow of artificial light. A peculiar thrill coursed through her, gradually unravelling the knots in her body. The Israeli bombardment of the Zahrani power plant had entailed severe rationing allowing for only a few hours of electricity a day. Evening light, along with peace, had become a rare source of pleasure, a luxury as fleeting as the countless cease-fires. Rasha switched off the lamp but kept it within reach on her desk.

Blaring television sets and radios replaced the taut silence. The Lebanese prime minister bellowed from the television next door calling for the people to unite in the face of foreign destabilization. Rasha paid no attention to his vapid oratory. Seven years of civil war had taught her that politics and diplomatic negotiations had no bearing on the daily happenings in the country. More telling were fatalities from crossfire, the numbers of injured as they scrambled for the last loaf of bread or litre of petrol, random victims of sadistic snipers and hostages of faceless kidnappers—ironically, events that took up no more than a couple of columns in a newspaper yet spoke volumes of the sad and brutal state to which her country had plunged.

A tap at the bedroom door gave her a start. She slid the journal back into its hiding place, locked the drawer, and reassumed her position at her desk, pen in hand.

"Yes?" she mumbled, head bowed over the exam papers.

The housekeeper peeped into the room. "*Sitt* Rasha, there's a young man for you at the front door." She spoke softly, her voice barely audible as the prime minister's televised speech reached a crescendo.

"Who is it, Umm Samir?"

"He didn't say but I don't think he's been here before."

No doubt one of her brother's friends. "Are you sure it's not Karim he wants?"

"He asked for you Sitt Rasha . . . and he doesn't speak Arabic."

Rasha's blood ran cold. "Where's Baba?"

"Watching the news."

"Did you tell him?"

"No," Umm Samir droned emphatically as if doing so would have been a breach of Rasha's confidence.

Rasha pushed her chair back. "I'll be right there."

She checked herself hastily in the mirror. Her sallow complexion was all the more pallid in winter, the dark rings around amber eyes more pronounced. A speck of red ink stained the bottom edge of her lip where she had been chewing on her pen. She tried to rub it off to no avail.

Racing down the long corridor, she contemplated the possibilities. Whoever the "foreigner" may be, she prayed his presence would not compromise her situation with her parents. Male friends were not always welcome.

With a firm grasp of the brass handle, she pulled the solid door wide open.

Chapter Two
Paris - July 1981

◆

The immigration official at Roissy-Charles-de-Gaulle frowned at the sight of yet another navy-blue passport embossed with the cedar, overtly disgruntled by the influx of Lebanese into his country. Rasha understood full well his indignation. France had been a popular destination for many Lebanese escaping the unrelenting turmoil in their homeland. Some only passed through Paris. Others stayed. In the process, the distinction between refugee and tourist had no doubt become blurred.

She smiled to lighten the tension. The French official's facial muscles contracted. That Parisians tended to be dour and derisive was not news to Rasha. Despite her impeccable French, she had been subjected to their intolerance on a couple of occasions during a pre-war visit with her mother.

Rasha did not dislike the French as a nation. Quite the contrary. Their twenty-three-year mandate over Lebanon until 1943 had brought in diversity and helped groom many Lebanese for life abroad. The mandate's lingering impact extended to her generation which continued to reap the pleasures of a European culture in a Middle Eastern country.

She waited silently. From her experience with "uniform," a classification under which she placed her father, Rasha had learned not to speak until spoken to. While the official leafed through the passport, she let her eyes stray, glimpsing a tearful older woman a short distance from the desk. Clad in black, she tugged nervously at her headscarf. What was visible of her face was furrowed with a web of fine lines and had the quality of parchment. She blotted bleary eyes with a crumpled tissue by lowering her head ever so slightly to a shaking hand. Now and then she made a subtle movement with her wrists as if, with a telling upward glance, she was pleading for divine assistance. Rasha gave her a compassionate smile. The woman strained to smile back, lips tremulous, her face contorted with disquiet and confusion.

Much as she may have wanted to, Rasha was in no position to help. She understood that all passengers on Middle East Airlines, herself included, were looked upon as anomic "people of the war," anarchists who posed a danger in any country where the rule of law still applied.

Reluctantly, Rasha averted her eyes from the shrouded woman to give the official her full attention. She let herself be scrutinized against the younger face pasted on her passport. The glasses were no more, and her hair now stopped at the nape of her neck. She had lost a few kilos, appearing more chiselled than the sixteen-year-old rounded face on the document. The characteristics were basically the same: hair, light brown (also, hennaed at the moment); eyes, hazel (with a black rim); height, 160 (sadly the same), scars, one across the left eyebrow (from a bicycle fall at age eight. Any others since were not visible). The passport did not specify religion, unlike the Lebanese identity cards which figured it prominently and thus became death warrants. In Lebanon, religious persuasion was considered an admission of ideological sympathies.

"*Le but de votre visite?*"

Rasha pouted to realize a near-perfect French accent, "*Ma tante habite à Paris. Je passe mes vacances chez elle.*"

"*Votre visa est bon pour dix jours, mademoiselle,*" he said dryly.

"*Tout à fait monsieur.*"

Having established that the purpose of her trip was purely a visit with her aunt and that it would not exceed the ten-day visa she was given, Rasha retrieved her passport and mouthed a *merci*. But the official had already looked away, scowling at the next person in line. She was not sorry he had not heard her. Gratitude was the last thing she believed she owed men in authority.

Knowing it unwise to loiter once cleared by the immigration official, Rasha moved on, stealing a last glance at the wretched woman. Pleading, rheumy eyes met hers, making Rasha feel abominable. For a split second she contemplated intervening when a gendarme accompanied by a civilian approached the woman in a seeming attempt to resolve the situation. Rasha walked away at a fast pace, eyes downcast, her heart heavy for the elderly woman and her uncertain fate.

The last time Rasha had seen her aunt Hana was two years earlier, in Beirut. Hana had come to stay with her brother Amin and to visit the rest of the family, including her other brother, Salim. Rasha, twenty-three at the time, had been struck by Hana's Parisian style and savoir-faire. Her distinctive almond-shaped eyes beamed from an angular face etched with maturity and intelligence. Imposing self-confidence compensated for her average height, and a raspy voice stopped others' conversations in their tracks. Deep parenthetical lines at the corners of her mouth were testimony to Hana's love for laughter. Rasha recalled how she had groomed herself with incontestable ease, how she tamed a black mane of hair with a couple of brushstrokes. Thick eyeliner highlighted her wide eyes. Jeans and a white blouse with a *foulard* thrown over the shoulders sealed her style with simplicity.

That was precisely the image that now appeared before Rasha. Two years on, Rasha still admired the woman who was to host her during her short stay in Paris. The aunt who, undeterred by her brothers' disapproval, had had the courage to give up security and home and single-handedly set up a future abroad.

Their long and warm hug spoke of painful separation. It communicated the unjust fragmentation of a close family in wartime. Rasha could feel Hana's arms tighten around her as if she hoped to draw, in one dose, on the affection of kith and kin that she had been starved of for so long.

Hana rattled on at the speed of Parisian traffic, though her driving was more halting than her sentences. Her disdain for punctuation aside, Hana's unwavering respect for stop signs was reassuring. Rasha was even more relieved that the journey to Hana's apartment in Saint-Germain bypassed the Champs-Élysées roundabout—an invention reserved strictly for the skilled local drivers. Rasha maintained that she would approach the "circle of death" with one hand on the horn and eyes shut. Pretty much the way she tackled dilemmas in her life— blindly and fearfully—waiting until they blew over.

Barely two hours in her new environment and Rasha was already overwhelmed by the hive of activity around her. The streets teemed with people striding purposefully; cafés spilled over with customers served by frantic and irate waiters; voices rose amicably or irascibly. Motorists ploughed on with little regard for pedestrians. Parisians' lives interlaced and unravelled within the throbbing pulses of their mother city. Living here suddenly struck Rasha as too exigent, requiring a level of energy that she doubted she possessed. She struggled to assimilate the normality and the mad scramble that clouded her vision as her head reeled from an onslaught by life itself, so impossibly normal, so unbearably right.

The only available parking space drew Hana's Renault 5 like a magnet, across two lanes of heavy traffic, under a hail of abuse from belligerent motorists. One protester, dissatisfied with a mere rant, pierced the air with his middle finger, his top half hanging from his car window. Unfazed and undeterred by the narrow gap, Hana nudged the car behind her and the one in front to wedge her own into place.

"A masterful demonstration of parallel parking," Rasha quipped.

Hana yanked the handbrake with undue force. "The key to survival in a big city, *chérie*. Push, shove and just grab." She let out an uproarious laugh.

Solid oak doors, adorned with brass leonine paws at shoulder-height, led to a heavenly courtyard paved in stone. Above hung balconies of wrought-iron latticework, brimming with pink and white geraniums. The mesmerizing trickle of water offered up by the centre fountain defied the nervous roar of traffic beyond the enclosure. This was a world apart, thought Rasha. Sadly, beyond Lebanon, any existence was a world apart.

Fitting what Rasha had thought was a standard suitcase into a lift the size of a shoebox took some manoeuvring.

"I'm afraid there's no Mustafa here," Hana explained with reference to the Halwani's concierge. "God how I miss Beirut!"

With the suitcase wedged into the lift, there was no room left for their slender figures. Hana pressed the button to the third floor and they scaled the stairs to meet it at the top. When she opened the front door to her apartment, a cat with a silky white coat wove its way between her shins, purring with contentment.

"This is Lulu." Hana affectionately picked up the white cat and stroked her. "Isn't she beautiful? Come on in. *Tu es la bienvenue ma chère. Ahlan wa sahlan.* You are welcome."

They walked straight into Hana's lounge where two, low, cream-coloured divans lined the square room. Dozens of cushions in Palestinian needlework of rich crimson and pale blue tied in with a Bukhara carpet of the same hues. In the middle, a brass Damascene tray rested on a wooden frame studded with mother of pearl. Unobtrusively, in the corners, low modern bookshelves displayed family photographs, a fern, blown-glass ornaments, and books—an eclectic mix of French and Arabic. A taste of home in a foreign land.

Hana took a left. "I'll show you to your room. I'm sorry, it's not much. Quite small in fact, but at least you won't hear me snoring," she added half in jest.

The room was as serviceable as any spare space would be for a single woman like Hana. A narrow bed lay flush with the wall. Cardboard boxes, piled high, cluttered up one corner.

"I haven't managed to unpack completely," Hana exclaimed, laughing, "seeing that I've only been here five years." Then conspiratorially, "Don't mention this to your father. He'd be horrified. Come, find a space for your bag and let's have a bite."

Amused by Hana's impossible instruction, Rasha dropped her suitcase where she stood, and took two steps to the window. She glimpsed a well-groomed mother in her twenties cross the courtyard with a pushchair. A dowager in a housedress watered the geraniums on her balcony. They exchanged a perfunctory *bonjour* with a sweep of the hand. A haunting vision of the old woman at the airport constrained Rasha's breathing. She brushed her face with the palms of her hands before turning to join Hana.

A female voice rose from the answering machine. "The documents have arrived. I've left them on your desk. I should be finished with my doctor's appointment by three. I'll come straight to the office. Expect a call from Nadim. He's panicking, as usual."

Click. A man's deep voice filled the small lounge. "Hana. We've received the legal documents. We've got a week. Don't let me down."

Hana stuck her head through the kitchen serving hatch. "My boss," She explained to Rasha, rolling her eyes.

Click. *"Hana . . . tu me manques . . . je t'en prie, rappelle-moi."* The man's husky tone was sincere, desperate.

"Jean-Baptiste. Doesn't give up easily!" Girlish embarrassment coloured Hana's cheeks as she came out bearing a marble cheese board of Brie, Camembert, and Crème des Anges, a loaf of Pain de Montagne, and a bottle of Chablis on a tray.

She eased herself onto the carpet, tucking her legs underneath her. "Tell me the news. How's everyone, your dad, your mom?" she asked, reaching for the wine.

Rasha broke off a piece of the warm loaf. "First Jean-Baptiste."

"My brother . . . your father . . . would kill me if he ever found out about him," she mumbled as she filled the glasses. *"Bien,"* she shrugged, "Jean-Baptiste and I have been seeing each other on and off for the past six months, since he walked into the office asking for a translation of a document. He's married. I knew it from the beginning. Unhappily married, though they all say that, don't they? *Bref,* as always after throwing myself blindly into a passionate relationship, I came to my senses, and decided this was going nowhere. So I sent him packing and ever since I come home to endless messages from him. Every other day he sends me a bouquet of pink roses, my favourites as you know. *Et voilà, c'est tout!* Nothing more to tell." She raised her glass.

Rasha scanned the room for evidence of Jean-Baptiste's offerings.

Reading her mind, Hana quickly remarked, "I keep them in the bedroom."

Rasha pictured herself relaying Hana's news to her father and grinned with amusement. Amin had opposed his sister's decision to leave Beirut for good five years earlier. He was adamant that they stick together in hard times, that the conflict in Lebanon would resolve itself, and that going it alone was turning one's back on the family. But Rasha, her mother Nuha, and Hana knew that what he objected to in essence was the impropriety of his unmarried sister starting a life on her own in Paris. A woman's place was with her father or her husband. Hana's departure, Amin knew for certain, would fire up gossip that would in turn reflect badly on him and tarnish the Halwani name. It was inevitable.

The family discussions that preceded Hana's departure confirmed to Rasha the extent of her father's obduracy which Nuha openly opposed, for once, fighting in her sister-in-law's corner. Amin's obsession with the family's honour and good name was so extreme that Rasha was convinced it bordered on paranoia. He did not stop to consider that his sister would be safer outside war-torn Beirut. He turned a blind eye to the anguish her fiancé's disclosed infidelity had caused her. Amin maintained that Hana's departure was a direct challenge to his authority when in fact it was a flight on the emotional front, an attempt at self-preservation. His handling of the situation foretold the difficulties Rasha would face in her twenties. As she approached womanhood, Rasha understood all too well Hana's desperate need to escape the clutches of male domination and establish a life of her own.

For the moment, Rasha intended to enjoy her aunt's fresh honesty. She would not question her judgement nor probe her on the propriety of her affair. She did wonder however how Hana could forget that it was her fiancé's duplicity that had led to the break-up of their engagement so many years ago. And here, Jean-Baptiste's marital bliss or lack of it notwithstanding, Hana was instrumental in a betrayal. Unlike Hana, Rasha preferred to steer clear of turbulent affairs: partly because she had an aversion to complications, and partly because she was brought up to believe that a woman earned respect through steady relationships. What she did not realize was that—in an effort to dignify her friendships with men— she had deceived herself into believing them to be meaningful and lasting. By the age of twenty-five, she had split her love life between two men only. Neither had been worth the time or the attention she had invested in them.

"So I won't get to meet him?"

"Well," Hana cocked her head to one side, a glimmer of mischief in her eyes. "I'm having a drinks party this evening in your honour. I could ask him to join us." She raised a brow, inviting her niece's opinion.

For fear of sounding judgmental, Rasha replied tentatively. "You said yourself that this relationship was going nowhere."

"*Tout à fait*. But you see, habibti, at my age, life, relationships . . . everything . . ." she opened her arms wide, "takes on different shades of grey. There really is no such thing as black-and-white. Is there, Lulu, besides you?" She lifted the bundle to her bosom. "What's right sometimes turns out to be pointless, and what's wrong hardly punishable. Especially when you're living outside your country. Then you realize no one pats you on the back for doing the right thing, and no one really cares if you go wrong. Ultimately, you learn to look after yourself, to think of yourself. Any gain will only be yours, and any loss yours alone."

"Are you saying that you can get away with almost anything because you have no one to answer to? Because no one knows who you are?"

"Not quite." She paused to take a sip of wine. "Not if you have a conscience. What I mean is that living in exile gives you a sense of anonymity, the perfect chance to reassess values that were ingrained in you and you never dared question."

Rasha doubted her aunt could so easily have discarded the mores inculcated by her family. They had led a cloistered, rural existence, until their father moved the family down to Beirut where he gradually acquired a juice-bottling factory. Hana's first taste of a cosmopolitan city life came at the age of nine when she was enrolled in a girls-only school.

Her father, Habib, was as his name denoted, amiable and kind. His paternal duty, conventionally, was to provide for the family and he threw himself totally into a business for his sons to inherit. The assumption was that Hana would take on her own profession, probably not a demanding one, and would rely on her husband to be the breadwinner. That was the custom. Just as her mother Amina was true to her nurturing duties, so Hana would one day have to fulfil her own for her fledgling family.

Hana and her brothers grew up happy, unruffled by the pressures placed on them for decorum and good behaviour. They were all equally subjected to restrictions which they attributed to fair parental concern. But Hana's path diverged from that of her brothers the moment the boys were extended privileges she was denied. Hana sensed the world closing in on her. Amin and Salim were charged with the role of chaperons on their outings together. Her dress and make-up had to be subdued, too much rouge dismissed severely as tartish and inviting. In all, she had to exhibit understated elegance and appear discouraging to the opposite sex. Unless she came upon a suitor who was deemed "appropriate" by her father. Only then would control of the manacles be passed on to him.

Naïvely perhaps, Hana expected her inbred sense of loyalty to be met with honesty in her relationship with Ghazi, her fiancé. Yet, even Rasha could discern that Hana was tempting fate with the impossible relationship. Because Ghazi was not only a Christian club-owner but also an infamous womanizer, it seemed to Rasha as if her aunt had gone beyond the pale to defy her brothers who had assumed their father's role after his death. Amin was incensed that his sister spent her evenings perched at the bar of her fiancé's club and the more outraged he became, the more determined Hana was to make her engagement to Ghazi work. She turned a blind eye to his flirtations with other women, reminding herself that he had chosen her to be his lifetime companion. All the while, Rasha sided quietly with Hana, admiring her courage to stand up for what she believed was true, if selfishly hoping that her aunt's battle would pave the way for her own emancipation. In particular, it pleased her to see her mother, Nuha, sympathize with Hana's plight. Once Hana had set a precedent, Rasha hoped that in the future she could inspire the same commiseration in her mother, making it harder for Amin to lay down the law.

Then as quickly as Ghazi and Hana's relationship had blossomed, it fell apart. It was through her parents that Rasha had learned of Ghazi's well-known affair with a married woman. Once Hana established the rumour to be true, she broke off the engagement.

Her life began to unravel. Her visits to Nuha, always when Amin was at work, ended up in long tearful sessions. While Hana bemoaned her bad luck, Nuha would try to boost her morale by extolling her single-mindedness and independence. Until one day Hana arrived dry-eyed, in full make-up, looking as if life had been breathed back into her. "I'm leaving for Paris!" She announced to Nuha and Rasha. "There's no future for me here, no job prospects, no security, no love life. So I've made up my mind. I'm going." No sooner had she spoken than tears welled up in Nuha's eyes putting the onus on Hana, for a change, to console her.

A call from the office brought Hana to her feet. Alone now, Rasha scrutinized the family photos on the bookshelves. A fading sepia portrayed a young Hana with her brothers picking figs in the garden of their childhood home. She inspected her father's playful expression as a young boy and realized how rarely it manifested itself in old age. The youngster looking forward to a feast of ripe figs could not have anticipated the fight over rightful property that Lebanon's future conflicts had in store for him.

Whenever Rasha questioned her father's reluctance to flee the country, she reminded herself of her friends' reports of life in exile. Most spoke of homesickness and loneliness. Others felt they had sacrificed their identity in return for physical security. Self-exile, she'd heard incessantly, was a form of alienation, a costly trade-off for survival. Ultimately, Rasha's options were either to go down with the ship or drift on a lifeboat in dark alien waters.

Hana cradled the handset. "Sorry habibti, that was Nellie, the office secretary. Lovely girl. You'll meet her this evening."

Rasha resumed her seat. "Is she Lebanese?"

"Lebanese father, Algerian mother. She joined the company a few months after I did. Young girl in her late twenties. They'd been living in Ashrafieh, and during one of the battles, a rocket hit their apartment. Her mother had shrapnel lodged in her back but fortunately nowhere near her spine. Nellie's father called it quits and put his family on the first available boat out of Jounieh. He's sworn never to set foot in the country again."

"And you, Auntie Hana?" Rasha inspected her over the rim of her glass.

"Oh I'd go back. For sure," she frowned. "I love the place. It's my home, Rasha. But when I do, I'll make sure it's at a time when I can leave *on a plane*, and *not* on a miserable excuse for a ship, bursting with people and reeking with vomit." Her brow unknotted. "I wish your father would bring you all out here."

"He can't give up the factory. Besides, I can't see him starting over at his age. Can you? Understanding European culture on your own turf and having to live by it are two different things. You know as well as I do that he'd never survive in Paris. To start with, he wouldn't want to."

Hana spread a thin layer of melted Brie on a slice of bread. "It's not a question of what he wants, Rasha. He's got you, your brother and your mother to think of. You're living under horrendous conditions. And what's worse is that you've learned to accept them. It's not normal to look at every rubbish pile or car on the street and half-expect it to explode. The world is not about sniper fire and car bombs."

"There are a lot of people who are worse off . . ." Rasha repeated the mantra of those who bordered on self-pity.

"And others who are better off!"

"When you came out here Auntie Hana, you did not have a family in tow. Could you honestly imagine Baba going around Paris on job interviews?"

Hana gave her a cloak-and-dagger look.

"*You* come out then. I'll get you a job. In fact, we need a proofreader at the office and with a little training, you'll move up to translations in no time. How's your Arabic?"

"Never been worse," Rasha giggled. "I want to teach, Auntie. And I specifically want to teach at the university, at AUB. I took a lot out of it and my country. It's time I give something in return."

"That's very noble of you, Rasha." Hana paused as if weighing what she was about to say. "But the truth is no one's keeping score."

"I am."

Hana tipped her head to one side. "It just tears me apart to think that you're missing out on a good life. It doesn't have to be Paris. It could be anywhere really, outside Beirut."

Clearly Hana had no intention of bringing up the difficulties she had faced when she relocated to Paris. But Rasha had heard of her period of adjustment through her mother. Nuha was always quick to relate Hana's grievances to Rasha in an effort to prove that exile simply replaced one set of worries with another which was harder to contend with in the absence of family support.

For the first year in her new home, Hana was on the phone to Nuha regularly, complaining of sleepless and tearful nights and wondering whether she had made the right decision. Uprooting herself, she'd say, had propelled her into a cold, unfriendly vacuum. The evenings were sombre and lonely, and her scant dinners in front of the television set contrasted brutally with the large gatherings and sumptuous feasts that had marked her years in Lebanon. No one simply dropped in, the phone rarely rang, and at times the distinct sound of her own breathing—and hers alone—accentuated her despair. Hers was not a home but a lifeless abode that bore no memories and uncertain hopes for the future.

Despite the physical distance between her and her family in Beirut, Hana's mind was consumed with details of their daily life. Often, she paused at her desk wondering what her brothers or sisters-in-law were doing at that very moment. She agonized over their safety, and on a daily basis combed the pile of Lebanese newspapers she received at the office. At night she wept alone at televised scenes of war-torn Beirut. While she shopped for her handful of provisions, flashes of her local and friendly grocer, Abu Munir, brought tears to her eyes. Aimless and solitary walks were devoid of the many familiar encounters she would have had in village-like Beirut. Her heart and her thoughts refused to succumb to her new environment. Hana knew that she would have to overcome her nostalgia and ruthlessly discard her beloved heritage to make her stay a success. Torn between the Lebanese Hana and her new Parisian counterpart, she had to make a choice.

In Beirut, Hana had felt weighed down as if by an old, heavy and tattered coat and could not wait to be rid of it. When she shed it, the chill pierced through her like shrapnel. Impersonal novelty usurped the place of warm familiarity. In her homeland, she had been the branch of a cedar, deeply rooted in ancestry. In Paris, she was a fledgling with no past. Sewn into the lining of that coat she so readily cast off was her identity.

She felt like a deserter, not only of her family, but of a country she held dear in her heart. Lebanon was being shelled to a pulp, her people victimized, kidnapped and slaughtered, her favourite haunts—preservers of sweet memories—obliterated.

Many a time she had thought of putting her trip down to experience and returning to her loved ones. But her eagerness to succeed pushed her to another year, and yet another, until before she knew it she had been in Paris long enough to adapt. Only partially though, because Hana had found refuge in a job that preserved ties with her past, and among people who understood her culture. Though she mingled with the Parisians, the core of her existence revolved around a microcosm of Lebanese friends. On a small scale, they managed to recreate the life they had in Beirut or bemoan the aspects they could not. They dined in Lebanese restaurants where camaraderie with the waiters came easily, where the familiar fragrance of crisp onions, mint, fresh parsley and grilled lamb filled the air, and where they were expected, as was the custom, to languish, perhaps smoke the *narguileh*, with little regard for a quick turnover. They spoke of areas they had seen change during the war, bemoaned the Green Line that partitioned the city into East and West, and made hushed comments on the unwelcome developments of events and the militias' atrocities.

Perhaps these details had been relegated to Hana's distant past and were not worth a mention. Perhaps she would not bring them up to avoid disheartening her niece. Rasha could not tell for certain. But she knew that her aunt's eventual success did not automatically imply that Rasha, too, would be happy in a foreign environment.

Rasha rested her head against a back cushion. "I shouldn't have had that glass of wine."

Hana reached over and took Rasha's hand in hers. "It's been a long day. Why don't you go lie down for a bit while I prepare a few snacks for this evening?"

"I'll be fine," Rasha mumbled.

"Habibti," Hana began softly, "I know why your mother insisted on this trip."

"What exactly did she tell you?" Rasha forced herself upright, gently withdrawing her hand from Hana's grip.

"Basically that you needed a change, a little break."

The tenderness in her aunt's voice unleashed a rush of sadness in Rasha. "You know I'm not the only one who's had a bad experience, Auntie Hana."

"Maybe not . . . But you're the only one I care about," she added with a faint smile. "Tell me what happened, Rasha."

Rasha hugged a cushion to her chest. "Seven months is a long time. I don't remember everything clearly," she lied. Her memory of the incident was so painfully vivid she had despaired of it ever fading.

Hana's intent gaze forced Rasha to avert her eyes.

"I was with Malek at the time," she began. "You never met Malek . . .," she added, turning to her aunt.

"No, but your mother told me about him a while back."

"I'm not surprised she did. She and Baba were besotted with him. Certainly more than I was. What more could they ask for, a Muslim, brilliant medical student with a promising career, good family, impeccable manners. They thought he was *it*, the ideal son-in-law. I sort of promised myself to him to get some breathing space and to please my parents. He was responsible, decent, and if I were safe in anyone's care, they were convinced it had to be Malek's. Little did they know . . . but anyway that's another story altogether."

Rasha took a deep breath. "I don't mean to say he wasn't a good guy. He was. But all men are the same aren't they? Determined that their own expectations be fulfilled, that every woman be moulded to fit their perfect image. They say they love you for what you are, but they very rarely do . . . Malek was like that. He wasn't in love with *me*. He was in love with the person he thought he could turn me into. Always a question of control, isn't it Auntie Hana?"

"That's our society, I'm afraid. Macho." Hana shrugged. "Did you love him?"

"I suppose I did in a way." She squinted. "I don't know."

"So what happened?" Hana peered at her over the edge of her glass.

"You mean with the two of us?"

Hana shook her head.

"That night? . . . We'd been to a dinner party in Ramlet-el-Baidah on the corniche. It was a beautiful summer evening. Clear skies, still night, and quiet. So quiet. The couple who had invited us lived quite high up, you know in those luxurious apartments that overlook the sea. From their balcony you could see the dark waters, you could just make out the ripples, ever so slightly, gentle waves lapping up against deserted beaches. It took you back to Beirut before the war. For a short while you could even be deluded into thinking that nothing bad had ever happened. That the war was a nasty figment of our imagination . . ."

"If only," Hana interjected.

"Yes, if only . . ." Rasha stroked the scar on her eyebrow. "There must've been about ten of us, laughing, telling war jokes. Just having plain fun." Visions of the boisterous gathering came back to Rasha, the laughter resonated in her ears. "As it got late, I became restless, tense. I told Malek it was time we left. I just had the gut feeling that we'd better be on our way. He kept on saying 'soon', but once I was set on going home, I became more and more agitated. When I looked at my watch, it was a few minutes past midnight, so I told him that if I were a minute later he'd have a lot of explaining to do to my parents. We said our goodbyes along with another couple we'd just met over dinner. Lovely people. She was beautiful, my age, with long curly black hair. Her name was Leila, an Arts student at the university. I remember her hands. She had long and fine fingers, a perfect specimen of creativity. Unfortunately, I'd spoken to her only briefly." Rasha paused, recapturing her image. "You know how at these large parties you never get the chance to talk to everyone you meet. But Malek still could not tear himself away. And it took a while before we headed down the stairs with a torch. From a distance, as we walked to our car, we shouted our goodbyes to Leila and her boyfriend as they got into theirs." She stopped. "His name was Akram, I think. Akram or Makram," she added pensively. "I had my back to them but could hear their car doors slam, one after the other. I heard the car starting . . . then . . . then, a split second later, there was this almighty explosion." She flung her arms in the air as if to demonstrate its magnitude. She swallowed hard. "It was horrible. I felt my heart had been ripped out of my ribcage . . . as if an electric shock had shot right through my body. I couldn't feel my legs. The next thing I know I'm crouched beside the passenger door, paralyzed, dazed. I think I was yelling. I'm not sure. Then came the shouting, the frantic screaming. It was like a televised scene being played out in front of me, except that this time I was part of it. I was there! Everyone came rushing out of their apartments warning us frantically of another bomb. It had happened right there in front of me. The other car was engulfed in flames and black smoke, lying there in a heap with those poor people trapped in it. And the smell . . . God, the stench of burning!"

Rasha covered her face. The words choked her as she fought back the tears. Emotions and memories she had suppressed for so long burst forth. Hana slid next to her, her arm firm against Rasha's shoulder. "There was no reason for it. It wasn't as if either of them was politically involved. And you know what the terrible thing was?" Her eyes locked with Hana's. "Instead of rushing to help I just knelt there, peering from behind the car, yelling hysterically, while Malek like everyone else circled the flames, trying to douse them, feeling at a complete loss. Deep down all I wanted to do was go home. I can still see their faces, around the table, by the car, smiling, making plans for the next day. And no one knew. *None of us knew.*" Her voice trailed off. "I blamed Malek for dragging his feet. I kept on thinking that if we'd left earlier, we wouldn't have witnessed the whole thing. God, I'm worthless!"

"It's perfectly normal to have reacted the way you did, Rasha."

Hana's comforting words fell on deaf ears. Rasha was already too far gone in her recollections. "There's more," she brushed her cheeks brusquely, scanning Hana's face to determine whether she should go on. Rethinking their conversation about Jean-Baptiste and her aunt's past experience with her fiancé, she became emboldened, half-hoping that her aunt would sympathize.

"I've never told a soul about this, Auntie Hana." She stared at her aunt communicating the need for confidentiality. "When we finally got in the car, I don't know what possessed me but I felt I couldn't go back home. I was hysterical. I couldn't face my parents. So, we went back to Malek's apartment. We had a drink and he gave me a Valium. I was in a heap crying, shaking all over. Then the combination of alcohol and sedative started taking effect. I mellowed and sat there feeling drained and numb. He took me in his arms . . . I let him . . ." Rasha examined Hana's expression for any signs of shock or disappointment and was relieved to find unwavering tenderness. She hoped Hana would surmise the rest without her having to go into detail. "Nothing that I'd been taught to be important was anymore. Everything was confusing, uncertain. Nothing mattered. When you could have your life stolen, cut short, from one minute to the next, everything else seems insignificant. I just gave in to him. Don't ask me why. To this day, I don't know why." For a brief moment, Rasha contemplated the shame she'd felt on giving up her virginity to someone she did not love.

"On the way home, we didn't speak. He sat with my parents explaining why we'd been delayed, leaving out the bit at his apartment of course. My mother came into my room when he left, bless her. She took me in her arms and held me tight. She didn't say a word but she knew. She must've guessed somehow."

"Your mother is a remarkable, perceptive woman, Rasha. I promise you nothing that goes on in her home escapes her attention."

"That's probably why she organized this trip for me. A month after the incident I broke off with Malek. Gradually, I just retreated into my own world. I stopped going out. For no reason at all, my hands would start shaking and turn sweaty." She rubbed them together. "Every morning, I'd wake up only to burrow deeper under the blankets. I had no desire to get up, no will to teach. Whenever I got stuck in traffic in a taxi, I'd feel my heart beating so hard, so fast, as if it were about to leap out of my chest. I'd imagine a bomb hidden in every rubbish pile. I'd jump at the slightest noise, any raucous, loud voices. I simply had to be able to anticipate danger and avoid it. I had this recurring vision of myself planning for the next day, then, just like Leila, having my life suddenly cut short. I was convinced my turn would come." Rasha looked straight at Hana hoping for enlightenment, words of wisdom.

She could go on and on about the anxiety bred by reality and fed by imagination. Her notions were not delusions. The threats were there, lurking in cars, garbage dumps, classrooms, and shops.

"Mama insisted I see Dr. Namih. He said it was nerves and prescribed a mild sedative. That was the only way I could go on."

"Listen, habibti." Hana held her by the shoulders forcing Rasha to face her squarely. "You've got ten days here . . . with me. I know it's not much, but you must promise me that you'll forget about Beirut for now and enjoy every moment in Paris. Make the most of it, habibti. Promise me you will."

Rasha nodded, trying to force a smile that would not come. Yet, she felt light, relieved of a heavy burden.

Lulu jumped up between them. Hana let out a half-hearted laugh. "Jealous, are we?" She picked up the cat and placed it on the rug. Pulling Rasha up by the hand, she brought her to her feet. "Come, let's get some snacks together."

Rasha had thought she could do without a nap, but as the evening approached her energy lagged. She had started off early that morning. Her eight o'clock flight from Beirut meant that she had to wake up at dawn to check in at least two hours before departure. She had taken a sedative to steel her nerves during the drive through dodgy parts of the city and to see her through the mayhem at the airport. All that and what little wine she had consumed at lunchtime made her feel unsteady and disoriented.

She helped Hana lay out some *mezze* of *homous*, grilled *hallumi* cheese, and a selection of *kibbe, fatayer bi sbanegh* and *lahm bi 'ajin* that Nuha had implored Rasha to carry with her. To go with it, Hana had set aside a selection of Lebanon's finest wines, Ksara and Château Musar, and a bottle of *'arak*, the anise-flavoured Lebanese spirit.

"How many people are you expecting?" Rasha asked.

"Let me see. There's Nellie, our secretary, you'll like her. Fadwa, a colleague and translator. Nadim, our boss . . ." Her face contorted with distaste. "Munir and Hayat, a Lebanese couple I met through work I did for Munir. Hayat is actually a lovely person. We became good friends. And finally Daniel and Sophie, my neighbours. Their flat is just beneath mine so I thought, since we're likely to make some noise, why not invite them. They're okay," Hana screwed up her nose, "not very forthcoming but harmless really. And . . . have I left anyone out?" She had counted seven on her fingers.

"Jean-Baptiste?"

"Nah," Hana let out with a swipe of her hand. "He's not worth the trouble."

At the sound of the doorbell she added, "That'll be Nellie."

Nellie turned out to be a round, little person, rosy-cheeked and affable. As she briefed Hana on the urgent documents that had come in that day, Rasha was struck by her joviality. From Hana's account of the family's tragedies and their hasty evacuation, Rasha had expected to meet a reserved woman racked by her horrific experience. No sooner had Rasha started warming up to the twenty-eight-year-old than everyone arrived. First were Hana's neighbours, Daniel and Sophie, then Munir and Hayat, and last Fadwa, who apologetically announced that she had been delayed at the office. At each introduction, Hana would throw an arm around Rasha and present her as *"Ma belle nièce."* Slightly embarrassed by her aunt's clearly biased compliment, Rasha nevertheless appreciated Hana's reassuring warmth.

Munir engaged Daniel in conversation as the women congregated in one section of the lounge. They all spoke French, out of consideration for Sophie, but could not help the odd aside in Arabic to report an incident in Beirut which they knew would be meaningless to her. An hour had passed when the doorbell rang. Hana rose from the rug announcing wryly: "Here comes the pièce de résistance. Our one and only Nadim!" Nellie and Fadwa giggled, understanding full well Hana's sarcasm when it came to their demanding boss.

Hana lingered at the door, as more than two voices mingled and her "welcomes" became more animated.

Fadwa bent forward to catch a glimpse of Nadim. "He's brought someone with him."

"Someone else's wife," Nellie ventured.

Fadwa clipped her playfully on the arm. "Shush."

The two men stepped in. Nadim, a tall and hefty man immaculately dressed in suit and tie, concealed his companion.

"Everyone," Hana cried out. "This is Nadim, whom you all know . . . and Luke. Let me take your jackets."

Nadim extended a brown manila envelope to Hana. "I need you to have a look at this."

"Later." She flung it unceremoniously on a side table. "Now gentlemen, what can I get you to drink? Nadim, the scotch is there. Ice in the bucket. Please help yourself. Luke, would you like some Lebanese wine, or some 'arak maybe. It's like Greek *ouzo*."

Rasha overheard him mumble "I'd love some, thank you" but she still could not see him clearly. Then, as Nadim turned to take his jacket off, Luke emerged from behind him. He walked into the room shaking hands all round. "Luke, hi," "Pleased to meet you," "Luke Elliott", "Sorry, I didn't catch your name." His six-feet compelled him to bend in half each time he greeted someone seated. He bore a light hunch in the shoulders, but when he straightened up, Rasha could see that a sinewy but solid physique helped him carry his frame well. As he approached her, her heart raced. He had a disarming smile, wide, generous, offset by narrow sky-blue eyes that disappeared when his face beamed in earnest. Shoulder-length chestnut hair, parted in the middle, swung freely as he nodded and expressed delight at meeting everyone.

"Hi, I'm Luke." He towered over her, making Rasha feel she was half the diminutive size she already was. Though her palm felt clammy, she had no choice but to accept his. When their eyes met, his had lost their jollity. Grave and searching, they pierced into hers and the diplomatic smile she had been admiring from across the room had faded.

Rasha was certain she had misinterpreted his star-struck expression. She was far from being a classic beauty. Her short hair and boyish figure were hardly inviting, and the clothes she wore, jeans and T-shirt, did nothing to redeem her shapelessness. Conscious that Luke's grip was unrelenting, she claimed her hand back as subtly as possible. An awkward silence followed as Luke searched for a place to sit. Dwarfed by his height, Rasha jumped to her feet, but felt herself practically at eye-level with his chest. Feeling herself blush, she looked down, wishing she had remained seated.

As if reading her thoughts, Luke said "I'll grab that chair over there." Rasha could not tell whether she was delighted or dismayed by his company. She felt self-conscious, flustered, and altogether unprepared for a tête-à-tête. This was certainly not the time for someone to try and get to know her better.

Hana handed Luke a glass of 'arak. As he stood up to take it, she pressed down on his shoulder. "No need for formality here, Luke. Please make yourself at home. I see you've met Rasha, my . . ."

Please, please don't say "my beautiful niece".

". . . niece. Just arrived from Beirut. She'll be staying with me for ten days. How long are you here for Luke?"

"I'm not quite sure. I just got in this morning from East Africa. I hope you don't mind Nadim bringing me along. He wouldn't take no for an answer."

"Don't be silly. I'm delighted you're here," she chimed. "Why East Africa?"

"I'm a photojournalist . . ."

"For?"

"I'm stringing for Reuters." Then he added for clarification, "Freelance." Luke took a sip of his 'arak and grimaced. "This is strong stuff!"

Hana burst into laughter. "Would you like me to get you something else? Some wine perhaps?"

"No, thank you," Luke let out between coughs. "This is fine really."

"Well, if you change your mind . . ." Then to Rasha, smiling, "You'll look after Luke for me, won't you, chérie?"

"Sure. With pleasure," Rasha stressed, hoping that Luke would catch on to the fact that she meant it. She waited until Hana had moved away, towards her guests, before reaching for the platter of kibbe. "Try some of this, it goes nicely with 'arak."

"Kibbe."

"You've had it before!"

He smiled. "Often actually, with friends at a Lebanese restaurant in London."

"Do you know many Lebanese?" Rasha found herself staring at his wide, white grin.

"One or two I met through journalists who'd been to Beirut."

"But you haven't?"

His mouth full, Luke shook his head. He swallowed hard. "No. I'd like to one day. Tell me, what's it like?"

"Beirut?" Rasha drew a breath. "Like any beautiful city ravaged by years of war. Chaotic, dirty, noisy . . . but still beautiful."

Rasha put Luke's curiosity down to polite conversation. Reticent by nature, she tried to describe it in a nutshell, sparing him the memories of old Beirut that invariably clouded her mind and seized her heart with unrelenting nostalgia—pre-war Lebanon that had been paradise on earth. She could ramble on about a childhood deliciously spiced with treks to the orchards and treasure hunts in virginal wooded areas of Dhour-el-Choueir. She could disappoint Luke by revealing that a Lebanese meal in High Street Kensington was a poor re-enactment of a sumptuous spread of mezze, grilled meats, and mouth-watering watermelon oozing with its cold juice. To experience the real thing he would have to hear the peal of kids' laughter in the forest, inhale the smell of the soil as it mingled with the crisp mountain breeze and the resinous scent of pines. She could reel off the rich history of her country, its strife, and the ancestors whose presence lingered in every speck of dust, in every stone, every column of its ancient monuments.

Sadly this was no longer contemporary Lebanon. Its beauty, like its people, had curled up in wartime, waiting for peace before it unfurled. There were now the ruins of time and the ruins of war. The first inspiring awe and fascination, the second pity and despair.

"I'm sure you've heard this ad nauseam. But they used to call it 'the Switzerland of the Middle East', didn't they?"

Rasha grinned. "*Used to* are the key words. Early spring you could be swimming in the Mediterranean in the morning and snow-skiing among cedars in the afternoon."

Luke's eyes narrowed. "How do you cope? I mean how can you carry on living there?"

The voice of this stranger rang with genuine concern. Rasha found this disarming and briefly considered dropping her guard. Could she tell him she did not actually "cope"? Could she confide in him the terror that plagued her every waking hour? Should she speak of the emptiness that had claimed her once purposeful and ambitious soul? Could she reveal to him that she could only carry on by numbing her senses with barbiturates?

One day perhaps, if she got the opportunity, but not just yet. So, she didn't admit she had to manage somehow but simply said "It's my home." Luke pressed her for details. He wanted a first-hand account of how people carried on with their lives in wartime: a question to which Rasha had a well-rehearsed but dispassionate reply. They took every day in their stride. They avoided certain areas and imposed their own curfews. In case of heavy shelling, they huddled in stairwells and only ventured out when all was clear. Beyond that, there was nothing much they could do.

Rasha had no desire to speak about Beirut or herself. Next to her sat an attractive young man who, by his mere presence, sent her heart thundering and her pulse racing. She took in the khaki shirt that hugged his biceps, the worn jeans that concealed long legs, his sturdy neck, his raspy voice. She yearned for the here and now, the chance of being drawn into his life, his world. Her mind reeled off a list of questions which would unveil the essence of the man who had so effortlessly stirred her curiosity: how many lovers he had had; the type of woman he appreciated; his fears, his strengths, his deepest secrets. But mostly, what he thought of her, Rasha.

Luke sat doubled up, elbows on his thighs, blocking Rasha's view of the gathering. "I presume all your family's there."

Rasha stared into her wineglass. "Everyone except for Hana."

"Brothers, sisters?"

"I have one brother. Karim. He's a couple of years younger than me. He's a medical student."

"Do you see much of each other?"

"Actually, we live together." She took a sip of wine, eyes dipped. "We both live with my parents," Rasha murmured, blood rising to her cheeks.

"Oh! Right." Luke grinned sheepishly, as if he had committed a blunder and stood corrected. He pulled out a packet of Gauloises from his shirt pocket and offered her one. She declined. She didn't smoke. But no, she didn't mind if he did.

Was he shocked? Did he expect that Rasha would be independent of her family? Or, a far-fetched thought, was Luke trying to find out whether she was married? Was he married?

Rasha turned the tables. "What about you?"

Luke drew on his cigarette. "Carol, my sister, lives in Paris with her husband and two boys. My father's in London. Works for a multinational oil company. My mother lives in Houston. They're divorced."

No wife. "So . . . you're here to see your sister?"

"Sort of," Luke grimaced, tapping his cigarette on the edge of an ashtray. "I thought I deserved a break before going back to London . . ."

"Where you live . . ."

"It's a base. But I wouldn't call it home."

Luke seemed reluctant to say more about himself or his family. Rasha summed him up as a loner, a wanderer who travelled on a whim and valued his freedom of movement. Unlike Rasha, he did not seem to have a family unit to speak of, none at least that kept them all in one place. Not that he spoke coldly of his relatives, but he sounded detached, dismissive, as if their lives had been severed from his and had become inconsequential. That was more or less the norm in Europe, though, wasn't it? Rasha placed him between twenty-six and twenty-nine. Of the foreigners she had met, very few stayed on with their families or parents much beyond their late teens. In Lebanon, as in most Middle Eastern countries, a woman rarely left home before she was married, and a man only did so when he felt financially self-reliant. To move out any sooner would be morally unacceptable or a slight to the parents whose sole purpose, out of deep affection really, was to keep the family together and extend unconditional security. That had been beyond question for Rasha in Beirut. But, here, now, with Luke, his independence made her feel self-indulgent.

"So, you're a photojournalist?"

Luke dragged on his cigarette, squinting. "News photographer, to be exact. That's what I do. You could call it a passion of mine." His eyes swung to Rasha's.

"But you work alone?" Rasha's question meant to underscore her grasp of Luke's free spirit.

"Only recently. About, let's see . . . five months ago. I was a staff reporter before that."

"Where did you study?"

"London College of Photojournalism. During that time I did my internship for a local newspaper then fortunately landed a job with a Sunday paper."

Rasha thought for a moment. "It must be difficult being a freelancer in such a competitive field. Do you manage to get work easily?"

"I have to graft. There's no doubt about that." He clasped his hands together. "Freelancers don't get the benefits or health insurance that staff reporters do nor access to pool equipment. So, we don't enjoy the same security and have to watch our expenses carefully." He tilted his head to one side. "On the other hand, working for ourselves means we can choose our assignments and have creative control of our work. I, for one, enjoy . . . actually, *need* that freedom."

"But why specifically photojournalism? Why not just journalism?"

"The camera never lies." Luke's face beamed in vindication of his profession. "Look at it this way, a photograph has more immediate impact on people than words. It's a mental picture, easily grasped and automatically retained. For instance, I'd much rather take a snapshot of you and show it to Carol, say, instead of struggling to describe your every feature, what you look like or how beautiful you are."

He said it with intent, straight-faced, waiting for a reaction. Rasha lowered her eyes focusing on his hand gesture as he stubbed out his cigarette. She had to come up with something to say. "But the picture, any picture," she specified to deflect any allusion to herself, "is one still reproduction. It doesn't reflect the context, the back-story. What went on before or after," she went on, ludicrously repeating herself.

"That's where the text and captions come in. But so can a quote be taken out of context. So what's stronger? Words or images?"

"Words, definitely." A smile tugged at her lips. "I'm partial to language and the power of self-expression."

Luke held his palms out. "Photography *is* self-expression. No two photographers can take the exact same picture, especially with the limited amount of time and resources we sometimes have."

Rasha was speechless. She gave him a look of sweet defeat.

He chuckled. "I'm right, aren't I?"

"Maybe . . . maybe," Rasha replied tentatively, a glint in her eye.

At that point, had either of them been bold enough, they would have touched. Rasha felt a physical pull towards Luke which, as quickly as it had surged, dissipated the minute he turned away.

In an awkward moment of silence, Rasha scanned the room. Nadim and Hana were deep in conversation, probably about work; Daniel, Munir and Hayat stood in one corner and it looked as if Daniel was holding forth; Nellie instructed Sophie on how to roll vine leaves. They were the only two seated across from Luke and Rasha.

The sultry voice of Edith Piaf filled the room—*Non, je ne regrette rien . . .*—sending shivers down Rasha's spine.

Rasha was relieved that her self-exclusion from the rest of the company did not come across as anti-social. Not wanting to leave Luke's side made her feel silly and childish. The interest she had gleaned from his expression when they shook hands seemed to have changed into careless charm. Perhaps it hadn't been there in the first place and she had misread him. Perhaps what she had assumed to be interest was mere flirtation, his indiscriminate way with women. She wanted to take in the contours of his face, the blueness in his eyes, and his full white smile. She wanted to say: "Stay there, let me have a good look at you, let me feel, once again, whatever it was that had passed between us."

"Are you working? Studying?" Luke covered both grounds, possibly to avoid the gaffe he had made in assuming Rasha's independence from her family, or because he had not quite figured out her age. She had often been told that she looked not much older than nineteen but she hoped that her demeanour displayed the maturity befitting her twenty-some years.

"I teach English at the American University." When Luke asked if it was literature, she said it wasn't, unfortunately, because she didn't have the right qualifications. She did not delve into the circumstances that stopped her from getting a higher degree. But she did mention that the university's inflexible stance on its policy typified a general denial of the changing times.

No sooner had she finished her tirade against the English Department than, in sharp contrast with Edith Piaf, the poignant lament of Fairouz filled the room. Bewailing her people's plight in lacrimatory lyrics won Fairouz European acclaim as a Lebanese singer. Her *Bhibbak Ya Lubnan* (*Lebanon, I Love You*) was a song about the torment of a country. Fadwa, Nellie, Hayat and

Hana huddled together as they chorused from the depth of their hearts, arms swinging to the music, eyes closed with yearning and nostalgia. Rasha excused herself and slipped quietly to the bathroom.

She needed time alone. Fatigue had made her emotional but she was reluctant to expose her vulnerable side to someone she had just met. Her mind was in a muddle, trying to make sense of the absurd yet uncontrollable nervousness that had seized her in Luke's presence. Her trip to Paris was meant as a reprieve from uncertainty and a revival of her faith in beauty and promise. Meeting Luke had disrupted her craving for numbness, stirring in her feelings that warred with the anxiety that already afflicted her. Setting out in calm waters, she felt as if she had been caught in the wake of a vessel bigger and mightier than her own.

She knew that the desire he had sparked in her gushed from a desperate longing to love and be loved, and its fulfilment, like all else, was precipitous. Otherwise, time would claim the moment before Rasha had had the chance to seize it. Ten days from now, she would be in Beirut again. If what she had read in Luke's eyes was true, they had less than a fortnight to feed and develop a romance. But she was not brazen enough to initiate it, and not too certain of the wisdom behind pursuing it.

She waited for the song to end before walking out to the more sober tune of Ella Fitzgerald. Luke followed her with his eyes, until she took her seat again by his side. He had not moved.

As if he had been party to her moment of seclusion, Luke surprisingly said. "You know, when Nadim invited me this evening, I thought it would be a good opportunity to get to know a few Lebanese and find out more about the situation in the country. Networking, it's what I do." He shrugged. "Instead, I've not budged from this chair. And the truth is I've loved every minute of it.

Which got me thinking . . . you can say no if you don't want to . . . since we're both free birds, since we're both visiting I mean, why don't we hook up tomorrow and see a bit of Paris . . . together?"

Before Rasha could answer, Hana cut in. "Sorry to have left you so long. Luke, you haven't touched your 'arak! You should've helped yourself to some wine . . ."

"No, I'm fine, thank you," Luke replied, jumping to his feet, hands outstretched to indicate he was wanting for nothing.

Just then, Daniel and Sophie stepped in to say their goodbyes, behind them Munir and Hayat who also had to leave. While Hana saw them to the door, Nadim joined Luke and Rasha apologizing for not taking the time to speak to Rasha.

"Luke, would you like me to drop you off on my way home?" Nadim asked.

Rasha's heart sank. She hoped he would turn down Nadim's offer.

Luke glanced at his watch. "Unfortunately, I'd better go. I didn't think I'd be long so I didn't bother to take a key. Carol's normally exhausted in the evenings and turns in early."

When Nadim had moved away to speak to Hana, Luke spun round to Rasha as he clutched his jacket. "Listen, there's something I have to do tomorrow morning. I should be free by lunchtime . . . Um, can I maybe give you a call then? We could do something?"

Rasha hesitated. "I should check with Hana first. She may have plans . . ." Stunned by her own reaction, she felt her heart swell with regret.

"Of course." He slung the jacket over his shoulder. "Well . . . I guess I could always get your number from Nadim." He gave her a tentative look.

Rasha nodded, her mind grappling with the foolishness of her reply and her fear that she may have stung his ego. Why couldn't she have just said yes, she would love to meet him?

As Hana and Nadim wrapped up details about the next day, Rasha and Luke held back. The silence that settled between them exacerbated Rasha's discomfort.

Not knowing what to say, she stammered, "I feel so short standing next to you."

He brushed her cheek with the back of his hand. "Petite!" he corrected her, "but beautiful." Leaning over, he planted a kiss at the very edge of her mouth. "Very beautiful."

With one gesture, one meaningful word, Luke filled Rasha's heart with hope and anticipation. It would have been enough for her to have just met him and seen him off again. What took place in between did not detract nor add to the unexpressed understanding that their eyes, their whole beings, had exchanged at those two moments. All the discussion, the polite conversation about her family, his family, life in Beirut, his work, her work, had been truly irrelevant and inconsequential. What could be more absurd, more difficult for Rasha than to feel weak in the knees for a non-Arab and a non-Muslim. It defied reason: a cry from the heart.

Chapter Three

◆

Over warm croissants and *cafés-au-lait*, Rasha and Hana reviewed the evening before. They rested side by side against the kitchen counter, Hana in a tailored grey suit, taking short and hasty sips of her coffee, her eye on the clock.

"What's Luke like? I saw you two talking for most of the evening."

"Very pleasant," Rasha tried to keep her voice level.

"Will you be seeing him again?" Hana glanced sideways at Rasha.

"In fact, he suggested we meet up later today. You know, for a bit of sight-seeing."

"And . . . are you going to?"

Rasha turned to the counter to tear off a piece of croissant. "I told him to give me a call." She refrained from telling Hana that she had used her as an excuse to play for time. Clearly her aunt was too busy and Rasha did not want her to feel guilty for leaving her behind. "I'll see if I'm up to it." She suppressed the rush of expectation that made her body tingle. "Do you think I should accept if he calls?"

Hana took a while to reply. "I suppose there's no harm. Just don't let it develop into something you can't leave behind."

Rasha stared into her steaming coffee, deflated by Hana's answer. Her family seemed committed to cautioning her against physical and emotional pitfalls. Though she understood Hana's concern, Rasha wished her aunt were the exception who encouraged her to be daring.

"You should know better than to ask Big Mouth Auntie for advice." Hana smiled broadly, detecting Rasha's disappointment. "Right!" She placed her cup in the sink. "I must be off. Will you be all right?"

Rasha nodded, offering her cheek to Hana. "I'll be fine."

"Oh, the cleaner Mme. Gilbert should be here about nine. She has a key . . . I've left an extra set for you by the front door. The code to the outside gate is 5432. Easy!" Hana picked up Lulu and gave her a kiss. At the door she shouted over her shoulder. "I'll try not to be late."

The door slammed. Then silence. The gentle trickle of the fountain outside alone reached Rasha's ears. She wandered aimlessly in the flat, coffee in hand, picking up and replacing books. A glance out the window revealed once again the young woman with the pram. Wondering what to do next—the possibilities in Paris were endless but none immediately spurred her on— Rasha ambled to the bedroom to dress.

Opening her suitcase, a whiff of home, of Ariel mixed with the intrusive and impersonal smell of the plane cargo hold made her momentarily nauseous. She checked herself in Hana's full-length mirror, too grand for her size, tousling her hair with frantic fingers in an attempt to revive it. It stayed there for a brief moment, on the *qui vive* before collapsing again, defiantly, over her oval face. Her outfit was nondescript: cream-coloured shorts, a light blue sleeveless T-shirt, canvas shoes and no make-up. Rasha puffed out her frustration. She was way, way removed from the come-hither goddesses that graced the glossies and sadly doubted she would ever hear from Luke again. Right then, Lulu brushed against her shins, her fluffy coat soothing against her skin. Rasha picked her up with both hands, her amber eyes at level with the cat's green irises. "It's easy for you to be loved, isn't it? Just the way you are."

Rasha checked the time. Nine thirty, and no sign of Mme. Gilbert. Without a moment of hesitation she set about cleaning the kitchen and washing up. When it came to the glass Luke had drunk from, Rasha brushed it against the corner of her lips. She hoped to revive a sense for the stranger who, for an evening, had chased away the sadness and dejection that had become second-nature to her.

The strident ring of the phone made her jump, and nearly landed the glass on the kitchen floor with a crash. Luke was her first thought.

"Rasha. It's me habibti."

She slumped against the wall. "Hi, Auntie," she murmured.

"What's the matter?"

"Nothing," Rasha replied in a high-pitched voice.

"Are you still in the apartment? Why aren't you out and about?"

"I was cleaning up. Mme. Gilbert . . ."

"I know. She phoned the office and gave me a sorry excuse for not coming. She always does that. It's infuriating." Hana spoke with the speed of lightning, her voice tight with stress and exasperation. "Just leave everything. There's a map of the metro by the phone. Just take it and head off."

Rasha's gaze swung towards the guide on her right. "Are you sure there's nothing you'd like me to do for you?"

"Absolutely nothing. Go on. You're wasting a beautiful day and they're few and far between in Paris."

When she hung up, Rasha had the uncomfortable feeling of having been caught out. She was not pressed to venture out alone and, had Hana not called, would've spent the day happily indoors. In spite of her aunt's instructions she finished off the washing-up, reluctant to leave any task incomplete. Sunlight filtered into the lounge, casting a prismatic glow over Hana's Bukhara. It was indeed a glorious day and Rasha would be foolish not to make the most of it. Meticulously, she examined the contents of her handbag, making sure her passport and the francs she'd brought with her were safely stowed in the inside pocket. She grabbed the keys to the apartment and the guide though she had no intention of going underground for the metro and had made up her mind to walk. She had already mapped out a route along the riverbank and then across to the Louvre.

However much she tried to assume the ease and insouciance of a tourist, a disturbing sense of vulnerability gnawed at her. The pedestrians pounding the sidewalks and the traffic whizzing past were one charged mass that accentuated her aloneness. She felt totally exposed with no buffer between her fragile self and the nervous energy surrounding her. So she resorted to the only tactic she knew and had pretty much mastered to quell her apprehension. She played a sort of a mind game whereby she debated with herself, questioned the reality of the threat and countered it with sound reasoning. What did she have to fear? Of all the people around her why should she be a target? And a target for what, really? This was Paris for heaven's sake. Relax, she told herself. Enjoy. Don't let your fears take hold. She forced herself to slow down, to admire the *patisseries*, the *boulangeries*, the *épiceries*, and the boutiques that lined her path. But all she could manage was a cursory glance at the exquisite displays that would entice any other to walk in, linger, and buy.

The Seine finally in sight, a wave of exhilaration washed over Rasha. Water, in all its forms, invariably soothed her. Its texture, its free unrestrained movement inspired tranquillity and promise, and the manner in which it wrapped itself around her body and selflessly moulded itself to her form immediately assuaged her. The river drew her like a beckoning lover, obliterating the mass that, only a short while ago, had put her on edge. Reassured, eyes fixed ahead on the riverbank with antic-ipation, Rasha failed to notice a few paces ahead the dishevelled heap resting against a stone wall disfigured with graffiti. She was pressing on when in one leap the creature was on his feet, extending a palm imprinted with the filth of *trottoirs* and garbage. A groan emanated from him, a plea for assistance, a *sou*. Rasha's heart raced, pushing her stride to a trot which she resisted, determined not to display her fear. Mustering the courage to face her pursuer and deliver a definitive "*Non*", Rasha's eyes crossed piercing grey eyes, feral, supernatural. In that one moment, the vagrant's intense gaze drove a chill through her, an iciness that was impossible to shake off, threaten-ing to freeze her mobility.

She clutched her leather handbag close to her waist. "*Je n'ai rien monsieur, je regrette je n'ai rien!*"

Her back to him, she sensed the brush of his hand as he reached out to grab her. She pulled back, turned away from the Seine and the riverbank and retraced her steps frantically to the haven of her aunt's apartment. Resisting the urge to look back, she sliced her way through the crowds, her surroundings blending into a soundless, aseptic world from which she was completely divorced. She could smell her terror, hear her heartbeat.

In her mind there was her and him, nothing and no one around or in-between. Before turning the corner off rue du Bac into the side street where Hana lived, she glanced over her shoulder to make sure he wasn't following her. Then she took to her heels, shunning caution and finally succumbing to her instincts. She lifted a shaky finger to punch in the code, 5-4-3-2. A brief click released the lock. As she reached forward to push the oak door open with her body, the weight of a heavy hand landed on her shoulder. She let out a cry, and leapt into the courtyard. Pivoting to wedge the assailant's arm in the gate—a rush of adrenaline making her moves precise and sharp—she braced herself for the haunting grey eyes that had unleashed her terror. Instead she saw blue. Crystal blue.

In the crack of the doorway, she glimpsed the left side of Luke.

"Christ, Rasha. If you don't want to see me, a simple no would do."

Relief, elation and surprise rumbled through her, threatening to erupt into a paroxysm of laughter or tears while a separate visceral emotion made her want to propel herself against him. Instead, her feet nailed to the ground, Rasha pressed a palm against her bosom and gasped. "You gave me a fright, Luke." Among the strange and hostile faces she had around her, Luke's was a familiar and welcome sight. Then, almost shouting, "What are you doing here?"

"I was on my way back from the airport and decided to stop off and see if you were in." Luke, bemused, craned his neck to see her. "Are you going to let me in or are you coming out?"

Her thoughts momentarily dimmed by a vision of her pursuer, Rasha eventually complied. "I'll come out."

Luke was as casually dressed as Rasha, a Canon with a long lens slung over his shoulder. He plunged his hands into his pockets, beckoning her with a head-tilt. "Let's grab some coffee."

Rasha scanned the street for the all-clear. "All right."

"Are you sure you're okay? You look like you've just seen a ghost."

"I'm fine," she reassured him in a high-pitched voice.

They took the narrow, winding roads, avoiding the boulevards. Rasha simply followed, only too happy to be led. She inhaled the sweetness of freshly-baked pastries wafting from quaint patisseries and lingered with Luke to admire the mouth-watering displays of gold- and silver-decked chocolates. In Luke's protective shadow she took in the antique shops, boutiques and cafés, the array that spoke of festivity and sweet indulgence. All around her, the basic pleasures of man were exonerated—pleasures of which Rasha yearned to partake.

They stopped at a small café, La Passion du Fruit, Luke's choice.

"La Passion du Fruit?" Luke began, tongue-in-cheek, "would that be the 'passion fruit' or the 'passion of the fruit'?"

"I think 'passion of the fruit.' Passion fruit is *fruit de la passion*."

"A French scholar, no less," he said, grinning.

"I wouldn't go as far as to say *scholar*. But I speak it."

"In fact, quite a few Lebanese are trilingual, aren't they? Because of the English and French influences."

"You seem to know more about Lebanon than you let on, Luke." Rasha moved aside to allow the waiter to place their coffees.

"History A-levels."

"Which covered Lebanon?" Rasha asked, dubious.

Luke threw his head back and let out a hearty laugh. Rasha thought she had been had when he said, "No. I admit I caught up with my research last night after I left you."

His occasional quips relieved the inevitable awk- wardness between two people getting to know each other. Luke appeared a great deal more relaxed than Rasha who felt under pressure to be engaging and jovial. She was like a released hostage blinded by the white glare of daylight, needing time to adjust to normality. It was different for Luke. At Rasha's instigation, he spoke of his travels in Europe and a substantial part of East Africa. He was a chameleon who seemed to adapt to whatever country or situation he found himself in. Though this was her second trip to Paris, the first having been with her mother before the war, Rasha had been nowhere save for Cyprus. She acknowledged that the only thing that could truly bridge their differences was Luke's brush with a panoply of cul- tures. Even then, her conservative background and unbending parents were a challenge to anyone's under- standing, including herself.

Halfway through an anecdote that took place on his last assignment, Luke stopped, seized his camera with one jerk, and proceeded to focus.

She reached for her coffee. "What are you doing?"

"Taking a snapshot of that old man over there," he replied absent-mindedly, his voice trailing off.

Rasha followed his line of vision. She detected an elderly man in a suit and hat, seemingly uncomfortable and overdressed for a balmy June day. He leaned immo- bile on a cane.

Slowly, she replaced her cup, eyes flitting between Luke and his subject. "He's not doing anything," she observed, baffled.

"Precisely," Luke answered from behind his cam- era, shooting off frame after frame.

"Luke, he's staring at you." It was a matter of time before the man would come across and make a scene. The Parisians were never too shy of a confrontation. Rasha sat bolt upright, hand creeping to her eyebrow.

"All the better. Makes a nice succession of frames, of changing expressions."

Rasha twitched. "You know, Luke, some people don't like their photo taken. It might get you into trouble one of these days."

Luke peeled the Canon away from his face, eyes wide. "What's he going to do? Shoot me? Accuse me of stealing his soul?" He bent towards Rasha and whispered conspiratorially, "Maybe he's a spy and the building behind him his agency's secret headquarters." He paused for effect. "This is Paris, sunshine." He leaned back in his chair, arms limp at his sides. "Relax!"

Rasha forced a smile. Her deduction was clearly out of place, almost ludicrous in their context. By his easy manner, Luke made her seem uptight and unnecessarily cautious. Yet his remark showed that he was keenly attuned to her line of thinking.

"So, what have you been up to today?"

Rasha reviewed her morning mentally. "Not much, really. And you?"

Luke winced, looking afar. "I had to take my mother to the airport."

"I didn't realize she was with you in Paris."

"She breezed in for a visit. That's my mother. Wakes up to the fact, once in a while, that she has children and without any forewarning expects us to drop everything and cater to her whim."

His bluntness made her uneasy. She thought him a little too harsh.

"Was she going back to Houston?" she asked, hoping he'd notice that every detail he had offered the evening before had registered.

"Back to Houston."

"So you're still in touch."

"Last time I saw her, before this trip, was let's see
. . . two years ago. Which suited me just fine."

Not seeing one's parents for a long stretch was
totally foreign to Rasha; not wanting to, inconceivable.
Though Luke had not actually expressed it, Rasha gathered that he felt no compassion for his mother. Was his
indifference actually tinged with regret, even sadness, or
was Rasha reading too much into a coldness in him that
she was unwilling to accept?

"How old were you when your parents divorced?"

"Eleven." Luke pulled out a packet of Gauloises
from the front pocket of his shirt. "I'm not surprised they
did, actually. They're like fire and ice. Literally. My mother is five-foot seven, a stunning woman with long jet black
hair. What you could call a 'dark' southern beauty. An
extrovert, a socialite, always well groomed, not a hair out
of place. My father," he cocked his head indicating the
other side of the coin, "is five-foot-five, beer-bellied and
balding. The ultimate executive who got his first job with
an American oil company, moved up the ladder, and stuck
to it for the rest of his life. For thirty-six years . . . thirty-
six, he lived in the same building, the same festering
environment! I swear his face eventually took on the
colour of his office walls."

Rasha giggled. "And what colour was that?"

"Emetic green." Luke gave her a lopsided smile.
"Honestly, I don't know how anyone could do that. Same
old thing, day in day out. It would drive me right round the
bend."

He hunched up to light a cigarette. A coil of
smoke rose between them.

"How did your parents meet?"

"On a flight from London to Houston. My mother
worked as an air hostess for Pan Am."

"And when they separated . . . where did you end up?"

"Neutral ground. Otherwise known as boarding school. The day my mother left, my father hauled me into his car and drove me as far from London as he could. 'Character-building experience, wot, wot. Cricket, the classics and all that.'" Luke mimicked in a gruff voice and exaggerated accent.

Rasha smiled, not letting on that she sensed the hurt behind the humour. "And Carol?"

His gaze drifted into the distance. "Carol must've been about seventeen or eighteen at the time. She dropped out of school and married Xavier, a teacher ten years her senior. I guess it was her way of dealing with the divorce. She didn't want anything to do with any of us. At least that's what I think." He shrugged.

"So you grew up apart. You and Carol."

Luke exhaled. "That we did. There's a big age gap between us, and I guess when my parents broke up, she had to think of herself. Now that she has kids, two boys— I think I mentioned them, Lucien and Dominic? Yes, well, since she's had them, she sort of softened towards me. I don't know, maybe she felt she'd missed out on a family life and wanted more for her boys. For them to get to know their uncle and all that. Which is fine by me. I really have a soft spot for those two." He stubbed out his cigarette, half-finished. "Listen, sunshine, my life history tends to have a soporific effect on me. I'm surprised you're not nodding off. So, another coffee or a walk? Your choice."

"Let's walk."

They strolled along the Quai de Montebello replete with stands selling mementos, books and painted scenes of Paris. Despite the breathtaking landmarks around them, Notre-Dame and Île-de-la-Cité close to their left, neither of them stopped to comment, too engrossed in each other's company.

Their conversation had somehow veered away from Rasha's object of interest. It was Luke she wanted to hear more about. "How did you feel about being sent to boarding school?"

She felt him cringe. Maybe she was being too rash.

Luke stopped and turned to face her. "I'll answer your question if you promise me it'll be your last."

"Okay. I promise."

He walked on. "I guess, under any other circumstances, I might have enjoyed it. But, given my home situation, I had no doubt I was being . . . how shall I put it? Disposed of." He said it coldly, avoiding Rasha's gaze. "My father had neither the time nor the desire to look after me. In fact, he had no clue. My mother, well, she soon packed up and left for Houston to look after my grandmother. Now, she claims she had no choice. I doubt that any child in my position would've seen it as anything less than being abandoned." Luke paused, bemused. "Satisfied?"

Rasha shrugged. "Satisfied."

Luke stole a glance at her, smiling, unconvinced. They stood by a large sign advertising Bateaux Parisiens cruises on the Seine. Out of what seemed to Rasha a desperate urge to stave off further mention of his past, he suddenly exclaimed, "Let's take one!"

She fell back a step. "I don't know. To be honest, I'm not too keen. Boats make me sick."

"You'll be fine. Come on. It takes an hour at the most."

Before Rasha could protest further Luke led her down the stairs to the ticket booth. She took a seat by the edge of the boat, Luke snugly at her side. He leaned over and extended a hand under the row of seats in front of them, searching.

"What are you looking for?" Rasha asked.

"A bucket. They have them on cruise boats in Amsterdam," he replied, matter-of-fact.

She frowned. "What do you need a bucket for?"

He gave her a wicked smile. "You did say boats made you sick."

Rasha laughed. "I didn't mean seasick, literally."

"What then?"

Heartsick, she thought. Instead she said, "Never mind."

"Listen, sunshine. You can't expect me to pour my heart out to you and then you clam up. You owe me one."

Over a loudspeaker, a guide welcomed the tourists on the Bateaux Parisiens: ". . . *Au fil de la croisière, vous allez découvrir les trésors de Paris. Le Louvre, Notre-Dame* . . ." As they pulled away from the pier, Luke's insistent gaze fixed on her, Rasha relented.

"I'd never been on a boat before then . . .," she began softly. "1976. The situation was at its worst in Beirut, the city in the throes of civil war. The shelling was incessant and we couldn't leave our homes." The boat's motion somehow drove Rasha to open up, more for her own sake than for Luke's. Although she was reluctant to dredge up bad memories, she dreaded that the conversation would otherwise come to a standstill. There was little she could reveal of herself without somehow bringing up the war that defined her. What else could she possibly talk about?

As they went down the Seine, the ever-changing scenery and the forward movement made her feel her words would lift, scatter like dried dead leaves, unheard, and unrecorded. "We huddled in the stairwell for hours on end, deluding ourselves that we were protected. The idea was to move away from the exposed front part of the building to the back, which was sort of shielded by other buildings. The more walls there were separating us from the mortars, the safer we were. That was our only shelter."

Her mind dwelled for a moment on a vision of herself, Karim, her parents, and a few neighbours on the staircase, their shadows flickering against dirty hand-printed walls. "Only when the battles were clear of our neighbourhood were we able to stay in one of the rooms. We whiled away the time playing cards until the early hours of the morning. We slept by day and stayed up by night."

"*Nous sommes à Paris du moyen âge, de Quasimodo. Voici Notre-Dame de Paris, entreprise en 1163 à l'initiative de l'évêque de Paris Maurice de Sully . . .*"

Rasha bent forward for a clear view of the gothic cathedral. "Breathtaking, isn't it? It almost looks as if it had been embroidered. Wasn't it Monet who painted it at different times of the day?"

Seemingly eager to hear her story, Luke followed her gaze with some disinterest. "That was actually the Cathédrale de Rouen."

"Of course. How stupid of me!"

"They do look similar though," Luke added in an attempt to minimize her embarrassment. "A lot of people make the mistake. It's no big deal." He waved it off with a flick of the hand.

But it was a big deal for Rasha. Her memory lapses had become more frequent and her concentration was dwindling. Lately, she strained to remember dates, incidents, and verses which years before had rolled off her tongue like water from a source. Whenever she tried to recollect something she had imbibed in her college days, it was like diving in murky waters, and more often than not coming out empty-handed. Her mind would wander as she read or corrected exam papers. She would find herself going over the same page time and again, and nothing registering. Looking back, the few events that had claimed chunks of her memory were exclusively incidents of war.

She spoke out in a daze. "Cathedrals are such havens. They're so . . . so . . ."

"Spiritual?" Luke sniggered.

"Calming," Rasha replied flatly.

"Carry on."

"Well, my father decided to whisk us off to safety. The airport was closed and we had to leave by the port of Jounieh, east of Beirut . . ."

"You and . . ."

"My mother and my brother Karim."

"How old were you?"

"Twenty."

"Go on," he said.

"My father had a driver from his factory escort us through the Green Line. You know about the Green Line?" Rasha asked.

"The dividing line between East and West Beirut."

She nodded. "Snipers' killing field. At the time Arab peace-keeping forces were manning most of the roadblocks but the situation was far from under control. We headed off at dawn with what little luggage we could take . . ."

"Why didn't your father go with you?"

"He was worried about his factory. He and his brother, my uncle, had taken over the family's juice-bottling business after my grandfather died. It was in East Beirut, you see, and it was too dangerous for either of them to cross over. They had to rely on their manager, who lived in East Beirut, to report back on any damage. Anyway, I suppose my father hoped for a cease-fire so he could see it for himself, or restart it. He promised he would meet us in Cyprus as soon as he could."

"Did he?"

"No."

*"Le Pont de la Concorde devant vous. La Bastille.
Sur vôtre gauche, l'Hôtel des Invalides et juste à côté le
Musée Rodin."*

"We should go there later. I love Rodin.
Especially *le Penseur.*"

"My choice would be *le Baiser*," Luke confessed
with a roguish smile.

In fact, that was Rasha's favourite as well, along
with *la Cathédrale*, but she was too timid to admit it
because of its sentient, palpable, passion. For a brief
moment, the image of the intertwined sculpted hands of *la
Cathédrale* revived a painful recollection of Leila, the art
student.

"Now will you please stop changing the subject,"
he snapped, half in jest.

"Where was I?"

"Crossing over to the port."

Rasha lingered to collect her thoughts. She transported herself back to Beirut. "The streets were deserted,
not a soul in sight. I was terrified we would be shot at. I'd
heard so many horrific stories about people killed by
sniper fire. There was this one report of a woman who was
running across the Green Line cradling a child in her
arms. Like a predator on the prowl, the sniper waited
awhile before he took a shot at the heel of her shoe from
the roof. He looked on as she hobbled for cover, wailing
and pleading for God's mercy. Then, when she probably
thought she was in the clear, he took one clean shot at her
head.

When the child dropped to the ground, he left him
to cry for some time before he . . ." Rasha could not bring
herself to say it. Her windpipe closed. "Have you ever
heard sniper fire, Luke? Its ring is singularly different. It
sounds like a needle hitting a marble floor, amplified a
million times. Pin-sharp." She pinched her finger and

thumb to illustrate. "Ping! Ping! Just like that. Icy cold, cruel, pointless." Rasha's stomach churned. She passed trembling fingers along her scar.

Luke swung an arm around her.

"Anyway . . . we made it to the port in one piece. It was pandemonium. People were jostling, shouting. Militiamen were everywhere, menacing and gloating over their power. They checked our passports and ordered us to the end of the pier. We passed several ferries, each time hoping that one of them was ours. We were so wrong. At the very end of the pier, a tug boat no more than twenty metres long and ten metres wide swayed in the waters. That miserable compilation of timbers was to carry us for sixteen hours to Larnaca. People scrambled aboard like cattle, determined to get a seat.

"We climbed on and managed to secure three chairs. Those were folding wooden chairs that weren't even fixed to the deck. They were set out in a circle, about fifteen of them for at least forty . . . maybe fifty, passengers. In the middle lay a filthy blue mattress that I swore I wouldn't sleep on. The bottom line was we were refugees and as you know beggars can't be choosers. We felt humiliated, frightened and disgusted at the same time. I tried to look out to sea, to ignore the persecution that went on around me, to ignore that I was a part of it. But there was no escape. Mothers cuddled their crying children, unable to provide them with any other comfort. Destitute men stared vacantly, having lost all hope, uncertain of their fate. The choking sound and rancid smell of retching was everywhere. One woman threw up on our supply of water. We had nothing left to drink. War is a great leveller, isn't it Luke?" she asked rhetorically. "I only had to look at my mother and brother to know that their thoughts were not far from mine."

Rasha grew impatient and frustrated that her words came out all wrong. Something stood between her and her ordeal, preventing her from conveying the extent of the terror and humiliation she had felt then. It may have been Luke or the distance that the beauty of Paris placed between her and her embattled country. Not able to reconcile her location now with the past she recounted, she preferred to stop rather than risk trivializing the misery that had speared her heart and her pride. Rasha was convinced that a breakdown in communication between those who had suffered a misfortune and those who hadn't made it impossible for the damaged to cross over to the unscathed. So Luke could never fathom the torment she had been through.

In a way she did not want him to, for she had also become perversely possessive of her fear. She almost could not live without it, and the normality that surrounded her now challenged her to relegate it to the past and move on. But she would not discard even one of the many significant episodes in her life that had cruelly exposed her limitations as a human being and had drawn out of her a brutish instinct for survival.

"*La Ville Lumière . . . ville de Picasso, de la Joconde, de Piaf . . . le Paris éternel.*"

"By the time we set out, it was dark." She spoke faster now, with some detachment. "The seasickness tablets I'd taken started to take effect. Suddenly, it was as if I'd been propelled forward, landing on the infested mattress I'd vowed not to touch. I slept through most of the trip. When I did wake up now and then and realized I was *still* on the boat, I shut my eyes as quickly as I could hoping that the truth would go away. Sixteen hours later, we docked at Larnaca. It must've been very early, sixish maybe, because the customs offices were still closed. We were made to wait on deck for an additional hour until our passports could be checked. There must've been an ice-cream vendor there, because I remember quenching my thirst on a lemon ice lolly . . ."

"Mille neuf cent. Matisse fait exploser les couleurs avec son impressionnisme . . ."

"I love the Impressionists, don't you?" she asked, intending to dissipate the black mood her account had spun.

"Who in his right mind doesn't? We'll go to the Jeu de Paume after this tour. Carry on."

"That's it. That's my boat experience," Rasha concluded with the tone of a dispassionate narrator.

"What happened when you got off the boat?"

"We asked the taxi driver to take us to a hotel. We ended up at the Holiday Inn or one of those chains. Fortunately, they had one room due to be vacated by one o'clock. So we waited. We looked terrible. We hadn't showered for two days. Our hair was fleecy, our skin scaly, and our mouths felt like sandpaper. We watched the tourists as we sipped silently on lemonade by the pool. I remember thinking how different we were, how removed we were from everyone and everything. We were destitute, figuratively speaking. We had lost what it took to frolic by the pool, to laugh wholeheartedly, to soak in the sun. We were like prehistoric cavemen looking on the twentieth century, baffled and uncomprehending. We were exhausted, miserable and in shock." She paused. She recollected her thoughts at the time without voicing them. It had pained her to see that life carried on as normal outside Lebanon. Time had been held captive in her home-country and she had naïvely expected the world to be commiserating.

"Le prochain pont est le pont Marie. Le plus romantique de Paris. Faites un vœu. Il se réalisera."

Luke waited to see whether she would continue. When she did not, he prodded further. "How long were you there for?"

"We'd meant to spend a couple of weeks, a month at the most, until the airport opened. That's always been an indication that the situation was under control. When the prospect of our return looked bleak we rented an apartment on a monthly basis."

"And your father?"

"We couldn't call him. The phone lines were down. We communicated by word of mouth, through friends or acquaintances leaving or returning to Beirut. In the end, we flew back in November."

Luke had assumed his usual attentive position, elbows on thighs, hands clasped, doubled over. He stared at Rasha with penetrating eyes, unwilling to shift his gaze. She wished he would take her in his arms and kiss her. She wished that by doing so he would dissipate her sadness. Yet she wanted him to know that her story barely scratched the surface of her despair.

He lowered his eyes. "I'm . . ." She expected him to say sorry, but he must've thought better of it. It was an empty word, a cheap filler for an awkward silence.

When he turned to Rasha, who looked at him quizzically, he murmured, "If you wouldn't think it insensitive, I'd take a picture of you right now."

"Why?"

"Because it exposes you . . . your hurt, your sadness," Luke said, his voice thick as molasses.

Rasha looked away. It was not that one incident alone that enfeebled her, but talking about any wartime experience triggered off a landslide of misfortunes, hers and others'.

"Compared with other people, we count ourselves lucky. We've been spared, you know." Rasha twisted the locket around her neck.

"What's that?"

"This?" She looked down at her chain. "It's a *sura* from the Koran. *Ayat 'l Kursi*. It's supposed to protect you, like the St. Christopher medal, I suppose."

"You're Muslim?" Luke sounded surprised.

"Yes, I am. Does it matter?" Rasha asked a little too sharply. Religion, with its political undertones, had caused unbridgeable gulfs among her people.

"Hell, no!" Luke blurted out. "Not in the f . . ." He did not say it. "Not in the least."

Rasha grinned, amused by his omission. When he caught her eye, they burst out laughing. Then suddenly, Luke's beaming face darkened. As had happened at Hana's when they first met, his smile was gone. His eyes communicated desperate longing, hesitation, sexuality, lust. It was his habit, Rasha soon noticed, to keep unbridled joy in check, controlling it with sobriety. The instantaneous change in his expression was a stopper that prevented him from drowning into imagined bliss. Carefree as he may seem, Rasha suspected that Luke had little faith or trust in others. His look begged for reassurance that his feelings were genuinely reciprocated, that Rasha or any other would not let him down.

"Just out of curiosity," Luke went on, "Are you Sunni or Shi'a?"

"My, you *have* done your homework." Rasha's admiration was genuine. "Sunni, originally from Tripoli. And you?"

"Neither."

Rasha looked at him askance.

"Anglican. Church of England!" He announced, crossing himself theatrically. "What's that scar from?" he asked, running a finger across his own eyebrow to demonstrate.

Rasha mimicked his gesture. "Bike accident when I was small. I slipped off and hit the brick around a flower-bed. It's my 'red badge of courage,'" she added superciliously, drawing a vague comparison between her sense of inadequacy, her cowardice, and that of Stephen Crane's character Henry Fleming. "You probably thought it was caused by shrapnel or something like that, didn't you?"

"Well. It would seem logical."

"I keep safe," she retorted lightly. "Sometimes, too safe."

"Where you come from, Rasha, I imagine you can never be *too safe*."

Their tour over, they headed for the Jeu de Paume, where Rasha was only too happy to linger at the Impressionists' works. Their resplendent landscapes, their uniquely dainty technique of capturing serenity were what she coveted. Renoir, Sisley, Monet, Pissarro engaged all her senses and offered up the invigorating promise that Rasha craved to harbour. Her appreciation of art, never professional, was unashamedly subjective, and she was only drawn to the works of artists that moved her. The Impressionists' vivid colour palette, their world, was what she needed, what she pined for. And for a brief moment while she eyed each and every masterpiece, she was transported by a splendour she had known only fleetingly.

She stood transfixed by Monet's *le Bassin aux Nymphéas: Harmonie Verte*, Luke close behind her. His warm breath caressed her neck.

"I wonder whether they got as much pleasure from painting their works as we do from viewing them," Rasha murmured, captivated by the iridescent surface of the water. "I mean, look at the texture, the water among all this lush landscape. You can feel the life in the stillness. It's remarkable."

"He actually had that little Japanese bridge built. When he bought the terrain in Giverny, it was a marsh,

and he managed to divert water from a tributary of the
Epte and dug the pond."

Rasha stared at him. "Quite the researcher, aren't
you?"

He shrugged. "Just read it somewhere." She felt
his chest lightly touch her back.

"I suppose one could derive equal satisfaction
from *staring* at a book," he whispered the sarcastic
remark in her ear.

Rasha looked over her shoulder at him. "Back to
the debate on pictures versus words, are we?" she began,
referring to their discussion on visual stimulation at
Hana's party. "You can be *as* enthralled by a story."

"Sure you can. But it'll take much longer, won't it?"

"Precisely, so your enjoyment is more lasting.
Instant gratification can be detrimental," she retorted
vaguely.

"Not in my books, sunshine. I'll take gratification
any way it comes."

As they approached Monet's *Cathédrale de Rouen*
series, Luke beckoned Rasha to come closer and drew
her attention to the nameplate. They were head to head,
his breath warm on her cheek. "Oops, look at that, they
must've made a mistake. This should read '*Notre-Dame*'!
I should go tell them," he announced, straightening up.
Rasha gave him a hard slap on his side and meant it. She
walked away, feigning irritation, when Luke rushed after
her, grabbed her by the hand, and slung his arm over her
shoulder. He pulled her to him and kissed her on the
forehead.

"Know something? I could easily fall in love with
you," he crooned, leaving her with the sensation that vel-
vet had brushed her sensitized skin.

Just like that. "I could easily fall in love with
you." The seed of promise planted by her viewing of the

great artists now bloomed into elation. Her own reality was changing into a dream, a wish that it would be fulfilled. If you ever do, Luke, she caught herself thinking, I'd love you right back.

From then on their intimacy grew like a rising tide that washed away their timidity and restraint. They touched incessantly, inadvertently, purposely, to draw each other's attention to this and that, to move away, to simply feel each other's skin. Ever so slowly, it was as if they were fusing into one, and it felt so right that Rasha had no compunction about surrendering to it.

By the time they had reached the Musée Rodin, the awkwardness between them had abated.

In front of *la Cathédrale*, Rasha intertwined her own hands, comparing them to the sculpture.

"What are you doing?" Luke asked.

"This is amazing. Look at this. I always thought they were the hands of one person, but they're not. They're two right hands and if you look closely, it looks like one's a man's and the other's a woman's."

Luke circled the stone sculpture. "You're absolutely right. How perceptive."

"Actually, I read it somewhere."

"Clever!"

They strode on to see *The Kiss*, viewing on the way the works of Camille Claudel, Rodin's student and mistress for nearly fifteen years. The couple embracing in *The Kiss*, Rasha read on the plaque beneath it, represented Paolo and Francesca, of Dante's Inferno, who were chastised because of their forbidden love.

"It's a shame that something so beautiful should represent a love that's condemned. I was under the impression that it symbolized pure, vindicated love."

"That's what makes it so passionate, so intense." His voice oozed sensuality. "How about we strip down to reproduce the pose . . . just to make sure this sculpture hasn't got a trick hidden in it like *la Cathédrale*," he added deadpan.

Rasha clapped her hand over her mouth to suppress an outburst of laughter. Unable to, she rushed out into the gardens, and let it loose, clutching her sides as she laughed like she had not done for a long time.

She grew to expect and enjoy Luke's banter, and took each and every one of his quips with the lightness it deserved. As they were about to enter Notre-Dame, Luke stopped her in her tracks and asked, flatly, "Do you think Muslims are allowed?" By sunset, Rasha could not recall having laughed so much in one day.

Just outside Hana's building, an awkward moment set in. They stood at arm's length, he with his hands in his pockets, she with her arms folded, shifting now and then to let people through on the narrow sidewalk. They were equally reluctant to part ways—it seemed almost unnatural—and each fumbled for something to say. When Luke suggested they get together for dinner, Rasha declined as delicately as she could, muttering that she had to spend time with her aunt for after all she was her guest. Deep down, though, Rasha was eager to take refuge in familiarity. Though Luke had gone several steps beyond being the "stranger", Rasha could not drop her guard completely. Everything about him was still too exciting, so debilitating in its novelty that she felt the need to retreat into comfort, to be with someone who knew her well.

For a split second, as Luke leaned forward to kiss her, Rasha made to offer him her cheek. But before she could, her mouth was his, her desire, his. His kiss, soft, greedy, his embrace possessive, suddenly revealed to Rasha his overpowering control and her lack of it. "I've got to see you tomorrow," he whispered at last, his face only inches from hers. Rasha nodded, speechless, then stepped into the courtyard, the caress of his eyes gentle on her back.

"Hi, habibti, your parents called." Hana was reclined on the sofa, a stack of papers on her lap.

Rasha held her breath. "Is everything all right there?"

"All fine." Hana tapped the side of the seat. "Come sit next to me. So, where have you been?"

Rasha perched herself on the edge of the sofa. "With Luke."

"Ah!" Hana's almond eyes widened. "Did you have a good time?"

"I had a great time," Rasha replied warily, recalling her aunt's cautioning words of the morning and suddenly beset by the inevitable reality of her parents' disapproval of Luke, should they ever find out. The entire day she had lived out a fantasy, a dream that would have been impossible in Beirut. Away from parental control, she had given in to the intoxicating passion that was Paris. It struck her that this was the first time ever she had been alone on a date of her choice, the first time that she did not have to report to anyone or dread her father's reception of a male acquaintance. From the moment the sun had risen to the moment it had set, Rasha had lived for herself only.

Hana raised herself on one elbow and stroked Rasha's cheek, snapping her out of her introspection. "Come along now, get changed. We're going out."

Rasha wondered where Hana got her energy. "Where to?"

"La Coupole."

"What's at La Coupole?"

"*Les fruits de mer!*" Hana declared grandly.

Right then, it dawned on Rasha that she had not eaten all day.

Chapter Four

◆

The sun that bathed Paris in its warm radiance that morning was hers, Rasha's. This was to be her day—the harbinger of a fledgling romance. Her own. And she was more than ready to embrace it.

Dinner with Hana had been a light-hearted affair. Neither spoke of Luke, dwelling instead on reminiscences, news of the extended family, and pleasing anecdotes. Throughout the evening, the exhilaration that had enveloped Rasha stayed with her, her heart brimming with anticipation of meeting Luke again and with redeemed confidence in herself. Between Hana and Luke, she was being lifted to new heights to which she surrendered unconditionally. Intoxicated by the freshness injected into her bloodstream—Luke, an untiring nightlife, her physical and social independence—her thoughts wandered but could not linger for more than a moment on her parents and Karim, on the paleness of their life edged with uncertainty and constant threat. An all-consuming, burning desire held all latent guilt at bay as Rasha revelled in the tantalizing promise of intrigue.

Gradually, she had become possessed by a selfishness she had never acknowledged before. A selfishness fuelled by infatuation and rapacious longing.

Each day forged another link in the chain that was to bind her to Luke. Their conversations flowed, marked by intermittent silences that were no longer awkward as their physical contact grew more frequent and natural. They rediscovered Paris together: Jardin des Tuileries, Bois de Boulogne, the Tour Eiffel—their exploits serving more as a conduit into each other's pasts, thoughts, likes and dislikes. They set aside days for long trips to Versailles and Fontainebleau and charted their course with the unspoken understanding that they would be together for the rest of Rasha's stay.

Rasha sat still on a stool as the bearded artist swept quick, adept strokes over the pearly white card-board. They were in Place du Tertre, Montmartre, on her fourth day in Paris when Rasha gave in to Luke's request that she have her portrait done. The tree-lined square, so vivid with colourful paintings and rich with talent, buzzed with untiring activity. Flashing a humble smile, the old man presented Rasha with the finished product and pocketed his fee from Luke, murmuring, *"Merci, monsieur."*

Rasha made a face. "It's not quite me."

Luke held the sketch in both hands, nodding. "It's close."

She ran her index finger over the upper part. "The eyes are too wide apart. Too large." She grimaced, "And the nose. It's too straight. The entire portrait is too . . . how shall I put it . . . too neat!"

"He draws what he sees. And what he did manage to capture is the image of perfection." He gave her a peck on the lips, rolling up the cardboard. "Here, you keep it."

Rasha was taken aback. "Me? What would I do with it? I thought you wanted it for yourself."

"I have you right here," Luke patted his camera. "And deep, deep in here," he added with a fist to his chest. "I don't need a Montmartre artist to do it for me."

By these frequent pronouncements, Luke had Rasha levitating. He touched her with a unique tenderness that Rasha had rarely known in a man before. His every move was liquid, his every gesture a delicate ripple that lapped against her senses. With the swift force of a strong current, he carried her away with his passion.

Luke made her feel that she was the best thing that had ever happened to him. Whatever had attracted him to her lay in her quintessential self, divorced from and untainted by her environment back home. His confidence made up for her timidity and in his shadow she began to believe that all was possible. Rasha pondered all this while she scrutinized him, always ending up with the same conclusion that she may have found a soul mate, fiercely brushing aside any misgivings over the durability of their relationship.

Hana's preoccupation with work and the long hours she spent on the rushed translation project gave Rasha the space she craved with Luke. So she dedicated her evenings to her aunt, to dinner at home or a quick meal in a nearby *brasserie*. On those occasions, whenever Hana mentioned Luke, Rasha circled the subject, determined to sidestep sober cautioning. She played down their relationship, labelling it as no more than friendship, companionship. At all costs, she would guard her feelings for him like a lioness would her cubs. Spellbound, Rasha was determined that nothing and no one should stir her conscience.

As she got to know him better, Rasha discovered in Luke a quiet boldness and spontaneity that reminded her of Malek's predecessor, Farid. Farid had verve, a joie de vivre that had attracted her and had given her a vicarious taste of freedom. He had challenged Rasha's restraint and prudence enticing her to take risks, which she did with exhilarating dread of being found out. They took secret rides to the mountains on his motorbike, and on a couple of occasions she had even let him talk her into smoking hashish. For the brief period they had spent together, Farid had reawakened in Rasha the adventurous spirit she had once possessed as a schoolgirl, an impulsiveness that had caved in to age and her father's strong hold. At the time, what had drawn her to Farid was precisely what her father had found to be reprehensible: a lack of responsibility and purpose. A year later, the tug of war between Farid's unbridled energy and her father's dogged resistance took its toll on Rasha, leaving her with no choice but to end the relationship.

The similarities between Farid and Luke, however, went no further than their tenacity. Luke was a man with a definite purpose, a man who exhibited a confidence bred by a necessity to carve his way through life unaided. His manner with people was assured and he managed to win over children and adults alike with disarming charm and flattery. His solitary travels had hardened him against any mishap that would have left another soul broken, dispirited. Once Luke set his mind on something, he would achieve it, undeterred. Rasha recognized that she was his foil, exhibiting none of his courage, none of his confidence. She had been conditioned to bow down to disappointments, to accept that eventualities could change the course of her life. While Luke believed he could shape his destiny and realize the impossible, Rasha maintained that hers had already been dictated by some celestial power and was therefore completely out of her control.

These were subtle disparities in their characters and their outlook on life that stemmed from their polarized backgrounds—differences that Rasha did not dwell on, enjoying instead the ease with which they communicated and the sustained attention they gave to each other's views.

A far more fundamental emotion linked them together, as if they had been two parts of a photograph finally brought together and rejoined with unmistakable perfection along the hairline tear. With the conviction that their dissimilarities were complementary, Rasha instinctively took refuge under Luke's wing.

Luke slouched against the steps just outside the Château de Versailles, Rasha by his side eyeing the buses disgorging American tourists in throngs.

He drew on a Gauloise. "Yanks!"

"Don't sound so derogatory. You're half a Yank yourself."

He winced. "But I'm a cultured Yank."

"A presumptuous one, too." Rasha watched him fling the Gauloise and immediately light another.

"You smoke too much. Gauloises are particularly potent, to boot."

"Odd observation coming from a Lebanese. If my memory serves me right, the only departure gate fogged up in cigarette smoke at Heathrow is normally the one crammed with passengers bound for Beirut." Then with the mock tone of an announcer, "All passengers on flight 631 to Beirut, please follow the fumes to your gate." He let out a hearty laugh.

"Very funny," Rasha retorted, smiling.

He looked at her intently. "Come on Rasha, you must've had a cigarette in your lifetime. A joint even, I'll bet. Tell me the truth. Have you?"

"No." She lied.

He raised an eyebrow.

"Once," she mumbled, eyes downcast.

"Hah, I knew it! My squeaky-clean little Muslim got high. Once!"

She nudged him with her elbow. "Why such a fuss? It was no big deal. It did nothing for me, anyway."

"Ever tried anything stronger?"

"Never! And I never will." A pause. "Have you?" She asked tentatively, hoping he had not.

"No. Jeez no. I'd never touch the hard stuff."

Rasha looked ahead, relieved. She knew of too many people years younger than her who had resorted to drugs during the war. It sickened and repelled her to converse with them in their half-comatose state. She thought back on Karim's girlfriend, May.

"Why so quiet?" Luke snapped her out of her reverie.

"I was just thinking of Karim."

"You hardly ever mention your family, you know that?"

"Coming from someone who pours his heart out," she remarked pointedly.

"Touché." He tapped the tip of her nose with his finger. "What made you think of him? Did he have an addiction problem?"

"Karim? Never! It was someone he knew long ago. A girlfriend. During the war, she became involved with the wrong people and they got her onto heroin. In no time at all she changed from a bright, witty young girl to a spaced-out, incommunicative addict."

"How did your brother deal with it?"

"In the end, there was little he could do really. He tried to move her away from the crowd, promising that he would see her through her withdrawal. Being a medical student, he was certain he could get proper help." Rasha wedged her hands between her knees. She knew it was not her business to divulge her brother's past but she assumed that the chances of Luke ever meeting Karim were probably nil. "She wouldn't listen. In the end he had no choice but to give her an ultimatum: him or the drugs. He lost, and it broke his heart to have to end their two-year relationship. Then one day May got caught in crossfire and died from a stray bullet to the head. Karim was devastated, inconsolable."

"That *is* tough."

"Yes, it is." Rasha squinted against the sun. "Speaking of girlfriends," she started casually, "I don't suppose you've ever had any?"

"No, none whomsoever," Luke retorted in a similar playful tone. "And I presume I'm your first as well?"

Rasha turned round to face him, grinning.

"Thought as much." He was silent, as if pondering his next question. "All this mushy, lovey-dovey, 'love at first sight' bull. You don't believe in it, do you?"

"Never have and never will," Rasha confirmed, smiling broadly.

"I'm glad we see eye to eye on this." He wrapped a palm around the nape of her neck and kissed her passionately. Placing his forehead against hers, he added in a hushed tone,

"Rasha Halwani, someone should've warned me you'd come into my life."

In the six days that they had been together, Luke and Rasha had woven for themselves a little cocoon, a timeless little realm that shielded them from unwanted cares and from unkind reality. In that snug world and by a sleight of hand, Luke had unwittingly managed to transform Rasha from the guilt-ridden, anxious daughter of Amin Halwani to the Rasha who embraced giddy abandon like never before. She never once brought up her difficulties with her father, and had almost forgotten the depths to which she could sink or the macabre pessimism that could take hold of her relentlessly. Her euphoria obscured clarity of vision and lucid thought, unreasonably leading her to think that time would stand still for the two of them. But as her departure date loomed close, whatever power of self-persuasion she mustered would not alter the fact that she and Luke would soon have to face a painful separation. Day by day, the dreaded prospect inched its way through her mind, threatening to dampen her high spirits.

Then the incident in Saint-Denis occurred.

Happiness, Rasha knew only too well, was a sublime, tenuous emotion, too brittle to withstand the onslaught of grief or lurking fears. It was only a matter of time before Rasha's demons would resurface, abruptly steering her behaviour, mercilessly slapping her into sobriety.

On that evening in the red-light district of Saint-Denis, Rasha glimpsed from afar a couple having a heated argument. She made out the woman to be in her late twenties, scantily dressed in a black hip-hugging skirt and an off-the-shoulder lycra top, her hair a mane of flaming red. The man looked a few years older, unkempt, one side of his shirt protruding from baggy khaki pants.

"Luke, I think there's a fight brewing over there," she said under her breath.

"Where?"

"Across the street," she replied, tipping her chin.

Luke's eyes zoomed in on the couple. It took him a fraction of a second to reach his own assessment of the situation. "Doubt it," he said decidedly. "I'll give you two scenarios. She's either his wife who's just found out that he has a mistress or caught him picking up a prostitute. Or . . . she's his mistress, possibly a regular, who's lost it because, it turns out, he's still sleeping with his wife!" Luke grinned widely, delighted with his comical interpretation. "Mind you, the way she's dressed, I hope for his sake she's not his wife."

His voice reached Rasha through a tunnel of muffled sounds and faceless shadows. Struck by the sparks of hostility that flew between the couple, she was already drawn into their sphere of tension and acrimony. She watched them from the corner of her eye, her body in position to turn away.

"No, Luke." Her voice faltered as the back of her neck prickled. "This is bad. Please let's go." Hooking her arm in his, she tried to pull him away from the scene.

"The bastard's pulled out a knife!" Luke snapped his arm free and whipped his camera off his neck. He darted across the street where passers-by had already intervened and managed to restrain the aggressor. Rasha did not budge, all the while crying out for Luke to come back. Shock waves of fear shot through her every limb, her heartbeat fast as a hummingbird's, her legs liquefying beneath her. The commotion, the strident screams cautioning, warning, were universal, transporting Rasha in a flash to the car bomb that fateful evening with Malek. The woman's persistent hysterical taunts at her assailant—who struggled to break loose and lunge at her—made Rasha's blood curdle. Cursing under her breath, Rasha desperately wanted her to stop instead of exacerbating the situation. She looked with abject scorn on the woman who, arms on her haunches and doubled over, rained insults and abuse on the aggressor.

Then came the flashing lights, the gendarmes, the arrest. Still, the redhead would not desist and, arms flailing, pursued the moving police car, her cries shrill and unnerving. With a jolt, without warning, she spun round to Luke and berated him for his voyeurism. A gendarme who lingered to take statements motioned him to move away. Luke slung the camera on his shoulder and, arms outstretched in a placatory gesture, began to backtrack.

Long after the situation was defused, Rasha could barely move. Her terror did not tame her, nor did it seep into her subconscious, but morphed into rage, blind fury. Before she could stop herself she was flinging angry accusations at Luke as if she had become afflicted with the redhead's temper.

"Are you mad?" she yelled, drumming her temple with her index finger. "What the hell did you think you were doing? They'd already got the guy." She flung an arm aimlessly. "Was it so important for you to get them on camera? What's wrong with you?" Acute anger mingled with shame. Anger because Luke would not heed her pleas to move away, leaving her instead by the sidewalk. Shame because she could not handle witnessing or being in the middle of conflict. By his curiosity, Luke had challenged her sense of self-preservation.

Luke froze. He faced her, rigid, stupefied. His astonishment dug deep into Rasha, churning her insides.

"You think I'm crazy? You think I'm overreacting, don't you Luke?" She ran off her badgering like machine-gun fire. "What's so titillating about a woman on the verge of being sliced up? Tell me, Luke! What is it that draws people to violence or . . . or accidents? What do people want to see, blood?"

Hesitantly, Luke stepped forward and reached out to touch her. With one jerk, Rasha repelled him.

"Don't touch me! I don't want anyone to touch me." She walked around in half-circles like a caged animal. Her voice was more like a croak. A lump in her throat constricted her breathing and a chill fanned to her extremities. Apprehension and shock, hot and cold, played havoc with her body. She was a few meters from Luke, standing alone, brittle, unprotected. She shook uncontrollably, until her only release realized itself. Tears streamed down her cheeks, thick, furious, unbidden. Quiet at first then turning into a paroxysm of sobbing. Like a wave of warm reassurance, Luke moved towards her and wrapped her against his chest. He said nothing, but Rasha could hear his heartbeat, loud and clear.

Head tucked against Luke as they walked away, Rasha could not stop weeping. The dam within her had burst and her woes came gushing out, unimpeded.

Gradually, numbness crept through her, drying out the source of her tears.

They stopped at a café. Luke gently pulled her away from him, hands steady on her shoulders, soliciting her gaze. "Are you all right?"

Rasha nodded, too feeble to reply. He led her to an outside table. She sat, rigid, eyes averted, suddenly self-conscious and contrite.

When the waiter brought the carafe of wine, Luke poured her a glass. "Here, this'll make you feel better."

Rasha sipped on her drink. A taut silence followed. Long and heavy. She prepared herself for Luke's rebuttal. She was now certain he would never want to see her again. Curled up to light a Gauloise—despite the fact that no breeze threatened to put out the flame—Luke's body language suggested a wish to turn inwards, away from her. An orange hue briefly washed over his face. Rasha felt a rush of tenderness towards him. He continued to look down.

"I'm sorry you felt threatened," he addressed the sidewalk beneath him as he blew out a cloud of smoke, "but there was no real risk. It was just an altercation. I'd never put you in danger, Rasha."

His words were vaporous, their significance too laden for Rasha to absorb. Her eyes, her ears, her whole being had shut down. Her facial muscles had hardened, and she was aware that she remained expressionless. A flicker of blame still burned inside her.

Silence again.

Rasha cleared her throat. "Unlike you, Luke, I steer clear of conflict, and I *don't* find it fascinating. There's plenty of it where I come from. Hostility, violence, are not things I want to conserve and put a caption to. They only make me want to turn away. I can't help it."

"I understand what it must be like for you . . ."

"Actually Luke, no," she interjected, trying to maintain a softness in her tone of voice, "you don't understand. You can *imagine* what it's like, but I doubt you can ever *really* understand."

"Could that be, perhaps, because you never talk about it?" His tone was laced with irritation.

"That wouldn't make the slightest difference."

"It makes all the difference, Rasha. It could bring us closer," he said tenderly. "But that's not the point here. What I'm trying to say is that, *for your own good*, you've *got* to try and control . . ."

That last word stung her. All Rasha had done, ever, was to control her feelings, stomp on her emotions. "Control what exactly, Luke? Being attuned to threat? Anticipating danger? Instinct? Do you really want to know the number of times this sense of intuition saved my skin? Vigilance, Luke, is my *only* means of protection." She gesticulated fiercely as if to drive her message home, all the while keeping her voice hushed. "I can't put it all behind me! Five days from now, I'll be back in Beirut. Back to car bombs, street fights and shelling," she blurted out acidly. "Back to where precisely this . . . this . . . *paranoia* helps me stay in one piece. All this," she flung her arms, "Paris, shimmering lights, outdoor cafés, music. That's not *my* reality. It's a fantasy. And the day I board the plane, it'll vanish! Poof. As if it never was."

Luke's face turned ashen. By her words, Rasha had as good as called their relationship a mirage. She knew he might interpret it that way, but she also knew it was tragically true. The impossibility of transposing themselves as they were now, in Paris, to her environment was beyond question. Theirs was a phantasmal romance that had no place in the chilling reality of her microcosm back home.

"That includes me, doesn't it?" Luke asked defiantly.

Rasha lowered her eyes. She did not have the answer.

Luke crushed the cigarette butt with the heel of his shoe. His knuckles blanched as he clasped his hands together, liquid eyes refracting Rasha's frustration and sense of injustice. "Don't you think I know all this?" The proximity of his harsh tone and accusative look made her recoil. Clenched teeth reduced his tirade to a murmur. "*I* know where you come from. Believe me, it hasn't escaped me that you keep a whole side to you completely bottled up. It doesn't scare me, it doesn't discourage me in the least. I'm not naïve. How could I expect anything more from someone who's spent the better part of her life in abnormal conditions?" He paused to catch his breath. "The last thing I ever wanted was to complicate my life, Rasha. Hell, I realize you have to go back to a sordid existence. I realize that what's going on here, between us, may have to come to an end. *We* might become a set of photos pasted in an album marked 'Paris. Summer of 1981'." His voice rose a notch. "But not just yet, Rasha. Don't shut me out just yet. Just remember, this is not only about you. It's also about me. And don't underestimate me. I don't give up that easily."

The whole incident had exploded in her face, and Rasha found herself uncertain as to how she should handle it. Both of them had let their emotions overtake them, and now they were even. Negativity hovered over them like a suffocating mantle, but it had brought in tow honest expression, stripped of embellishment and euphemisms. Somehow, Rasha felt that their quarrel was inevitable, the only possible outlet from the serene, yet so transient, world they had appropriated. From her experience, the bubble that rose eventually had to burst. She wanted to apologize. For what? For underestimating Luke, really. Because, in truth, she had foolishly assumed that she had pulled a blindfold over his eyes. She was almost certain it would take a long time before he got to her core. One thing she could not deny, though, was this: their responses to peril were oceans apart. Luke was the observer behind the lens and Rasha the subject in front of it. He would always see her world, soulless and scentless, minimized through his glassy cold viewfinder.

Yet wasn't his detachment what had drawn her to him? The reason Luke had captivated Rasha was precisely because he was so far removed from her daily life. Luke was to her a gust of fresh air that awakened a life dormant within her. And she, by reproaching him for what she termed as voyeurism and insensitivity, had broken the spell. If the bubble had burst this time, it was simply because Rasha had pierced it with a pin.

Sadly, when fear possessed her, as it often did, Rasha's fierce attempts to quell it always came to nothing. She could thwart anger, hide disappointment and temper joy, but terror invariably overcame all reasoning, turning her into a demented prey. To apologize would be to assume responsibility for something that was stronger than she was.

She felt light-headed. Noticing the empty carafe of wine in front of her, she realized why. She had no recollection of having drunk it all.

"There's a lot about me you don't know, Luke," she finally said in a daze, her index finger on her scar.

"No shit!" Luke blurted out.

Her lips slowly formed into a smile. "There's a lot you might not want to know."

"I'll be the judge of that." A pause. "Do me one favour, though. Next time, just before you do one of your Jekyll-and-Hyde tricks," he twirled his forefinger, "give me a warning, will you?" He glanced at her obliquely.

She gave him a sheepish look. "If I can."

For the rest of the evening, they spoke to each other as if they were treading in a minefield. To Rasha's relief, Luke did not speculate on the future of their relationship nor did he question her conviction that it would soon end. He seemed deep in thought, distant, wounded, for once uninterested in bouncing back with a quip to lighten the tension. The effect Rasha's outburst had had on him was greater than she had expected, and his silence bored into her soul.

She was now convinced that their feelings for each other were not something she could belittle or easily leave behind. But for either of them to confess that their emotions ran deeper than they cared to admit would entail a downward spiral into reality. For Rasha, it would raise certain issues she had so far skillfully avoided, such as the logistics of a lasting relationship and their cultural differences. Delving into the secrets of magic would take away childlike amazement, and Rasha was reluctant to relinquish that rare sense of wonder.

By the time they reached Hana's apartment, it was midnight. They stopped at the gate and, without a word spoken, Luke drew her to him. His chin rested against the top of her head. She felt him swallow hard. When he pulled away, he gazed at her intently, as if trying to record mentally her every feature. Then, briskly, he brushed his lips against her forehead, mumbled "See you tomorrow" and turned to leave.

With sadness trapped in her throat and with a burdened heart, Rasha shuffled her way into Hana's apartment.

"Rasha, is that you?" came the cry from the bedroom.

"Yes, Auntie Hana," Rasha murmured, loitering by the front door. She dragged her feet to her aunt's bedroom, stopping in the doorway. Hana was in bed surrounded by a pile of papers. She peered over reading glasses perched on the bridge of her nose.

"Nice day?"

Rasha nodded.

"Listen," Hana set the papers on the bedside table and removed her glasses. "I've nearly got this document wrapped up. Tomorrow, I'm taking you out for lunch!"

Lunch! On one of her last days with Luke!

"That'll be great, Auntie," she feigned excitement.

"Now come and give me a kiss."

Hana locked her niece in a bear hug. "I'm going to miss having you here."

By ten o'clock the following morning, Luke had not phoned. Rasha contemplated all courses of action: to try to contact him, wait for his call, or leave it alone. Perhaps it was the way their relationship was meant to end. Perhaps it was a blessing in disguise that did away with a tearful separation. To let it simply fizzle out.

Dismissing all thought, she looked up Carol's number and dialled. No reply. No answering machine. She replaced the receiver and sank into the chair, staring at the telephone. She tried again and let it ring longer this time. Nothing. She glanced at her watch. Twenty-five minutes past ten. If Luke were en route to see her he would get there before she had to leave for the restaurant.

Rasha endured Mme. Gilbert's vapid talk, relocating from room to room as the cleaning lady forged her way with a roaring vacuum cleaner. Twelve o'clock came and no sign of Luke. With the conviction that she got no less than she deserved, Rasha grabbed her bag and set out for the restaurant.

They were lunching at Le Soufflé, on rue du Mont Thabor, off rue de Rivoli. As the taxi circled the Place de la Concorde, Rasha admired the hieroglyphics on the obelisk from the temple of Luxor, offered by the viceroy of Egypt Mehmet-Ali to Louis Philippe in 1831. It was again a beautiful, crisp day, yet nothing could lift her spirits.

It did not help that the restaurant appeared stifling. With no view, as curtains and a solid door concealed
the clientele from passers-by, Rasha had no escape.
Seated in front of Hana, her attention was guaranteed,
unlikely to roam.

Hana examined the menu.

"Habibti, did you find it easily?"

"I took a taxi," Rasha replied as she sat down and
accepted the menu being handed to her.

"What do you recommend, Auntie?"

"All the soufflés are absolutely delicious, but I
warn you they're big."

The waiter brought along a bottle of Chablis,
uncorked it and poured a touch for Hana to sample. Once
they had placed their orders, Hana and Rasha made a
toast to absent loved ones.

"When do you have to get back to work?"

"By three, we have plenty of time."

"Is it going well?" Rasha asked, her mind dis-
tracted by where Luke was at that moment and whether
she would succeed in reaching him after lunch.

"I'm meeting with the client tomorrow. I don't
think we should have any problems. I'm just so furious
this came up while you were here." Hana screwed up her
face with irritation. "I've hardly had the chance to see
you, and I had all these plans. Things we would do together. I'm really so sorry."

"I could use it as an excuse to come back," Rasha
forced a smile.

"Oh! I'd love to have you here again." She sipped
on her wine. "I have a feeling though that you didn't have
such a bad stay after all," she fixed Rasha with inquisitive
eyes.

"It's been nice."

"Too nice to walk away from?"

Rasha gazed out the window. "Everything here is too nice to walk away from."

"That's true." Hana rested her elbows on the table, closer to Rasha. "So, tell me, where have you been so far? What have you seen?"

Rasha trailed her fingertips over the rim of her glass. "Most of the sights, really. Notre-Dame, les Invalides, Montmartre, quite a few galleries and museums. I've loved every minute." Her face beamed. "It's been so refreshing. A good break. And Luke has quite a sense of humour too. He's good company." She stopped herself at that. To gush any further would, without fail, pave the way for a sermon from her aunt.

Hana gave her an earnest smile, the lines around her mouth forming deep grooves. "He struck me as being quite a decent young man. Handsome too." She sat back in her chair, rearranging her cutlery. "You remember the village church round the corner from our old stone house? Well, as a little girl, whenever there was a wedding, normally on a Sunday, I'd follow the crowd all decked in their finest whites, the little girls' hair tied with pearly silk ribbons," Hana raised her hands to demonstrate, "Their dresses trimmed with their mothers' lacework. They looked like little angels. At the time, I so wished I'd been born a Christian so I could turn out looking like those girls, sweet as the coating on sugared almonds. Back then I made a vow . . . I promised myself that when I grew up, I'd be married in church, just to be able to wear a gown in brilliant white with a veil trailing behind me, and to have my own bevy of little angels." She paused, lost in thought. "Imagine that?"

"Well, you nearly did marry a Christian."

"A complete disaster," Hana giggled.

"That wasn't because he was Christian, really Auntie, was it?" Rasha asked, pre-empting the argument that religion could subvert a relationship.

"No, it ended badly because he was a night-club owner and a womanizer," Hana replied with a sad smile, her fiancé's deception and her gullibility clearly moving her after all those years.

"He didn't deserve you."

"He was a shit," Hana murmured, laughing.

The waiter came forward with two large soufflés. *"Un soufflé de saumon à l'oseille pour Madame et aux asperges pour Mademoiselle. Mesdames, bon appétit."*

Hana had her spoon poised. "My mistake was to ignore all the signs. Everyone, your father included, tried to warn me about Ghazi. But I wouldn't listen."

"Baba only objected to the relationship because he was concerned about the family's reputation," Rasha retorted matter-of-fact.

Hana pursed her lips. "That's true."

"Besides, you were a grown woman. You were quite capable of looking after yourself."

"Evidently not." Hana put down her spoon and locked her hands together. "Which is the point I'm trying to make here. When you're in love, you might think you're in control of the situation. You put your trust entirely in the hands of the man you're besotted with, and you can delude yourself into thinking that 'love conquers all'. But it doesn't, Rasha. It can chew you and spew you out like a pip."

Rasha kept mum, lifting her eyes only when Hana placed a hand on hers. "I tried to warn you as soon as you met Luke. I could see it in your eyes and in the past few days I've noticed, with the little time we've had together, how you've changed. You look so happy now. So different from the nervous, uptight niece I picked up from the airport. That's why I didn't want to say anything. I didn't want to spoil it for you. Still, I'm your aunt, I adore you and I don't want to see you hurt." She stopped, waiting for a reaction. None was forthcoming from Rasha. "Just tell me, where do you go from here?"

Rasha shrugged. "What happened to the 'shades of grey,' Auntie?" She asked with some smugness, recalling Hana's observation on her arrival.

"You memory's too good," Hana laughed, wagging a finger. "I'm not used to anyone marking my words."

Rasha's spoon cut into the soufflé as if through a cloud. "What if I were to stay here with you? Find a job as you suggested. Simply not go back to Beirut." She was surprised that the idea had not crossed her mind before.

Hana's almond eyes darkened. "You'd be making the biggest mistake of your life," she said unequivocally. "Take it from me, life out here is not easy. I can tell it to you straight now. I may have been the first woman in the family to have broken the mould. I've done well, I can't deny that I have. But if I could go back and relive my decision, I'm not so sure I'd go through with it. It was not worth the family rift. It was not worth the empty days and nights I've had to spend away from my brothers, my sisters-in-law, my nephews, my nieces . . . my home." Her voice quivered. "When I suggested on your arrival that you leave Beirut to come to Paris, I meant for you to do it with your parents' blessing. Only with their blessing, because to do so in spite of them would be like slicing off a whole side of you. You'll lose all sense of belonging, Rasha. And trust me, you should never, *ever* take such a massive step as a result of a week's whirlwind romance."

Dejection shaded Rasha's face. "Of all people, Auntie Hana, I thought you'd understand. Given the way you stood by your decision to marry Ghazi. Even your . . . your relationship"—she steered away from saying affair—"with Jean-Baptiste." Her eyes narrowed. "I sort of expected you to appreciate what it was like to be so . . ."—hopelessly in love was what she wanted to say—"attracted to someone."

"I'm probably the last person you should look up to for vindication, habibti. It's no secret all my relationships have ended badly. What did you expect from me? Encouragement? Did you think I'd throw you into this young man's, what's his name . . . Luke's arms." She replaced her spoon, putting her hands forward. "Listen, I don't agree with your father's attitude. I think he's wrong in dictating whom you should spend the rest of your life with or how you should conduct yourself. Especially at your age. Rasha, *I* respect your right to make your own decisions. I'd encourage you to live your life. But I can't, with a clear conscience, let you get yourself mired in a situation that *will* end in heartache."

Rasha stared out the window, above the curtain tracks, at the heads of a young couple who entertained walking into the restaurant. It was as if she were watching a puppet show. Resentment rumbled through her. It was all very well for Hana to preach to her on moral correctness. Hana, who has been physically removed from the hell that Rasha had to endure daily. In her view, her aunt—like all emigrants—had, with every day spent estranged from her country, lost a fraction of her right to comment.

"You know, Auntie Hana. Despite all the goodwill that's perpetually being directed at me, despite the family advice, sometimes unsolicited, and everyone's good intentions . . . Despite it all, sometimes I wish I'd be left alone to care for myself and make my own mistakes. I know that my parents' motivation is to avoid any slurs on the family. And I realize," she pre-empted Hana who seemed on the verge of objecting, "that that's not the case with you." Rasha strained to confine the issue to Luke without bringing up past restrictions that had eaten away at her all those years. "For the first time *ever*, this trip, I haven't had anyone look over my shoulder. That is what has made me happy. It's not just Luke. It's the fact that I could come and go as I pleased and for once allow myself to be honest about my own feelings."

It was out. All out. Relief enveloped her as she emptied out her grievances without a second thought. In that very moment, she felt totally in control. Yet deep down she knew that voicing her objections would not eradicate the obstacles.

Her eyes stung. Hana was silent, no doubt to give her the chance to compose herself. "All I'm saying Rasha is just take your time. You *have* to go back to Beirut. Think this over, away from him. If . . . if then this . . . Luke . . . proves to be the one, I promise you here and now that I will do my utmost to mediate for you."

Rasha was certain that Hana made that commitment anticipating that her niece would need someone to watch over her. She turned away as the waiter approached with the dessert menu. Hana took it and placed it on the table. She enfolded Rasha's hands in hers, smiling.

"Isn't it just horrible how men always manage to control our lives? First it's the father, then the boyfriend, then the husband . . . It's criminal isn't it? Our society is not macho, it's a bloody military camp!" She laughed, managing to claim a crooked smile from Rasha. "I feel for you, habibti, but if there's little I can do now, just remember you'll always have me to talk to."

Rasha had to admit that she did indeed feel she had an ally in her aunt. She, certainly, recognized her feelings to run deep and did not dismiss them as foolish infatuation. There was no doubt that Hana's advice was sound. In the long run, at least. If anyone really knew what Rasha was up against with her father, it was Hana.

After lunch, they walked along the leafy Champs-Élysées towards Hana's office near the Arc de Triomphe. The sappy scent filled Rasha's lungs, a simple luxury she longed for and had long ago lost in her home-country. Her entire adolescence had been about deprivation. She recalled her stroll with Luke in the Bois de Boulogne where their path through lush greenery and manicured gardens had exhilarated her. Soon, in Beirut, she will be sidestepping rubbish piles, potholes and, remorsefully, maimed victims of the war. The safe track of the Bois with its ambrosial rose gardens and ponds studded with waterlilies will by then be a fond memory. With a stab of pathos, Rasha had to brace herself for a world where humanity was not as well tended to as vegetation in Paris.

When they parted, she drifted along, pondering her conversation with Hana. She appreciated her aunt's concern and, were she in her position, Rasha would've probably done the same for her own niece. A certain resolve on her part, however, had clothed her in an armour that rebuffed salvos of sensibility and caution. Throughout lunch, her emotions for Luke had amplified ten-fold, filling her with a rush of warmth and longing. His words resonated in her mind. "It's not just about you Rasha. It's also about me." For all the people looking after her interests, who was looking after Luke's? She had won his heart, and she had every intention to handle it as she would china. Here was a man who cared for her deeply, who was good to her and she would be foolish to let it all, as he said, be reduced to photos in a scrapbook.

She stopped at a phone booth and pulled out a piece of paper. She dialled. At the first ring she heard his voice.

"Luke, it's me, Rasha."

Chapter Five

◆

"Rasha, hi," Luke's voice came back as a drone that suggested despondence or perhaps reserve but not, as far as Rasha could tell, lack of interest. It didn't escape her though that he hadn't called her "sunshine".

"Is everything okay?"

"Define 'everything'."

Rasha didn't know what to make of his reply so she simply said. "I tried to call you this morning to let you know that I was having lunch with my aunt. There was no reply."

"Sorry, I didn't hear the phone. I must've been asleep. And Carol's away for the day."

He was being curt, or so it seemed to Rasha. He had every reason to sulk after her outburst the evening before. It was now her turn to try and remedy the situation.

"I'm sorry about last night," she finally said.

"Ancient history."

A cold silence threatened to freeze the conversation.

"Anyway," Rasha picked up her tone a notch, "Hana's back at work. I thought maybe we could meet up." The phone beeped. She rummaged for a coin.

"Where are you calling from?"

"A phone booth.Rue . . . I'm not quite sure. I can't see the name. Somewhere near the Arc de Triomphe."

"To tell you the truth, I'm not feeling up to wandering the streets of Paris. A bout of flu, I think . . ." He muffled a cough.

"That doesn't sound too good. Have you seen a doctor?"

"It's not that bad."

"Too many cigarettes, maybe? . . . Well, would you rather we left it to tomorrow?" She proposed, heart pounding.

"Would you?"

The ball bounced in her court. She thought fast.

"No," she confessed.

"You could come here, if you like."

"Okay. Unless you'd like some rest."

He hadn't heard her last sentence or maybe chose to ignore it. "Do you have Carol's address?"

"Yes, I've got it here. Three avenue de Villiers. Apartment 2B?"

"That's it."

"Do you need anything from the chemist?"

"Any chemist's stock would pale by comparison with Carol's medicine cabinet. Just bring yourself. And Rasha . . .?"

"Yes?"

"Don't be long."

The sensuality in his tone sent shivers down Rasha's spine. Without for a moment considering the metro, she hailed a taxi. She was outside of herself, as if the person going through the motions were totally separate from the Rasha she knew. A better woman who went after what she wanted.

She pressed the button on the intercom and made her way up to the apartment. Luke was waiting at the door in a white T-shirt and shorts, unshaven, eyes bloodshot. He pulled her to him and she could feel his fever searing her body. Moving away ever so slightly, she placed a palm on his forehead.

"You're burning up."

"I've just taken some painkillers. They'll take effect soon."

She walked in, brushing against him, and scanned the lounge. It was impeccable, sparsely furnished and clearly childproof with not one glass ornament in sight.

"Carol obviously likes order."

He grimaced. "That was me actually. Boarding school conditioning. My sister's in fact the messiest person you're ever likely to come across. A drink?"

"Some water, please."

She waited there until he re-emerged from the kitchen, glass in hand.

"How was lunch?"

"Very good. We went to Le Soufflé. Do you know it?"

He shook his head. "Never liked the stuff. I always thought it was like eating air."

Rasha moved towards a framed photograph of a little blond girl hugging a baby. "Is that the two of you?"

"Yeah, taken yonks ago."

"You look so cute," she remarked, examining it at close range.

"I'd like to think I still do. So what did you two talk about?" He asked as he flung himself on the sofa.

"This and that," she replied straightening up.

"Me being 'this'," he tilted his head to one side, "or 'that'?" He repeated the motion in the opposite direction. He reached out for a Gauloise.

Rasha let out a laugh. "Neither. Should you really be smoking?"

He coughed.

"You're not feeling well, are you?" Rasha moved up next to him.

"I've been better."

She sipped on her water, stalling. "I'm sorry about last night," she finally said in a small voice.

"You said so on the phone."

"I meant it."

"I know you did, sunshine." His eyes locked with hers, communicating a reluctance to dwell on the dispute and a yearning for the here and now.

Before he had even approached her, before he had even touched her, a bolt of electricity shot through her every limb, scorching her nerve-endings. Passion burned through her, melting into love, hungrily consuming all will and awareness. Nothing within sustained her frame.

He moved slowly towards her, cupped her face and kissed her long and hard. His lips felt almost too hot to the touch.

"What about your sister?" she whispered.

"She won't be back until late this evening," he replied with a glint in his eye.

He led her into the bedroom which she presumed he was occupying, kicking the door shut behind them. Alone at last, Rasha could surrender to the body that possessed her.

Her mouth was hungry for his, her whole being yearning to be taken. He brushed his lips down her neck and across her collarbone, as he gently unbuttoned her blouse. He moved upwards again, along her chin, her cheek, back to her lips. With his hands, he re-sculpted her body, stroking curves she never thought she had. Luke not only brought out the woman in her, he reinvented her.

With delicate fingertips, Rasha gleaned the affections of the man who had won her heart. With every touch, she furtively gathered grains of his passions one by one, with the hope of reconstructing his innermost being. By this act of love alone could Rasha entice the man averse to words as a form of self-expression. By this act of giving, she could stealthily take what he would not willingly relinquish: himself.

Their lovemaking was gentle and slow. A dialogue of hope and reassurance, pleas and promises. It was an interfusion of two people whose waking thoughts and sober fears were diametrically opposed. Their bodies together defied mind and reality, crystallizing a domain where satiation came from feeding off each other and nothing else. They were willing captives of the moment that made them one.

Rasha rested her head against his warm chest, her arm slung across his waist. For a while they said nothing for fear that the spoken word would fail to live up to the divine expression of their souls. A light aura hovered inches over Rasha. So long as she lay still, it would not shift nor abandon her. The powerful emotion the invisible spirit emitted was rare and precious. It was rapture. A feeling she had never experienced before in the arms of a man.

Now, Rasha was certain she had never known love before. Whatever it was that she had felt for the only two men in her past, Farid and Malek, was a sham, a confused attempt to escape, or at least defy, the restrictions imposed on her. She chased the thought away before it took hold.

Luke lay motionless, eyes fixed on the ceiling. "How do you say 'I think I'm in love with you' in Arabic?"

"In simple terms, '*biftikir inni bhibbik*'," Rasha said in the impersonal tone of an interpreter. Her heart raced.

"So what's 'I love you' in this unpronounceable sentence?" Luke chuckled.

She raised her face to Luke's. "'*Bhibbik*'."

A pause.

"Are you trying to tell me something?" she asked, searching his eyes.

Luke contemplated her question. "Actually no. Just thought it would be a good start to an Arabic lesson on a lazy afternoon."

Rasha nudged him lightly. "You're incorrigible."

"I wish I were." He turned to her, adding. "In fact I think I liked myself a lot better before I met you."

Rasha lifted herself up on one elbow. "What's that supposed to mean?"

"Don't move away!"

"I want to know what you meant by that."

Luke pressed her against him, but kept his eyes averted. "You must've guessed I'm a loner at heart, Rasha. From the day I left school, I lived with friends in digs and with a few odd jobs and a grant I saw myself through a photojournalism course. I enjoyed being alone, unencumbered, free. With time I guess this self-sufficiency extended to relationships . . ."

"Any of them serious?" Rasha ventured with a tinge of jealousy.

"All very casual, trust me."

She wanted to believe him.

"Tell me about your mother."

"What do you want to know?"

"What's she like?"

"I thought I'd told you. Dark, tall . . ."

"That's not what I meant."

He let out a sigh. "My mother was absent, Rasha. When my parents divorced, she let my father whisk me off to boarding school without as much as an objection. She rarely came to visit and only occasionally made an appearance at my cricket matches. In the first few months at school I wrote to her every day, and in the end tore up every single letter." He shrugged. "I guess it was a child's desperate reaction to being hurt. I wanted to cut her off and make her suffer for it. Now she claims she had tried to stop my father from sending me away but had no power to do so. With no income and no security, she was in no position to offer an alternative. She figured that, anyway, I'd get a better education in England."

"That shouldn't stop you from trusting, Luke."

"When the only person you truly love turns her back on you, Rasha, it's difficult to bounce back. It's just become second nature to me to be wary. I refused to be tied down and the minute I felt a woman getting too close, I'd think up a trip and scurry off like a weasel. I was comfortable the way I was, me, my travels, and my camera. It was all I ever wanted, all I ever needed. Why would I want to complicate my life?"

"Too scared to fall in love, maybe?" Rasha suggested, recognizing the cause for Luke's guardedness, the significance behind his sombre expression. She considered his behaviour in hindsight, the sudden shifts in his mood, from laughter to gravity, from abandon to caution. All the while, he must have been wondering whether he could entrust Rasha with his naked soul. She realized, with stinging regret, how her entire tirade about the transience of their relationship would have disheartened him. It only confirmed his suspicion that nothing was lasting and no one was worthy of his trust.

"That's exactly what Carol says." He smiled wryly as if expressing his disagreement with the two women's like reasoning. "Since she took a psychology course, she attributes all our hang-ups to my parents' divorce. She's convinced I see all relationships as hopelessly doomed. What a load of bull!"

The irony that she and Luke strove to protect themselves in their own way against their demons did not escape Rasha. Both avoided hurt, Luke's being emotional, hers physical.

"How has that changed then, Luke? With me, I mean."

His chest rose and fell underneath Rasha's head. "Somehow, you've managed to break down my defences. You make me feel . . . vulnerable, I guess." She heard him swallow. "Rasha, I think I *bhibbik*."

His attempt made her smile with amusement but her eyes were red-rimmed, moist. She craned her neck to get a glimpse of him. "*Ana keman bhibbak.* I love you too Luke."

"If I'd been in love with me, I'd be crying too," he said to lighten the mood.

"What are we going to do, Luke?"

"We'll work something out. I'll come to Beirut if I have to."

"No, you can't do that."

Luke was taken aback. "Why not? Is there someone else?"

"No."

"Look Rasha, I'm obviously not the first . . ."

"That was a mistake. Long ago."

"Actually I'd rather not hear about it," Luke blurted out. "Why couldn't I just come and see you?"

"There's my family, Luke. I never went into my background in detail, but my parents are not what you would call liberal. They expect me to marry a Lebanese Muslim. They would never tolerate me going out with a foreigner."

"Rubbish," Luke exclaimed. "They can't make you do that! Hell, Rasha, this is the twentieth-century. Just put your foot down."

"I can't just put my foot down. It doesn't work that way." The lens came up once again between them, blurring Luke's understanding. "We're brought up to respect the wishes of our parents. We have a responsibility towards them, towards their standing and their reputation in society. It's not easy just to go against their word. Besides, there's a clear demarcation line between us that we simply don't overstep. We don't argue with them or raise hell. It's just not done. Call it respect, reverence maybe."

Luke was incensed. "More like emotional blackmail if you ask me. You can't just discard your desires and ambitions because they don't happen to correspond with theirs, Rasha."

"It's not that simple. I happen to believe in some of our values. They're a part of me."

"Like what?"

Rasha fumbled, trying to focus in the daze that enveloped her. "Like being there for them. Making them proud. Consideration for other people's beliefs and creeds. Being circumspect and not flaunting riches," she reeled off. "I don't know Luke, there's a whole list."

"Self-effacement. Living for others."

"No, that's not true. There was a time when I went strictly by their rules. But the war has since turned our lives upside down. Now, what they can't handle to know, I keep to myself," she explained. "It doesn't necessarily stop me from doing what I want, but I don't need to confront them with it either."

"Hm. And I thought all along that the Lebanese were open-minded, more European than Arab in their mentality."

"Most are, to some extent. But you do get families, like mine, who lean towards the conservative. It's partly the religion, partly the upbringing, you know. My father came from a traditional, well-established, Muslim family near Tripoli. His parents were stern and did not believe in any display of emotions. They led a simple life and taught their children that nothing comes easy. As expected, my father dedicated his whole life to his father and the family business. That's the way it worked then, and still does, family and honour first, everything else last. He won't accept anything less from his children."

"Sounds like the bloody Mafia," Luke chuckled. "And to think that all along I was under the false impression you were a Halwani and not a Corleone."

"Funny," Rasha retorted.

"Don't get me wrong. I don't think it's funny at all." Luke brushed his hair back with the palms of his hands. Rasha could tell he found it difficult to accept her stoicism. He struggled to make sense of her culture.

He lit a cigarette and drew on it with force. "So, where do we go from here, Rasha?" he finally asked, exhaling smoke and deep frustration along with it. He let out a heavy cough.

"I don't know."

"What would *actually* happen if I were to follow you to Beirut?" Luke presented his hatched plan hypothetically.

Rasha's chest tightened. "All I can say is that it could be detrimental . . . to us both." She imagined having to explain Luke to her father. She shuddered at the thought of Luke being her guest in a country where some militias considered a foreigner persona non grata. Rasha's previous boyfriends had both been Lebanese, were responsible for their own safety and fully understood her household rules for dating. Luke was likely to resist them.

In order to circumvent possible complications with her parents, she tried to placate him.

"We'll work something out," she said pensively. "I could maybe come and stay with Auntie Hana. We could meet up here, in Paris. In the meantime, we can talk on the phone, or write. The telephone lines are not very reliable but I have a postal box at the university, so I'm sure to get all my mail. You never know what could happen."

"Nothing will, sunshine, unless you make it."

"Luke, please . . . give me time. I'll think of something."

"Think all you want, Rasha, but know this. I won't give you up without a fight." Soulful but determined eyes shot through her. Silently, he stroked her cheek and made to plant a kiss on her eyelids. She recoiled.

"No!"

"What's the matter?"

"Don't kiss me on the eyes."

"You *are* joking!" He retorted, incredulous. "Why the hell not?"

"They say that if a person were to do that, you'd never see him again."

"Rasha Halwani. You never cease to surprise and confuse me. But I'll go along with you, simply because I don't want to take any chances." He worked his mouth along her temples down to her ear where he whispered, "I love you."

The days that had run into each other at the beginning of Rasha's stay henceforth gave way to numbers. The countdown to her departure date had begun. Her mind had already travelled the distance as her thoughts were forcibly reclaimed by the life and the people awaiting her. Yet her heart lagged behind, reluctant as a stubborn child to wrench itself from the new being it had found and loved.

Wakefulness sought out the spell in an effort to destroy it. In the time Rasha had spent with Luke, fortunes had been reversed, her reality becoming Paris and Luke, her illusion Beirut and her family. Without a second thought, she helped it along. She avoided the news bulletins and only glanced in passing at newspaper headlines. Unless something major had happened in Beirut, she no longer cared for daily reports. So long as her parents were all right and no news arrived to the contrary, she did not seek details. She shut herself off, knowing that otherwise her elation would be superseded by apprehension. Not only had her faith in good and beauty been restored, Rasha had let herself be sucked into a spiral of desire and unprecedented joy.

But today was day eight. On day ten she will be making her way home.

She was out shopping with Hana at Galeries Lafayette for presents to take back home. The list was long. First and foremost something for her parents, Karim, her beloved brother, her grandmother Amina, her uncle Salim and her aunt, her cousins, and down the line, Umm Samir, their maid, Mustapha the caretaker, and knick-knacks for her associates at the university. A little something for everyone, a token of her appreciation for their kindness, their friendship, or their services. It was a simple enough task rendered laborious by Rasha's inability to focus on anything that disassociated her from Luke. Every moment spent away from him was a moment lost. Her seconds were golden, time priceless.

She managed to get together leather wallets for the men, a silk blouse for her mother, a scarf for her aunt, and children's clothing for the help. As she and Hana explored the goods, a sour taste crept into her mouth. Bile rose in her throat, and the walls of the massive Galeries closed in on her. All at once, an unrelenting urge to flee the premises gripped her. She flung a silk foulard back into its pile and turned to Hana.

"Auntie, let's go have a coffee or something to eat." She tried to sound calm, though food was the last thing she desired. "I've had enough of this."

"That's more or less it," Hana reassured her, noting her edginess. "You can always pick up a few more items from duty free if you need to."

As she stepped out of the store, Rasha inhaled a gulp of fresh air. They walked down the busy boulevard Haussmann for a short span before turning into a quieter side street. Rasha moved towards the first table available in a shabby sidewalk café, adjoined to a sleazy bar where inebriated bodies draped themselves over the counter while ogling the new arrivals.

"Don't you want to look for something better?" Hana queried, casting an eye at the clientele.

"No, this is fine. My feet are aching. I really can't face going any further." It was a white lie. The constriction Rasha actually suffered was higher up, closer to her chest. "Besides, I'm actually not that hungry. I just needed to sit down."

"Are you sure?"

"Positive, but you go ahead and have something, Auntie."

Hana ordered a *croque monsieur* and a *ballon* of white wine, as safe a choice as she could possibly make. Rasha hoped a Perrier would help unravel the knots in her stomach.

Her mind wandered to the two days she had left in Paris—the path to her journey's end long and excruciating. Perversely, and instead of planning to make the most of it, she wished she could bring her departure day closer. What she felt was akin to a death wish that frequently seized her in war-torn Beirut. The build-up of paralyzing fear was at times so intolerable, so intense, that she invited, even prayed, for the end. Cowering under a barrage of artillery, she often caught herself hoping one would tear through the ceiling and put her out of her misery. Now, equally stifling was the dreaded prospect of leaving Luke behind.

Little by little, the figures of pedestrians swam before her eyes. Her vision was blurred, her lashes moist. A sudden heave escaped her lips. Quietly, she rummaged through her bag for a tissue, determined to conceal her face from Hana.

"Rasha?" Hana's voice was unbearably soft, pulverizing what little composure Rasha struggled to muster.

She turned slowly to her aunt, her gaze honest and desperate. "I can't go back."

Hana laid a warm hand over her niece's. "You want me to speak to your father?"

The question hung in the air then vaporized, a hollow offer that they both knew would yield no results. Rasha shook her head, dabbing her eyes. "I've just had such a good time, here," she sniffled. "I don't remember ever being happier." A vision of Luke appeared before her. "What am I going to do, Auntie? What *am* I going to do?"

"Nuha will understand, she'll listen."

Rasha's mother was not the answer. "You know she won't. She has never stood up for us. She has never opposed Baba. She won't do it."

"I'm so sorry," Hana whispered, "I feel responsible for this."

"Why?" Rasha's eyes settled on Hana's.

"I should've tried to stop it. I don't know, maybe I should've spent more time with you. Kept on warning you."

"Stopped me from seeing him?"

"I'm not so sure I could've done that."

"I don't regret a single moment I've spent with Luke. There was nothing you could do to stop it."

Hana nodded, beaten. Rasha could see that this time her aunt was at a loss. From this point on, Rasha was on her own and whatever solution she designed had to be one she could live with. However, it was clear that she could rely on Hana's support and assistance should she need it.

"Where is the fairness in all this? Is it so criminal to want happiness, gratification? What am I really going back to, really? Fighting, mayhem, destruction . . . insanity?" Gun-toting militiamen, gaping holes in tattered buildings, streets that bared their bellies flashed before Rasha's eyes. "I don't have the strength or the will to put up with it anymore. I feel . . . I feel like I've emptied my chambers and now have to reload, be ready to fire back." Rasha looked pleadingly at Hana. "I'm tired, Auntie. So tired. I don't think I can do it, give up what I have here to return to hell on earth."

"Habibti, take it one step at a time," Hana finally said in an attempt to alleviate her distress. "Let's see how things go after you get back. Like I said, think things through, first. Maybe with time I'll be able to talk your parents into sending you here, to stay with me. You've still got a couple of days left . . ." Her tone of voice rang with optimism and hope.

"A couple of days . . ."

"Look, why don't you give me the shopping bags. I'll drop them off at home. Now that there's no turning back, you may as well go see him."

Rasha managed a shadow of a smile, once again disarmed by her dear aunt's goodwill. "Are you sure?"

"Positive. Now let's get out of here." She pulled out her purse to pay.

"But you haven't touched your food!"

"In this place? You must be kidding."

Rasha made her way to Carol's at Luke's insistence. Over the phone, he let her know that Carol was getting ready to leave for the country with her family and that she just *had* to meet Rasha. With a stab in her heart, Rasha agreed. Despite the fact that she would have wanted to know Carol, she felt that all of a sudden, Luke's and her world was being intruded upon by "real" people they had so far succeeded in shutting away.

The hustle-bustle of Carol's home, the boys' giddy laughter and their mother's drowned instructions reached Rasha before she had entered the apartment on avenue de Villiers. The female voice, barely audible through the door, was calm and steady, the tone of a woman in control and unfazed by the chaos boys tend to wreak.

Luke opened the door for her. He took her in his arms and kissed her.

"How are you feeling?" she whispered.

"Never better, sunshine. Carol has been plying me with antibiotics."

Rasha broke away as she saw Carol approaching. Carol was Luke's antithesis: short, fair and plump. Hair cropped, she appeared in loose white summer pants, a long T-shirt, and no makeup. She spoke with the authority of a manager, an adept homemaker, intent on everything ticking along like a clock.

Her home environment sucked in the guest like a tornado. Carol's greetings were interjected with instructions for eleven-year-old Lucien to get off his brother, and reproaches towards Dominic for starting the fight. She flung her warnings at her kids, without lingering to make sure they were heeded.

"Excuse the mess," she said to Rasha, stooping to pick up a tennis racket. "We're getting ready to leave. Holidays with the kids," she explained rolling her eyes.

"Dominic, you keep teasing him and he'll kill you," she let out neutrally. "Then don't come crying to me."

"How can I if I'm already dead!" bellowed the nine-year-old.

Before he had finished his sentence, Carol had hooked her arm into Rasha's. "Coffee?" she asked as she led the way to the kitchen.

To the sound of hysterical laughter, Rasha glanced over her shoulder and saw Luke haul the two boys under his arms and twirl them round the room. These were not merely the antics of an uncle, she gathered, but of a man with a genuine love for children.

"Are you sure this is convenient? You're in the middle of your packing . . .," Rasha began.

"Of course it's convenient. When would I have the chance to meet you otherwise?" Carol cried out over the rattle of the coffee grinder. "You leave in a couple of days, don't you?"

"That's right. Yes." Rasha swallowed, but the lump in her throat would not budge.

The clamour from the lounge built up, calling for another word of caution. "Lucky! You get those boys all worked up and *you're* stuck with them for the holidays. There's no way I'm having them jumping around in the car. Lucky!" she yelled.

"I'm right here, and please stop calling me that." Luke leaned languidly against the kitchen doorframe.

"Lucky?" Rasha raised an eyebrow at him.

"As in Lucky Luke," Carol explained. "The boys' nickname for their uncle. What can I say? It stuck." She poured the coffee. "Do me a favour, could you take the boys out for a croissant or something, so we can enjoy our coffee in peace? Rasha, milk, sugar?"

Luke appeared reluctant to leave the women alone. "They've just gorged themselves on cereal, Carol.

Besides, where's Xavier?" His question came out more as a desperate plea to be relieved of his task.

"He's gone to get some fuel, check the car. You know. Be a sweetheart, Lucky. Do this for me?"

"All right," Luke drawled. "Where do you keep their collars and leashes?"

Carol looked at him sideways. He ignored her, walked up to Rasha and gave her a peck on the mouth. "I have it on good authority that my sister was a witch in her previous life. Don't let her cast a spell on you."

He started for the kitchen door, then turned back and gave Carol a hug. "I didn't mean that, you know. Still, watch you tongue." He wagged a cautionary finger.

"Get out . . . now!" Carol retorted playfully. "Oh and Luke," she cried out, "don't hurry back."

A muffled reply was followed by the click of the front door closing.

Then, bliss. Carol swept her hair back and let out an exaggerated sigh. "Goodness! To think I wanted four kids. Just look at this mess!"

Rasha scanned the kitchen, silted up with state-of-the-art equipment, the worktop space taken up with a mixer, a blender, a deep-fryer, a coffee-machine; the sink bursting with plastic cups, plates and cereal bowls. Something told her Carol would have it no other way. The mess she pretended to spurn was indicative of her laissez-faire, a testimony to the fact that her children and their happiness overrode a meticulously tended home. Rasha could picture Carol elbow-deep in flour, baking and cooking to her boys' hearts' content. Perhaps influenced by Luke's mention of their parents' divorce, Rasha deduced Carol made every effort to give Lucien and Dominic the home she never had.

Rasha sipped on her coffee. It was too strong, bitter. "I can help you clean up."

"Are you sure? You wouldn't mind?" Carol sounded delighted.

"Not at all."

"I'll wash. You dry."

They moved to the sink, at close quarters. Rasha was grateful for something to busy herself with. "So where are you going for the holidays?"

"L'Aiguillon-sur-Mer just north of La Rochelle. Friends of ours have a place there and asked us to join them for a couple of weeks. They have two boys as well, more or less Lucien's and Dominic's ages so it normally works well." A pause. "Are you looking forward to going back home?"

The question was meant as an attempt at conversation, but it was too laden with significance for Rasha.

"Not really." She could not help being honest.

"It must be hard for you. Have things quietened down a bit?" Carol searched Rasha's eyes.

Rasha reached out for a wet plate. "On and off. It's not too bad really. We carry on as best we can."

"Luke's already in a state about you leaving." Carol obviously did not mince her words. "I'm sure he's already told you that he and I were never too close. But I can safely say that I've never seen him like this before. So . . . so . . . besotted."

Carol turned to Rasha and smiled warmly.

"He's a very special person," Rasha's voice broke. "Where do these go?" She held up a stack of plates.

"Top right-hand corner," Carol motioned with her chin. "I let him down badly after our parents divorced. I regret it now. But it was my way of dealing with the reality of it, I suppose. When you're young you believe that adults can always 'fix' things and if they didn't, it was because they didn't want to. I thought then that my parents were being selfish and cared little about how the separation would affect Luke and me. So I just turned against the whole family. I didn't want anything to do with any of them. That, unfortunately, ended up including Luke. Poor Luke!" Carol's voice trailed off.

"He told me you were seventeen at the time," Rasha said, hoping that Carol would carry on.

Carol nodded. "What else did he tell you?"

"Not much," Rasha mused. "He hasn't actually said much," she added, suddenly struck by Carol's openness in stark contrast with Luke's reserve.

"It doesn't surprise me."

"I did get the impression though that he . . ." Rasha could not find the right word and regretted having started, ". . . had problems with your mother," she muttered the end of the sentence, unhappy with her choice.

Carol's eyes stayed fixed on the foamy water. "He won't go see her. It's his way of getting back at her, you see. He resents her for having left him to go to Houston. In retrospect, now that I'm a mother, I recognize her distress to be genuine. He reckons that since she'd never been around, he's under no obligation to please her. It's sad because I know for a fact that he worships her. He has too much anger in him, and very little trust." She paused. "That's why I had to meet you, Rasha. I had to know the woman who managed to win his heart and have him admit it to me, of all people." She looked at Rasha in earnest. "I hope it works out for the both of you." She stopped, yet Rasha could tell she hadn't quite voiced what preoccupied her. "Do you think," she started slowly, "that Luke might be thinking of following you to Beirut?"

"He brought it up once, but I discouraged him."

Carol chuckled with relief. "I must tell you, I'd hate to see him go there. I'd be terrified for him. Perhaps you could come back to Paris instead." Clearly, Carol would propose any alternative to Luke ending up in Beirut.

Rasha was lost for words. She detected in Carol a woman whose maternal instincts knew no bounds. She shielded her grown brother as she did her own children. More than guilt, it was her grand capacity to love that drove her to do so. Carol's affection was veracious and unbridled, and for no discernible reason, Rasha suddenly felt a great weight had been laid on her shoulders. Perhaps because she knew that it was entirely up to her to ensure that Luke's first-ever plunge into trust was not breached, and she had to do so while curtailing any plans he might have of a trip to her homeland. How could she avow her love to the man and in the same breath insist he stay away from her?

"I could probably come back to Paris," Rasha said, unconvinced, but determined to allay Carol's fears.

A man's voice bellowed from the lounge.

"Xavier's back. Listen, Rasha, I'd rather you didn't mention this conversation to Luke. He'll be furious with me for meddling. Unfortunately, I couldn't help but say something," she shrugged.

Rasha stepped out to meet Xavier, a bespectacled, round-faced and relatively unattractive mathematics teacher. Though he was courteous, Rasha noted his eagerness to set off. Charged with impatience, he proceeded to load the car while Carol, with Rasha's help, gathered the last few items. By the time Luke returned with the boys, everything was set for their trip.

"Luke," Carol scanned a list she held taut in her hands, "Spare keys are on the table in the hallway. Gas. Don't forget to switch off the gas after you've used the cooker. Garbage is collected every Monday . . ."

"Carol, give me that," Luke snatched the paper and pasted it on the inside of the front door. "Anything else?" He turned to face her.

"*Carole, m'enfin dépêche-toi!*" bellowed an irate Xavier.

"*J'arrive!*" she snapped back. Then softly to Luke, "No. All right, no, there's nothing else." Carol looked around to make sure she hadn't forgotten anything. "Well I suppose I must be off." She walked up to Rasha and hugged her. "Don't worry too much about what I told you. Just look after him, while you're here." Then out loud, "Call me when you're in Paris again."

At the door she stole a kiss from Luke. "Take care of yourself. I'll see you in two weeks. Thanks for looking after everything."

"Don't thank me yet. You might come back to find the place trashed," he yelled to her back.

"Don't you dare, Lucky. Don't you dare!" Her boisterous laughter receding as she ran down the stairs.

Rasha stood motionless, her stomach churning at the first farewell, however inconsequential, that she had to contend with. The landslide to her departure had been unleashed.

Luke rested against the front door. "Now that you've met my sister," his mouth in a half-smile, his azure eyes clear, enticing, "any regrets?"

"None," she replied, unable to budge. She touched her belly. "I don't feel well."

Luke approached her and took her in his arms. "You must've got my bug. Sorry. Is that all I've managed to give you to remember me by? The flu?"

"I just need to sit down for a minute," she said, inching her way to the sofa.

"In fact I do have something for you." Luke disappeared into the bedroom, re-emerging with an enlarged black and white photo of Rasha taken in Versailles.

"That's me. Again!" She exclaimed disbelieving. "First you ask me to keep my own portrait and now this."

"This is different, sunshine. When you look at it," he explained looking down at the photo, "I'm hoping you'll remember who was standing behind the camera."

Rasha rested her head on his shoulder and they sat there for a while lost in reflection. They made love, this time with pulverizing despair over their imminent parting. But once satiated, their hunger for each other would fire up again. Hope as they may, they both knew that no time spent together would be sufficient—that, however successfully they may have escaped it, reality in the end had the upper hand. In the final two days, each drank in the other's every look, every word, to defy the distance that would soon dilute vivid recollections of their sensuality. As best they could, they stored in their minds and hearts the fire of romance that no camera could eternalize. The intangible can never be contained and retrieved when the heart craves it. Once they were apart, Rasha feared, she would not only lose Luke, but would find herself dispossessed bit by bit of any memory of his lips on hers, his warm embrace, mesmerizing voice and musky scent. Would she forget the intensity of the love she felt for her soul mate?

Her trip to the airport became the centre of much discussion and debate. Hana had insisted she drive her up, the responsibility to see her niece off safe and sound paramount in her mind. Luke was determined to stay with Rasha until the last possible moment. To have the two of them, Hana and Luke, at the airport would have been awkward and inhibiting to Rasha.

On the last evening together, she made her gift to Luke. A Zippo lighter with the words *Remember Paris, 1981* minutely carved at the base.

"There were two things I could get for you. Equipment for your camera, which I know nothing about, or this lighter. It had to be something you would use every day. Since you seem intent on smoking, this should be a constant reminder of the time we had together."

As she lay huddled up in Luke's arms, Rasha thought back on the first time she had set eyes on him. He was the stranger back then, yet there had not been a moment when she had felt she did not know him. It was as if the man who claimed her heart had been lying in wait, her love for him virtually dormant within her being. If they were destined to fall for one another, how was it to end? Since she had had no power over what grew between them, would she be capable of controlling their fate?

In their last private moments, Rasha's heart welled up so, she could hardly breathe. She barely spoke, snug in his arms, shedding tears of hopelessness and imminent loss. Whenever he spoke, whenever he touched her, the only thing that sprung to her mind was that this would be the last time. So it was for the last time that Luke would walk her to Hana's apartment, stand by the leonine paws that adorned the gate, and hold her against him with unspoken possessiveness.

The long drive to the airport was shrouded in silence, broken at intervals by arbitrary reminders from Hana. "You haven't forgotten anything?" "You've got your passport and ticket?" "Make sure you give everyone my love." "Will you be all right?" However, Hana did ask for Carol's number, which Rasha gave gladly. Would her aunt act as a go-between?

As Rasha stepped into the sobering atmosphere of Roissy-Charles-de-Gaulles, day ten was coming to a fast close. Mechanically, she went through the motions of checking in her luggage, requesting a non-smoking aisle seat. (If she had been travelling with Luke, would they have opted for the smoking section?) She looked over her shoulder constantly, wondering whether Luke would surprise her. A part of her had been severed, leaving her with overwhelming grief and an unbearable emptiness.

She hugged Hana, thanking her for her hospitality, her understanding, tears threatening to break loose. Rasha's every moment had been so consumed with Luke that she had forgotten the wrench her aunt would suffer. Hana clung to her for the last contact with family. Tears streaming, she entrusted Rasha with the task of conveying her love to her mother, her brothers, sisters-in law, nephews and nieces, listing them by name. As Hana walked away with a scalded heart, Rasha envisioned her stepping into her empty apartment with nothing but solitude to look forward to. At the very thought of not only abandoning her lover but also an aunt so selflessly devoted to her, Rasha felt her own composure crumble.

Through a film of moistness, she thought she glimpsed a vision of Luke moving towards her. She blinked to focus on the apparition, unable to divorce illusion from reality. Not until she flung herself in his arms and sensed them tangible and firm around her did she know that what she had seen was indeed true.

He pulled away from her slightly, brushing away her tears. "Mafia or no mafia, sunshine, there's nothing on earth that will keep me away from you. Don't cry, Rasha. I can make the world stop if I have to."

In that one moment, Rasha was injected with new hope that fanned through her, steeling her with confidence. What she had perceived to be a mirage was Luke, in the flesh. She knew, for certain, that he would never give her up.

Their long embrace silenced the throng around them, shut off life itself beyond their two beings. When she turned round to bid her last farewell, Rasha saw on Luke's face the very first thing that had reeled her in so hopelessly: a wide white smile. Beyond Passport Control, at the mouth of the journey that she would have to undertake alone, Rasha could not resist the urge to catch a glimpse of Luke Elliott for the last time. She turned once more and from afar could make out his silhouette. His face was indiscernible, fading away in the distance that splayed itself between them.

It was over in a heartbeat.

Chapter Six
Beirut - July 1981

◆

U nder any other circumstances, a woman in love would be allowed the time to nurse her wounds after a break-up with a loved one. She may for a period wallow in her sadness, grieve for the intimacy they had shared and console herself with the promise of a reunion sometime in the very near future. She may dwell on recollections of their lovemaking, conjure up her lover's face, and imagine his warm breath, his sensual caress. Once in a while, she may even succeed to revive the closeness and passion now made impalpable by distance. Tearful moments of dejection would be assuaged by a sympathetic confidante or by the reassuring voice, bridging the seas, of the man she had pledged her heart to. In normal times, a heartbreak of such colossal proportions would be a legitimate ailment which deserved and received due care and attention.

Rasha, however, returned to a gritty nation where mourning and despair had become exclusive to the death of a relative or a friend; the dispossession of home and property; or personal injury—tragedies of irrevocable loss and damage. She was once again in a state of perdition where resilience hinged on denial: denial of the barbarity that was rife, denial of any emotion that might weaken one's resolve, denial of a love once so true and now beyond reach.

Her dread that she may someday forget Luke, that his features would become a fading vision, his light touch a fantasy, presupposed that she was empowered to safeguard him in her mind and soul, that her life was her own and her thoughts were of her own making. Yet the second her plane touched down at Beirut International Airport, Rasha collided with the stark reality that lingered beyond her reprieve in Paris. The instant she stepped onto the tarmac, she was divested of excessive sentimentality and gratuitous self-pity. In the grand scheme of things, her shattered heart was flotsam in a sea of cadavers.

It was unwise to dither in war-torn Lebanon. One never stopped to ponder one's destiny and never idled without a task to finish or a job to complete for fear of breaking the momentum. To come to a halt entailed confronting a situation that was unbearable and that fiercely challenged any human being's tolerance. Rasha knew this. She knew that to pause and muse on where she was and what she had left behind in Paris may very well destroy her ability to carry on. She was now back in Hobbes' "state of nature," that malevolent anarchy whose dictates she could not forget after just a brief hiatus.

Despite all this, she felt herself charged with an uplifting sensation of being in essence a woman in love. She hovered in a haze of emotional anesthesia that for a while shut her off from the pervading hostilities. Her corporeal body had been transported back to Beirut but her senses were in limbo, stubbornly clinging to a sublime emotion they had grown dependent on. Sadly, it was not long before the effects of the analgesic wore off and affliction drove itself through her like a darting pain. Her stash of stolen joy depleted, she was left bereft in an unforgiving void.

Back in the fold, she never once uttered Luke's name out loud. Relayed accounts of her trip were restricted to the times she spent with Hana and to her aunt's wellbeing and state of affairs. From having been the hub of her everyday thoughts and actions, Luke was relegated to her guarded subconscious, his memory exhumed in private moments when a tear would go unnoticed and a sigh unheard. Back in the fold, an invisible hand had reached into Rasha's insides and ripped her heart out, offering her no choice but to endure unrelenting emptiness in self-imposed silence.

When her mother was finally able to reach Hana by phone, Rasha sat by her side on tenterhooks hoping she would get the opportunity to speak before the fickle connection was cut off. Under the pretext that the line in her bedroom would be clearer, Rasha picked up the handset.

"I've got it Mama . . ." She waited for her mother to hang up. "Auntie Hana, how are you?"

"I'm fine habibti. Missing you terribly." Her voice came through with tantalizing clarity.

"I miss you too. I miss Paris. Thank you for all you've done for me, Auntie. This was one trip I'll never forget."

"Anytime, habibti. Anytime."

Rasha cupped the handset. "Have you heard from Luke?"

"He's phoned twice since you left. He's been dying to hear your news." Hana's voice trailed off.

Rasha felt relief and joy at the same time. "Auntie, I need you to do something for me. Is he still in Paris?"

"Yes, at his sister's. I have her number."

"Would you please call him and tell him that I'll try to phone him at nine o'clock our time tomorrow evening?"

"Nine o'clock Beirut time," Hana confirmed.

"My parents will be having dinner at the neighbours'. Just tell him that it might take a while before I get through. Please ask him to be patient."

"I will. Anything else?"

"I don't think so. Have you thought of seeing him sometime?"

"Would you like me to?"

"Well, you never got the chance to know him."

"All right, I'll see when he's free."

"Just don't take him to Le Soufflé. He doesn't like soufflés. He says it's like eating air."

A peal of laughter. Then, "Soufflés are out."

The line went dead.

Rasha lingered on her bed, motionless. Until she spoke to Luke, she would not be able to shake off her intractable anxiety. She would have to wait an entire day. She glanced across at the papers on her desk. Summer school tests. Without contemplating her duties, she paced her bedroom, wringing her hands, gazing out into darkness. What if the phone lines were cut off? How would she cope with not getting through to him? She took a pill to calm her nerves and lay on her bed. Sleep would not come as she mulled over everything she would want to say to Luke before their conversation was cut short by unreliable communication. She yearned to tell him how deeply she loved him, how empty she had felt since they had parted, how unbearable it had been to keep her thoughts and feelings to herself and pretend that nothing had ever happened to change her life so drastically. She would solicit his confidence in their future together and his assurance that nothing would come between them. He alone would be able to comfort her and reconfirm his presence, in spirit at least, in the seclusion that had haunted her days and nights.

At 8:45 the following evening, Rasha picked up the handset and waited for the tone. Five minutes passed and dread rumbled through her. She moved the receiver from one hand to the other in order to wipe the moistness off each of her palms onto her jeans. She looked at her watch, 8:55. Frustration turned her body into a rigid mass. She had the handset pressed so hard against the side of her face that her ear throbbed. Then, a tone. She could hear a tone, and a shiver coursed up her arm. With infinite care she dialled Carol's number, slowly, making certain that each digit was accurately recorded, judging by the echo that each had been electronically completed. Then a long pause as a sound like that of a gust of wind finally yielded a ring, then a click.

"Hello?"

"Luke?" she squealed. "Luke, it's Rasha."

A pause.

"Hey, sunshine. You got through. Is everything all right? Your voice is faint."

"I'm fine. It's just the line. I miss you Luke." A rush of longing washed over her.

It took a while before he responded, and Rasha gathered it was because of the line delay.

"Not half as much as I miss you. I love you Rasha."

"I love you too Luke. More than I ever imagined." She tried to keep her voice steady.

"Did you get my letter?"

"Not yet. The mail has been slow. When did you send it?"

"I must've posted it about an hour after you left." He laughed at his silliness.

His beaming face flashed in front of her. She could visualize his head flung back, his eyes narrowing. She smiled, even though the sadness she felt was all-consuming. Everything she had intended to profess fell by the wayside as Rasha longed to hear his voice and relish it in total silence.

"Nothing has changed between us Luke?"

"Nothing, sunshine."

"I just needed to hear you say it."

His tone turned grave. "Rasha, we've been getting bad reports on the wire. How's the situation?"

Rasha understood his allusion to the escalating Israeli-Palestinian conflict.

"I can't go into details over the phone, Luke. But we're okay. How long are you in Paris for?"

"I'm due to leave for London when Carol gets back. Another week. When can I call you?"

"I'll phone you. I'll try again day after tomorrow. What's today? The fifteenth. I'll try same time on the seventeenth. Luke? Are you there?" Her heart skipped a beat.

"I'm here. That'll be great. If I can last that long."

"To be honest, Luke, it's been difficult being back. I don't think I've ever felt so miserable, so . . ." They were disconnected as she was about to pour her heart out. "Luke?" No reply. "Luke?" She repeated in a plea, the tone of a flatline boring defeatism into her eardrum.

Although she had half-expected it to happen, she was incensed by her bad luck. She hung up then retrieved the handset in hope for a tone. It came quicker this time. No sooner had she formed the second digit than a power failure severed the line again and plunged her room into blackness. The handset slammed down on the hook with a force Rasha did not recognize as hers. Blind fury seized her. Profanity spewed out of her ricocheting off confining invisible walls. Her rage was too great to contain, claiming a life of its own, erupting from deep inside her. She ranted at the injustice, the cruelty, at her pathetic helplessness. Beaten, she collapsed in a heap by her bed, dropped her head into shaking hands and sobbed in deathly darkness.

As dawn broke on the seventeenth of July 1981, a thunderous crack jolted Rasha into consciousness. Recognizing it as the all-too-familiar sonic boom of Israeli reconnaissance jets, she pulled the sheet over her head in desperate need for a few more moments of slumber until the door to her bedroom flew open and Nuha's urgent voice reached her with absolute clarity through the covers.

"Rasha. Up, quickly."

Staggering on limp legs and feeling peculiarly groggy, she followed her mother down the hallway. "What's happened?"

"Israeli attack. They're bombing the hell out of us. Bastards. May God forgive them." Nuha's propensity to use foul language under stress was not unusual, and Rasha quite enjoyed seeing her upright mother lose her composure.

While they frantically collected provisions to sequester themselves, Rasha could make out the heavy footsteps of neighbours as they scrambled down the stairs to safety. Umm Samir, the maid, muttered off her prayers as she soberly followed Nuha's instructions. Rasha's father had the radio blaring in the entrance hall.

"Where's Karim?" Rasha asked with alarm, a bottle of water in her hand.

"He's gone to the hospital," Nuha replied.

"When?"

"About half an hour ago."

"How could you let him go, Mama?"

"He's a medical student Rasha. The hospital will need all the help it can get."

"How was he getting there?"

"Ali the taxi driver took him."

"How is he supposed to get back?"

"God is merciful, Rasha. He'll see him through safely."

"But how are we to know when it's safe for him to get back? We can't even call him!"

Nuha stopped in her tracks and turned to Rasha. Her face was flushed, her eyes lacklustre with unspoken dread.

"Rasha, don't get me agitated," she said in a measured tone. "Besides, I told him to go to his friend Fuad's. He's close enough to the hospital. Karim should be fine there." She paused. "He'll be fine," she finally reiterated as if to convince herself rather than Rasha.

The sky groaned as Israeli Air Force Phantoms sliced through it. Pointlessly, the three women ducked as if the jets had just skimmed the tops of their heads. Nuha mouthed a curse.

"Let's move. This is getting worse. Amin!"

"Coming!"

"Rasha, grab a chair for your father. Umm Samir, did you leave the balcony doors ajar?"

"Yes, Sitt Nuha."

"Mama, I'm not even dressed."

"Hurry then. Quickly!"

They made their way to the first floor in a file, Amin sauntering behind, his ear tuned to the running update on the radio. There was a time, at the very beginning of the war, when they would have been reunited with the forty-odd residents of the building. Since then, however, that number had dwindled to fifteen at the most as the rest opted for safety in exile. Seven years ago they whiled away the time playing cards and telling jokes. There had been something magical in the bond that brought them together and a thrill in the disruption of their routine, despite the dreaded and unfamiliar threat that had crept into their existence. Seven years on, determination gave way to lassitude, and incomprehension to ambivalence.

No one was interested in the minutiae of a battle, its cause or its ramifications. Nor did they care, or so they thought, if death were to come too soon. In essence, they were up against yet another storm of artillery that they had to wait out, wan and dejected, until it blew over so they could resume their lives.

Nevertheless, reflexes prevailed, manifesting themselves in a cry or a start when a missile hit too close or a jet flew too low. The reactions were involuntary, visceral, while the mind remained idle, ossified by many years of unspeakable violence. When the war began, they had all predicted its end in a day or two. As soon as the conflict exceeded its "days of grace", they conceded to another week or two. Before they all realized, it had been years, many years that had killed in their wake any hope of deliverance. Yet they still stubbornly referred to what had clearly become a full-blown war as *al hawadeth*, "the incidents".

On that particular morning, their sequestration was imposed by a strife that in its very nature was anything but Lebanese. It was the culmination of clashes between Palestinians and Israelis that had thus far been contained in southern Lebanon and had come to a head in a bombing campaign of the central district of Beirut. The Israelis were intent on weakening the Palestinian stronghold in Lebanon. Rasha, her family and their neighbours were sitting out a vicious battle with no end in sight, no victor and no vanquished.

The distinctive thud of Umm Fadi's step echoed through the stairwell, mingling with the persistent salvos of missiles. She stopped at the landing, a Bette Davis lookalike with the pounds piled on, clutching a mongrel the size of a pug. Her forty-eight-year-old daughter Suha lingered by her side, true to her role as her mother's crutch.

Umm Fadi drew an emphysemic breath. "These stairs are going to kill me," she heaved. "By God, I'd be better off staying put in my own home and risking a mortar."

"Exercise is good for the heart, Umm Fadi," the occupant of the first floor apartment remarked from a seated position, his protruding belly a poor evidence of physical exertion.

"*Sayyed* Munir," Umm Fadi retorted flatly, rigid. "Do I look like Jane Fonda to you?"

Rasha burst out laughing. The eighty-year-old widow had long been her favourite neighbour, conjuring up in her mind Chaucer's Wife of Bath. The stalwart dowager had a razor-sharp humour and spoke her mind with unashamed candour, traits that Rasha relished and her father looked upon with distaste. Having birthed seven children and lived through the Second World War, endless skirmishes and a fair share of family tragedies, Umm Fadi had seen it all.

With a vociferous declaration of God's might, she waddled to the landing where Amin, Nuha, Sayyed Munir and his wife Aliya stood up in polite consideration.

"Thank you all for your kindness but I fear you're being premature. By the time I get to you I may very well need a stretcher, or a coffin, God forbid."

She sank her weight into an armchair Sayyed Munir had actually reserved for her, knowing full well that a narrow folding chair could not accommodate her corpulence.

"Coffee, Umm Fadi?" Aliya offered.

"And a glass of water if you please." She paused to catch her breath. "These accursed people. Shelling the daylight out of us. Why don't they fight on their own territory and leave us alone?" She produced a handkerchief from her ample bosom and dabbed her chin.

"We must stand by our stateless brethren, Umm Fadi," Sayyed Munir preached.

She sneered at him. "At this rate, *we* may very well end up *stateless!*" she blurted out, one arm flailing, the other steadfast around the tyke. "You want to die, Sayyed Munir? Then, be my guest. Go out there and fight with them. But don't expect us all to go with you. I didn't survive two husbands and little wars in between to die in a dingy hallway. It's civilians, like us, who pay the price, sitting here like ducks. And for what? What good has it done so far?" she wheezed. "Do I need to remind you that all the casualties out there will be innocent victims and not the targeted militias?"

Sayyed Munir shrugged. Rasha had no views on the matter. She was not a fighter but rather, as Umm Fadi had labelled them all, a sitting duck, hoping to get through the shelling unscathed.

Umm Fadi's brow contracted into a scowl. "Don't talk to me about causes. Do you honestly think every four-teen-year-old toting a machine gun out there is doing so for 'the cause'? Hogwash. Nothing and no one in this bloody war is noble. They're all a bunch of self-serving, hypocritical assassins. Am I right, Sayyed Amin?"

Her outburst was followed by a heavy silence. All eyes were now on Amin. Given her father's aversion to political debates, Rasha knew he was the last person Umm Fadi should've turned to for support.

"God provides, Umm Fadi," Amin replied ambiguously in an attempt to circumvent a delicate issue.

"Wish that the heavens would mark your words, Sayyed Amin. To start with, I wish God would heed our need for electricity and water. Speaking of which, I was under the impression that we had collected the necessary funds to fuel the generator. Why isn't it running?"

"Not everyone has paid up," Aliya admitted as she held out a coffee cup to Umm Fadi.

"Who hasn't?"

"Sixth and eighth floors."

Umm Fadi slapped her free palm dramatically on her thigh, producing a distinctive clap of hard flesh on flaccid skin. "Of course they wouldn't! How could you possibly hope for the squatters to foot the bill? I'll pay their share, if only to get the lift working and spare myself heart failure."

Rasha all along sat mum listening to the conversation. The squatters, refugees from bombarded homes in Beirut, had simply broken in when they were tipped off on vacant apartments in the building. Each man for himself was the practised creed in wartime when government assistance was not forthcoming. The two large families kept to themselves, never mingling with the paying residents.

She thought back on the early days of the war when they had to buy ice blocks off savvy pedlars for the egregious sum of five Lebanese liras apiece to keep their food fresh. When they had relied on candles for light, and transported buckets of water up several flights of stairs. Since, they had graduated to generators to operate the lift and pump water, and chargeable battery lamps as a safety measure when fuel was scarce. Gas heaters and electric fans—when those could be used—replaced the more sophisticated central heating and air conditioning systems. She often wondered whether it was a good thing that they surmounted every obstacle so resourcefully. Doing so had made everything seem all right, as if they could take more and be challenged with a lot more, because ultimately they would devise a solution to every complication.

"Rasha, you're looking too gaunt. Haven't you been eating? Nuha . . ." she drawled to emphasize the obvious. "Feed your child. She's disappearing."

Nuha lifted her eyes to the ceiling while Rasha simply smiled. The hours had ticked over and the heat held them hostage in the stifling hallway. Rasha suffered, though, from a heat that raged within her, dulling her senses.

"Shame on you Amin for keeping these youngsters in this godforsaken country. Send them away! There's a world of opportunities out there. My children speak highly of Canada, where they're at least in the heart of civilization. This is no life for a young woman like Rasha. And Karim . . . he could be finishing his studies at a medical university in Montreal or Toronto. The very best."

Rasha sensed her father tense with exasperation. A private man, he never discussed his children's future with anyone but his wife.

"We have top medical schools in Beirut, Umm Fadi. All the doctors who've been educated and trained here have excelled abroad."

"Provided they got out in one piece," she retorted. "And Rasha? Such a young and beautiful girl should be married by now. At your age, my dear, I was mother to three children. May God keep them safe."

Rasha's cheeks tinged crimson. She glanced at her father who had brought the radio to his ear in order to discourage further give-and-take.

"The time will come, God willing," Nuha finally said, hoping no doubt to bring the conversation to a close.

"So long as she doesn't end up with a no-good bastard like my son-in-law." Umm Fadi looked sideways at her daughter Suha who, clearly embarrassed, dipped her head. "Had he been my husband, he would've had his arse whipped for his despicable behaviour. All he cares about is his whisky and his women. No shame."

"Mama, please," Suha muttered.

"You should never have married him. I could tell from the minute he set foot in my house that he was a good-for-nothing. But as we say, *kul fooleh msawseh bit la'i kiyyal a'ma*—for every weevil-infested bean, God provides a blind man to dish it out— . . . Look at me, the very mention of him makes my blood curdle. I'll say no more."

Suha's inability to silence her mother elicited Rasha's sympathy. She wondered how well the young woman coped with a failed marriage and a stalemate. The similarities with Hana were evident, as Rasha saw in Suha an image of her aunt had she remained in Beirut: a woman in her forties with no hope for long-lasting happiness and broken by betrayal. For no obvious reason, Rasha could sense though that for all his insensitivity, Suha still held hopeless affection for a heartless opportunist. An urge to speak to Luke came over Rasha. It struck her that she may not be able to call him after all, as agreed, on the evening of the seventeenth.

The screech of a flying jet incurred a barrage of anti-aircraft artillery, shocking Rasha back to reality. The cup of coffee slipped through her hand, crashing on the steps, thick dregs splattering into an inkblot on grey marble. She clasped her ears in an effort to shut out the din. Nuha got up to clear the broken porcelain.

"Sorry Mama. I'm so sorry Auntie Aliya."

"You know what they say: break a cup, break an evil spell. Don't worry. These things are a dime a dozen."

"Calm down my dear," Umm Fadi interjected. "The bombing is nowhere near us. May God preserve those who are in the middle of it all."

No sooner had she spoken than the ear-splitting whistle of a mortar ended abruptly in a deafening bang. Not too far from them, the clang of glass shattering could be heard. Within minutes, the wail of sirens, accompanied by a volley of machine-gun fire, reverberated through the streets.

The mongrel's hysterical yelps drummed on Rasha's nerves.

"I take that back. They're getting closer. May God spare us," Umm Fadi pleaded, voicing a collective but silent thought.

Sentiments ran high as the air putrefied with acrimony mingled with mortal terror. Rasha noticed her father straining to follow the news. She read explosive impatience on his face. Or was it a peculiar demonstration of fear?

In the end, he piped up with blatant disdain. "Umm Fadi, with all due respect to you and your precious mutt, if you could manage to silence that *rat* for a moment maybe I could catch something of this broadcast. Then we might find out where we stand."

Rasha cringed, mortified that he should be so blunt.

Probably deeming it wise to ignore the slur, Umm Fadi clung to the mongrel, one hand clasped around its muzzle.

Amin raised the volume, placing the radio on the floor strategically for all to hear. "The Israeli air attacks on our land do not seem to let up in Tyre, Nabatiyya, Hasbayya and the Beqaa Valley. In the central district of Beirut, the headquarters of Fatah, the Democratic Palestinian Liberation Front and the Popular Palestinian Liberation Front have come under continuous shelling resulting in a heavy loss of civilian lives . . ."

Vigilant eyes fixed on her father in order to anticipate and pre-empt another outburst, Rasha sidled up to her mother. "I don't feel well, Mama."

Nuha touched her forehead with the flat of her hand. "You're burning up. I'll get some Paracetamol . . ."

Rasha held her back by the arm. "Don't go to the apartment."

"I've got some here." Nuha pulled out the tablets and a bottle of water from their bag of provisions.

A rumble shook the building. Everyone stiffened except for Rasha who fidgeted in search of a spot to cool off her body on cold tiles. Her joints began to ache and she could not tell whether it was a result of taut muscles or an oncoming illness. She yearned for a soft mattress and cool sheets.

Acid bile burned through her insides and her throat, souring her thoughts and hopes. A cursory glance at the people around her and an honest assessment of her situation filled her with a sense of doom. In an epiphany, she came to the conclusion that nothing good could germinate from her circumstances. Her gloom cast its shadow far and wide encapsulating her future with Luke. Whether she liked it or not, she was fated to a barren existence and lacked the courage to escape it. She, like Suha, had become subjugated to her tormentor, in her case the war, that had persistently and brutally intruded on her being. There was nothing unusual anymore about the days and the nights she spent sheltering in hallways. Even if by some miracle she should be able to flee the war, she could never purge her mind of its haunting, parasitic reality.

For one simple reason. One glance at her parents and deep love gushed out of her like an open source. Their past as a family was too interwoven, not simply by name and nurture, but by immediacy and the matter of life and death. Under a hail of missiles, she could not stop and consider whether her love for Luke would ever be fulfilled, but whether she would be able to tend to her parents in their old age. The normalcy she so craved had to be on her own terrain, a return to tranquil gatherings under pine trees and family journeys through the winding roads of her beloved country. She looked around and knew in an instant that, here, she belonged. She also realized with a pang that Luke could never find his way into her arcane world. Rasha and all who surrounded her had become incarcerated, involuntarily, in a state of being and a state of mind impenetrable to outsiders. Today, as each of her days could be fashioned, the threat of mortars flying overhead, the gnawing fear for her life, and overriding anguish over her brother's safety made her conditions impregnable and, in their singularity, too far removed from the man with whom she had felt complete.

These thoughts came to her in fragments like shrapnel, leaving her confused and despondent. The fever had crept through her body fast, stultifying her mind. As the heat ate its way through her like tongues of fire lapping against her limbs, she tilted her head backwards against the wall, the voices receding as she slipped in and out of consciousness. The sound of muffled shellfire, now in the distance, was her lullaby.

She is a child again. Her forehead has just landed against the red brick edging white and pink impatiens. She reaches out for a man's outstretched arms. When she looks up, she sees Luke. Just then she is miraculously transformed into the young woman she is today. Her brow is not bleeding nor does it bear a scar.

"What are you doing here?" she murmurs.

"I saw you fall. You're hurt," he replies plainly, perplexed by her question.

She looks around, fretful, the rumble of mortars in the far distance.

"You can't be here. You can't stay."

"Why not?"

"It's wrong."

Wordlessly, he takes her hand and with a tilt of the head motions her to follow him.

"Where are you taking me?" she asks.

"For a walk."

Ahead of them is the path in Bois de Boulogne. Behind her an indiscernible mass watching her, waiting for her next move. The road snakes its way into a dark tunnel. She pulls back.

"I can't go with you. I won't be able to reach my parents. The phone lines are dead. I can't go." She pivots to a vision of her father, her mother and Karim standing rigid, their faces suffused with sadness. Her hand feels light. The grip has been released. She turns round to explain to Luke. But he's gone.

Karim is calling her, not with a sense of urgency, but flatly.

A whisper. "Rasha?"

She whipped her head straight. "Huh? Is Karim back?"

"Not yet," Nuha murmured. "You need to take more painkillers." She handed her two tablets and a fresh bottle of water. "Can you eat?"

Rasha shook her head, swallowing the medication. "What time is it?"

"Four o'clock."

Muttering excuses to Sayyed Munir with whom he was engaged in a backgammon game, Amin approached them. "How's she feeling?"

"Not well. She may need something stronger, like antibiotics."

"Let's get some then," he said in a sweet tone that brought to mind his delicate care of Rasha in her childhood.

Whereupon, Umm Fadi offered from her throne, "What's wrong with the child?"

Nuha turned to her. "The flu, I think."

"I have a cabinet full of medication. For headaches, muscle aches . . . even heartache." Umm Fadi flung back half in jest. "Suha. Go up and see if we have any antibiotics left."

It was common knowledge that the war and breakdown of order had led to a slackening in pharmacies. All medications, from antibiotics to the strongest sleeping pills were available over the counter without prescriptions and in endless supplies. The city had turned into a hypochondriac's haven. Civilians relied on themselves for everything from self-diagnosis right through to self-protection.

Within minutes, Suha was back. Nuha pulled out the brochure from the box to check on the dosage and side effects. Satisfied that they would be suitable, she handed one to Rasha.

"Thank you Umm Fadi," Rasha said feebly.

"*Tikrami tislamili. Bil 'afia Inshallah.* You're welcome my dear. I wish you good health."

Her benevolence and earnest concern touched Rasha to the core. She felt herself growing emotional and struggled to rein in her melancholy when a loud commotion rose from the ground floor of the building. Angry threats mingled with the muffled pleas of the caretaker.

Sayyed Munir stood up. "I'd better see what's going on."

His wife Aliya held him back, cautioning him.

"I'll go with you," Amin said pushing away the backgammon table.

Rasha reached for her mother's hand. Nuha took it absent-mindedly, her eyes fixed on her husband as he disappeared down the stairwell. Surprised that no sound had emerged from Umm Fadi's dog, in spite of the clamour, Rasha turned to find his snout concealed by his owner's hand.

The women sat motionless, holding their breath. Then, with one jerk, Nuha was on her feet.

"Mama, where are you going?"

"I need to have a look."

She draped herself over the balustrade for a clear view of the entrance to the building and reported what she saw. Three men in fatigues and brandishing rocket-propelled grenade launchers were standing outside the building's locked iron gate. Mustafa the caretaker, Amin and Sayyed Munir were inside, talking in turns, reasoning with the armed men.

"What the hell do they want?" Umm Fadi uncharacteristically whispered to Nuha.

"They want to be let into the building."

"To get up on the roof?" Umm Fadi asked, now in her usual high-pitched voice.

"It seems so."

"May Gold help us if they get in and start launching their rockets from here. We'll be bombarded to a pulp."

Rasha clasped her hands to stop them from shaking. Cold sweat trickled down her arms. All of a sudden, a bellicose rant split her ears.

"Mama, what's happening?"

"Sayyed Munir is trying to placate them, but one of them has lost it completely."

A rattle of machine-gun fire forced Nuha to take cover. The rancid smell of terror filled the hallway as the threat of unseen aggression permeated it. The women, speechless and incapacitated, exchanged petrified glances. Nuha rose slowly, craning her neck to get a view.

"Mama, be careful."

"Nuha?" Aliya begged for reassurance, a hand flat against her bosom.

"Everyone's fine. They must've fired in the air. Oh my God, he's pointing a gun at the lock!" Nuha hunkered down, hands over ears.

The women waited out the silence that filled up the space between them. No one dared move. Then, in a brusque display of frustrated impatience, Aliya lined herself up with Nuha. Like a child afraid of witnessing an unwanted sight lest it haunt her for life, Aliya inched her head over the balustrade.

"There's someone else there, now."

"Can you see who it is?" Aliya enquired.

"He seems to be one of them. He's shaking hands with . . . I think Sayyed Munir through the bars. They seem to know each other."

There was a long pause while the women prayed that the situation would be defused. The awful stillness in the end pushed Rasha to break it.

"Mama, what's happening?"

"They're still talking. Hold on, they seem to be leaving. They're moving away."

A few minutes later the men returned from the ground floor.

"Amin, what was all that about?"

"They wanted to climb up to the roof for a good vantage point."

"Who was that man Sayyed Munir was talking to?"

"It turns out I knew his father from the village," Sayyed Munir replied, still catching his breath. "Aliya, do you remember Nabil Sadawi?"

"Of course."

"That was his eldest son, Hisham."

"Good God."

"Oh yes! We were very lucky. The others were almost ready to break in. I tell you that putting in that iron gate was the best thing we ever did."

"It wasn't the gate that stopped them, Sayyed Munir," Umm Fadi objected, recovering her capacity to argue in a heartbeat. "It was your acquaintance with this Hisham's father. They could've easily blown that piece of metal off its hinges."

Rasha leaned her head against the wall, her body numb with exhaustion and relief. What a brilliant puppet she was! What a remarkable pawn! Her range of chameleon-like emotions fired up and deadened by callous and self-serving militiamen. She was a predator's dream prey.

The raids carried on for another week, shifting back from West Beirut to Zahrani, Tyre, and West Beqaa. Karim returned home on the second day of the clashes, unshaven and with dark rings under the eyes. Rasha had great admiration for her younger brother, and had often wished she, at the very least, had the fortitude to help as a volunteer at the hospital. Karim avoided talking about his experiences in the trauma unit and had the ability to shut them out. As soon as his head touched the pillow, nothing seemed to mar his sleep. At times, it took him no more than four hours to recharge. Rasha was adamant that the haunting sight of gaping wounds and mangled limbs—compounded with the stress of having to tend to patients in dire conditions—had to impress itself on her brother's subconscious. In light of all that he had just endured in the emergency ward, Rasha played down her symptoms though they had left her debilitated and mired in self-pity.

"Are you sure you're not pregnant?" Karim asked when they were alone.

Rasha was stunned by his quip. "Karim!" she exclaimed feigning affront.

"You're keeping something from me."

"What makes you so sure?"

"I know you like the palm of my hand, dear sister. Never mind, you'll tell me one day when you're ready."

"There's nothing to tell."

On July 24, a cease-fire was finally reached at the intervention of the US envoy, Philip Habib. A day later, mid-afternoon, the phone rang. Rasha picked it up. It was Hana.

"Rasha, finally! God I've been worried sick about you all. How *is* everyone?"

"We're all fine . . ."

"Thank God!" Hana interjected. "It's been a nightmare trying to get through to you. Has it been as bad as they led us to believe?" Evidently, her aunt had fallen into the trap of taking news coverage of Beirut at face value. Footage of Lebanon under bombardment often left expatriates with the impression that their country had been reduced to rubble. Discerning Lebanese and those closer to the situation, though, knew that that was not the case.

"It was worse than it had been for a long time. But we got through it by the grace of God."

"Is your mom there?"

"She's just gone out. Auntie Hana . . ."

"Before you ask. I did meet with Luke. We had lunch about a week ago. He's a lovely boy, Rasha. He really is. Very sharp too. It was a few days into the attacks, and he grilled me on the situation. Very inquisitive boy! Charming. He's mad about you."

"Have you seen him since?"

"No. He did call though the day he was leaving for London. He said he'd wanted to phone you but you asked him not to. I guessed it was because of Amin."

"Well . . . he wouldn't have been able to get through anyway."

"That's what I told him. In any case, I've got his number and address in London if you want them."

"I have them. Thank you."

"Habibti. It's *so* good to know that you're all safe and sound. Give my love to everyone."

"I will."

The unexpected phone call and the speed with which Hana had spoken left Rasha reeling. In her daze, she tried to imagine herself in Paris again, in vain. She had even reached a stage where she was at pains to visualize Luke's face. What had occurred since her trip superseded the precious memories she had tried so hard to cling to. Yet she felt incomplete, perpetually hungering for fulfilment.

On the off chance that her aunt's phone call was an indication that the international phone lines were functional, Rasha retrieved the handset from her bedroom and managed almost immediately to dial the London number.

"Luke?"

"No, it's James. Luke's not . . . Oh, hang on a minute."

A second later. "Rasha?"

The sound of his voice carried her away like a retreating tide. "Luke? How did you know it was me?"

"I wasn't sure. I just hoped it was. God, Rasha, it's so good to hear your voice."

"I'm so glad I found you at home," she whispered, all the qualms she had had during the protracted attack dispelled at the mere thought that he was at the other end of the line. How could she ever have doubted her deep love for him!

"Believe it or not. I *just* walked in."

Then, as if darkness had stolen the light of day, out of nowhere and for no apparent reason, tears welled up in her eyes. Her fist tightened on the handset.

"Rasha, are you there?"

She shook her head. Invisible hands locked around her neck, choking her. She came apart like a house of cards.

"Rasha?"

"Yes," she managed to say in a thin voice.

A pause.

"You're crying." He put it in a statement rather than a question, uttered with the gentleness of a ripple.

Her vocal chords were leaden. "A little," she said at last, straining to smile in reassurance, as if he could see her.

"Has anyone been hurt?" he asked delicately.

I've been hurt, Luke, she thought.

"No."

A heavy silence relayed mutual love and longing. They communicated wordlessly.

"Damn it! Rasha, listen to me. Are you listening?"

"Yes." She reached for a tissue.

"We can't go on like this."

"I know."

"I mean it Rasha." She sensed he had stopped short of saying what was on his mind. "Just for now I want you to remember . . .," he added in a tender voice, "I'm watching over you every minute of every day . . . I love you, sunshine."

As he uttered his last sentence, a male voice came on the line. "Hello?"

Rasha jumped, dabbing her eyes hurriedly. "Karim, I'm on the phone!"

"Sorry." Then a click.

"Who was that?"

"My brother."

"Does he know?"

"No, I haven't told him." She drew a breath of relief. What would she have done if it had been her father who had cut in? Then, for fear that Luke might assume she was ashamed of their relationship she added hastily. "Not yet."

"Keep your chin up, sunshine."

"I will," she assured him, unconvinced. "Luke, this time I want to say good-bye properly before the lines fail. I hate it when we get cut off."

162

"When will we speak again?"

"I'll just have to try whenever I can. I can only hope I get lucky."

"Rasha, don't give up on me."

"I won't . . . I think of you too Luke every minute of every day. I won't forget."

"Keep out of harm's way, sunshine."

"Bye, Luke."

Then, a gnawing stillness. Whatever tricks her mind had played on her when the fever burnt through her were pulverized by the mere sound of Luke's voice. Any contact with him, however impalpable, fulfilled her. Whatever her intellect had debunked as an impossible fantasy, her heart knew was real, and right.

A knock at her bedroom door broke the spell.

"One minute." She turned to the mirror, wiping away any traces of her emotional outburst.

"Yes?"

Karim stood in the crack of the door, his soft hazel eyes refracting sympathy. Rasha waited. He stepped into the room and as he took her in his arms, she laid her head snug against his chest. "You could've told *me*," he whispered.

Rasha shook her head repeatedly, but could not speak.

Following the cease-fire reached on July 24, the violence did not abate. In lieu of air attacks, it took the form of bloody combats in Tripoli and a series of bombardments in the capital. On September 4, the French ambassador Louis Delamare was assassinated, and September right through to October saw a wave of kidnappings and car bombs that spread throughout the country. In spite of it all, the state-run baccalaureate exams took place on August 18 without disruptions and Rasha resumed her teaching at the American University.

She finally received Luke's letter three months after he had posted it. It was no more than a note scribbled in tight handwriting on a paper napkin and undated.

Sunshine, I've just seen you off, and find myself alone in a café with no one to talk to. I guess I got so used to having you with me that I had to communicate with you right then, hence this napkin. Let me tell you that you seem as competent in destabilizing people as you did your own country. And you, Rasha, have left me feeling hopelessly destabilized. I miss you, and I know now that there won't be a single day, a single moment, when I won't be thinking of you and wishing you were with me. Keep safe, for me. With all my love. Luke.

She re-read the note until she had practically memorized it, then replaced it in the envelope and stowed it away safely in her desk drawer. She pulled out an airmail pad and wrote:

Beirut, October 7, 1981
Dear Luke,

I've only just received your note. On a napkin! How French! If you've written to me again since, I'll probably get it next year at this rate. Still, I count myself lucky to have been able to call you, although I do find it quite ridiculous and frustrating not to be able to talk at length. It just occurred to me the other day that I have no idea what you're working on or what assignments you have in the pipeline. I just hope that you're not angling for a trip to Beirut. Not yet at least. The situation's been very touch and go and there's no way of telling what's going to happen or when the next car bomb will go off.

Fortunately, the university has reopened and my classes keep me occupied and focused. Despite the fact that nothing is sacrosanct here, I still consider the campus a haven. I laugh within when I see students with guns tucked under their shirts biting on their lower lip over an essay or battling to construct a sentence that's grammatically correct. They may display bravado outside the classroom but are miraculously humbled in class. I get the odd thug of course who'll try to weasel himself out of a bad test, but in the main they're good people who I guess have known nothing but warfare since their adolescence. It's uplifting to see a few of them determined to better themselves and secure a profession, in spite of the dim future of this country. The other day I was stunned when one of my students, Youssef, approached me for extra lessons. He's a reserved, shy kind of guy, who lost his father sometime during the war. Little gestures like that make me proud of my profession.

I'm rambling, sorry. Unfortunately, by way of news, except for my teaching, I have none. By channelling my frustration and loneliness through my work, I can just about cope. Not a day goes by when I don't wish we'd had more time together, although I know that no extra time would've been enough. If I had the power, I would get on a flight to London this very minute. But I know that to do so would be rash and might end up being more detrimental to the two of us. I won't bore you with the long list of complications. I'm in quite a predicament, Luke, yet I have no regrets and I hope you don't either. I keep telling myself that there's *got* to be a reason we were brought together and whatever happens, it can only be for the best. So many people around me are grieving daily for a lost child, parent or relative that I'm immediately reassured by the fact that at least *you're* okay. Unfortunately, other people's pain doesn't detract from mine, and I feel every bit as miserable, as empty as the day we said good-bye at the airport. But I have to count my blessings, Luke, and only hope that the world will be kind to us and bring us together before long.

I re-read this and I question whether I'm as resigned and calm as I make it sound. Somehow it doesn't ring true. I feel like I'm trying more to silence my frustration, the sense of being incomplete without you. If I were to admit to every moment of longing, of feeling short-changed and cheated out of love, I would crumble. Luke, you've left an empty space in my soul. Reliving in my mind the precious moments we had together invariably turns into self-flagellation, and before long I feel I need to let go of them to purge myself of an excruciating sense of loss. I *want* to believe . . . I *need* to believe that I will see you again. And I *will* wait.

But will *he*? The thought struck Rasha like a thunderbolt. She had been so sure of his love that she had not allowed herself a moment of doubt. Now, uncertainty gnawed at her. Luke had a dynamic lifestyle, busy in a job he was passionate about, and predestined to travel to different corners of the world. She, on the other hand, waded in a stalemate, stagnant in a second-rate job with no prospects of change or advancement. Why would any man resist temptation for the sake of an absent woman? What kind of man would want to?

Rasha rubbed her scar fiercely. What stood between her and Luke was not only distance, nor her traditional father, but time. Time that dragged along enticing experiences and stimulating change. Beyond the passion that Luke had exhibited towards her were two other loves: a love for his profession and a love for his freedom. Could she honestly expect to compete? And with what? Empty promises and impassivity?

Her mind shut down, her hand poised over the paper. She entertained the idea of destroying the letter. She considered for a moment whether she could be wrong. The hurt on Luke's face during their quarrel in Saint-Denis flashed before her. This time she would rather risk a rebuff than disappoint him. She tried to revive her enthusiasm but her reasoning had left her emotions in disarray. In the blink of an eye, and with the destructive power of her mind game, she had managed to quench honest feelings that had sprung from the bottom of her heart and spilled out on the white sheets of paper.

She could say no more.

With all my love, Rasha, were the words that sealed her letter.

Chapter Seven
Beirut - November 1981

◆

For five months, and since her return from Paris, Rasha's mind had been saturated with thoughts of Luke and designs on when and how she would see him again. Yet the evening she walked down the long passage and pulled the front door open, she was oblivious to the far-fetched possibility that the foreigner at the door could have been—Luke, himself.

A leap back in time, forward into the present and a reconciliation of two different continents at once was required of her to believe her eyes. She felt like she had been spun around, stopped, and left to find her bearings in the dark. In a split second, disbelief mingled with elation and nervousness. The minute she set eyes on him, immobile on her doorstep with backpack and duffel bag, the air itself became redolent with mystification. The intoxicating scent and the peculiar taste on her tongue were indefinable, a blend of the familiar becoming extraneous and the inconceivable proving real. Since Luke and her home, together, were not possible, it seemed as if her well-known environment had become instantaneously unrecognizable.

All this swept through her consciousness as she flung herself into his arms. Without thinking, she submitted to his ardent kiss, time suspended. She lingered in his embrace, too shaken to meet his gaze, head tucked against his chest.

Bracing herself, she finally looked up. "What are you doing here?" she asked inanely, her eyes brimming with childish surprise and satisfaction.

"What do you think?"

"Oh Luke, why didn't you call and tell me you were coming?"

"I thought I'd surprise you."

Before she could come to grips with the sudden turn of events, her father's sobering voice tore her away from Luke. "Who's at the door Rasha?"

Ears tuned to the approaching rustle of her father's 'abaya, she raised an index finger up to her lips. "Let me handle this." Her thundering heartbeat shook her body from within, leaving her in doubt as to whether she would be able to regain composure. Still at the door, she steadied herself and introduced Luke to her father a touch too elaborately as a friend of Hana's boss, a freelance photojournalist for Reuters on assignment in Beirut. She was relieved that her qualification was in essence accurate, and that there had been no need to lie. Only after he had cast an appraising eye on the stranger did Amin accept the extended hand. Then true to custom, he invited him in, hospitality being paramount in Arab culture. One admitted one's guest first and asked questions later. Rasha avoided her father's gaze, sensing silent bewilderment on his part. No doubt he would demand an explanation when it suited him, more likely in the absence of the foreigner.

Amin ushered Luke into the lounge instructing Rasha to call her mother. From then on Rasha knew, and doubted Luke ever expected, that communication between the two of them would be curtailed by her father who would take it upon himself to converse with the male guest. The opportunity to revel in Luke's arrival had been plucked too soon. That one brief euphoric moment on seeing him, now stolen, never to be retrieved.

Eager to rejoin them in the lounge, Rasha, virtually incoherent, related what had just occurred to her mother and pressed her to follow.

"I'm surprised Hana didn't mention any of this," Nuha observed as she and Rasha started towards the lounge.

Rasha shrugged. "She must've forgotten." The urgency to contact and alert Hana, in order to pre-empt being discovered, was foremost in her mind.

Uneasy is too weak a word to describe how Rasha felt in the presence of Luke and her parents. Everything she did or said appeared contrived. Her own skin, her own voice, were no longer hers. Her every word to Luke was laden with a hint or a cue. When she offered him a drink, she suggested a lemonade, a Coke, water maybe, hoping that he would latch on to the fact that a beer or whisky would be out of the question. She fought the urge to stare at him and single out anything different in his appearance and demeanour, to reacquaint herself with the lover who had been refashioned by her imagination. She did so only when it seemed natural, on the occasion when he spoke and everyone else's eyes were on him. Bit by bit she gleaned subtle changes: his shorter hair, a slight weight loss, and his manner of warm dress with a T-shirt underneath a shirt. Yet she strained to remain expressionless and to conceal any sign of attraction. She crossed and uncrossed her legs and never seemed to get comfortable as the ticking of a grandfather clock rapped on her nerves.

Amin and Nuha were pleasant and courteous. Despite the fact that everyone in the room, bar her, appeared contained and congenial, Rasha could not shake her edginess or stop herself from stroking her scar. The ironies in the course of the chitchat were too obvious to her. Luke was challenged to reveal everything about himself, his background, his parents, his work, relatives who had dwindled into insignificance in the course of his life, all subjects that he preferred to circumvent. Amin dwelled particularly on Luke's father. In a patriarchal culture, one's father defined one. To Rasha's amazement, Luke answered Amin's queries satisfactorily, betraying the fact that he was more in touch with his family than he had led her to believe.

Every question that Amin put to Luke was calculated and purposeful.

"Do you have any colleagues in Beirut?"

"A few," Luke replied. "I expect they should be quite easy to find."

"Do you know anyone else in Beirut?"

Short of an affidavit and reliable references, Rasha mused, her father would not be satisfied.

"No, actually I don't . . . Except for Rasha."

Amin stiffened, as if Luke's innocent addition pronounced indecency. He would not probe the stranger on how and where he met his daughter. That would be undignified. Such information he would have to prise out of Rasha. She watched her father, majestically reclined on the sofa, the camel-hair 'abaya wrapped around his bulk, and read his mind. The man who had shown up unexpectedly at his door had no connections in Beirut, which made it difficult for Amin to turn him away. His expression turned into a scowl which only Rasha could detect.

"You say you're here with Reuters."

"Yes, sir."

Amin took an inquisitor's pose, mulling over his next tactical question when Karim walked in. It was as if a window had been flung open and a gust of air had swept into the stifling room. Overjoyed, Rasha could count on Karim to take the edge off the conversation. Luke stood up to shake his hand, and as she observed them face to face, Rasha assured herself that there should be no obstacle to their compatibility. Eventually, it was Karim who brought up the question of accommodations.

Luke seemed taken by surprise and looked questioningly at Rasha. She grasped his meaning with a tinge of horror. He had actually intended to stay with her.

Luke cleared his throat. "I'd heard of a hotel in Beirut where it seems most journalists stay. I hoped you might point me in the right direction."

Rasha suppressed a sigh of relief. Maybe he had come well prepared after all.

"That would probably be the Commodore, just off Hamra Street," Karim confirmed. "They're quite jacked up on communication and have telex machines which is why the hotel is popular with the press."

"It's far too late for you to wander the streets," Nuha interjected, having by eye contact acquired her husband's approval. "You must stay here tonight. We have a spare room."

"You're very kind, Mrs. Halwani, but I wouldn't want to put you out."

"It's no trouble at all. I'm certain your parents would do the same for my children."

Heavens, Rasha thought, aren't we all talking at cross-purposes!

"I'll go see to dinner," Nuha rose smiling. "I'm sure you're very tired."

Luke respectfully rose to his feet as he mumbled his thanks. Instead of regaining his seat he asked to freshen up. Rasha got up to show him the way to the guest bathroom. Out of sight, he grabbed her and made to kiss her. She pushed him away.

"Not here," she muttered, casting a quick glance down the passage.

"No one can see us."

"No, Luke."

He lingered to argue with her but she interrupted him. "I have to go back. They'll start wondering where I am."

He shrugged. "So . . . you're with *me*."

Rasha looked him straight in the eye, to emphasize what her tone of voice could not. "Luke, listen to me," she whispered, "No one is to know about us."

He went ashen, his expression reminiscent of his reaction to her outburst in Saint-Denis.

"Rasha, I've been planning this trip for months. Do you know what it took for me to get here? The networking, the financing?" His voice seemed on the verge of breaking. "And now you tell me no one must know about us?" His facial muscles tensed.

"I'll have to explain later. Please, Luke, just listen to me this once."

Without a backward glance, she turned to the lounge where she found Amin alone with Karim. Nuha was busy setting the food on the table. Rasha sat down and wedged her hands between her knees.

"Whose friend did you say he was?" Amin enquired again like an interrogator setting a trap for the accused, expecting the final answer to contravene his original plea of innocence.

"Nadim's. Auntie Hana's boss."

Amin nodded. "Why weren't we told to expect him?" His steady gaze challenging Rasha.

"Auntie Hana probably forgot. She might've mentioned something to me. I don't know, Baba. The last time we spoke the lines were not clear."

Amin dropped his head once more, hands locked in a fist. "He can stay here tonight. One night," he said, extending a forefinger. He held it there long enough to ascertain that Rasha had taken note of his gesture and its significance, then reiterated, eyes darting, eyebrows like a vulture's wings. "One."

"Yes, Baba."

The way her father delivered his instructions implied that, because of the closeness in age between her and Luke, Amin suspected there was more to the newcomer than Rasha had admitted and therefore held her responsible for the intrusion. An intrusion it was, for Rasha recognized that her father had found himself in a quandary: he could not turn Luke away nor was he too happy to admit him into his home.

"I'll have to talk to Hana," he snarled.

Rasha's heart sank. The joviality they had all assumed in Luke's presence was, as she had guessed, fleeting and insincere. In one instant, she plunged into despair, the sight of Luke back in their midst, unsuspecting, accentuating her guilt and covert duplicity. It was cold-hearted of her father to spurn him because he was a stranger and a foreigner, and because he believed that Rasha's involvement with him possibly ran deeper than she cared to reveal. Amin's proscriptions in Luke's absence were a check on where she belonged and where her allegiance lay, and at that very moment she detected no less than hypocrisy and prejudice in her father. She was placed in an unbearable position of having to deceive the man she loved.

They moved to the dining-room where a generous platter of chicken with chick peas and Lebanese rice occupied the centre of the table, accompanied by a bowl of *tabbouleh* at one end. Amin enjoyed food and Nuha with little effort satisfied his insatiable appetite. It was her habit to produce time-consuming dishes with no fuss and always in abundance just in case someone dropped in.

Amin headed the table and motioned for Luke to sit to his left, next to Karim. Nuha faced Luke with Rasha at the very end, far from him.

Luke flashed the diplomatic smile Rasha had first noticed at Hana's cocktail party. "This looks delicious, Mrs. Halwani." His tone was flat, and Rasha surmised that he was at pains to keep his disappointment in check.

"I hope you'll like it. It's one of our traditional dishes. If you don't like pine nuts just push them aside."

Luke did nothing of the sort and dug hungrily into his plate, chick peas, pine nuts and all. Rasha recalled their brief mention of Lebanese food when they first met and was pleased that Luke could finally get a taste—though culinary at first—of her culture.

She was quiet over dinner, her father's scrutinizing gaze unrelenting, inhibiting her gestures and speech. By his silence, he managed to reawaken in her the self-reproach that she had managed so far to repress. The conversation was far from animated, yet Luke appeared oblivious to the undercurrent of restraint and tension to which Rasha was well attuned.

Her saving grace was Karim, who quizzed Luke on matters that had intrigued her: How had he made his way from the airport and what were his impressions on landing in Beirut?

"Unfortunately, I couldn't see much from the air because of the blackout. That would've been an interesting sight. Otherwise, it was all pretty much as I'd imagined," Luke replied, resting his fork on the side of his plate. "I expected the airport would be swarming with militiamen and although it was a little chaotic, it doesn't compare with the mayhem in Africa. I got a cabbie who spoke a smattering of English. He managed to get me here, despite my poor pronunciation." Luke paused in thought. "What I didn't expect though was to have so many buildings still standing. When you see Beirut coverage on TV, you get the impression that the whole country has been razed."

"Did you have any problems at the roadblocks?"

"Actually, none," Luke said between mouthfuls. "We were stopped at a couple on that stretch just outside the airport, but as soon as the driver mentioned that I was with the press, they waved us on. What was that word he used in Arabic?"

"*Sahafi?*" Rasha offered.

"That's it." In what seemed to be an effort to keep the conversation flowing, Luke carried on. "He was quite a talkative little chap. He rambled on about the Israeli raids and kept pointing at bombed-out buildings all the while saying 'Israeli attack.' Funny chap. He wouldn't keep his hand off the horn although there were hardly any cars around."

"That's the taxi drivers' reflex here," Karim clarified. "They do it more out of habit than necessity. It's really irritating."

"You could tell, though, that Beirut must've been a truly spectacular city. The driver took me along the promenade . . ."

"The corniche," Rasha interjected.

"The corniche," he repeated after her, a glint in his eye recognizing Rasha's obsession with accuracy. "It was still a bit eerie. In its heyday, I can imagine it may have looked very much like Cannes."

"It did, actually," Nuha said. "Not that I've been to Cannes but I've seen pictures. I think it's the palm trees that line the road, really."

Luke turned to Karim. "It went fine, I'm glad to say. No hitches."

Rasha wondered in silence what Luke's thoughts had been as the driver weaved through shrouded streets, their guts blown up by rockets and mortars. What went through his mind when they skirted apartment blocks that appeared as flimsy as papier mâché, peppered with bullet holes and displaying curtains of unsightly clotheslines. If she knew, she would take his every impression to heart for it was a reflection on her homeland and by extension a reflection on her. Being exposed to Rasha's surroundings had to have had an impact on the way Luke now perceived her. She had been stripped naked. In Paris, she could censor any aspects of her background as she chose to. In Beirut, her existence was bared and self-explanatory. Whatever she may have effaced, Luke would be able to discern for himself without her guidance or help. She no longer had the power to channel his vision.

"Karim, Rasha tells me you're a medical student."

"That's right."

"What are you specializing in?"

"Cardiology," Karim replied with a tinge of pride, then added in jest, "Mender of broken hearts."

Luke raised an eyebrow in admiration. "So are you still doing theory or practical work?"

"One of the courses in the fourth year required an internship in the Emergency Room. Now I've moved on to residency for training in internal medicine."

"The ER? That must be tough. Especially under the circumstances," Luke said.

"One has to look on the bright side. The experience I'm getting is exceptional. Extremely valuable." Karim smiled in earnest.

The conversation nearly ground to a halt when Luke asked, "What made you choose medicine?"

"Masochism," Karim replied, eliciting a laugh from Luke. "Seriously, I have no clue. I think it was the other way around really. You could say medicine chose me."

"That's actually how I feel about photojournalism." Luke beamed as if he and Karim had fallen on common ground.

"Now *that* must be exciting."

"Not always. It depends on the work. I've had quite a few dreary assignments. Still, I can't see myself doing anything else."

Rasha's gaze flitted between Karim and Luke. She desperately hoped they would not only get along but also end up liking each other.

"I regret not being able to cover the Israeli incursion," Luke carried on. "It took place in July, didn't it?"

Karim nodded as he swallowed.

"Anyway, I couldn't manage it. I still had some work pending from a recent trip to Africa. The whole episode must've been horrendous for all of you, and yet nothing definitive came out of it." Luke chanced a look at Amin.

"It's a protracted and complicated strife that will take years to resolve," Amin stated curtly. "We've learned not to expect instant solutions."

Luke set his cutlery on his plate, without the faintest clank, and sat ramrod-straight. "I don't mean to be presumptuous, Mr. Halwani. I know very little about the situation here, so please correct me if I'm wrong . . . but it does seem to me that non-Lebanese issues are being fought out on Lebanese soil." He waited for an answer. Rasha stared at her plate. Although her father may very well agree with Luke, he would never admit it. Revealing his views would be exposing a side of himself which he was adamant not to with anyone, least of all Luke.

The pause that followed was like a lit fuse, and Rasha braced herself for the blast. "What's going on in Lebanon is beyond anyone's comprehension."

Luke rested his forearms against the side of the table. He rubbed the tips of his fingers together. Rasha guessed that he was itching for a smoke. "I presume the Lebanese are quite divided in their views, some supporting the Israelis, others the Palestinians."

Amin delayed his response by requesting another helping of rice. "Have you heard of the tenet, 'My enemy's enemy is my friend'?" he finally asked.

"Yes, sir, I have."

Amin dipped his head with some exaggeration, implying that there was no need to elaborate.

Luke went no further. With a tinge of sorrow, Rasha had watched him try hard, since his arrival, to ingratiate himself with her father. Between her rebuff and Amin's recalcitrance, Luke must have been wondering why he had bothered to come to Beirut. Her inability to reassure him, to accept him into the fold, left her bristling.

Luke leaned back as Umm Samir cleared the table and brought out a platter of fruit. Rasha broke her silence. "You can smoke if you like."

Luke turned to Amin for concurrence. "Certainly, be my guest. An ashtray if you please, Umm Samir."

Luke produced his packet of Gauloises and the Zippo lighter Rasha had given him from the front pocket of his shirt. He lit a cigarette and drew on it with hunger. The pungent smell, and the sight of her gift, transported Rasha back to their intimate moments in Paris. She brushed them aside briskly lest anyone should read her thoughts.

"That was a delicious meal, thank you Mrs. Halwani."

"I'm glad you enjoyed it. Help yourself to some fruit. Please."

He lifted a flat palm to his chest. "I'm actually quite full. Thank you all the same."

Another pause, as if all possibilities had been exhausted. Rasha was at a loss. Her pretence not to know Luke well prevented her from asking after Carol and his mother, and how he had spent the time after she left Paris.

"How long do you expect to be in Beirut?" she asked, hoping her tremulous voice would go undetected.

"A week. Ten days maybe," Luke fixed her with enticing eyes.

She looked away.

Karim came to her rescue. "Luke could stay with Fuad! I'm sure he'd like to have company."

"Who's Fuad?" Luke asked.

"He's a good friend of mine, half-French half-Lebanese. His father passed away just before the war, and only recently his mother decided to go back to France with his sister. But he insisted on staying behind. He now lives alone in the family's apartment. If anyone has room to put you up, it's Fuad. It beats staying in a hotel, unless of course you'd rather have access to their facilities."

"Does he live far from the Commodore hotel?"

"Only fifteen minutes away on foot."

"I wouldn't want to impose . . ."

"I promise you Fuad won't mind. In fact, I'm meeting him tomorrow at nine. Why don't you come along and I'll introduce you to him."

"Thanks. That would be great."

Amin slapped the table with the flat of his hands, rising. "If you'll excuse me, it's getting late. Karim, would you show our guest to his room?"

"Yes, Baba."

Luke towered over Amin as they exchanged a handshake. "It was a pleasure meeting you, sir. Thank you for everything."

"It's my pleasure."

Amin disappeared without addressing Rasha, his silence more portentous than spoken reprobation. She set about clearing the table with her mother and Umm Samir, to occupy her mind.

"He seems quite decent," Nuha remarked.

"He does, doesn't he?" Rasha concurred in an even tone. "I'm sure Hana wouldn't have suggested he contact us otherwise." She felt abominable for laying the duplicity on her aunt and hoped for the opportunity to apologize to her.

"It's unfortunate we can't put him up for the duration of his stay, but your father won't have it."

"Why, Mama?" Rasha asked at the risk of inviting reproach.

"Well, Rasha," Nuha said in a tight voice, "It's certainly not the time to have a foreigner in the house. Your father's trying to get his factory back and with the raging conflict he wouldn't want to be seen playing host to an American and a journalist to boot."

"He's a photographer, Mama, and he's English, not American. That hardly has anything to do with it."

"English, American. You think the people out there who have their teeth sharpened against Israel can tell the difference? All westerners are not welcome at the moment. You know that, Rasha."

The irony that Nuha was debating a point they both believed to be true did not escape Rasha. She would not have wished for Luke to be there under those circumstances but now that he was she could not turn him away.

"Did Baba actually tell you all this?"

"He didn't have to."

Of course he didn't, Rasha thought. Amin communicated telepathically with Nuha. As his wife, she had been conditioned—and in fact was expected—to intuit his train of thought.

"He should be fine with Fuad," Nuha said conclusively, but her tone of voice betrayed concern for him. Rasha could tell that, her mother's categorical agreement with Amin aside, Nuha already felt responsible for Luke. To her, he was no more than a young man in a strange city without a soul to look out for him. Her maternal instincts rose to the fore.

Nuha continued. "What surprises me is, if he's with Reuters, why wouldn't they have organized his accommodations?"

"He freelances for the agency, Mama. He's a stringer and stringers don't get the same benefits as staffers," Rasha replied ambiguously as she drew on Luke's explanation, not certain that what she said was altogether accurate.

"Put this away in the fridge for me will you?" Nuha extended the *tabbouleh* to Rasha. "What if something were to happen to him, God forbid? Would the agency look after him?"

Rasha would not let herself dwell on the sinister thought. "I don't know, Mama. You'd have to ask him. Let's just hope that it doesn't."

Rasha loitered in the kitchen, waiting for her father to fall asleep so she could seek out Luke. That was what she had told herself even though she suspected she was buying time, too shaken to face him. She dreaded his reaction to their reception and what she anticipated as a confused impression of her family. She had a lot to explain while at the same time threading her way through the maze of her own emotions.

Rounding the corner to the guest room, she walked straight into him. A familiar warmth surged in her.

"I was on my way to get a glass of water," Luke said, eyes glistening.

"I'll get it for you." She made to turn when he held her back by the arm.

"Rasha, wait. That was actually just an excuse to look for you."

She glanced over her shoulder then led him into the family room. Out of propriety his bedroom was out of bounds.

Leaving the door ajar, she stood facing him. She drew a breath, at a loss as to where to start.

"Rasha, do you mind telling me what's going on here?" he began rather loudly until she motioned for him to whisper. "Why should I keep my voice down, for Christ's sake?" he retorted, nevertheless heeding her gesture and lowering it. "You carry on as if we'd done something wrong!"

"Luke, do you remember when in Paris you suggested coming to Beirut? Can you see now why I thought it was a bad idea?"

"Rasha," he only used her name when he was vexed or irritated, "you're behaving like a teenager. You haven't said a single word to me the whole evening. You act as if I lived next door and popped in for a coffee. Christ, Rasha. I've come miles to see you, at my own risk and my own expense. This place is swarming with journalists! One less, one more wouldn't make a bloody difference to media coverage!"

"I'm sure being here would do no harm to your career, Luke."

He stared at her fiercely. "I can't believe you just said that. You think I'm here because of my bloody career?"

She lowered her eyes. "It's not what I meant, but would I be wrong to assume you shot a whole film on your way here?"

"So?"

"So . . .," she stammered, " So . . . nothing. Listen, Luke, it's all coming out wrong. I'm not saying what I mean."

Luke passed tensed hands through his hair. In a dramatic show of dejection, he slumped against the wall, arms crossed. "Okay . . . Take your time then. Explain it to me."

"Explain what?"

"Everything, Rasha. *Enlighten* me on why I have to endure a stilted conversation with your father, sit miles away from you, and hope against hope that you would look at me, acknowledge me."

"I *did* explain it to you, Luke. In Paris. Weren't you listening? I told you about my parents' mentality. I tried to warn you."

"I don't expect you to jump in my lap and shower me with kisses in front of everyone Rasha. But to act as if I wasn't even there is a bit extreme."

"I couldn't let on that we knew each other, Luke. I introduced you as a friend of Nadim's and pretended that I never knew you were coming here. Which is true, I didn't!" she exclaimed in earnest. "If my father had found out about us, you wouldn't have even been let into this house."

"So where do we go from here? Am I supposed to pack up and leave? Do *you* want me to leave? Do you?" he bombarded her.

"No." A door slammed. Rasha tensed.

"Look at you," he shot back, palms upturned, "you're so strung out you're about to snap."

For one brief moment, she looked at him and all else seemed to vanish. In that instant, her passion for him flared up from smouldering embers.

"Luke," she finally said softly, "You can't begin to imagine how happy I am to see you. But, here, it's different. It's difficult. My home, my environment prevents me from acting like . . . from openly being the woman you fell in love with . . ."

"So was it a *mirage* after all Rasha?" he interjected, dredging up their argument in Saint-Denis.

She fixed him with imploring eyes. What went through her mind, at complete odds with the yearning she felt in her heart, was too complicated for words. Something stood between her and Luke. Something barred them from getting closer to each other, from touching. The restraint came from her, as caution seeped through the porous walls, pungent and repelling. In her home, she was no more than a puppet who anticipated and acted out its controller's wishes, even when the strings were long and the puppeteer's eyes were averted. Yet, before her stood a man whose presence was testimony of his love. The reunion she had dreamt of over and over had been realized and all she could do was cave in to prudence and self-control.

Desperate, she said without thinking. "Please try to understand," all the while recognizing that she perpetually asked him to make the effort to accommodate her.

Luke tipped his head towards the ceiling. "Rasha, you know it's not in me to play into other people's hands. I'd do it for you. I'd do anything for you. But I know that ultimately I'd be doing it for your father's sake. That's not right! Christ, Rasha, you know I don't even answer to my own father!"

"Luke, I realize this couldn't have been easy for you either. Being grilled about your family and your background. Feeling cornered maybe . . ."

His face unexpectedly awash with understanding, he observed. "That's not unusual, Rasha. It happens the world over. I am a stranger to your family after all, and of course I appreciate that they took me in this evening. But you know . . . I wouldn't have been that much of a stranger if you'd admitted to our relationship."

"That's what I've been trying to tell you. If I had 'admitted to our relationship,' you wouldn't be here now. You'd be staying at the Commodore."

Luke puffed out a sigh. "I need a drink! But I suppose that too is out of the question." He looked at her sideways, flashing his roguish smile. "You should've seen yourself trying to make me understand that alcohol was a no-no. I half-expected you to walk in with a glass of milk and chocolate chip cookies."

Rasha burst out laughing then instinctively covered her mouth.

"Yeah! Be careful no one hears you. They might think we're up to something," he said in a stage-whisper.

She suppressed another outburst. Then eyes beaming at him with love and unfettered trust, she simply said, "I'm sorry."

His back flush against the wall, he extended an arm and pulled her to him. She had forgotten the sweet taste of tobacco on his lips, their fullness, their warmth. Her memory had failed her to the extent that it had undermined the passion she had felt every time Luke held her in his embrace. Her body, though, would not yield and remained stiff, reining in desire.

"I missed you, sunshine."

"I missed you too, Luke."

Nuha's slippered shuffle sounded in the passage. Rasha pulled away and opened the door, just in time to walk out and meet her.

"Rasha, does Luke need anything?"

"No Mama, he's fine." Her cheeks were aflame.

"Thank you, Mrs. Halwani," Luke pronounced over Rasha's shoulder.

"You're welcome, Luke. Well, Good night, then." Nuha gave Rasha a quick glance then disappeared into her bedroom.

"You'd better go on," Rasha said softly.

Luke had not missed Nuha's prompt. "Looks like it, doesn't it? Sweet dreams, sunshine."

"I'll see you tomorrow, Luke," she said finally, eyes radiant.

On the way to her bedroom, Rasha passed Karim's, then on second thought retraced her steps. She tapped on the door. Without waiting for an answer, she walked in and found him flat on his stomach in bed, reading. He craned his neck to get a glimpse of her. Before she could speak, he said: "I knew you'd come . . . It's him, isn't it?"

Rasha shut the door behind her. "How did you guess?" she asked, concerned that what was obvious to him must have been equally so to her parents.

Karim shrugged, his face back in the book. "Just a feeling."

Rasha sat at the edge of his bed. "Do you think Baba suspects something?"

Karim chuckled. "He *always* suspects something! He suspects *everything*!"

"Karim, I need your help."

"I thought I'd already been a great help," he threw back, eyes stubbornly glued to the book. "I came up with the idea of putting him up at Fuad's, didn't I? This way you two can meet without half of Beirut knowing about it and Baba finding out."

"I know, thanks. That was great. Please leave your book for a minute and listen to me."

He slammed it shut and propped himself up on one elbow. "I'm listening."

"Why are you acting so nonchalant, Karim? You know this could land me in big trouble."

"I didn't mean to, sorry. But don't you think Luke is the one who should've thought of your situation before appearing at our doorstep?"

"He doesn't really understand what it's like for me."

"I guess he couldn't, unless you'd warned him."
"I did."

"So what is it that you want me to do?"

"Karim, Luke is here for ten days. You've got to be with me whenever I meet with him."

Karim dropped his head on an outstretched arm.

"It's no big deal, Karim. You and Rula go out anyway, quite often too." Rasha's reference to Karim's busy

social calendar with his girlfriend as opposed to her stagnant life was meant as a dig, a reminder of the fact that he
had more freedom than she did. "Maybe we should also
ask Fuad to join us. This way it wouldn't be obvious that
Luke and I are a couple."

"Rasha, do you have *any* idea how much work I
have this week?"

"Please, Karim. I can't do this without you."

"I promise to try my best. okay?"

"I love you, Karimo." She gave him a peck on the
cheek.

"The feeling is mutual."

Ignoring the sly remark intended as a dismissal,
she asked, "What did you think of him?"

"He's a nice guy."

"Is that all?"

"He's great! *Admirable*! Now will you please let
me get on with my book?"

Rasha persisted. "What time did you say you'll be
leaving tomorrow morning?"

"Half past eight, quarter to nine," Karim replied
impatiently.

"I'll set my alarm clock. By the way, where are you
meeting Fuad?"

"West Hall. Anything else?" He cocked his head
to one side.

Rasha mentally reviewed her agenda for the day.
"I'll meet you there. I'm not teaching until twelve."

She did not leave his side. At once overcome with
self-doubt, she had to ask, "Karim, do you think what I'm
doing . . . what I've done . . . is wrong?"

"You're not a child, Rasha. You're entitled to
make your own decisions."

"I feel like such a hypocrite."

"Quite frankly, you did get yourself into a bit of a
mess here. Couldn't you have found a good Lebanese

Muslim to latch onto instead of *him*?" He put it to her half in jest, aware of her predicament.

"Stupid, isn't it? Now, what do I do?"

"You can either confront Baba and Mama with the truth, making sure first that you've packed a bag and booked a one-way ticket. Or keep quiet about it and see how it goes. You've only known the guy for a short while. Who knows? You might discover you don't actually love him."

"I love him."

"Then tell them."

"I can't do that!"

"Right then, don't tell them!"

She scowled at him. "You're such a big help, Karim. You're lucky you've never had to deal with the issues I've been plagued with."

"Here we go again." Karim rolled his eyes.

She changed tack, softening her voice. "All I'm asking for is your advice, your help. You know I have no one else to turn to."

"Rasha, I *will* help. You can come to me anytime, okay? I'm sorry."

Rasha smiled victoriously. She opened the book at the marker and placed it in front of him. "Enjoy."

Once in her room, Rasha glimpsed her desk intact as she had left it four hours earlier to make her way down the passage. In that short span, her existence as it was remained suspended, waiting to be resumed as if nothing had happened, as if Luke had never arrived and had never disrupted the drudgery of her quotidian life. In a way, she bemoaned the predictable monotony of her existence, the comfort of inertia. Had Luke not shown up, she would have finished correcting the exam papers, had a quiet dinner with her parents then slipped under her covers unruffled by the day's events. Now, her torpor had been challenged, the developments calling for quick decisions and galvanizing her into action. The secret she had harboured so skillfully and for so long threatened at any moment to disclose itself, and Rasha had to muster the energy and the deviousness to tame it.

This all led to the fundamental question: was she pleased to see Luke? Luke who had assumed the role of an *agent provocateur*? Picturing him again in the midst of her family, being interrogated, and virtually put on show, she had to say no. Rasha loathed disruption. She would go as far as to say she disliked surprises which invariably presupposed unmitigated joy. Did she feel exhilarated? Save for the brief instant when he held her in his arms, no she didn't. Her insides had been a cauldron of emotions, her thoughts a mad scramble governed by rising contrition. Where in all this could she place the satisfaction that seeing Luke again had given her?

Never *ever* before had she caused as much as a ripple in her family situation. Now, because of her, the waters raged, crashing against the very foundations of her nucleus. And no one, but her, could quell them or plot their course. Like it or not, Rasha was placed in the position of arbiter, between Luke and her parents—a role that demanded conviction and fortitude, neither of which she could boast of.

Blood rushed to her head, her veins pumping a dull ache in heavy doses. She sneaked off to the bathroom to retrieve a painkiller, careful that no one, not even Luke should hear her, for fear of any intrusion on her thoughts. Back again in her room, she lay on her bed in darkness, assailed by an inner voice: Luke is here, asleep under your roof. He is here, in the flesh, the man you thought you would never see again. So what do you feel? Warmth, restrained pleasure maybe, but unbridled passion only momentarily. How could I? He's a guest in my parents' home. He and I are playing out a charade, deceiving the people I've always held dear. The only two people who have nurtured, protected and loved me. I feel vile and to want him would be beyond contempt. I've silenced my senses and allowed my instincts to be trampled upon and pulverized. All in an attempt to salvage whatever decency I could.

Her answers were lucid and indisputable. Yet when she conjured up Luke's face, she was overcome with despair. The thought of him close to her shattered her resolve into smithereens. He asked for no more than to reclaim her love. He had made a great effort to come to Beirut and see her, in spite of her cautioning. Then a thought. Did Carol know where he was? Did he tell any members of his family where he was going to be? What if, indeed what if, as Nuha wondered, something were to happen to him?

Rasha reached for the switch on her sidelamp and depressed it. She pulled out a sleeping pill from a box in the drawer and washed it down with water. In darkness again, she waited for it to take effect. If this didn't work to slow down her racing mind, nothing would. She curled up against the wall, in the fetal position, beckoning sleep. Then it came, fitful and laden with visions, but it came to her, nevertheless.

Chapter Eight

◆

As the cacophony of mid-morning street life gathered momentum, Rasha sat bolt upright in her bed. She had overslept. Half past nine. They were most certainly gone by now. The roar of the vacuum cleaner in the adjoining room brought her to her feet.

"Umm Samir, is Karim still here?" She had to shout to be heard above the din.

"No, Sitt Rasha. He left with the guest a while ago."

Rasha scurried to the kitchen, unnerved, the whine of the machine persisting behind her. The after-effect of the sedative had left her mellow and listless, yet exasperation fermented inside her.

While she waited for the water to boil on the stove, she calculated that if she were to dress quickly enough, she might still be able to meet Luke and Karim on campus. She strode, mug in hand, towards her room.

"Rasha?"

"Yes, Baba."

"Come in here."

With awe overriding impatience, Rasha made a double turn and entered the lounge. The time had come. She knew it.

Her father pored over the daily *An-Nahar* and did not acknowledge her.

"Sit down," he said in a level tone of voice. He removed his reading glasses and placed them meticulously over the folded newspaper.

As usual, Rasha did as she was told, no questions asked, no protestations.

Amin took time to speak, for effect. "Your brother left with the Englishman this morning to arrange for his accommodations."

"Yes Baba."

"We needn't do any more for him."

"Yes Baba."

Silence stretched between them. A metallic taste of dread hung on Rasha's tongue.

"He was not invited here." He stopped. "His reasons for coming to Beirut are his own business and his alone, not ours . . . I see no purpose in him visiting this house again," he stated with finality.

He may as well have driven a knife through her chest. Often she wondered whether he had to consider his words or whether they sprung out naturally blunt and to the point. What irked her most was the manner in which he spoke for the whole family as if it were a monolithic unit whose opinions or stances fell under one umbrella: his. He would not say that Luke's business in Beirut was "not *his*", but "not *ours*", encapsulating in his own view Nuha's, Karim's and Rasha's.

Rasha acknowledged the ban with a nod, her knuckles blanching around the mug.

When she chanced a glance at him, his eyebrows met in a frown. She looked down at her coffee and sipped.

"I will not take charge of him. He's neither my responsibility nor this family's. Is this understood?"

"Yes Baba."

Another pause.

"I'm not interested in the details of how you got to know him . . ."

"There's nothing . . ."

Amin held out a flat hand, stopping Rasha in her tracks. The meaning behind his gesture was manifold: he will not hear what she had to say; he will not be lied to; and anyhow, whatever the explanation, the ban on Luke will hold.

That was her father, succinct, unequivocal and steadfast. His words were invariably well chosen, his arguments watertight, and his instructions brief and to the point—even when they were insinuated and not voiced. What made it simpler of course was his intolerance of debate and discussion. By denying his opponent free scope, Amin invariably emerged triumphant.

Rasha sat rigid, seething yet incapacitated, as if a firm hand had gripped her vocal chords.

"As for what goes on outside this house, you know the rules."

By rote, Rasha thought. Not to be seen alone with Luke, never to give the impression that their relationship was based on anything more than acquaintance, never to overstep the lines of propriety and decency.

"Yes Baba."

With a single nod signifying the end of the one-way discussion, Amin replaced his glasses on the bridge of his nose and retrieved the newspaper. His all-too-familiar dismissal was Rasha's cue to leave.

Amin's reaction was no less than what she had anticipated and what she had prepared herself for. She imbibed it and stored it mentally in the doctrinal heap that had accrued over the years. Her track record left her in no doubt that she would abide by his restrictions. For now, though, she would go about her plan undeterred. In any case, she told herself, she had to go to the university to teach.

She scoured the upper campus for Luke, Karim and Fuad, checking out the cafeteria, the Oval, West Hall, Nicely and College Halls. No sign. With little time left to make her way to the medical school or the hospital, Rasha reluctantly abandoned her search. She would head straight for Fuad's apartment once her classes were over.

She walked across the leafy campus to the English Department in Fisk Hall. Her office on the second floor looked over the grassy Oval and was adjacent to that of the secretary she shared with a professor of English Literature.

"Any calls, Surayya?"

"No, Rasha."

"Messages?"

"None. But . . .," Surayya pointed her pen towards the corner.

Rasha pivoted to find Youssef waiting, a handful of books and notepads in his lap.

"Youssef, I'm so sorry. I didn't realize I was late."

"It's okay, Miss Halwani," replied the spindly undergraduate.

"Come on in."

Rasha motioned for him to sit, shutting the door to the office behind them. She deposited the papers on her desk and proceeded to find his in the pile.

"I read your essay. It's good. I see improvement."

Youssef's face beamed with delight mixed with embarrassment. It had not escaped Rasha that the young man harboured a soft spot for her.

"You were asked to describe a sad episode in your life . . ."

Youssef gave a nod of acknowledgement.

"And you wrote about your father passing away," Rasha could not bring herself to say dying. She opted for the euphemism as if it could mitigate the tragedy.

"Yes, Miss Halwani." Youssef reddened, not with emotion, but acute shyness. It was his habit to do so whenever he was spoken to.

"You didn't mention when this happened, Youssef."

"The 10th of May 1976, miss."

Rasha was not after the exact date but the period. His clear-cut answer, an instinctive articulation of a trauma branded onto his memory, drove right through her heart.

She cleared her throat. "At the very beginning of the war."

"Yes, Miss Halwani."

"You say he was shot by Christians." At the time, Rasha recalled, animosity had flared up between Muslims and Christians leading to criminal acts of revenge and recrimination.

"Yes miss, they took him from the car and shot him." His finger rose to his temple. "That's what they told us, Miss Halwani," he said in Arabic.

"English, Youssef."

"They tell us that, Miss Halwani."

"That is what we were told," she corrected him, smiling encouragingly.

"Yes, miss."

His soulful eyes, his hopeless timidity, and his struggle to learn the language and do well touched her to the core.

"How old were you, Youssef?"

"Thirteen, miss."

"I'm so sorry."

He smiled.

"Do you have any brothers or sisters, Youssef?" The danger of being sucked into his bereavement and of delving into his personal life did not deter Rasha.

"Four sisters, miss, and one brother," He held up five fingers. "I'm the smallest." A flat hand parallel to and only half a metre away from the floor indicated his place among them.

"The 'youngest'. And what does your brother do?"

"He fight, miss."

Rasha overlooked his grammatical error. "And you don't?" She looked at him quizzically.

"I study, miss, to do good, to get a job. I take care of my sisters and mother. My brother, he fight because he is . . ." At a loss for the word, he shook clenched fists.

"Angry?"

"Yes, miss. Angry, very angry," Youssef let out, with discernible relief.

Which militia his brother belonged to was insignificant. It was the brothers' distinct reactions to their loss that intrigued her: one had chosen the path of revenge and violence while the other opted for self-improvement and responsibility. Youssef had a long way to go before he achieved his goal and Rasha felt no less than great admiration for the young man who had assumed his absent father's duties.

"I think it's very good of you to ask for private lessons," she finally said smiling. "I'll help you, Youssef. I can help you get through this course."

"Thank you, Miss Halwani."

"Let's go through the corrections."

Rasha's dedication to her profession was nearly all-consuming. During the whole hour she spent with Youssef, clarifying grammatical and syntax errors, Luke never crossed her mind. Her office had always been her haven. Brimming with books and redolent with the hypnotic, sappy scent of pinewood, this was one place where

Rasha could languish undisturbed. When she took time to stare out the window at the lushness that had become peculiar to the university grounds and no longer character- ized her city, she could delude herself that its peace was sacrosanct. On campus, birds sang, music rose from West Hall during auditions, and the denizens of this cradle of knowledge strode with a purpose that was realizable and commendable. Within the nineteenth-century stone walls of the institution, history and extolled learning challenged time and aberration. It was a mausoleum of great minds and lofty feats that haunted and breathed through ancient stone.

In her hideaway, Rasha would lose herself in Shakespeare, Keats, Yeats, Coleridge and William Blake, and draw on their wisdom to endure her hell. Imagination has no boundaries, and nothing could bar her way back in time. When she found herself bound and gagged, she reassured herself that inspiration at least could not be fettered.

Hours would pass while she pored over the anthologies weighing down her shelves. In this manner, when she emerged from her sanctuary, her mind saturated with literature, she was almost desensitized to the rubbish that littered the streets and the aggression that plagued them. Fantasy preserved her sanity. That this was escapist was irrelevant so long as it achieved the desired end: endurance.

The tutorial over, Rasha looked out the window as a phalanx of silver clouds threw a shadow over the Oval. Her heart tightened so, that not even the thought of Luke in Beirut could ease it. In a brief moment, the campus and her office bathed in greyness, the prospect of heavy rain portentous and hostile. She turned her back to the oppressive sight, collected her books and proceeded to the classroom.

Fuad leaned against the door, barefoot, dressed in a loose sweater and creased jeans, smirking.

"Come to see your friend?"

"Let me in, Fuad."

He swept an arm in an exaggerated welcoming gesture as Rasha walked past. She did not particularly like Fuad and thought him immature and vain. She tolerated him only because of his long-lasting friendship with Karim.

"He's not here."

"Did he say when he would be back?"

"I don't think he'll be long. He was expecting you." A smirk again. "Coffee?"

"No thanks." Rasha's eyes wandered to the centre table in the lounge. An ashtray overflowed with cigarette stubs and an unfinished joint.

"Listen, I've got a lecture to go to. Do you mind waiting here alone?"

"Not at all. You go ahead."

He turned to leave when Rasha added, "Thanks for putting Luke up."

"It's nothing. Oh and, make yourself at home . . . I'm not expecting anyone," he said with a wink.

Rasha momentarily sat on the edge of the sofa but nervousness forced her back to her feet. Arms braced, she paced the lounge. She noted all the evidence of a young man living alone. Wrinkled clothes hung on chairs. Rugs lay askew on the tile floor. Papers and books covered most surfaces, weighed down by mugs of unfinished coffee and peppered with crumbs. She assumed it was the cleaning lady's day off.

She heard a key turn then the front door squeak on its hinges. Her heart gathered pace before he had time to see her. Unable to contain her excitement, she threw herself in his arms. His camera, in its usual place around his neck, dug into her bosom. He slung it off, while he

pulled her to him with a free arm. With one swift movement he picked her up and carried her to his room. His
body clinging to hers he lowered her gently to the bed,
his hands rediscovering the woman who had left him
behind. He made love to her with the fervour and hunger
of a man reclaiming what he believed was rightfully his.
The sounds of street life beyond their own enclosure
heightened her passion. While life outside the four walls
ground out in normality, she rose to exhilaration in her
lover's embrace.

As she rested her head on his bare chest, she
experienced a déjà vu.

"I still can't believe you're here," she murmured.

Luke lit up a Gauloise. "You never thought I'd
follow you, did you?"

She thought awhile. How could she not expect
the strife in Lebanon to grasp the curiosity of a news
photographer? "I wasn't sure," she mumbled. "Did you
tell anyone you were coming?"

"Anyone, like who?"

"Carol."

"Why would I do that?" As he looked down at her,
his bristly chin brushed against her forehead.

"I think she may have wanted to know."

"Did *you* tell *your* parents you'd be here making
love to me?"

Rasha slapped him lightly on the forearm.
"Seriously Luke, you've got to promise me to be careful.
You're a foreigner here. You don't know the city or what's
going on . . ."

"Hold on a minute," he interjected, "news coverage
is what I do, sunshine. Remember?"

"What you hear out there doesn't prepare you for
being in the middle of it. You're not familiar with the mentality of the people. You don't know your way around here.

There's sniping at the port, along the mountain roads, downtown. How would you know where to go?"

"I can figure it out."

"You may figure it out too late."

"I could ask your father."

"I like your sense of humour."

"So do I," he said smiling. "More to the point Rasha. I'm here to be with you. How will you manage that?"

"Karim said he would help us out."

Luke stubbed out his cigarette with force. "This is so wrong."

"You have to go along with it, otherwise I'll never be able to see you."

"Play by the rules? Is that it?"

"Exactly. And while you're here, you'll discover that there are more rules than you'd care to know about."

After a long pause, Luke finally began. "Suppose . . . suppose I were to ask you to marry me?"

Rasha's eyes beamed back at him.

"I said *supposing* I were to ask you, what would I have to do?"

"Hypothetically speaking," she repeated, playing at his own game, "if you were to propose, you'd have to convert to Islam."

"And if I don't?"

"We wouldn't be able to register our marriage. Technically, it wouldn't be legal."

"And if I were willing . . . to convert that is . . . would that be acceptable to your father?"

Rasha sniggered. "Unlikely."

"Christ! What would it take to win him over?"

"Arab ancestry."

"Is that all?" he retorted superciliously.

"My father is comfortable with what he knows, his own people's customs and way of thinking. Even if I were to marry an Arab and a Muslim he would have to meet certain criteria. 'Being one of us', so to speak, at least covers basic ground."

He reached for another cigarette. "You're talking shit."

"Not very well put, was it?" she giggled. Then in a serious tone, "I was only trying to explain him to you."

"You'll have to do a lot better than that. It sounds to me like you're defending him."

"I understand him, yes. But I don't agree with him."

"If you 'understand him', then what are you doing here with me? In fact, what the hell am *I* doing here?"

His tone of voice, laced with anger, stung her. She felt herself grow equally impatient. From the moment Luke had arrived, he had almost expected her to reconsider her entire past, her background, and cast them away. Her ideas, although not entirely in tune with her father's, bore the stamp of the same society. The environment that Luke urged her to stand up to was the only one in which she knew she belonged.

"Luke, don't you think you're being a little unreasonable?" she asked gingerly. "I mean, you appeared yesterday out of nowhere, without warning, and you want me, overnight, to set everything right?"

"No, Rasha, I don't. But I took chances to come here, to be with you. All I want in return is for you to meet me halfway. If, and a big if, you still feel the same way towards me."

"You know I do."

"We're going round in circles, you know that?"

"If you wanted to keep it simple, you should've just forgotten about me the minute I boarded the plane in Paris."

"Believe me when I tell you, sunshine, if I could've . . . I would've."

"I wish I could spend every minute of the day with you," she reflected. "You said over dinner you'd be here for about ten days, right?"

"Actually, I've got an open ticket," Luke said turning away.

Rasha searched his eyes but he would not look at her. They were on new ground now, under circumstances that unmasked a side to each of them that had not come into play in Paris. Luke was up against Rasha the conformist, she against the man who resented obstacles to his goal.

Later in the day and after much deliberation with Karim and a couple of phone calls to Fuad, it was agreed that they would all meet at The Backstreet, a pub in the vicinity of the university that Karim and Rasha frequented with groups of their friends. When they arrived, they found Fuad and Luke seated at a corner table, laughing, a number of empty bottles of beer between them. Rasha felt mildly jealous and disappointed that Luke should seem to enjoy the company of someone as shallow as Fuad.

Judging by Luke's bloodshot eyes and his frozen smile, Rasha surmised he had had too much to drink. When he reached out for her, she flinched, casting a cursory glance all round to make sure no one had noticed. He retracted his arm and took a swig of his beer, staring straight ahead.

"Luke was telling me about his first brush with militiamen," Fuad began. "Go on, tell them."

"I don't think that's such a good idea."

"Go on. There's nothing to it."

Rasha, seated next to Luke, looked at him quizzically. "What happened, Luke?"

"Nothing major," he retorted curtly, arms folded.

"I'd still like to hear it," she said simply, though she believed she had a *right* to know.

Luke pulled out a Gauloise, stalling. He exhaled the smoke towards the ceiling. Then with a flick of his cigarette, he said dismissively, "I was shooting a few frames and, well . . . a couple of guys went berserk."

His smirk triggered Fuad's laughter.

"Who? Where were you?" Rasha pressed, irked by his sang-froid.

"Where was I again?" Luke directed his question at Fuad, smiling.

"The Hotel District, by the St. Georges," Fuad chuckled.

Rasha's irritation spread to the two of them. "Why don't you just tell me and get it over and done with, Luke?"

When he finally turned to her, her eyes met his with dogged determination. By then she did not care that her impatience was evident to Karim though Fuad seemed oblivious to it.

"All right," Luke said in a tone indicating he would forgo his little game. "I went down to the bombed-out Hotel District to take some photos. In the background there was a building with a flag at the entrance—some militia's headquarters. I thought nothing of it." He continued with a swipe of his hand, "Then through my viewfinder I see a couple of gunmen emerge out of the blue, waving their Kalashnikovs and shouting. I have no idea what their problem was, so don't ask. They were after the camera, and they began tugging at it, threatening. My neck nearly snapped I swear. Anyway, I insisted I was keeping it, all by sign language, mind you, they pointing and pulling frantically at the camera and me at my press card. It was quite comical actually." This last utterance aimed at Fuad, patently his captive audience.

"Hilarious, I'm sure," Rasha commented dryly.

"Yes, well, *I* thought it was. Anyway, this went on for a while, before they decided that they would take me with them! They started pulling at me. I resisted. Then this man comes out of the building and starts mediating. Nice little chubby chap with a mean moustache that curled up at the edges." Luke demonstrated with a twirl of his forefingers at the corners of pouting lips. "They were yapping in Arabic, and the only two words I could make out were '*Abu* this' and '*Abu* that' and again '*Sahafi, sahafi.*' In the end, this chap runs back to his car and produces a couple of cartons of Marlboro which he hands over to the gunmen. They all shake hands, and they let me go."

"Go on." Rasha locked her hands together, her wine untouched.

"Well . . . it turns out he's the taxi driver for the Commodore Hotel. All the journalists apparently use him. He knows everybody and everybody knows him. He saw me as a customer in a bit of a jam and came to the rescue! He drove me back to the hotel, rambling on about how I should be careful, that I should stay away from certain areas and that I should call on him anytime because he knew his way around . . . On and on . . . Finally I ended up at the bar of the Commodore sharing a few beers with others of my ilk."

Rasha's head pounded. How was she to respond to such a benign rendition of a grave incident?

"You were in fact lucky you got away with it this time," Karim finally said.

Luke shrugged. "Yes, well. Goes with the job, Karim."

Fuad stood up. "I need another beer. Luke?"

"Sure, why not."

"I'll come with you," Karim offered. "It'll be my round."

Left alone, Luke and Rasha sat still, not touching. Horrendous scenarios ran through her mind. And the emotions they fired up were so intense that she battled to make sense of them. What if they had managed to grab Luke? What if the driver had not been passing by? In this muddle, she was only conscious of being potentially explosive. She opted to stay silent rather than blurt out something she would regret later.

"Are you going to talk to me Rasha?"

She stroked the stem of her glass. "What do you want me to say?"

"That you told me so." Luke smiled at her.

Rasha sipped on her wine. "What's the point of repeating myself? You never listen to me anyway."

He reached under the table and placed his hand on hers. He sought her gaze but now it was she who evaded it.

"It's my job, sunshine. 'A man's gotta do what a man's gotta do'," he added with a twang.

"Don't be so flippant," she snapped back.

"I'm just trying to get you to relax."

"You're going about it the wrong way. Making light of a serious situation is not the answer."

"Nothing happened."

"It could've."

"But it didn't," he said emphatically. "Look, I know you think I've had a few beers . . ."

Rasha looked at him obliquely. "I suppose I'm wrong there too."

"Let me finish, will you? You *are* the reason I'm here, sunshine. But we don't live in La La Land, and by the end of this trip I've got to have something to show for it. I *need* to do this. Don't you understand?"

She would not admit that she did. "I worry about you. I feel responsible for your safety."

"You're not." He squeezed her hand.

"Easier said than done."

"Relax, sunshine. I'll be fine."

"You're not invincible, Luke. You can't make things always turn out your way."

"As you keep on reminding me."

When Karim and Fuad approached them, Rasha slipped her hand free of Luke's. Instead of responding with like circumspection, Luke would not shift his gaze, holding it long on her, while she redirected her attention to her brother and his friend. In the end, from the corner of her eye, she glimpsed him grudgingly give up.

"Guess what we just heard?" Fuad exclaimed. "Apparently, last week, this place was robbed. A bunch of guys walked in and stripped the customers of their valuables . . ."

A shiver ran down Rasha's spine. "It's a fine time to be telling us, Fuad."

Ignoring her remark, Fuad persisted. "I promise you. Alfred the bartender just told us. They just strode in at midnight, guns flashing, ordered everyone to lay out wallets, watches, jewellery, scooped out the lot and walked out!" he concluded, eyes wide with disbelief.

Rasha looked over her shoulder at the entrance to the pub. Had she not been there to see Luke, she would have left on the spot.

"Was anyone hurt?" This from Luke.

"No, fortunately. Not this time."

"What do you mean not this time? Does this sort of thing happen often?"

"Most shops and businesses, even some individuals pay protection money," Karim offered. "In principle, it shouldn't. Still . . ." he shrugged.

"Do they know who the robbers were?"

"It wouldn't make the slightest difference if they did," Karim replied.

"I suppose it wouldn't." Luke leaned back and swung an arm around Rasha's chair. "How can you guys live like this? Why don't you just leave?"

"Crime's everywhere," Karim said. "Besides, once your card's up, it's up. I could tell you stories of people who fled the war only to die in an explosion elsewhere or in car accidents. You can't escape your destiny."

Luke would not subscribe to such a fatalistic rationale. "Is that how you feel about it, Rasha?"

She construed his question to mean: If I asked you to come away with me, away from all this madness, would you?

"Pretty much, I guess. As Karim just said, how are we to know where we're really out of danger?" She raised her eyes to his and read bemusement mixed with pain.

Fuad burst out laughing. "You could call us brave or plain stupid. I can tell you pal, I for one *am* plain stupid," to which Rasha said nothing but could not agree more.

For the rest of the evening, Luke and Rasha barely addressed each other. To all intents and purposes, their meeting proved to Rasha to be futile and almost damaging to their relationship. A distinct gulf stretched between them and she recalled that, ironically, she had felt closer to him when they were physically apart. On the phone, they had been more capable of baring their emotions than they were now when the possibility to demonstrate their love for each other was within their grasp. A part of her reasoned that Luke's odd behaviour was a reaction to her aloofness. But the other wondered whether she was not gaining insight into his character. Her conversation with Hana came to mind. Time, Hana had said, would tell whether Rasha's love for him ran deeper than a whirlwind romance. The optimal test of a relationship was being in one or the other partner's environment. That was when complications and disagreements set in.

She could not ignore the fact that she and Luke, together, alone, were right for each other. His touch, his voice, his mere presence stirred in her emotions that she had never experienced with a man and doubted would ever again with any other than Luke. Sadly, however, they did not live in a vacuum.

"What time is it, Karim?"

"Half past eleven."

"We'd better be on our way." She made to stand up.

"Pumpkin time already?" Luke quipped.

"Not Thinderella . . ." Fuad slurred, a finger in the air. ". . . But werewolf time!"

"That's really funny, Fuad," Rasha retorted flatly, then to Luke. "Can we give you a lift?"

Luke turned to Fuad. "I could do with another beer. How about you?"

"I'm in." Fuad stretched his legs across the chair Karim had barely vacated.

"I guess we'll stay."

"Fine."

"Hold on a minute, Rasha," Karim said. "I just need to settle the bill."

"I'll wait for you outside," she heard herself say knowing that never would she, by choice, linger on the sidewalk, alone, at night.

No sooner had she spoken than Luke jumped to his feet to escort her out. They stood in the total stillness of the side street.

Luke dug his hands into his pockets. "Will you call me tomorrow?"

"I've got a class at eleven and then at two," she replied, scanning the alley.

"How about lunch then?"

"Meet me on campus at twelve. Nicely Hall."

He moved up to her and ran a finger along her cheek. "It's good to be here, sunshine. To know that you're around and not miles across crackling telephone lines."

Rasha held his hand against her and with one look hoped he would gather all the thoughts she had failed to articulate during the evening—foremost among them that no harm come to him.

Chapter Nine

◆

"I spoke to Hana last night," Nuha told Rasha over morning coffee as she checked provisions for the day and prepared her shopping list. The intention to pre-empt her parents' call had slipped Rasha's mind.

"She apologized for not letting us know beforehand that the Englishman was on his way," Nuha continued to Rasha's relief. Hana had come through for her. "Apparently she had just given him the address as back-up, out of courtesy really. Naturally, she never expected him to stay here."

"Nor did he, Mama. You're the one who invited him, remember?"

"You're right, I did. What do you feel like having for dinner?"

"I can't think of dinner right now."

"Lunch?"

"I'm teaching. I won't be back home till late this afternoon."

Nuha consulted her shopping list then scribbled.

"Have you seen him since he arrived?"

"He has a name, Mama, like everyone else. His name's Luke."

"Have you seen him?" Nuha repeated obstinately as she got up and opened the fridge. "The tomatoes have gone bad already. Can you believe it?"

"Karim and I met with him and Fuad at The Backstreet last night," Rasha replied casually.

"I see. So he's comfortable at Fuad's, is he?" Nuha resumed her seat and added "tomatoes" to her list.

"I didn't ask. But they seem to get on well."

Nuha put down her pen and sipped on her coffee. She appeared lost in thought but, familiar with her mother's mannerisms, Rasha gathered she was providing a gap for her daughter to speak—perhaps to confess her association with Luke. Rasha's lips were sealed.

After a long pause, Nuha reclined in her chair and eyed Rasha. "If there were more to you and this guy . . . Luke. Would you tell me?"

Rasha so loved her mother's finesse. She never forced an issue or belligerently argued her point. Those were qualities that served Rasha well when she, herself, was under scrutiny but helped her poorly in her battle against her father, which called for persuasion and assertiveness on Nuha's part.

"Would you want to know?"

Nuha's mouth curled up at the edges. "A mother always wants to know, Rasha."

Hana must have said something to Nuha to prompt this conversation, Rasha deduced. She was not too sorry. Whenever she could, Rasha avoided keeping secrets from her mother. She not only needed but wanted her support and concurrence in all matters.

Rasha cast her eyes on the kitchen clock. "I should go. I don't want to be late." She planted a kiss on Nuha's cheek. "I love you Mama."

"I love you too, habibti."

Luke and Rasha were in the queue at the students' cafeteria. It was a better choice, she thought, than the smaller and formal faculty dining room. Here, at least they could lose themselves in the crowd and their conversation would be muffled by the boisterous students.

Trays in hand, they made their way to the outside area and installed themselves on a wooden bench awash with sunlight. It was the first time, since Paris, that Rasha had seen Luke in natural vibrant light. The rays seeped through his chestnut strands of hair, refracting in his pellucid irises. His complexion, now sun-kissed, had started to conceal the gauntness Rasha had attributed to recent weight loss. He appeared a vision of serenity.

A group of young female students at the adjoining table stole a few glances at him. He was none the wiser, but their admiration bolstered Rasha's pleasure and her smugness at being the woman of his choice.

She must have been staring at him, smiling, for he said between mouthfuls, "What is it? Is something wrong?"

"No," she dipped her head. "Quite the contrary."

"So this is where you work?" He waved his fork in a circular motion.

Rasha nodded.

"Nice campus."

"I think so. What have you been up to this morning?" She watched Luke consume his meal with boundless appetite and surmised he had not had anything to eat that morning.

"This and that. Went down to the hotel. Met a few guys. Journalists, of course."

"Of course."

A pause. "Did you ever think you'd be sitting here having lunch with me?" he asked.

"Never."

"I could live in this country, you know?"

"You've only been here . . . what . . . a day and a half?" Rasha picked at her food. "How can you be so sure?"

Luke's eyes lit up. "Gut feeling."

A passing shadow briefly cast itself on their table. "Hello, miss."

"Hello, Youssef."

"A student?" Luke asked following Youssef with his eyes.

Rasha nodded. "I wrote to you about him. Don't you remember?"

"Vaguely."

"He . . ." Rasha contemplated retelling his story then decided not to. "Never mind."

"I'll bet all your male students have a crush on you."

"Every single one of them," Rasha said in jest, giggling.

Luke bent forward and whispered, "I'd *kill* to have an English teacher like you."

"Stop it, Luke," she said half-heartedly, enjoying his banter. "So have you met anyone interesting?"

Luke tapped his shirt pocket for his cigarettes. He produced them along with the Zippo lighter and lit up. "There's this one journalist, Michael, who works for an English paper." He exhaled. "He's been here for years and the hotel has become his second home. He tells me he knows this place inside out. Great guy actually. On two occasions now I've seen him at the bar with a group of foreign and local journalists. I think he's quite popular. He has a wealth of stories, none of which you'd care to hear."

"I'll take your word for it." Rasha took a bite. "In any case, I very much doubt that the world is losing sleep over us. We're old news nowadays."

"To be fair, sunshine, the war has been going on now for five . . . six years?"

"Technically six, yes. But I remember skirmishes and incidents disrupting our lives as early as 1974."

"No item of news makes page one for that long, you know."

"I guess not. But from my subjective point of view, as someone who's had to live through the war, it seems to me we only make headlines when they're sensationalized. Or when it involves the superpowers." She pushed her tray aside.

"That's not altogether true, is it?"

"It's more often the case than not."

"What about all the journalists who are still here, like Michael? Some of them don't even want to leave."

"I don't doubt that, Luke, but media coverage has gotten us nowhere. We're still in the same mess we were in seven years ago, and most international intervention is half-hearted and in the end futile. I wouldn't be surprised if this war carries on for much longer. Then the media will have really tired of us."

Luke reached across the table and placed his hand on hers. "All the more reason why you should come away with me."

It was a choice she would have to make between Luke and her family. Her heart swelled at the implications. Either way, she risked losing someone.

"Let's go for a walk," she said, slipping her hand free to collect her bag. "I'll show you around."

She led the way down a meandering path between the upper and lower campuses, her destination a park bench in a sunken and private area, out of view and overlooking the sea. There, where they could not be seen, she leaned against Luke and held his arms tightly around her waist. Beneath them, the red-tiled roofs of college buildings peeked through a carpet of foliage that stretched beyond to the azure expanse.

This was one of those rare moments she wished she could hold on to for an eternity.

Rasha started softly. "Is there a place, a moment, in your childhood maybe, that you wished you could go back to?" She turned away from Luke, and unable to see his expression, patiently waited for his answer.

"One, maybe," he replied pensively. "Our home in Hampstead, when my mother was still around. The smell of burning wood from the fireplace. She always had a fire crackling away . . . God, how she hated the cold." For the first time ever since they met, his voice rang with nostalgia.

Rasha tried to imagine a young Luke in school uniform revelling in the warmth of his childhood home, enjoying a security that was perhaps even then teetering on uncertain grounds. A mental image of herself in her tender years followed, leaving her marvelling at how the paths of two people from polarized parts of the world unexpectedly converged and fused.

Luke planted a kiss on her temple. "And you, sunshine, what do you hanker for?"

"From my childhood? All of it," Rasha replied, deep in retrospection. "Its order and predictability. The delusion that nothing can be taken away and evil can be kept at bay so long as I was good. The feeling of being snug and secure. Not worrying about long-term possibilities," she shrugged. "Just being able to live in the moment."

"You could have it back you know."

"With you?"

"With me."

In what capacity? Rasha wanted to ask him, but could not. Luke perhaps thought they could live together, without being bound by marriage, but such an arrangement in her culture was taboo.

She heaved a sigh. "I could have a semblance of it. Something like it, maybe. But the real thing is gone. Long gone. Circumstances have changed. And even if they hadn't, even if we still lived in a time of peace, my perspective would not be the same."

"You could have something better," he remarked.

"I could," Rasha concurred, unconvinced. A vision of herself married to Luke with a family of her own—her own children whom she would cocoon in the pleasures of innocence—made her smile. "I certainly could," she admitted, looking up at him.

Luke cleared his throat. "You know, Rasha, we never really spoke about this . . . but . . . weren't you at any time happy since then . . . What I mean is, haven't you ever met anyone who meant something to you?"

Rasha took time to answer, scrutinizing again past relationships to make sure she delivered nothing but the absolute truth. "Up until the moment I met you? No."

"So would it be safe to say that your attachment to the past, to the good old days, to use a cliché, is purely because they'd really been the best times of your life?"

"You're confusing me with your lucidity, Luke," she giggled. "I suppose that's partially true." She paused, then added, "What are you driving at?"

"To put it bluntly, sunshine, I'm fighting for my own corner here. What I'm hoping you'd realize is that if you were to leave all this behind, you'd have nothing to lose and everything to gain."

How simply he put it, Rasha thought. Luke was not so determined that he overlooked all obstacles. He refused, from the outset, to recognize that there were any. His vision tenaciously fixed on his goal, he was blind to the pitfalls along the way.

"Maybe you couldn't improve your life. Maybe it was easier for you to conform to your family's wishes and just accept an abnormal war-time situation." He continued,

"I'm now giving you the choice, sunshine. But it's up to you to act on it. It's your chance to take charge of your life."

The blood rushed to Rasha's head, pumping. She raised her fingers to her forehead, stroking her scar. She had long waited for this opportunity to escape her circumstances and sever all parental control. Her dreams had been laden with visions of normality, freedom and self-assertion. Now, faced with that "chance", as Luke had put it, she was overcome with paralyzing fear and a premature sense of loss.

Did Luke understand her trepidation and choose to ignore it or did he not see it at all? The gulf in communication widened again and Rasha withdrew once more into her own shell.

"Are you going to say something?" Luke asked.

"I have to think about all this," she replied straightening up. "I need time."

Luke sat hunched over, jaws clenched, staring into the far distance. "It all boils down to one thing, Rasha." He turned to face her. "Is it me that you want? That's all you have to consider. Nothing else."

Karim's girlfriend, Rula, was his ex's antithesis. Unlike May, she was a clear-headed, well-groomed young woman set on completing a bachelor's in Business Administration. She was responsible, sensible and kept well clear of politics and drugs. She came from a Druze family who had fled 'Aley during the troubles and had taken refuge with close relatives in Beirut. For lack of space, Rula resided on campus, and conducted herself in a way that made her parents proud.

Rasha maintained that Karim had fallen for Rula on the rebound. His heartrending loss of May had pushed him into the arms of a woman unlikely to upend his world or spring unwanted surprises on him. He had opted for a safe relationship and showered on Rula the affections he had not had the chance to bestow on May. But he did so, Rasha noticed, to excess.

Seeing her brother as the giver in the relationship, Rasha could never warm up to his new girlfriend. Nevertheless she accepted her, keeping her impressions to herself, because Rula had been Karim's choice. Rarely did they socialize together. But on that occasion, Rula was a necessary cover-up to Rasha's date with Luke. They agreed to meet at a private club close to the Hotel District.

That evening, like the time when they had met at The Backstreet, Rasha noticed a pattern develop in Luke's behaviour. Whenever the two of them were in company, he drank too much and appeared charged, tense. He no longer reached out for her and sometimes ignored her altogether. He was punishing her, Rasha deduced, for not being openly affectionate towards him. Luke took her distance to heart, seeing it as further proof of her acquiescence to her father's old-fashioned scruples. She had no doubt he saw it as a weakness and he had made it quite clear how he loathed inaction.

In her eyes, the outing was yet another failure. Luke had become mercurial and their relationship volatile. Nothing about their love was simple any longer, nothing was pristine. It had gained depth, yes, but in doing so had sunk below still waters to murky depths in which they struggled to see each other for what they really were.

Luke's ambivalence saddened and at the same time angered Rasha. They were caught in a vicious circle where her detachment turned him cold, and his sullenness tested her patience.

They were on the dance floor, Rasha rigid in his arms.

"I may as well be dancing with a broomstick," Luke remarked.

A nervous giggle escaped Rasha's lips.

"I actually don't mean it as a joke, Rasha," he added sternly.

"To be honest with you, Luke. I really didn't take it as one either."

The tension between them had built up to such an extent that when they got into the car they sidled up to the windows, a wide space between them. Karim was driving. Rula occupied the passenger seat. The tape played Joan Armatrading, Karim's favourite.

Rasha drifted in thought, growing tearful at the sound of the crooning voice and touching lyrics. She looked out the side window into blackness, her mind assailed by visions of her and Luke in Paris, momentarily oblivious to where they were in the present and where they were headed. She saw no one. But the sharp sound of metal against metal, of firearms being cocked on either side of the car, was unmistakable. The halting threat issued from total darkness, a rasp amplified by the stillness around them. All thoughts dashed out of her mind like mice scurrying at the sight of a cat. She ducked as a terrified "Stop, Karim. For God's sake stop!" emerged from her gut. Mercy, God's alone, froze the shots that may have been fired in the time Karim took to slam on the brakes.

"I didn't see him," Karim murmured. His voice was steady, flat, though the low tone that made it barely audible was heavy with anxiety. His wide, alert eyes shifted in the rear-view mirror.

They waited in mortal silence as the hurried thump of boots drew closer. In a flash, a khaki-clad forearm came down in a thud on Karim's door. Another militiaman intently clasped a Kalashnikov that ran the length of his leg.

"You're in a hurry, aren't you?" he growled.

Karim's smile meant to exonerate him. "I apologize. I didn't see the roadblock . . . it's so dark . . . and . . ."

"IDs!"

Rasha extended a palm to Luke. "Give me your passport. Quick!" she urged him through her teeth.

The khaki arm reached into the car for the documents. The man straightened up, flung the firearm over his left shoulder, and held three green identity cards and one British passport in both hands.

Rasha glanced at his compatriot who loitered disinterestedly by the passenger side of the car. His terrorist tactics had worked: the car had come to a jolting halt, its occupants had stiffened in awe of the almighty power of his gun. This being his ultimate aim, he relinquished the thrill of torturous questioning to his superior.

"Where are you coming from?" The question reverted Rasha's attention back to the man who held their destinies in the palms of sullied hands.

"Ain Mreisse," Karim answered.

Experience had taught them to let one person speak: invariably the driver, whose reflexes and manoeuvres displayed or betrayed obeisance to the supremacy of pure scum. Karim had heeded their authority by stopping. His soft-spoken and apologetic manner further placated the creature whose identity lay in a mortal piece of steel.

He peered at Luke. "What are you doing in Beirut?"

"He doesn't speak Arabic," Karim proferred. "He's just visiting."

"Where is he staying?"

"With us, in Ras Beirut."

"You're all locals."

"That's right," Karim ventured, not wishing to offend the man by stating the obvious.

The man stood erect again as he leafed through Luke's passport.

"What's he doing that for?" Luke muttered. "If he can't speak English, surely he can't read it."

He suppressed a groan as Rasha's stilleto heel dug into his shoe. His face contorted with anger and disdain.

"And he's British."

His flat tone suggested Karim had better not reply this time.

"Countrymen with a foreigner, a journalist. Not good!"

"I assure you, he's our guest. He's staying with us and won't be in the country for much longer. He probably shouldn't have come in the first place."

"Probably not."

Then sardonically, to Rasha, "And you, young lady. Aren't local men good enough for you? You look for the company of foreigners?"

His face was now visible. Cavernous eyes stared back at her through a leathery expanse of pockmarks half-concealed by bristle. Before her was the face of loathing, defiance, and sworn revenge. It had become a familiar face, versions of which graced posters of martyrs in the name of too many causes and too many vendettas. Consciously, she relaxed her facial muscles to achieve the poker face she'd learned to assume while playing cards by candlelight.

She picked up on his playfulness and, disguising her disgust, went along with it to end their nightmare.

"He's a family friend, really."

Suddenly, the man seemed to mutate into a human being. A sly smile revealed a set of teeth in desperate need of attention. He handed the IDs back to Karim and, with a flick of the hand, motioned for them to go. Karim waited to ensure his gesture meant dismissal.

The weary confirmation came in the form of a drawl. "Go, go."

Karim handed the documents to Rula. Before the car had moved on, Luke burst out, "Bloody fool."

"Shut up, Luke," Rasha fired back. "They might hear you."

"I don't give a damn."

"You'd better give a damn. We're lucky we got out of this one. Bravado will only get you into trouble."

Taken aback by Rasha's curtness, Luke spoke to Karim. "Who were these guys, do you know?"

"Leftists." Unsolicited, Karim volunteered the details. "Their archenemy is the US of A, my dear friend." He glanced at Luke in the rear-view mirror. "*Amreeka* to them. And along with Amreeka, any English-speaking national, which means you. So if I were in your shoes, I'd take Rasha's advice and keep my mouth shut. Until, at least, you're safely on a plane out of Beirut."

The car rolled slowly along the deserted corniche, headlights cleaving its way through Beirut by night. In gentle swerves to avoid potholes, the Mercedes waltzed along a straight road in a dance of death. Sick palm trees and parched grass divided the tarred road of civilization. The sea alone, sprawled like a black mantle, was testimony to God's beautiful creation. But in its belly, corpses, limbs, garbage, and ordnance mingled with a sea life on the verge of extinction.

Beirut by day, Beirut by night, doom hovered unrelenting over the Paris of the Middle East. And in the heart of that city, Rasha no longer dreaded that harm would come to three people dear to her, but four.

The following morning, Rasha stopped by Fuad's apartment on her way to the university. Luke was there alone. He picked up where they had left off the night before.

"You nearly crippled me!" Luke exclaimed.

Rasha rolled her eyes. "You exaggerate. I barely touched your shoe with my heel."

"You call that a heel? It's a bloody ice pick!"

"I had to warn you. I was protecting you."

"Protecting me or yourself?"

"You and by extension all of us, Luke. If they'd decided you were suspect for whatever reason, we would've all landed into trouble."

She watched him line up his camera, lenses, and film on the bed. She had her back to the bedroom window, arms folded.

"I'm not prepared to kowtow to these people, nor should you. The fact that they have guns means nothing to me."

"It should mean everything to you. Don't kid yourself into thinking you can beat them Luke. You're nothing to them."

His attention was focused on cleaning a lens, delicately, with a cloth. "It's only your predictable reaction that allows them to gloat over their power, Rasha. Putting fear in people's hearts is what keeps them going."

"So what you're saying is that if all civilians stand up to the militiamen, they will be *so* taken aback that they will choose to make themselves scarce. Poof, just like that!" She snapped her fingers.

"No . . ." he drawled. "What I'm saying is if you don't act scared, they won't see you as an easy target." His face was now hidden behind the Canon.

"What do you think this is, a psychology workshop? There's a war going on out there!" She gestured towards the window. "There are no laws, no dos and don'ts. We're not talking self-fulfilling prophecy here, Luke. Their actions are not a direct consequence of our behaviour," she articulated in a mocking tone. "You know, for a news photographer, I thought you'd have a better understanding of conflict."

"Of course I do, Rasha . . ."

"That of a bystander, Luke, and not a participant. When you land yourself in a dangerous situation, it's by choice. When you've had enough or done your job, you get out." She slapped her palms together. "Take my advice, Luke, and change your attitude. Try looking through *my* viewfinder. Things would look a lot more blurred then and quite different. My lens is *way beyond* being polished clean."

Luke snapped his head up, mouth agape. Taking his time, he replaced the camera carefully on the bed then walked up to Rasha.

He laid his hands on her shoulders. "If I do that sunshine, I lose my objectivity."

Her eyes met his, hard and translucent. "Then don't preach, Luke. While you and your classmates were being lectured on conflict situations and photography techniques, I was dodging bullets." She stabbed her chest with a shaky forefinger. "So don't fool yourself into thinking that you have the ultimate philosophy on survival. It doesn't work in this place. It certainly doesn't work with me."

"Touché. Just calm down," he said, rubbing her shoulders.

She shrugged him off, not having finished. "What makes you an authority about what's going on here? You come in with your ideas of how things should be and try to force them on a situation you know nothing about!" Rasha not only had in mind the political stalemate but also her culture, her standoff with her father, which she could not express in one breath. "We've seen this happen with reporters time and again. They simplify matters to make sense of them. Black and white, Christian against Muslim, Palestinian against Israeli. It's far, *far* more complicated than that. You have ancient vendettas being settled, personal grievances, attempts at destabilization. Not every bomb that explodes in a hotel owned by a Muslim is the doing of Christians, and vice versa. It could've been put there by someone who wanted to settle a score. Simple. And, contrary to what you may think Luke, there is no right way to safeguard oneself but to admit that in the large scheme of things, we're all dispensable and insignificant. And the wisest way to handle it is to accept our sorry state of affairs and do as we're told."

Her body shook. And almost as soon as she had finished her tirade, she was regretful. She was not in the habit of giving her thoughts free rein without weighing the consequences. Now, she feared, Luke might take it all to heart.

Instead, he cupped her face and looked her in the eye. "Now, would you like to hear what I see? I see a beautiful young woman, consumed with worry over whether she's behaving the right way, whether she's betraying her family's trust, whether she's going to be hurt or have anyone around her come to harm. And in so doing, I see her running roughshod over her own aspirations. All I'm asking of you is not to accept things the way they are. Don't let them dictate your life. Whether it's your family or the hoodlums on the street. That's all." He shrugged. "What concerns me, Rasha, ultimately, is *you*."

"And me, you." She paused. "And what hurts me the most is knowing that whatever I say you'll still carry on as you see fit. And if something were to happen to you . . ."

"Nothing'll happen to me."

"Let me finish, Luke. Don't you realize that no one knows you're here? Not even your sister."

"She wouldn't be able to help anyway," he said, enfolding her in his arms. When he could feel her body relax against his, which took awhile, he asked if she could stay.

"I have a class."

"Miss it. Call in sick," he whispered, his breath hot against her cheek.

"I couldn't do that," she retorted unconvincingly, a shiver running down the nape of her neck as his lips brushed her ear. "I'm helping a student out. He's struggling with the subject." She meant Youssef. "I also have a faculty meeting." Her agenda for the day ran through her hazy mind. "But I could come by later."

"I'll be here."

He kissed her softly, and in that kiss Rasha recalled why she was so drawn to him. She could lash out at him, she could argue with him, he could sulk, or play cold towards her. But in the end, the moment he touched her, he did so with infinite tenderness. Should she ever move away from him, Luke would reel her in effortlessly with kid gloves.

From the time she left him, she felt serene, contented, a sensation that stayed with her and buoyed her up throughout the day. Her outburst was self-purging, and though she did not address the issue full on and refrained from underlining Luke's oversimplification of her family situation, she had said exactly what was on her mind, and he had not been offended. That day, she could admit she was pleased he was there, in Beirut. And if she were to tread carefully and wisely, she may be able to insure a future for them together. How she would convince her father, she did not yet know. But she was optimistic she would find a way.

So it was a day when Rasha believed nothing could touch her or deflate her spirits. Her efforts with Youssef were paying off and in the faculty meeting she was commended on her class's performance. Anticipation to see Luke that afternoon propelled her through her duties, and though the morning seemed to stretch agonizingly, the time finally came when she found herself once again at Fuad's doorstep.

It was close to four o'clock in the afternoon when she rang the bell, smiling fatuously to herself. She waited. No one came. She pressed the button again, and listened for footsteps. Silence. She hesitated then rapped on the door with her fist. Still nothing. She clutched the books tight against her, wondering where Luke could be, eyes fixed on the door as if it bore the answer in invisible ink. It had not occurred to her to ask him what he had planned for the day, and regretted it, too late. He said he would be waiting for her. He may have just been delayed. Reluctant to go home, she sat on the steps and opened up a book. He would be along shortly. She was sure of it.

She replayed their exchange that morning, trying to pinpoint any indication that she may have upset him. Could he have been angry with her and not shown it? Did he not want to see her? With absolute certainty she dismissed those possibilities. Had there been anything amiss, she would have known. Luke would have told her, straight. She stood up and tried the door again. To no avail. She consulted the time—four thirty.

With a thump, the lift sank through the shaft as it was called to the ground floor. She watched, heart pumping, as the numbers lit up above it. First, second, third. It stopped. From the level below, she heard children being ushered out of the lift by their mother. The key turned in the door, then a slam.

She breathed out disappointment. Crestfallen, she collected her books and made her way down. She would call later, and by whatever means she could conjure up, she would meet with Luke.

Barely a few paces out of the building, she was caught in a downpour. Rasha took cover under the canopy of a cinema entrance. Her vision blurred, thoughts in a muddle, she did not notice the taxi stop in front of her.

"Rasha! What are you doing here?"

Nuha peered out the car window.

Rasha ran up to the taxi, the rain pelting down on her. "Mama! Are you going home?"

"Get in. You're getting soaked."

Pre-empting her mother's questioning, Rasha rambled on. "I was on my way home when it started raining. I thought I'd take cover until a taxi came along. Where were you?"

"Visiting with your aunt." Nuha looked at Rasha dubiously. "Aren't you a bit late? It's nearly five o'clock."

"I had a faculty meeting."

"You don't look well."

"I'm just a little out of breath. Tired, I guess."

"What time did you get home last night?"

"Midnight, as usual. And not a minute later," Rasha added pointedly.

"I must warn you, Rasha, your father's not too happy you've been out two nights in a row."

"I've just been going along with Karim. Since I also hadn't seen Rula for a while, I thought I'd take the opportunity to spend the time with her and Karim," she lied. "Is that a crime?"

"There's no need to use that tone of voice with me," Nuha retorted sternly.

"Sorry. I didn't mean to."

Rasha placed her hand on her mother's and turned away. For no justifiable reason, tears stung her eyes. She sniffed.

She vaguely heard her mother ask whether she was getting a cold.

Rasha cleared her throat. "Probably. It's my fault. I should've taken an umbrella."

No sooner had they arrived home than Rasha headed for the phone. She dialled Fuad's number.

"Fuad, it's Rasha. Is Luke there?"

"Hold on a minute, I'll go check. I've only just walked in."

Rasha's clammy palm tightened around the handset. She heard the clank of the receiver being retrieved at the other end.

"He doesn't seem to be."

"Fuad," she began in a measured tone of voice, "Did he by any chance tell you where he was going today?"

There was a moment of silence.

"No, he didn't."

"Are you sure?"

"Positive. Relax, Rasha. I'm sure he'll turn up."

"Let him call me as soon as he does." She remembered her father. "No. In fact, *you* call and ask for Karim. Did you get that?"

"I'll ask for Karim, don't worry."

"You're not going out?"

"I'll be here. I'll call as soon as Luke comes back."

Dinner with her parents that evening was pure torture. Karim had phoned to say he would be late, and every time the phone rang, Rasha had to restrain herself from jumping up to answer it. Amin did not mention Luke, nor did he have any reason to do so. As agreed with her father, Rasha had not invited the "Englishman" back to their home and to all intents and purposes she had disassociated herself from him. In her state of mind, completely on edge, Rasha was incommunicative and if challenged by any other than her father—whose wrath she dreaded still—was capable of outright belligerence. Blame gnawed at her. Had it not been for her parents, she would have been at Fuad's waiting for Luke's return, until the break of dawn if necessary. Instead, she was cast in her seat, lifeless and gagged.

"You're not eating, Rasha," Amin remarked.

"I'm not hungry, Baba."

"She has a cold. She might be getting sick," Nuha explained.

"Could I be excused? I have work to do," she said, avoiding eye contact.

Amin nodded.

"Would you like a cup of tea?" Nuha asked.

"Not now, thanks." Rasha got up and made it straight to her room.

Trying to keep calm, she sat at her desk and took down notes for her lecture. Now and then, she stared at the phone as if she could will it to ring, or picked it up to make sure there was a tone. The muezzin's call to prayer rose from the minaret of the nearby mosque. The television set blared next door, grating on her nerves. Rasha cupped her ears and rounded her lips as if to let out a scream. The wail built up inside her like lava ripping her from gut to throat. She slapped her hands on the desk, and stormed out to the balcony. A breath of cold air penetrated her lungs, drops of rain sprayed her hair. Neither assuaged her sensation of being constrained in a straitjacket.

Where was Luke?

As quickly as it arose, all sound died down. She re-entered the bedroom, feeling oddly depleted, her nerves frayed. From the hushed tones beyond her door, she gathered that her parents were preparing for bed.

She picked up the phone.

"Fuad? Why on earth didn't you call?" she snarled, desperate to vent pent-up fury.

"You said that I should only call when he shows up . . .," he replied sheepishly.

"And?" A touch of acid contaminated her voice.

He stalled for a brief moment before saying hesitantly, "He's not back yet."

Chapter Ten

♦

Rasha stared at the undisturbed bed, the slight depressions where his camera and rucksack had been the day before still there. His clothes, a little too scant for his intended stay, were neatly stowed away in the closet. She reached for the sleeve of his shirt and held it against her cheek, the scent of musk painfully familiar. His passport and press card, which she had noted he had taken the habit of keeping on the dresser, were gone.

She sat on the very edge of the bed, pointlessly scanning the room for clues when she knew there were none. Luke must have left just after she had. She imagined him flinging his bag over his shoulder, stowing his passport and Gauloises in the front pocket of his shirt, and setting out. But where to?

He had asked her to stay, but obligation had compelled her to refuse. She had a class to teach, a faculty meeting to attend, she had said. Had she for once given in to her heart, to her wishes, she may have been able to hold him back. Had she done so maybe he would not have gone missing.

Her hand swept around the slight ripples on his bed, careful not to disturb them, not to erase the last trace of him. Sheets of rain hammered against the window challenging her to find her beloved lost in greyness. There were no clear paths, no telling clues. Rasha would have to embark on her search in hostile darkness. She would not lose heart, not so soon, and would go about finding him in a logical, calculated, manner on the premise that he may be unharmed, that he may actually be safe. That last glimmer of hope was all she had to go by.

She rubbed her eyes to alleviate the exhaustion from lack of sleep. No sooner had Karim arrived the night before than she had cornered him with Luke's disappearance and her fear for his safety. The hours ticked away with speculation, reassurance, and doubt, debilitating and inconclusive. Karim had tried to allay her anxiety but in the end got sucked right into it. Her concerns, now reflected in her brother's eyes, plagued them both. Both of them realized that the difficult task of locating Luke rested primarily on Rasha and, in the event of any complications, possibly Karim.

For reasons she could not determine, she decided to throw caution and circumspection to the wind, and go it alone. She would only call on Karim if she needed him for she was adamant not to expose him to the perils she anticipated in her search for Luke.

She instructed the taxi driver to take her to the Commodore Hotel, her voice ringing with urgency—a sense of urgency that one felt at the beginning of a quest and based, at times unrealistically, on a presentiment that resolution could be imminent.

She crossed the reception area of the hotel which was teeming with journalists and cacophonous with the rattle of telex machines and the overlapping ringing of telephones. A turn to the left brought her in full view of the bar. She circled it purposefully to discourage the inquisitive glances of staff and a few guests. For a split second she considered approaching the barman for information then opted for assistance at the front desk.

"I'm looking for a guest by the name of Michael. I'm afraid I don't know his surname. He's a correspondent for a British newspaper."

The male receptionist studied her and without consulting the register, picked up the phone and said a few words into the mouthpiece.

"He's on his way down, miss. Please take a seat." He motioned to two armchairs flush against the wall, in full view of the street.

"I'll wait here, thank you." Rasha paced the lobby, inspecting everyone who emerged from the lift. She wished she had asked Luke for a description of Michael so she could recognize him unaided and dispense with the curious clerk more quickly. Her eyes set upon a bespectacled, thick-set man in his late forties who ambled towards the front desk. The clerk indicated Rasha with an outstretched arm and the man turned towards her. As he moved her way, Rasha stepped forward stopping short of the receptionist's earshot.

He extended a hand. "Hi, I'm Michael. I believe you're looking for me."

"Rasha," she said simply, doing away, as he had, with surnames.

Without relaxing his grip, Michael nodded, his eyes betraying a flicker of recognition. "Rasha . . . Rasha . . ." he thought out loud. "Are *you* by any chance Luke Elliott's friend?"

"He's told you about me," Rasha mumbled, abashed.

Michael gave her a crooked smile. "Without being indiscreet."

Gingerly, Rasha reclaimed her hand, Luke's devotion rendering her weak and dizzy.

"I . . . um," she battled to find her words. "Michael," she grinned, embarrassed by the informality, "Luke had mentioned meeting you . . ."

"Once or twice, yes."

"The thing is . . . he hasn't returned to the apartment where he's staying since yesterday. I was wondering whether you might have an idea of his whereabouts."

Michael's expression was indecipherable, either contemplative or grave. He would know, Rasha was certain, of the risks reporters and photographers ran in Beirut. If, as Luke had told her, Michael had been in the country for years, he would appreciate her concern and would not put it down to her being alarmist.

"Hm . . ." Michael lowered his eyes, running thick fingers along his chin. "When did you last see him?" he asked, squinting.

"Yesterday morning," Rasha replied, already warming up to him. He seemed solid, capable, and above all, sympathetic.

"And he never said where he was going?"

"No."

"Rasha, why don't you wait here?" He led her by the elbow to a seating area in the lobby, by the Chinese Restaurant. He bent over as a doctor would to a concerned relative in a waiting room. "I'll ask around."

Her eyes followed him as he made his way back to the front desk. By his body language, she strove to guess the nature of the news he was receiving. He gestured with his arms indicating a height, a frame, which led Rasha to believe he was giving a description of Luke. The receptionist volunteered a few words then turned to Rasha. Finally, she saw Michael tap a palm on the desk and move outside. Craning her neck to glimpse whom he was talking to, she recognized the taxi driver by his distinctive moustache. The one who had helped Luke in the Hotel District. He stared at the sidewalk, racking his brain, then shook his head. Michael gave him a friendly slap on the shoulder and turned into the lobby.

Rasha sat rigid in the armchair as she watched him approach her, her breathing suppressed. When he was a few paces from her, she stood up. Michael motioned her to sit down again as he occupied the armchair beside hers. Elbows on the knees, he leaned forward, as Luke often had when he spoke to her.

"It seems Luke had made enquiries yesterday about getting to the South . . ."

Rasha's heart skipped a beat.

"Apparently Hassan, the hotel driver, was not available. The receptionist believes he saw him hail a taxi off the street."

"When was that?"

"He couldn't say for sure. Mid-morning?"

"And no one saw him after that?"

Michael shook his head. "I'm afraid not."

Rasha was at pains to process what little, yet so significant, information Michael had gathered. Undefinable and erratic thoughts spun in her mind with such speed she could not hold them long enough to articulate them.

"What are you going to do?" Michael asked.

What was she to do? "I don't know," she replied, shoulders slumped.

"Do you have any connections?"

"None . . . I've never needed them before."

Michael's head dropped. "Listen. I'll keep on asking around. Most of my mates have already gone out on assignments. I might know more by this evening, but I can't promise anything. If I do, where can I reach you?"

She, and now Michael, knew this could be serious. Both secretly recognized that Luke should have relied on Hassan and no one else for transport.

"I'll give you a friend's telephone number." She rummaged for a piece of paper and pen in her handbag. "His name's Fuad," she explained as she scribbled his details. "He'll give me the message."

She tried to steady her hand as she gave Michael the paper. He stowed it in the front pocket of his shirt, as Luke would have done. She caught herself staring at him.

"I'm sorry I haven't been of much use. But if there's anything else I can do . . ."

Rasha shook her head, pressed to move on. "On the contrary, you've been a great help. Thank you. Now, at least I know where he was headed."

"He hasn't been in the country for long, has he?" Michael asked. Rasha read in his question an insinuation of Luke's inexperience and unfamiliarity with how things worked.

"No. He hasn't."

She could not move, not yet. Her legs were limp, her head swirled.

"You know," Michael offered, "He could still be there. In the South, I mean. It's quite . . . how shall I put it? . . . complicated getting there in the first place. He may have just decided to spend the night."

"Possibly." She did not mention they had made a date to meet the previous afternoon. There was no point. Michael's reassurance was natural, an attempt to keep up her spirits. But she did not believe he was convinced of his theory.

"I should go." Rasha supported herself on the arm of the chair to stand.

On her feet, she shook hands with Michael. Again he held hers for a while. "Would you please let me know if you come up with anything?" he asked.

"I will." She strained to smile. "Michael, thanks for everything you've done. It was a pleasure meeting you."

"Likewise. I only wish it had been under different circumstances."

"So do I."

As she made her way out of the hotel Rasha felt all eyes fixed on her. No doubt, in no time at all, rumours will fly of a foreign journalist gone missing, and a local girl looking for him. So far no one but Michael knew her name. Then again not even he had her family name.

Outside the hotel she watched a group of journalists pile boisterously into Hassan's taxi, encumbered with cameras, bags and equipment. At that moment, she would have taken back all that she had said about the futility of their efforts. She considered their presence in her embattled country no less than commendable. Whether it was to meet their job objectives or satisfy their curiosity, they were ultimately risking their lives to do so.

She stepped in a puddle and strode off aimlessly, impervious to the insistent honking of taxis offering her a lift. The rain came down with force, unforgiving, wetting her to the core despite the umbrella she held shakily. Her mind reeled off the many horror stories she had heard before. People who had gone missing and were never found. Others who only reappeared months, years after they were taken captive. Rarely were their destinies disclosed, and rumours of their whereabouts always remained questionable.

Rasha's resolve was already crumbling, after only one enquiry, one stone block. She had secretly hoped Michael would have the answer. He did not, compelling her to formulate a plan, a next step. It would take time, time that she was unwilling to spare and Luke could not afford. Every minute, every second counted, any delay prolonging his misery.

If indeed he were alive.

Somehow she got home, not recalling which route she had taken. It was not a decision she had weighed up or taken consciously, but she found herself on the line waiting for Hana to answer the call.

"Rasha?"

"Hi, Auntie Hana."

"What a surprise! I haven't heard from you for so long! Nuha phoned me the other day . . ."

"She told me," Rasha threw in. "Thank you for coming through for me."

"So Luke's there?"

"Yes . . . and . . . no."

"What do you mean? What's happened?"

Briefly, Rasha recounted the events to her aunt, dwelling not so much on the facts but the course of action she should take. Should she let Carol know? Whose help could she call on? One thing for certain, she had to confront her parents and tell them the truth. She had no other choice. Did Hana agree?

"I'm afraid you'll have to, habibti. They must be aware of what's going on."

"It's the only way isn't it? At this stage, there's no point wondering what they might do. Besides, I may never see him again . . ." Rasha's voice quavered.

"Don't think of the worst just yet, Rasha. If you want me to speak to your father, I will."

"No, Auntie. I have to do this myself. So you think I shouldn't say anything to Carol."

"Wait until tomorrow. As Michael the journalist said, Luke may have decided to spend the night away."

"Maybe you're right," Rasha concurred, sceptical nonetheless. "Auntie Hana?"

"Yes?"

"Thank you."

"For what?" she asked, astonished.

"For listening . . . for everything."

Next, Rasha phoned the university and told Surayya she was not feeling well. Surely someone would be able to take her class. She tried Fuad only to have her worst fears confirmed. Luke had not returned. Despite Fuad's lack of involvement, Rasha relayed her meeting with Michael should he call. She desperately sought someone to talk to. As she replaced the receiver, there was a rap at the door.

"Rasha, I thought you were at AUB. What are you doing home?" Nuha stood in the doorway, her new coiffure an indication that she had just returned from the hairdresser's. "Aren't you feeling well? Is it the cold?"

"No Mama. It's not the cold," Rasha replied wearily. "Do you have a minute? I need to talk to you."

"I need to prepare the rice for lunch . . ."

"Mama," Rasha interjected, "The rice can wait."

She had remained seated throughout the exchange. Nuha shut the door behind her and moved next to Rasha on the bed. She was silent. A silence that this time Rasha would fill, that she would accept as a cue to pour her heart out.

Eyes downcast, she told her tale. How she had met Luke, how they had spent their time in Paris, and how deeply they were in love, without elaborating on the extent of their intimacy. She stressed that Luke's idea to come to Beirut was entirely his own. She had discouraged him from doing so, detailing her parents' views and the political risks. The day he showed up at the door, Rasha confessed, she was taken as much by surprise as her parents were. It had not been a wise move on Luke's part, and Rasha apologized to her mother for their dishonesty. For not having been forthright from the beginning.

But surely her mother understood Rasha's motivation. And in any case, in the final analysis, Rasha did abide by her parents', or father's, wish and had refrained from inviting Luke to their home.

What made Rasha decide to tell all? Because Luke had gone missing and she fears the worst. At that point she broke down, tears streaming down her cheeks. Revealing the whole truth to her mother required exposing emotions that she had so far contained. Going through her history with Luke brought back sweet memories now soured by a terrible development. And regardless of his past protestations, she did feel responsible.

Nuha stared straight ahead, hands interlocked, no doubt mulling over the complications that the family now faced. Then, perhaps realizing that Rasha's need to be comforted was far more immediate, she swung an arm around her and pulled her close.

"Is there anyone you can talk to Mama? Can't we ask around? Maybe someone can find something out for us."

"I'll try my best," Nuha murmured. "But Rasha, you do realize that I'll have to tell your father."

"Yes." Rasha dabbed her eyes with a tissue. "I do."

"I wonder how he'll take the news," Nuha pondered out loud.

They both knew exactly how he would. Badly.

"It doesn't matter any longer, Mama. I have nothing to lose."

"He should be back within the hour. Should I speak to him then?"

Rasha shook her head. "He'll take it out on you. He always does. He'll accuse you of having known about Luke and me long ago and keeping it from him." She paused, summoning the courage to voice her decision. "I'll do it. I'll speak to him. But I'd like you to be there when I do."

"I will be, habibti," Nuha said in a daze. Then, decisively, "Of course, I will."

Whatever courage Rasha had mustered to confront Amin disintegrated the moment she found herself before him, his expression inscrutable and intimidating. She toned down her association with Luke to friendship, admitting that she had actually met him more than once in Paris. She could not divulge that his visit to Beirut was to see her, and reconfirmed that he was indeed in the country on an assignment. Nevertheless, by the mere fact that Luke knew no one besides them in the country, she felt obliged to ascertain his safety.

Amin was silent as Rasha painstakingly recounted her story. He did not interject nor did he respond, thus amplifying her solitary voice in the lounge, and sending mild tremors through her limbs. There was no way she could guess what went through his mind.

When she finished, a shroud of tension hung low above them. Nuha sat still, eyes trained on her lap. Rasha, ridden with unjustified guilt, assumed the posture of a defendant awaiting the dreaded verdict.

Amin turned to Nuha. "Did you know about this?" His voice boomed in the oppressive stillness.

"Baba . . .," Rasha interjected.

He lifted a forefinger in warning. "I'm talking to your mother."

"I only found out when I came in an hour ago," Nuha finally confessed.

Silence.

"I hold your aunt"—he refrained from referring to Hana as his sister—"directly responsible for this. We entrusted her to look after you in Paris."

About to intercede on Hana's behalf, Rasha restrained herself when Nuha cautioned her with a subtle movement of the head.

"What a fine mess you got us into, Rasha." He looked her squarely in the eyes. "I thought I'd made it quite clear from the beginning that I wanted nothing to do with this foreigner. What *exactly* do you expect me to do now?" he challenged her with a raised eyebrow.

Rasha swallowed. "Baba, I was hoping you might know of someone who could help us find him."

Amin leaned forward, a flat palm against his chest. "Me?" Then to Nuha, "Where has *your* daughter been all these years?"

His meaning unclear to the two women, neither of them responded.

"Since the beginning of the war. For seven years now," his voice oozed bitter anger, "I've been struggling to secure the factory my father poured blood and sweat into. Our livelihood! I've been cajoling, doling out protection money and using every means I can think of to resume the business. After seven long years . . . there's finally a light at the end of the tunnel. And you . . .," the accusative finger again, "expect *me* . . .," palm on the chest again, "to jeopardize all my efforts by associating myself with an irresponsible Englishman who should've known better than to come here?" His voice hit a high decibel. "Never!"

His last utterance rang in Rasha's ears, striking her like a thunderbolt. Hearing him was agonizing enough that she could not bear to record it visually as well. She looked down on her sullied boots, prepared for more salvos. She wrung her hands with such force, they ached. At that very moment, she despised him, and wished she had the courage to tell him so.

"And you! I presume you condone this sort of behaviour?" This to Nuha.

What behaviour? Rasha thought. What had she actually done?

"Amin . . ." Nuha began tentatively, "Honestly, this is not Rasha's fault."

"Then whose is it exactly. Mine? Yours?"

"These things happen," Nuha muttered.

"This is happening by association!" He tapped on the coffee table. "An association brought upon us by *your* daughter!"

Eyes lowered still, Rasha could feel her father's stare slice through her.

"Rasha!"

She snapped her head straight.

"I will not allow you to drag this family into this. Is that understood?"

"Yes, Baba," she said in a weak, inoffensive, tone.

One more accusative glance—as if that had been absolutely necessary, as if his condemnation had not been enough—and he stormed out.

Rasha's lips quivered, her body immobile. She could not remember the last time she had enraged her father so, if indeed there had been a precedent. His reaction, however, confirmed that her fears had not been misplaced and had not been amplified by her imagination. He was every bit as unforgiving as she had expected him to be.

Her mother was by her side now, equally helpless. "Let's face it, we both knew he wouldn't take it well."

"Don't tell me you agree with him this time. I couldn't bear it."

"Rasha, habibti, maybe I should . . ."

"No, Mama." Her eyes locked with her mother's, rage taking hold. "I don't want you to do anything. He'll only turn against you. I accept this whole disaster as my responsibility and mine alone. I don't *want* anyone's help." Rasha stopped. "Imagine if I'd actually told him what Luke really means to me."

"I'm glad you didn't go into details."

Rasha felt her features harden. "You know, there's one more thing he's not aware of."

"What's that, Rasha?"

"Whatever happens to Luke . . . Amin Halwani has already lost a daughter."

For the rest of the day, Rasha confined herself to her room. A sleepless night, anxiety, and her confrontation with her father had debilitated her. Sleep would have come even if she had not taken the sedative she thought she could not forgo. Contrary to her habit of unplugging her phone when she craved a rest, this time she left it untouched. If it had rung at all, she did not hear it.

She heard her name in a ripple, as if she were underwater. It was a man's voice. She could not lift her head. Then again, "Rasha." In her daze, she made out Karim's silhouette by the side of her bed. She rose to consciousness with the hope that sleep had washed away the nightmare, that Luke's disappearance had been dreamt up, unreal.

She raised her palms to her eyes, reluctant to move. "What time is it?"

"Half past eight."

"In the evening?" she asked wearily.

Karim nodded.

She propped herself up against the pillows.

"Mama asked me to come in and check on you. They've just finished dinner and she wanted to know if you needed anything."

"No. But thanks anyway. Has Fuad called?"

"Not to my knowledge."

Rasha fiddled with the lace edge of the bedsheet. "You've heard." She referred to the lunchtime debacle.

Karim nodded.

"Do you think he would've reacted the same way if it had been you instead of me?"

"Rasha . . ." Karim said in a pleading voice, not wishing to go into the inequality between them that his sister invariably brought up.

"Maybe I'm being unfair. But you remember, Karim, when you heard of May's death how solicitous and sympathetic he was to your loss?"

"That was different, Rasha. She was killed." His tone of voice was subdued with unrelenting grief.

"No, Karim it's different because you're his son, not his daughter," she pointed out. "How would you have felt if he'd told *you* to pull yourself together and stop acting like such a fool?"

"I don't think, in my state of mind then, that I would've cared."

Rasha let go of the lace, murmuring, "Maybe that's my problem. Maybe I care too much. Nothing had been more important, more precious to me, than Baba's approval. Until now . . ."

"What are you saying, Rasha?"

"Put yourself in my place, Karim . . . what would you do?"

Karim considered the wisdom and implications of his advice, but in the end could only be candid with his sister, as he had always been.

"I'd try to find him."

"At the risk of antagonizing Baba?"

"If I had no choice, I would. Yes," he replied unequivocally.

"Why?"

Karim took a deep breath. "Since you've mentioned May . . . one thing I've always regretted is having been so hard on her, out of principle. I so loathed her drug habit that I deluded myself into thinking that I'd rather give her up than have to put with it . . ."

"You gave her the choice."

"I should've given her more time. I loved her, Rasha. And I've never felt the same way about anyone else. Not even Rula. But you must've guessed that."

Rasha nodded.

"If I hadn't been so proud, so hard-headed and given her an ultimatum . . . I expected too much of her. I should've been more patient, more supportive. We'd been together for so long I suppose I'd started taking her for granted." He grimaced. "I never imagined something like this would happen to her."

"And if it hadn't?"

"The fact is it did," Karim retorted plainly. "What I'm trying to say is, whether Luke is the man you'd risk everything for or not, he's that man at the moment and you should go by your gut feeling. Do what you believe is right, otherwise you'll never forgive yourself."

"What if it turns out he's okay after all, but just acted irresponsibly . . . didn't think of phoning for instance to let me know that he wouldn't make it back by the evening. He never really listened to me or heeded my warnings."

"Are you prepared to take that chance? Of assuming he's unharmed?"

"No."

Karim cupped her hands in his. "You have all the answers, Rasha. If you'd been irresponsible and reckless I'd watch what advice I give you. But you're not. You know what you want, what you *have* to do. If you're prepared to take the risk, then think clearly, act wisely, and don't let anyone influence your decision. Because if it ever got to the stage where you regretted not having done anything, nobody's commiseration will make the slightest difference."

Rasha contemplated her options. "I'd do anything to find him, Karim. The problem is I have no idea where to start."

There was a long silence while each considered viable options.

"Maybe I should go down to the South," Rasha said matter-of-fact.

"Bad idea," Karim let out, alarmed. "You wouldn't know how to go about it. You'd be jumping into the fire along with Luke." Then he added, "What I could do is phone around the hospitals tomorrow, the emergency rooms."

"That's something." Rasha envisioned Luke injured and bloodied. She swept her hands over her face to wipe out the distressing image. "You know the feeling, Karimo, when you've lost something, that it *is* there somewhere and can be found if you were patient enough to look, as opposed to that sinking feeling that it's gone forever?"

"Yes."

"I have that feeling. Something tells me Luke's out there. I know it. I can feel it in here," she said with a fist to her chest.

When all was still at home and Rasha assumed the coast to be clear, she made her way to the kitchen. As she passed her parents' bedroom, she overheard them arguing, in their usual manner: Amin's voice stern and bordering on anger, Nuha's hushed and placatory. Rasha had no interest in eavesdropping. If they chose to dwell on the difficulties the family was in, so be it. She had neither the energy nor the desire to deal with it.

She made herself a cup of tea, then tiptoed back to her bedroom. Under a solitary light focused on her desk, she placed the pile of essays from English 201. It had seemed like ages since she had faced her students although it had in fact been no more than one day.

She looked through them distractedly, her attention as elusive as mercury. In spite of all her cautioning, Luke had managed to step right into peril. It did not escape her that the dread of him ever coming to harm not only stemmed from a concern for his own safety but a fear, equal in measure, that she would not be able to cope in such an eventuality. She had every justification to feel angry towards him for being reckless and over-confident, for placing her in a position where she had to challenge her parents and risk her own life looking for him. But she did not. What she experienced now was a strength that sprouted from grim determination. Knowing Luke, he probably would not expect her to jeopardize her own safety to find him. The motivation to do so was hers alone, and she would stop at nothing.

She leafed through the essays and stopped at Youssef's. Compared to him, and many like him, she and her family had had a good run. No immediate tragedy had touched them and, relative to others, they could still enjoy some of the comforts of their pre-war lifestyle. Recent events were sucking her into an underworld she had so far managed to avoid. They brought her closer to the brutal existence the majority had endured for years.

A lot closer.

Stunned by this epiphany, Rasha stared vacantly at the blank wall. Her mind schemed frantically, in a disjointed manner, glossing over details and feasibility. But her original premise was logical. She had mistakenly searched for the answer in her immediate circle when help actually lay in the hands of someone way beyond it. Power did not rest in the hands of those she knew well but one person whom she knew the least.

Feeling suddenly charged, she dug out the red pen from her briefcase and began her corrections. First thing in the morning she would phone Fuad, then she would make her way to the university. Not only to take her class but to gain access to a world unknown—to confront her demons.

Chapter Eleven

◆

She bounded up the three flights of stairs and rushed into the office, breathless, forgoing the customary morning greetings.

"Isn't Youssef here yet?"

Dumbfounded by Rasha's uncharacteristic zeal, Surayya shook her head.

"He's late."

"Actually, you're early," Surayya remarked, a flicker of a smile on her face.

"Please show him in as soon as he arrives."

"Obviously," she said flatly.

Rasha did not have to wait long. Barely had she made herself a coffee and installed herself at her desk than the knock at the door came.

"Good morning, Miss Halwani."

Rasha jumped to her feet and rounded her desk to meet him. Her zeal startled him as it had Surayya earlier.

"Youssef! Come in. Take a seat."

Instead of resuming her place behind the desk, she pulled up a chair next to him.

"How are you, Youssef?"

"I'm fine, miss."

"Good."

Leaning forward, hands locked, and itching to broach the subject, Rasha came straight to the point.

"Youssef, there's something I'd like you to do for me."

He stared at her briefly, for as long as his shyness permitted, wondering perhaps how he could possibly be of any use to his teacher.

"Do you remember the day you saw me at the cafeteria with a friend?" She was in no doubt he would guess whom she was referring to.

"Yes, miss," Youssef replied, looking dejected.

"Well, this man . . . who happens to be a friend of the family . . . has gone missing."

"Really, miss?"

"Sadly, yes. And I want you to help me find him."

Youssef's eyes widened. "Me?" he gasped.

"Yes Youssef, you. Listen," she hastened to add in order to dispel his fears, "I've thought this through carefully and I wouldn't ask you to do it if it endangered you in any way. It won't." Rasha gave him a reassuring smile.

"But . . . but . . . what can *I* do?"

"Arrange for me to see your brother," she declared plainly.

"My brother?"

Rasha nodded. "You did say he was a fighter."

Youssef paused to take everything in. "Is my brother responsible for this man's disappearance?"

"No, no," Rasha put out a hand. Maybe she had been too hasty in her request, and in her eagerness had not explained the situation adequately. "I'm not saying he or his militia is responsible, Youssef. What I meant was he might be in a position to find out more about what happened to Luke."

"Luke?"

"That's the man's name." Rasha felt the need to elaborate. "He hasn't done anything wrong. He's just a foreigner who didn't know his way around. I think somehow he got into trouble."

"You think that he has been kidnapped." It was a statement rather than a question.

"I'm not sure. But it's possible."

"And you would like me to arrange for you, miss, to see my brother—to ask him if he has heard of this man," Youssef recapitulated, no doubt to make sure he understood her correctly.

Rasha sat back in her chair. "Precisely." She waited while he considered her request, eyes steady on him.

"Where should I arrange for this meeting to take place?"

"Anywhere. I could even go to the headquarters."

"No, miss," he replied, embarrassed, ashamed even. His cheeks turned crimson. "I could not take you there. It is not a place for a lady."

Touched by his high regard for her, Rasha murmured. "I'll be fine, Youssef." Then added, "I'm not asking you to get personally involved. I don't expect you to come with me. I just want you to act as a middleman. That's all."

He retreated into his own thoughts for a brief moment, but Rasha was confident he would not turn her down.

"What my brother does has really nothing to do with me, miss," he said in a small voice, peering at her through thick black eyelashes.

"I understand, Youssef," she stressed, acknowledging his need to dissociate himself from his brother's militancy.

He flipped the edges of his book. Rasha watched him intently.

"Will you do this for me, Youssef? Will you ask him to see me?"

"If that is your wish, miss."

"It's my wish."

He gave a definite nod of acknowledgement. "Then yes, I will."

Rasha beamed. "Good. Good. Naturally, there's no need to mention this to anyone else." Her concern was essentially with staff and students.

"No, miss."

She paused before springing on him her second request. Her words came out slow, emphatic. "One more thing, Youssef. I don't want to waste too much time. So we need to do this today."

"Today?"

"Yes."

He thought awhile. "I will see what I can do."

"Good. And thank you, Youssef." She touched his hand gingerly. "I appreciate it."

The meeting was set for late in the afternoon. Youssef had insisted that he escort Rasha in a taxi and they agreed to meet in an alley near the university at five o'clock sharp. That allowed her enough time to go to the hospital and find Karim.

"Have you gone mad?" Karim exclaimed once she had divulged her plan.

"I expected you to say I was ingenious."

They had taken up a corner table in the American Hospital coffee shop. It was shortly after lunchtime and the place had begun to empty. Karim cut a distinguished figure in a white coat, his name tag pinned to its pocket. On this rare occasion, he was clean-shaven. Two cups of coffee were set before them, yet they left them untouched.

"Rasha, there must be another way. Why doesn't this Youssef just speak to his brother on your behalf? Or even make a vague query, without mentioning you. There's no need for you to meet him."

"There's every need, Karim," Rasha gritted her teeth. "I've *got* to do this, I've *got* to make sure he has all the right information. I *have* to be there!"

"You've lost your mind."

"No I haven't," she stated calmly now. "On the contrary. Everything's perfectly clear. I know it's the right way to go about it. It's the only way."

Karim leaned back in his chair and puffed out a sigh.

"Don't worry Karim. Youssef will be there. Besides, what would they want with me?"

"You're sounding more like your boyfriend every day."

Rasha cocked her head to one side. "Come on. I'm just going to talk to the guy."

"When was the last time you had any dealings with a militia, Rasha?"

Never, she thought. She could not give him an answer.

"My point exactly," he observed.

"I have no choice." Rasha enunciated every word for emphasis. "Have *you* come up with anything?" Her tone challenging.

"No," he replied, at pains to conceal his disappointment. "None of the hospitals have any record of a Luke Elliott."

"So, can you suggest any other way?"

He did not reply, his eyes steady on hers. Instead he asked, "What time are you expected there?"

"Five o'clock."

"Where?"

She opened her mouth to give him the location then stopped. "I'm not telling you."

"Rasha!"

"You're not coming with me. It would only make matters worse."

"How's that?"

"A woman has a better chance at this than a man."

"So you'll go there all alone, ask questions about a foreigner's whereabouts and expect to come out of it clean?" he scowled at her.

"I'm still more likely to get away with it alone than if you were with me. Besides, Youssef can vouch for me. I'm his English teacher, for God's sake! How could I possibly be suspect?"

"And if something were to happen to you? How would I know where to look?"

"It'll never come to that," she mumbled.

"Spoken like your boyfriend, again."

"Courage is not my forte, Karim, you know that. I wouldn't be doing this if it didn't feel right."

Karim scrutinized her, baffled. "What's come over you anyway? You seem . . . different."

"I'm not any different, Karimo. I'm just cornered." She looked at him straight. "I'd still have avoided getting into this mess if I could've. Besides, you encouraged me to find Luke, remember?"

"I didn't mean for you to walk into a lion's den." His tone of voice betrayed regret.

"However determined I might get, my sense of self-preservation is too strong to be pushed aside." She reached out for his arm. "But to tell you the truth, Karimo, at this very moment my life means little without Luke. And, don't forget, he has no one, not a soul to count on in this godforsaken place but me."

He clasped her hands. "Rasha, I'm asking you, please . . . please, let me go with you."

"No, Karimo. I didn't watch over you in all the years we were growing up to get you embroiled in this now."

"Let me have Youssef's telephone number, at least."

Rasha stalled. "I don't have it," she confessed, adding hastily, "In any case, you can get it from the university."

Disconcerted, Karim sank back in his chair. He took time to collect his thoughts. Then, his face suffused with impatience mixed with dread, he leaned across the table and pronounced sternly, "If you're not back . . . at home . . . by seven, I'm coming after you." He tapped a finger on the table to punctuate his remark.

"I'll be there. You'll see. I'll be there by dinner time."

Truth be told—and despite her assurances to the contrary—when she hugged Karim as they parted she secretly wished he had been going with her.

Five o'clock on the dot, Rasha climbed into the sunken back seat of the battered Mercedes. Putting up a brave front, she exchanged pleasantries with Youssef, consciously distending her facial muscles in an effort to disguise her trepidation. But her body, a solid block, would not yield and her hand, taut against the strap of her handbag, would not relax its stiff grip. Her heart beat at an uncontrollable pace. A sick feeling in the pit of her stomach shot up to her throat each time the driver forged forward or slammed on the brakes. Distractedly, she listened to Youssef's replies on the wellbeing of his sisters and their family situation, none of it registering. Her attention was on the arteries the Mercedes was following to the heart of war-torn Beirut. A meandering route that gradually revealed the immeasurable destruction in areas she had not visited for years.

Those were suburbs transformed into battlefields that Rasha had only seen in pictures. What she knew of them, the atrocities they had suffered, cold statistics of their dead and wounded, she had in the past gleaned while leisurely reading the newspapers over morning coffee. However much she had tried to picture them, what unfolded before her eyes now put imagination to shame. Garbage littered the streets that teemed with pedestrians suspicious of one another and disdainful of speeding motorists. Buildings of solid concrete tottered in shreds, their cavernous holes like gaping mouths, wanting to denounce the calamities of their residents and bewail the eternal torment of their souls.

A pervading stench of fear and anger scorched her throat. Her limbs seized every time the Mercedes skimmed a pedestrian, or when other drivers exchanged threats and abuse with a bellicosity as pointless as it was offensive. Scattered around her were paltry remnants of civilization: ghosts of vanished lives, carcasses of cars and construction—snapshots of humanity and barbarity.

Rasha was being sucked into the black hole of a large crater.

Gradually, resentment, even anger, surpassed apprehension. That her country, her people should come to this! That unfettered anarchy should be allowed to eat away at their dignity and wellbeing! That she should have unwittingly turned a blind eye to it. How is it that she had escaped the carnage, the day-to-day dehumanization? How had she managed, for nearly a decade, to hover on the fringes of many such craters?

As her father had said: where had she been all these years? Indeed, where?

All at once she was overcome with a sense of bereavement. She saw cold brutality in the faces of the perpetrators and hurt resignation in those of the victims. She watched transfixed, wanting to retain a mental image of the palpable manifestations of war, uncertain whether the misery she perceived in the demeanour of her people was real or a mere projection of her own wretchedness. How could she be so naïve as to think that in the midst of such dire existence the disappearance of one faceless foreigner should be significant?

Her steely resolve began to weaken. Her mission was neither ingenious nor fail-safe, but an undertaking that had sprung from blind optimism and the presumption that Luke's salvation rested in her hands.

Youssef tapped the driver's shoulder indicating for him to stop and wait for them. As he held the door open for Rasha, she stretched her neck to get a full view of the headquarters, a bullet-shot building draped with flags and plastered with faces of dead fighters, the militia's martyrs. Children played alongside it in puddles of rain. It was all right, she told herself. There were people around, children even. She would be all right.

At the entrance, some militiamen stood chatting and smoking. Rasha's appearance momentarily caused them to stop and stare. She wrapped her jacket around her waist, feeling suddenly exposed and icy cold, her gaze shifting to avoid eye contact. With a warm greeting, the militiamen took turns to shake hands with Youssef or give him a friendly slap on the back. Still, Rasha could see that he was nervous, intimidated. As they proceeded down a dingy corridor past other armed men, and as more threatening and lascivious leers sliced through her, she made sure she kept in step with Youssef.

They stopped at a gaping door which revealed a gathering of three men, one reclining behind a steel desk, the others seated on the other side of it at either end. All were in battle gear, the two men in attendance clutching AK47s that rested against the arms of metal-framed chairs. Youssef tapped at the door to draw their attention.

"Youssef, come in!" the man behind the desk yelled, beckoning him forward with a hand gesture but not getting up.

The other two, subordinates perhaps, stood up, retrieved their weapons with one hand and extended the other which Youssef accepted cordially in succession. No introductions were made. It was as if Rasha did not exist. The militiamen took their leave from their commander addressing him by his *nom de guerre*, and shut the door behind them.

"Ahmed, this is Miss Halwani."

"*Sitt* Halwani," Ahmed declared, only half rising to exchange a handshake, his grip strong as a vice. "Please take a seat. Can I offer you a coffee, a juice?"

"No, thank you." She crossed her hands over the handbag in her lap, as Youssef had often done in her office with his books. A coffee cup left behind by one of the militiamen—its bottom caked with black, thick, dregs—made her a little sick.

For a while, Ahmed, dismissive of Rasha's presence, chatted with Youssef. She looked on, noting that he was considerably larger than his younger brother, and tougher. Flinty dark eyes were rimmed with deep wrinkles, his jaw peppered with bristle. She made him out to be in his mid-thirties, and from his tone of voice detected a patriarchal, almost authoritarian attitude towards Youssef. Incredible as it seemed, she was in the presence of a man who probably killed countless others without flinching. She, an amateur at war, had come to appeal to the professional—to one, of many, who had dedicated himself to a cause, the sum of which was hapless civilians' lives.

With no forewarning, he swung to Rasha. "Sitt Halwani, Youssef tells me you're looking for a friend." Calloused fingers interlocked on the desk.

"Yes," she said plainly, not knowing how to address him. She shifted uncomfortably in her chair. "He's been gone a couple of days now."

Ahmed dropped his chin to his chest, as if deep in thought. Rasha had no doubt that he enjoyed the power of his position.

"What's his name?" He shot her a sideways glance.

"Luke Elliott . . . He's a British photographer."

"Ah!" He flung his head backwards as if he had been delivered some divine revelation.

He waited awhile. For impact, she thought.

"And he's your guest in Beirut," he declared.

"Actually, he's staying with a friend. I met him through an acquaintance in Paris. He was sent here by a news agency."

"Where was he last seen?" he asked in the same drone that implied a certain weariness and made Rasha wonder whether any good would come of the meeting.

"At the Commodore Hotel . . ." She proceeded to relate what Michael had told her, without naming names, assuring him that Luke had no ulterior motives and was simply doing his job. He was hardly a suspicious character and probably got into trouble through sheer ignorance.

"What makes you think we can help you?"

Rasha heard the hostility in his voice. She could even sense Youssef grow uncomfortable.

"Well. A man of your standing and with your connections . . . I thought you might be able to find something out for me."

She addressed him with a contrived tone of admiration and reverence. That would flatter him, she knew, and perhaps ensure his collaboration. Contrary to what Luke maintained, feigning subservience was more likely to yield results.

There was a long, heavy pause. Then, as though chatting at a party, Ahmed mused, "Halwani . . . Halwani . . . from Tripoli, right?"

"Yes, that's right," Rasha answered, irked that he had abandoned the subject of Luke. She shifted in her seat.

His eyes narrowed to slits. "The daughter of . . ."

"Amin Halwani," she offered reluctantly.

Ahmed picked up a pencil and proceeded to tap its end on the desk. Tap, tap, tap . . .

"What does he do?"

Youssef flinched, aware like Rasha, that his brother's questioning was senseless and unnecessary. His purpose was clearly to display his clout and underscore that wealth and status fell miserably short of the might that he, once among the oppressed, now had. It was precisely because he was being manipulative that Rasha drip-fed him the information he was after.

"He has a business."

"What sort of business?"

"Juice-bottling." Enough! she thought. There was no point pursuing this. She would say no more.

As if he had read her thoughts, Ahmed said, smirking, "Is this Englishman important to you?"

"We feel responsible for his safety," Rasha replied, using the collective to divert attention from herself. "He hasn't been in Beirut for long and doesn't know anyone besides my family."

"So how did it happen that you're here alone? Why didn't your father accompany you?"

Get personal, Rasha thought.

"*Sayyed* Ahmed, I came to you because Youssef is my student, and a good one at that." She smiled at Youssef. "He's a kind person, who comes from what I believe is a respectable and decent family. I expected you to be equally compassionate. So it was my idea to appeal to you." She stopped. "My family in fact doesn't know I'm here."

Ahmed flung the pencil on the desk, as if Rasha's praise had gone straight over his head. He appeared unmoved and unimpressed, insulted even that she should think him so gullible. Expecting him to lash out, Rasha tensed.

"Very well." Ahmed shifted his gaze away from her with palpable contempt. "I'll see what I can do. Youssef will keep you informed."

Rasha glanced at Youssef for a cue. He nodded meekly. She jumped to her feet and mouthed her thank yous. She started to walk away then turned to see if Youssef was following. Ahmed had rounded his desk and was holding his younger brother by the shoulders. "You stay out of trouble," she heard him say. Had she not known any better, she would have let herself warm up to the smug and phlegmatic Ahmed. But deep down, she suspected his compassion only extended to his closest kin.

They stepped out into the twilight as a purple haze skimmed the rooftops of Beirut. The city rang out with discordant prayers from scattered mosques while a foreboding stillness that followed rush hour mania enveloped the neighbourhood. The children Rasha had noticed on their arrival had vanished. To all of them, including her, it was an end to another uncertain day, a precursor to many more to come.

Wordlessly, Rasha and Youssef climbed into the Mercedes. For a while she could not speak, she could not even bring herself to thank him. What worried her was whether she had done the right thing by soliciting his brother's help. She replayed the exchange with Ahmed over and over, reviewing her utterances and her reactions. The mindset of fighters was beyond her comprehension and an impassable gulf separated them from the silent minority to which she belonged. Ahmed's disdain for her and her ilk was unmistakable. She just hoped that her mediation would not jeopardize Luke's chances.

It was only as they dropped Youssef off at home that she remembered to express her gratitude. By then, her mind saturated with visions of hostility and deprivation, she no longer cared to inspect the slums on her way home, yearning instead for the comfort and security of her own neighbourhood. Only once the taxi had entered a familiar district did she ask the driver to stop. She walked into an ancient grocery shop and purchased a bottle of cold water, downing it in one slug before she had even paid.

But the sour taste on her palate could not be washed down.

Karim received her with overt relief. Briefly, exhaustion catching up with her, she recounted her meeting with Ahmed. He listened attentively, intent, or so she suspected, on following the developments closely to preclude another foolish idea on her part.

"By the way," he began, "Fuad got a message for you from Michael. He wants you to phone him back."

"When was that?"

"This afternoon."

In no time at all, she had Michael on the line.

"Rasha. I'm afraid I have a bit of bad news."

She held her breath and from his silence gathered that he was giving her time to collect herself. "Yes, Michael?"

"Of the journalists I know, no one has come across Luke in the South . . ."

What did that mean?

"Rasha, are you there?"

"Sorry Michael, I'm listening."

"I don't want you to think of the worst, but my guess would be he never made it there."

"So . . . what do you suppose happened to him?" Rasha asked, almost pleading for reassurance.

"Whatever I say would be mere speculation."

Rasha dragged her fingertips along her scar, her eyes shut with weariness. "I understand," she murmured. "You know, Michael, I can't help but wonder whether the taxi driver was involved. Otherwise, why wouldn't he have come forward?"

"You're assuming Luke was taken from the taxi?"

"It's possible."

"He could've made a stop on the way."

"He could've." Or, a theory she did not wish to entertain, Luke along with the driver may have been hurt, even killed. Something told her Michael thought along the same wavelength but neither of them dared say it.

"And no word's come out about a journalist being harmed in any way?" she asked tentatively.

"None," Michael replied.

An awful silence set in.

"I haven't even thought of informing the agency," Rasha pronounced suddenly, a sober thought issuing from a confused mind.

"They already know."

She was keeping Michael on the line for no other reason than to bounce ideas off him. His patience made her all the more reluctant to let him go.

"Michael, has anything like this ever happened to you before?"

He let out a nervous laugh. "Not yet."

"I hope it never does."

"Rasha, hold on a sec, I've got another call."

She covered the mouthpiece and heaved a sigh. The rapport she had with Michael, which had developed with incredible ease, was sadly fleeting. Their common denominator was Luke. Once the crisis was over, however it may end, their acquaintance would die out the very moment they had no more to say to each other. Lately, events had led her to gravitate out of necessity towards people she would otherwise have no dealings with, from Michael and Youssef to the likes of Ahmed.

"Sorry about that."

"It's my fault," Rasha said, "I've kept you too long. You've been very understanding."

"To be honest, I'm doing what I'd hope a fellow journalist would do for me." His voice rang with compassion. "Any of us could be in Luke's shoes at any time."

With absolutely nothing more to go on after she had hung up, Rasha was at the mercy of her mind and her imagination. The way she saw it, she had two options: to recognize that she had reached a deadlock and assume the worst, or to beat the sinking feeling that threatened to take control, and hope for the best. Either way, it was neither the information nor lack of it on Luke's whereabouts that would be the deciding factor, but a reasoning which could sway dangerously to delusory optimism. It was entirely up to her to steer the thoughts and emotions that would in turn determine her actions.

It was the hardest mind game she had ever played. She was not in a situation where she attempted to anticipate danger and evade it, but in a dilemma where the threat had been realized and she had to test her competence in dealing with it. She could hold on to faith and the hope that Luke would be found. Against that, the brutal possibility that he might not would prepare her for the worst and attenuate the shock, if and when it came. While she endured this infernal torment, Luke's fate was unknown to her. Out there lay the truth of what had happened to him, and she, the only person desperate, so desperate to know it, did not.

She sat at dinner with her family only because Karim urged her to do so. Excusing herself would be a slight to her father, and Karim warned her that further antagonism would be counter-productive. To her surprise, it was her mother who initiated the conversation that had been understood to be out of bounds.

"Have you heard anything yet, Rasha?"

"Nuha!" Amin snarled.

"I'm just asking. There's no harm in that, is there?" Nuha retorted, palms upturned.

Rasha examined her father, trying to judge whether it was safe to reply. Eyes downcast, he stabbed his food with a fork.

"Well?" Nuha insisted.

"No, Mama. Nothing. Just that he was on his way to the South and never made it." Rasha mumbled her answer as if to assure her father that, in doing so, she did not mean to defy his authority.

"May God protect him."

"You stick your neck out, your head gets chopped off," Amin stated coldly.

"You don't *have* to stick your neck out in this place. They'll yank it out if they want to," she snapped.

Nuha's tone of voice brought the entire table to an abrupt silence. Rasha glanced at Karim who had stopped chewing, his eyes like saucers. This was as close to a quarrel that their parents had ever reached in their presence, their mother's overt defiance uncharacteristically manifest.

"He's just a young man doing his job. Neither he, nor anyone for that matter, deserves to be punished for it."

"He had no business coming here."

"People have been going missing since the beginning of the war, Amin. They didn't go out asking for it. This could've happened to anyone." She added softly, "It could've happened to one of us, God forbid."

"So now you're taking his side . . . and your daughter's," his voice rose a notch.

Rasha watched them silently, not wishing this standoff on her account.

"I'm taking the side of reason. At this very moment," she said tapping the table, "I feel sorry for the young man, regardless of his relationship with this family."

Amin's eyes darted back at her. "He has *no* relationship with this family."

Nuha would not give in. "We're not masters of our fate, Amin."

The way they carried on led Rasha to believe that this was not the first time they did not see eye to eye. Nor was it the first when Nuha dared speak her mind. Rasha and Karim may not have been witness to previous altercations between their parents but something told Rasha that they must have occurred, more often than she had imagined, behind closed doors.

She watched her mother intently, as if reacquainting herself with the woman she thought she knew. Nuha's body language spoke of sadness and despondency. She ate with distaste, pausing now and then to stare ahead vacantly. What had happened to Luke had struck close to home. Her preoccupation did not end with him, but extended to the safety of her own children. With danger at their doorstep, Nuha's maternal instinct drove her to rally her family together, intuition far surpassing regard for her husband's hardened stance.

What struck Rasha too was that Amin did not seem so headstrong, so obdurate. He let Nuha have her say when he could've just as easily stopped her. It was as if he had resorted to silent detachment to distance himself from the calamity. Not because he did not want to get involved, but perhaps because he knew events were bound to take a certain course which he wanted no part of. He could try to prohibit Rasha from interceding on Luke's behalf, but he had no power to crush everyone's empathy. So he waited on the sidelines, refraining from expressing approval or opposition because, deep down, he could not wish the worst on his adversary. The young Englishman was a victim, and Amin was not so callous as to disregard the tragedy that had befallen him.

Rasha looked on her parents and saw two people who had shared a life together. They had met, fallen in love, and taken their vows as husband and wife long before she and Karim had intruded upon their bond. In a moment of truth, she saw herself apart, separate from them, as a mature woman who should have established her own life. Witness to her parents' differences, it struck her that by now she should have been concerning herself with her own marriage and not theirs.

Her senses completely overloaded, they shut down, leaving Rasha hopelessly numb. She was no more than a shell, hollow within. The resolve she had experienced at the outset was dwindling, burning determination doused to dying embers. Whatever resources she could invoke to carry on were no longer evident when even in the home of her youth, in the bosom of her own family, she had become a dispassionate observer.

So the decision to take her class the next day was more escapist than conscientious. Of the twenty faces that gazed at her diligently, only one claimed her attention with magnetic force, Youssef's. His blank expression however implied that he had nothing significant to tell her.

"Describe in no more than two hundred and fifty words a person who has influenced your life. You have half an hour."

She had it all planned out. She would stay at her desk for a while then would circulate among the students as she had the habit of doing.

She ambled down the rows, stopping now and then to pinpoint a spelling or grammatical error. Dallying a little so her move towards Youssef would not be obvious, impatience mingled with expectation rumbled through her, tempting her to quicken her step. She resisted the urge, reminding herself that he may have nothing for her yet, that she may be in for a let-down. Finally at his desk, she lingered, trailing her fingertips along its worn edges. Then, casually, she leaned over his shoulder, her lips a little too close to his ear. "Have you heard anything?"

He did not look up, discomfited by the proximity of his idol. The tip of his pen steady on the paper, he mumbled, "No miss. Not yet."

Hesitantly, his eyes rose to hers. Rasha smiled in a way to assure him that her interest in him as a student surpassed his recent usefulness to her. Straightening up to move on, she nearly lost her footing as she caught a glimpse of Fuad and Karim outside the classroom, deep in conversation.

She could have walked out to them then and there. A part of her wanted to. But when she noticed them looking her way, she averted her eyes. More than that, she turned her back to them. Whatever it was they had to say, she did not want communicated through glances or gestures. She needed to hear it in plain words.

What she put herself through was unnecessary torture. But she dreaded that once she had heard them out, the moment of revelation would be irreversible. How could she possibly face it? How could she confront the truth?

She hid behind her students, like a child holding his breath underwater, in a standoff against time, looking forward to that sudden rush of air in his lungs when he decided to surface. But what if there was no air? What if Fuad and Karim's news were to push her under, suffocate her and leave her thrashing about in unforgiving waters?

Surprisingly, she stayed calm, composed. The bell sounded, and as the students filed out placing their essays on her desk, she took time to gather them in a pile and stow them neatly in her briefcase. Collecting her handbag and her books, she finally edged along students scrambling into the classroom for the next course.

With slow and easy steps she approached Karim, clasping her books against her bosom. The expression on his face was indecipherable, a forced grin that failed to disguise its gravity. He reached out for her, bracing her shoulders. She could not move.

"Rasha, he's back."

A wave of relief and confusion washed over her. She felt cleansed, light, as if new life had been breathed into her. She lowered her eyes, thinking, sifting the news she had just been given. Is it true? Please God, let it be true! Luke's face, unharmed and pristine, flashed momentarily before her, causing her lips to curl up in a half-smile.

"Where is he?" Her words reached her as if they had been someone else's.

"At the apartment," Karim replied.

Rasha's eyes, unusually hard, at once alert and accusative, swayed from Karim to Fuad. "And you left him there alone?"

Fuad began eagerly, "We had no choice. He . . ."

Karim abruptly flung out an arm to silence him. "I had to give him something to help him sleep. He . . . he was exhausted." He would have stopped at that had it not been for the ferocious look she gave him. "Rasha . . . he's in a bad way," he added at last.

Plunged straight back into doubt, Rasha reeled as blood rushed to her head. First there was a lightness, different from the one she had experienced only a minute ago. As if a syringe was driven through her, an overdose of iciness coursed through her veins to her fingertips, freezing tactile sensation. Her books slipped through a weakening grip and landed with a thud. Specks of white danced before her eyes. She was levitating.

Then, in one moment . . . there was blackness.

Chapter Twelve

◆

There are instants in one's life that seem to stretch to eternity, but seldom are they the gilt-edged moments one longs to cling to. More often than not they are splinters of time suspended by grief, sudden revelation or a sense of loss. As when, for instance, in this ongoing game of musical chairs, one finds oneself without a seat, confounded by a punishing isolation—patent humility and defeat visible to all.

The minute Rasha set eyes on Luke was a watershed that propelled her into a future forever branded with one such epiphanic moment. It was a leap into another realm insulated from an irretrievable past.

She had asked to be left alone with him. For hours, she had sat motionless by his side, tears trickling soundlessly down her cheeks. What she beheld was no more than a heap. A few strands of unwashed hair protruded from the blanket that concealed his body but clearly delineated two fists clinging to it for dear life. For hours on end, she stared at this shape, trying to imagine and anticipate the state she would find him in once his shroud had been cast off. When she heard a painful and muffled groan, she reached out with shaky fingers calling out his name. The bundle recoiled with palpable terror, furling, letting out a chilling wail of fear Rasha could not believe was Luke's.

Rasha's patience had worn thin. Now that Luke was back, she wanted him awake, lucid, able to soberly and coherently relate to her what had happened. Since his disappearance, time had ticked by at an agonizing pace and now she was unwilling to hold out for much longer. What she wanted, unrealistically, was for Luke to tell all so they could put the experience behind them and move on. What she pined for the most was the solid Luke—the man who had tried to cajole her with irresistible charm into staying with him four days prior in this very room.

She heard a gentle rap on the door and got up to open it, not daring to speak.

"Is he awake yet?" Karim whispered.

Rasha blocked his path in the doorway. "No, Karim. What in the world did you give him?"

"A mild sedative. Nothing too strong. It can't be the reason he's still asleep."

"No?" Rasha retorted a little too harshly. "Then what do you think it is?"

"Fear of where and what he would wake up to," he said outright. His stern expression implied that he would not tolerate unwarranted blame.

Rasha turned in Luke's direction. "Do you think that I should wake him?"

"No, don't." Karim consulted his watch. "Rasha, I know you need some time together, but . . . I'll have to look him over sometime."

Her eyebrows knotted. "What for?"

"Cuts, bruises." Karim cleared his throat. "He'll need some care."

Much as she may have wanted to, Rasha was painfully aware that she could not accelerate the healing process.

"Anything you need?"

Rasha shook her head.

Karim placed a palm over her shoulder. "Will you be okay?"

Would she? For one protracted moment she could not answer. She dipped her head. The door shut, she walked towards the window. The curtains were drawn and she so craved sunlight. Her chest was closing in, the air in the room oppressive, putrid. The only sound that reached her was Luke's heavy and muffled breathing. Vows she had made in exchange for her wishes coming true ran through her mind. Promising never to complain about power cuts if she were to be seen safely through gunfire. Pledging to want for nothing provided she and her family were unhurt in fierce shelling. What would she vow now in return for Luke's recovery? What promise would rise up to the priceless restitution of her love?

"Rasha?"

She pivoted, her legs leaden, a lump solidifying in her throat. She held her breath, making no sound.

"Rasha?"

"Luke?" she rasped, "Luke, I'm here." In one movement, she was by his side again. She held back, waiting for him to peel off the blanket.

Sullied fingers reached over the cover, pulling it down. First she saw his full mane of hair, glued in sweat and dirt against his skull. Then his eyes, bloodshot, cavernous. His cheeks were sunken. His lips cracked and dry, framed by bristle. Worst of all was his haunted stare, as if Rasha was a wolf in sheep's clothing.

She extended a hand and ever so lightly placed it over his fingers.

"You're safe now, Luke." She choked on her words. "You're safe."

He did not blink. His gaze steady, yet uncertain. Tears trickled from the corners of his wide terrified eyes, leaving in their wake streams of black. With trembling fingers, Rasha brushed them away slowly, carefully, her own lip quivering, sobs lodged in her throat.

"Oh, Luke," she whispered, looking to one side. Then, overwhelmed with his pain she lay against him with infinite care. She felt his every heave against her own body, painfully mingling with her sobbing. Sadness, suffering and relief locked them together in one knot of deep emotion. Gradually, Luke's body began to give way and Rasha tried to lift herself to face him but he pressed against her firmly, unwilling to let go. When her tears had dried out leaving her drained and speechless, she lay still, waiting for him to speak.

After a long silence, she called his name. He did not answer. She raised herself slowly, her head close to his, his breathing warm against her cheek. His eyes met hers, sober but vacant. He did not utter a word.

"Can I get you something to eat?"

Luke began to shake his head then stopped, grimacing with pain. One side of his neck revealed a swelling of dark purple and blue. She ran her fingertips along its edges.

"Hey, sunshine," he finally said smiling, as if to reassure her.

Rasha leaned over and placed her lips on his, tears welling up in her eyes.

"I'm sorry, Rasha. So sorry."

She nodded, her voice failing her.

"Will you help me up? I desperately need a shower." He began to lift himself off the bed but sank back, wincing.

"Where does it hurt, Luke?"

Face contorted, he waited for the aching to pass. "Everywhere," he groaned.

"I'll go get Karim."

Rasha looked on as Karim, with the precision and compassion of a medic, informed Luke of the course of the examination. He would be checking for broken bones, bruises, internal bleeding. Luke blinked to give him the go-ahead.

As he was about to remove the blanket, Karim turned to Rasha on the verge of speaking.

"I'm staying," she declared, pre-empting him. She straightened up crossing her arms defiantly.

She was a few feet away from them, to allow her brother some space to conduct his examination. With dextrous touches Karim pressed his fingertips along Luke's head, his face, ears and glands. He inspected his eyes, mouth and throat. As he worked the shirt collar down, Rasha was close enough to glimpse the bruise in the shape of the butt of a gun imprinted on her lover's skin in angry shades of purple and black. A brown stain—congealed blood—had stiffened one edge of his collar. Her eyes traced his body. His knees were grazed, coated in dirt and swollen. His legs lay immobile and limp against the soft mattress.

"Help me take his shirt off," Karim instructed her. "I'll lift him up."

Rasha began to unbutton Luke's shirt, all the while watching him, and at one point detecting a glint in his eye. Karim placed one knee behind Luke's head, slipped his hands under the arms and slowly hoisted him up. Luke bit his lip to suppress a cry. Carefully, Rasha pulled off one sleeve, then the other. Against the whiteness of his skin was a kaleidoscope of brutality.

"Luke, can you hold yourself up for a moment?" Karim asked under his breath.

Luke's head dropped, and Karim interpreted it as acquiescence.

"Come this side Rasha and help him."

She rounded the bed and took over Karim's spot. He tapped and listened then reached for the stethoscope, warmed it against his hand, and laid it against Luke's back.

"If it's my heart you're looking for, your sister's got it."

Luke tried to turn his head and get a glimpse of Rasha but couldn't. With a slight squeeze to his shoulder, she acknowledged his poignant remark. Karim glanced at Rasha, and smiling said, "I think we all know that by now Luke."

Karim conducted his examination in silence, breaking it now and then to ask Luke which areas felt tender to the touch. When he had finished, he gave his diagnosis.

"Well, you're not in great shape, but we can fix you up. One of the lower ribs may be fractured. I'll have to immobilize it. The best thing for it is rest, of course." Karim paused. "I'd like you to come in for X-rays, blood and urine tests—just to make sure. We also need to keep those cuts clean. Some are already infected. Probably better to get you on antibiotics as soon as we can. In the meantime I'll leave you with some painkillers. Take one every four hours." Karim placed a box on the bedside table. "How's your appetite? Are you hungry?"

"To be honest, what I desperately need right now is a shower," Luke replied.

Karim grinned. "I can see that. Right, let's get you up. Nice and easy."

In the bathroom, Rasha helped him undress, suppressing gasps over his frailty. She checked the pockets for any items that needed to be salvaged and finding them empty, not surprisingly, rolled his clothes up in a heap and threw them in the washing basket. He languished under a hot shower while she perched herself on the edge of the bath waiting, a towel, a clean T-shirt and a pair of shorts at the ready in her lap. All the questions that tormented her would have to wait. Wait until Luke was in a fit state to talk.

"That felt so good," he pronounced as he emerged from behind the shower curtain.

Rasha helped him get dry, dabbing the towel along his back, shoulders, down to his legs. As he found it painful to bend over, she crouched at his feet holding out the shorts for him to step into.

"I'm sorry to have you do this, sunshine."

"Not half as sorry as I am to see you like this Luke."

He swung an arm around her shoulder as she led him back to the bedroom, into bed, and covered him with the blanket.

"Karim insisted you have lots of liquids. I'll get you some juice. Something to eat maybe?"

"Sure," he replied, clearly drained from the effort he had put into getting up and moving around.

"I'll only be a minute."

"Rasha?"

She swivelled. "Yes?"

He took her hand and kissed it. "I . . . don't be long."

Rasha leaned over and planted a kiss on his forehead. Before he could notice her eyes redden, she turned away and headed for the kitchen. The house was empty, Karim having left, promising to be by later, and Fuad having made himself scarce. The hustle-bustle of the streets, of life going on outside the apartment penetrated through open windows with tantalizing clarity. In the fridge, Rasha found a piece of cheese riddled with green fungus, half a litre of orange juice, a couple of soft apples and a stack of beers. Frustration and anger welled up in her. She flung the cheese in the bin and poured juice into a glass. From the larder she pulled out a can of chicken soup and emptied it into a pan. She popped two slices of bread into the toaster and smeared them with the last bit of butter she could find. As she stirred the soup over the stove, her stomach churned. Chicken soup was for the sick, not the sick at heart.

As she re-entered Luke's bedroom, she found him trying to get out of bed.

"What are you doing?" she asked, hastily placing the tray on the bedside table.

"I need a cigarette."

"I'll get it for you." She helped him raise his legs back onto the bed.

"They're in the dresser . . ."

"I know where they are," she interjected. From a half-full carton of Gauloises she retrieved a packet and tore it open. She handed him one.

"The bastards took my lighter," he said between clenched teeth, eyes drifting. "The lighter that you gave me . . ."

"It's all right, Luke. I can always . . ."

"No Rasha. It's not all right," he snapped, "It's not bloody all right! They had no right!" His eyes looked feral. "It was *my* lighter. You gave it to me. They took my press card, my camera, my passport. Everything!"

"I'll get some matches," she muttered as she rushed out, not knowing how to handle his outburst or what to say, but determined to appease him.

Back at his side, when she extracted a match from the box, he took it from her gently, "I can do that."

He drew on the cigarette a little too eagerly and started coughing. He gripped his chest.

"Christ," he blurted out.

She watched him, speechless, letting him vent his frustration at being so helpless, and worst of all, so dependent on her.

"The soup's getting cold," she said hesitantly.

Luke did not respond, his gaze fixed on nothingness, past her, the cigarette poised between his fingers. With one swift movement, his eyes swung to hers.

"They had a blue mattress."

Had he gone insane? What was he going on about?

Rasha gaped at him, deadpan. "Who had a blue mattress?"

"In my cell. There was a blue mattress." He looked at her with alert eyes. "It made me think of the one you'd told me about in Paris. Remember, the one on the boat you took to Cyprus?"

There *was* method in his madness.

"Oh that," Rasha acknowledged.

"It was filthy too. I'll bet yours wasn't stained with blood, though." He shot her a sideways glance.

The macabre remark made her shudder. She steeled herself. "No, Luke, it didn't."

"I didn't think so." He flicked cigarette ash in the direction of the ashtray and missed.

Luke's grimness was strikingly out of character. Rasha faced the daunting task of reacquainting herself with the man—remnants of the man—she once knew intimately.

She finally mustered the courage to voice the question foremost in her mind, "Are you ready to tell me what happened?"

He exhaled a thick coil of smoke. "I need a drink."

"I've got some juice . . ."

"Not exactly what I had in mind."

"Beer?" she ventured. "There's some in the fridge."

"Now you're talking."

She returned with a bottle of Amstel and handed it to him. He took a long swig.

"Luke," Rasha began, her hands clasped, "the day after you went missing, I went to see Michael." She stopped, awaiting a reaction. There was none. "Eventually, I found out through him that you were on your way to the South and had taken a taxi from the street. Is that right?"

Luke took time to answer. "Yes, pretty much."

"Then what happened?"

"Any chance of me getting another beer?"

"You haven't even finished this one," Rasha tried to contain her irritation.

"It's going to be a very long story." He gave her a roguish smile.

"Fine."

This time round she took away the soup, now cold, and produced two more beers and a bottle opener. She took every measure to deny Luke the opportunity to circle the issue. Intent on extracting the details of his disappearance, she sat by his side refusing to speak until he did.

"Are you giving me the silent treatment?" he quipped.

"Don't joke, Luke. I've been worried sick about you."

An unlit cigarette hanging from the corner of his mouth, he struck a match and made to light it. The brief flicker revealed a ghostly face in a darkened room. Neither of them had thought of pulling the curtains open.

"Michael got it right," he began pensively. "I did grab a cabbie off the street. I was so eager to get to the

South and cover the events that I got careless. That was
stupid, I know. There, I've said it so you don't have to. It
would've been a whole lot different if I spoke Arabic,
which I don't. Except for *bhibbik* of course, which as you
can imagine never had a context." He took a long drag of
the Gauloise. "Just on the outskirts of Beirut, we were
stopped at a roadblock. The militiamen went wild when
they saw my passport and no questions asked hauled me
out of the taxi, shouting abuse and threats, and forced me
into a beaten-up BMW. I was sandwiched between two of
them who took my head for a speed-bag, laying their fists
and the butt of their guns into me every time I spoke. They
kept on accusing me of being a spy. 'Spy, *jasoos*, Zionist'"
he mimicked. Ash dropped on the blanket. Neither he nor
Rasha made a move to clean it off. "At some point, it
must've been as we drew closer to their destination I suppose, they blindfolded me. Just to toy with my nerves I
guess. I mean, really, there was no way that I'd be able to
find my way back there again. I remember thinking that
the sooner they get this over and done with, the sooner I
can get back to meet you at the apartment. How naïve!"

He leaned across to the bedside table for another
beer but could not reach it. Rasha opened and handed one
to him. After a long swig, he continued.

"I felt like a stuffed pig on a silver platter with an
apple in its throat. *Not* its mouth. Christ, Rasha, I tell you
they did rattle me. All I could do was blabber on, hoping
that somehow I might hit on a few words they would
understand like 'innocent', 'no spy'. There were four guys
in total and once in a while the one in the passenger seat
would say something and they'd all burst out laughing. It
was all a joke to them, I swear. That same bastard had
snatched my camera and ripped out a whole film." Luke's
face reddened with rage. He put out the cigarette that had
burned right down to the filter.

"I have no idea how long we'd been driving when we finally stopped. I remember thinking it must be hell to be blind. I was being jostled in all directions. I didn't know where we were, what was going on, and couldn't put any faces to the voices around me. There was a huge commotion as they pushed me through some entrance to a building. I think there were only two guys with me then, one at either side. They threw me into a room, whipped off my blindfold, and left me there." He smacked his lips. "Christ, my mouth is dry."

"Try some juice," Rasha suggested as she extended the glass to him.

Luke downed it in one gulp. Unexpectedly, his eyes shimmered. "That's when I saw the blue mattress." His lips formed into a smile laden with sadness and hurt. "The room was bare except for that one soiled blue mattress." Feebly, he lifted an index finger. "That's when I thought of you, your trip on the tugboat. A flash of the two of us on the cruise in Paris hit me right there." He brought a fist to his chest. Taking her hand into his, he muttered, "At that point it hadn't occurred to me that I might not see you again. I was certain that once they'd realized I was of no use to them, they'd let me go." His voice trailed off and he would not look at her.

His obvious distress constricted Rasha's breathing. There were no words.

Luke cleared his throat. "Anyway, some time later . . . two . . . three hours maybe, I couldn't tell . . . they had taken my watch along with the camera, the passport, press card and . . . the lighter . . . bastards! One of the guys, with an AK47 slung over his shoulder, yanked me off the floor and handed me the blindfold to put on. He pushed me towards the exit. He kept on pushing me down this long corridor, just shoving me with the flat of his hand." Luke demonstrated with his palm, pressing it against thin air, his expression demonic. "I swear, Rasha, I nearly lost it.

Right there and then, I could've killed him. The way he kept jabbing at my back I felt like grabbing his AK and sticking it right down his throat." His eyes oozed rekindled loathing and a hunger for revenge. "We went along what seemed like a passageway towards another room. He removed my blindfold and I saw two other militiamen waiting. One of them seemed to hold a higher rank. I became hopeful. Maybe I'd have a chance to communicate with him. He spoke to me in broken English as he held my passport in his hand. He asked me where I was from. I remember thinking England, genius. It says so right there on my passport. But I held my tongue. You would've been proud of me, sunshine." He grimaced.

A little too late, Rasha thought to herself. All the same, she smiled back at him.

Luke tried to recollect his train of thought. "He asked . . . um . . . well, he started grilling me. Why did I come to Lebanon? Whom did I work for? Did I know any Lebanese? Where was I staying? I gave him the half-truth. I kept you and Fuad out of it, and claimed I was staying at the Commodore. I admitted I was a photojournalist and my intention was to report their plight to the West." Luke finished his beer and pulled out a Gauloise. He resumed as he exhaled the smoke, "So he walks up to me and lands a fist across my head. Gwah! Just like that." He demonstrated with a sweep of his hand. "'You think I am stoopid?'" he growls. In fact, by then I was certain he was just that—stoopid. But again I said nothing. From then on he became quite belligerent. No answer would satisfy him despite the fact that I was actually being quite truthful. After a few beatings they dragged me back to the room and left me there to stew. By sundown—I could tell by a small crack in the window that had been boarded up from the outside—I started giving up hope. It dawned on me that I might be there for quite a while. If, that is, I were ever to be freed. A guard brought me sandwiches and water. 'You eat' he said. Fattening me up for the slaughter, no doubt." Luke stopped to reflect. "By then I was finished." His eyes lowered. "Like you, sunshine, I was so exhausted I also ended up on the filthy mattress." He looked up at her, grinning.

Rasha had sat motionless, listening, reluctant to interrupt lest he lose momentum in his narrative.

"It went on like this for three . . . four days? Beatings and isolation, then more beatings. Sometimes, they'd come to the room, peer at me through an open door, as if I were a specimen on show. I had no clue what they were saying but hoped, against hope, that they were debating my release. I'd given them all the information they needed to check my credentials. I even expected the British Embassy at some stage to intercede on my behalf. It hadn't dawned on me that my incarceration could be long-term. Up until then, I couldn't accept the possibility that I might never see you again." His eyes locked with hers. "I shouldn't be telling you this, but now that I'm here I guess there's no harm." He stopped. "I could hear them . . ." he began vaguely. "I could hear their pleas and cries as they were beaten up. The other captives." Pity flashed across his face. He shook his head as if to dispel his recollections. "Anyway . . . I had a lot of time to think. I realized how right you'd actually been in cautioning me. How short-sighted *I* had been not to listen. It dawned on me that I'd come along like a moron expecting you to snap out of your situation when, there I was, in my cell, totally incapacitated. I understood what you meant by being helpless. You see, sunshine, when you live in a peaceful, stable country like I've been, you can't imagine that order, humanity and decency can be pulverized so completely." He stopped. "I sound pedantic, don't I?"

She passed her fingers through his hair, "No, Luke, you don't." Her voice was hoarse.

Luke stared ahead, lost in thought. "I came face to face with the Luke that I'd been and didn't much like what I saw . . . A presumptuous, arrogant guy full of grudges and reproach. One who expected family, friends, and lover to live up to his standards. His mother should've been more loyal, more loving. His father, less conformist, more demonstrative . . . more motivated. And Rasha, dear Rasha, with a bit of tweaking, could be the perfect woman for him. The Luke I saw understood you better than you understood yourself, and had your family sussed out in the blink of an eye. Clever Luke thought he had a solution for everything. But there he was, ironically, trapped in a snare of his own stupid making."

When he stopped, Rasha feared he wouldn't go on. "How did you get out?" she prodded him.

"They let me go." Luke lit up and opened another beer. "Oddly enough, it was when I'd decided to come to terms with my actual situation full on. Every time I'd heard the key turn in the lock, I'd braced myself for more beatings. But this morning, I was hauled into a car and driven for miles. Again blindfolded. I thought to myself, that was it. I was dead meat. We sped through traffic and busy streets, the driver laying on the horn like a lunatic. The car took a sharp turn and stopped with a jerk. The man beside me pulled me out, threw me on a sidewalk and gave me a kick in the ribs for good measure. Then . . . then I heard the door shut and the car move away, a tyre screeching very close to my ear. I just stayed there for a minute, not knowing what was going on. I half-expected to be facing an execution squad. When nothing happened I lifted the blindfold off." Luke took a swig of his beer and swallowed hard. "Across the road, a bunch of young kids had gathered, watching me. I got up and walked across to them. They weren't a bit fazed by my appearance. As if it were commonplace for men to be thrown out of cars and left for dead." He drew on his cigarette. "Guess who I thought of right then and there?"

"Lucien and Dominic."

Luke smiled. "Clever girl."

Rasha shrugged. "Where were you?"

"One of them told me I was in Msaitbeh. Is that how you pronounce it?"

"That's right, Msaitbeh."

"I asked where I could find a taxi and they led me to a café where a couple of men were playing backgammon and sipping coffee. I remember thinking then that they may very well have been doing just that for the period that I was holed up in my cell. Even now, as we sit here and talk about it, Rasha, there are countless hostages dreaming of, desperate for, their freedom."

"I know, Luke. That's the tragedy."

"Anyway. The two men sized me up. Then, ironically, the one with the lame leg turned out to be the driver. I told him I had no cash. But he knew the Commodore, understood that I was a sahafi, and was only too willing to take me back and pocket his fee from the hotel. When I got there, I called Fuad and he came to pick me up with Karim. And here I am."

"Didn't anyone tell you why you were being released?"

Luke smirked. "No, sunshine, nor did I care to ask. Remember, I didn't know that was the case until after they'd left."

Rasha thought awhile. "And you saw no new faces there? No one else came to see you?"

Luke frowned. "No, not that I recall. Why do you ask?"

"Just wondering." Rasha had hoped to establish whether Ahmed had anything to do with Luke's release, but she felt it was not the time to mention her intervention. They were quiet for what seemed a very long time, each lost in thought.

"Do me a favour, open the curtains," Luke said at last, snapping them both back to the moment.

"Sure." Rasha jumped to her feet and walked to the window. The fading daylight cast up her lean and diminutive silhouette.

"You're so beautiful, you know that? Come here. Lie down next to me."

She did.

Wincing with pain, Luke wrapped an arm around her. "It feels so good to hold you." He took a deep breath. "Did you ever think you'd see me again?" he asked hesitantly as if her expectations could have had any bearing on the final outcome.

"I never lost hope, Luke. I couldn't . . ." she said quietly, craning her neck to catch a glimpse of him. A tear hung in the corner of his eye. He turned her face away gently, so she would not see.

"The strangest thing is I . . . I can't tell whether I was actually scared at any point. I mean, really scared. At first, I couldn't accept what had happened. I couldn't believe *I* was now a hostage. Then different thoughts and emotions came over me. I thought of you over and over. Not all the time . . . more in fragments . . . I'd have flashbacks of us in Paris . . . sometimes of myself in boarding school. At times I'd see your face, stern and pained, warning me about situations my recklessness might get me into. First and foremost in my mind was to get out, apologize to you for all I'd said, all I'd claimed to know. Make amends." His hand brushed against hers. "You'd think that fear overtakes you on its own, with its own force. But it doesn't. It drags along confusion, helplessness and disbelief. It's as if it equips itself with different emotions that serve to sustain it and disguise it all at once." He stopped. "Never had I tried to manipulate my mind so strongly. Never before did I have to prime it to interpret and accept my predicament. As if my survival, my life, depended on it."

"Mind game."

"What did you say?"

"You were playing a mind game."

"That's it." Then he repeated pensively, "I was playing mind games."

Rasha jerked her head.

"What is it?" Luke snapped, alarmed.

"Sorry, I didn't mean to startle you. I just heard the front door. It must be Karim."

She rose from the bed and walked towards the entrance.

"How is he?" he asked.

"He hasn't eaten."

Karim held up a bag of sandwiches. "*Shawarma*! You also look like you could do with some food."

"I'll get some plates."

"I need to bandage his chest."

"Can I get him to eat first?"

"Sure."

They gathered in Luke's bedroom heartily consuming the sandwiches drenched in *tahini* and bulging with onions, tomatoes, radishes and parsley. Karim had the presence of mind to bring along some Cokes to wash down the saltiness of the meat and vegetables. He refrained from asking questions, presuming perhaps that Luke would have already reported his ordeal to Rasha. In all likelihood, he was counting on getting the details from her in due course.

Wordlessly, he and Rasha proceeded to bandage Luke's chest. She holding him up while Karim wrapped the gauze around him.

"Not too tight," Luke urged them.

"It'll have to be up to a point," Karim objected. "Otherwise, it serves no purpose."

"Hang on," he blurted out.

Before Rasha had had the chance to help him, he had hauled his legs off the bed and sat up. She guessed it was because he could not bear lying down and being tended to. It was as if he was gasping for air.

"Okay," he finally said feebly. "You can go ahead now."

Karim glanced over at Rasha behind Luke's back and winked, perhaps as a warning that unusual or sudden reactions from Luke were to be expected and should go unheeded.

"How does that feel now?" Karim asked when he had finished.

Luke tried to straighten up then screwed up his face. "Like a bloody corset."

Karim reached into his case and pulled out a box of tablets. "Some antibiotics. To be taken three times a day after meals." He pulled one out and handed it to Luke who swallowed it with a swig of Coke.

They eased him back onto the bed.

"Can I get you anything?" Karim asked.

Luke shook his head.

"I'll see you tomorrow then. Fuad will be back shortly. Give me a call, anytime, if you feel the need to."

"I appreciate all you've done, Karim" Luke said, extending his hand.

He took it. "Don't mention it." With a subtle tilt of the head, Karim motioned for Rasha to follow him outside.

"Has he said anything?" he asked.

"Only that he was taken at a roadblock. He doesn't know who they were. It's irrelevant anyway. They accused him of being a spy and confiscated his passport, press card and camera." She crossed her arms. "As for the beatings . . ." Her eyes stung. "Well, you've seen the damage yourself."

"He can't stay, Rasha. We'll have to get him out of the country," Karim murmured.

Rasha nodded, palms to her eyes.

"The consulate will have closed by now. I'll phone tomorrow morning and find out what documents they require. Has he still got his return ticket?"

"I suppose so. I doubt he would've had it on him. In fact, yes," she said, recalling that the day he went missing she had rummaged through his room. "It's there. I've seen it."

"We'll have to look into earlier flights. If you get the chance, check when he's booked for. We'll contact the airlines once we know how long it will take for his travel documents."

Rasha leaned against the wall and let out a heavy sigh. "He had an open ticket," she said, more like an afterthought.

"It's getting late. When will you be home?"

Rasha paused, aware that her reply would be badly received. "Tomorrow."

"Rasha . . ."

She held out a hand. "I'm not leaving him in this state. I need to see him through one night. That's all."

Karim theatrically scratched the nape of his neck. It would be up to him to deal with his parents. "What should I tell Baba and Mama?"

"The truth," she retorted unequivocally. "That Luke is back. That he's badly injured and beaten up and that he needs care. I'll be here to provide it."

"Are you sure about this? Don't get me wrong, Rasha, I'm all with you. But are you absolutely certain that's the way you should go about it?"

She swallowed, but apprehension and deep sadness stuck in her throat. "There's no turning back now

Karimo. What's done is done. And whichever way they decide to take the truth, it won't change things. I'm not giving him up. Not for Baba, not for Mama, not for anyone. Ever."

Karim watched her intently, then, with some resignation, he nodded. "I'll see you tomorrow," he finally said, planting a kiss on her cheek.

She gave him a hug. "Thank you Karimo. Thank you for all you've done."

Rasha stopped outside Luke's bedroom, knowing that the minute she stepped in she would be crossing the Rubicon. She had made her choice, but had yet to experience its repercussions in the form of her father's wrath and her mother's disappointment. Nevertheless, that very moment, she knew beyond doubt that it was with Luke that she belonged on his first night of freedom.

There was silence. Blackness had seeped through the glass panes mingling confusedly with the darkness within. She approached him on tiptoes and could just make out his face bathed in serenity, eyes shut. On the bedside table, one of the foil casings of the sedatives lay empty. He must have taken one when she and Karim had their backs turned. He would not admit exhaustion or acute pain to their faces, concealing them deftly along with other scars that one day would probably rise to the surface.

She settled as comfortably as she could in the armchair by his bed. For a long stretch, she listened to his groans, whimpers, and empty protestations. He twisted and turned, letting out a cry of pain as he did so. This time round, instead of jumping up to comfort him, she let him be. Touching him might startle him into wakefulness. Speaking to him might rouse him when sleep could prove more cathartic than reassurance. Perhaps in his fitful sleep he would relive and cast away his torment.

Consolation will come by daylight when he realizes it was now just a bad dream.

Chapter Thirteen

◆

"Will you marry me?" The startling words reached her as she rose to consciousness. Her body uncoiled in halting movements, aching and stiff. Her eyes felt heavy, crying out for rest, spurning visual stimulation. When she managed to force them open, she saw Luke propped up against a pillow, watching her.

Rasha straightened up with a jerk and felt her lower back seize. She winced.

"Luke! Have you been awake long?"

"Long enough to think things over."

She twisted in the armchair. "How are you feeling?"

"Enchanted. Overjoyed," he replied, flashing an earnest smile.

"Isn't it a bit early to be flippant?" Rasha retorted, tired and on edge.

"Absolutely. That's why I can only be resolutely dead serious."

Her eyes narrowed to slits. "How many sedatives did you take, Luke?"

He let out a hearty laugh, then clutched his side in pain. "Are you going to answer my question?"

"What question?" Rasha asked, the conversation proving laborious in her daze.

"Rasha Corleone a.k.a. Halwani. Will you be my wife?"

She sat up, her gaze steady on him.

"I'll serenade you from a minaret," he quipped with an enticing voice.

A nervous laugh escaped her throat. She stayed pinned to the armchair, savouring the face of her lover, the brightness that had come over it, the unmitigated joy it exuded. How she loved it, how she adored its gentleness, its beauty! A sense of euphoria crept through her, and she could barely pronounce the word that would always fall short of the intensity that she felt.

"Oh yes, Luke Elliott. Yes!"

On impulse, she jumped up and carelessly threw her weight by his side, showering him with kisses.

"Oh and the minaret part. You do realize I was only joking?"

She giggled. "I certainly hope so."

Luke caressed her cheek. "Are you sure you'd want to spend the rest of your life with a wilful, hard-headed bigot?"

"You're not a bigot," Rasha replied smiling.

"But wilful and hard-headed, is that it?"

"We all have our shortcomings," she giggled.

"Thanks," he said flatly. "Well, now I suppose I'll have to ask your father for your hand in marriage." A sigh escaped his lips. "Do you think I'm up to the challenge?"

Rasha thought of the impossible hurdle they had to overcome. What Luke did not know was that she would first have to justify to her parents her spending the night away from home.

"I'll have to pave the way," she finally said out loud. "By the time you get to speak to him, who knows, I may have done all the hard work for you."

Her new confidence sprang from the fact that the improbable had already occurred with Luke's release. Who is to say she would lose out in the oncoming battle? There was a chance, and a good one, that she may fare well. Perhaps she had become a good negotiator.

Outside the entrance to her building, Rasha looked up at their apartment, shielding her eyes from the mid-morning sun. So much had happened in the short span since she had left it a day ago that she already felt removed from it.

She turned the key in the door and stepped into ominous stillness. Trepidation made her wish momentarily that her father was out, and that she would be allowed the time to steel herself for the confrontation. Despite the fact that since she had left Luke, she had been rehearsing her speech ad nauseam.

She shut the door gently, trying to make no sound. When she turned, her mother stood facing her, in her nightdress, rheumy-eyed and careworn.

"Mama, you startled me," Rasha exclaimed, palm to her chest.

Nuha dipped her head. Without a word, she walked up to Rasha and wrapped her in her arms.

Rasha settled in her embrace, baffled. "What's wrong? Has something happened?"

She heard Nuha snivel. "I was worried about you," she replied in a weak voice.

There was more to her admission, Rasha knew. Nuha's anxiousness was unjustified, almost excessive, when she knew Rasha was at Fuad's. There was no reason to be concerned about Rasha's safety. She must have had a premonition that their home situation was about to change, that their family unit was teetering on uncertain ground.

Nuha drew a deep sigh, moving slightly away, her hands steady on Rasha's shoulders. "How is he?"

"As well as can be expected under the circumstances."

Nuha nodded. "Your father's been waiting. He's in the family room."

Rasha cast a glance down the passage.

"Do you want me to come in with you?" her mother asked.

"I think it would be best, yes."

Contrary to what Rasha would have wished, there was no time to prime her mother for the news.

Had she not been told that her father was in the living room, Rasha would never have guessed that he was there. As she approached, the familiar crackle of the radio and the rustle of the newspaper were absent. With no forewarning of a presence, her mission grew more portentous.

She entered the room, her mother on her heels, and glimpsed her father seated in a corner, an open ledger neatly placed on the coffee table before him. He did not look up. It must take an iron will to resist impulse, Rasha thought.

"Baba?" she started tentatively.

He eyed her over his reading glasses, eyebrows hovering high above their rim.

"Sit down, Rasha."

He was already groomed for the day in grey pants, a navy blue shirt, and clean-shaven. Rasha guessed that he had postponed any meeting he might have had until such time as she came home and he had his say. Her actions had clearly disrupted his schedule. A dreadful start.

"If your intention is to test my patience, Rasha, you've succeeded," Amin began sternly.

"It isn't, Baba. I never meant to disrespect you or Mama." She stopped, half-expecting him to interject, as he often did. But he sat immobile, eyes darting. His reaction, or lack of it, tripped her up, leaving her hopelessly tongue-tied. She cleared her throat. "My intention was simply to lend my help where help was needed."

"At the cost of placing the family's reputation at stake."

"Nothing improper took place, Baba," she said, meaning to vindicate herself, but uneasy with her statement.

Amin removed his glasses and placed them squarely on the ledger.

"I will not be lied to anymore, Rasha."

"But, Baba . . ."

"Before you dig a deeper hole for yourself, be aware that your mother has informed me of the truth."

Rasha sought her mother's gaze, but Nuha kept her eyes lowered.

"Call your mother a liar if you wish, but according to her, this Englishman means more to you than you led us to believe."

Silence was Rasha's best defence. She dropped her head and before she could stop herself, the words slipped through her lips, "He wants to marry me."

"I beg your pardon?" Caustic cynicism tinged his tone of voice. His neck stretched forward in disbelief.

Rasha looked at him demurely. "He asked me to marry him."

"Out of the question!" Amin blurted out.

During any other exchange, this would have been the point where Rasha would resign herself to her lot and retreat. But not this time. The stakes were too high to fold her hand.

"Why not, Baba?" Her voice was soft. She forced back the tears.

"Well," Amin proceeded in a tone that came across to Rasha as mocking, "Let me see . . ." He spread the fingers of one hand in the air. "One," he pressed a forefinger to the other, "Because we know nothing about him or his family, or where he comes from . . ." By that, Rasha understood that he did not simplistically mean the country of origin. "Two, because he's not one of us," signifying Lebanese and Muslim, "And knows nothing about our culture. Three, for the simple reason that I, personally, don't know him." His palm struck his chest. "And . . . and if I were *ever* to do so I cannot guarantee that I'd want him for a son-in-law. Does that answer your question?"

All at once, Rasha's confidence in her negotiating skills crumbled. Her father's case, though predictable, was difficult to contest. She resorted to a different tack. Instead of Luke, she put herself in the forefront of the discussion.

"Habibi Baba," she began in an attempt to cajole him, "I understand your concern. I appreciate your wish to ensure the best for me . . . and for Karim. But I'm a twenty-five-year-old woman and not getting younger. The husband you may have dreamt up for me hasn't come along and may never do so. At my age, Mama had already had one child . . ."

Amin interjected, "That's a poor reason to settle for second-best."

"I'm not settling for second-best." The words flew out of her mouth before she could stop them.

He frowned. "Do you mean to tell me that you're in love with him?"

"Yes," she mumbled.

"Impossible!" He exclaimed sitting ramrod straight.

"Why is it so impossible? He's a decent, honest, kind person . . ."

"Because," Amin leaned forward, "I cannot believe you would choose a man who will come between you and your family."

"He won't."

"Oh yes he will. And if you must know why, It's because I will never sanction this marriage."

When Nuha, at last, tried to object, he stopped her. "You approach this any way you want," he said to his wife. "I *am*, and will always be against this marriage," he reiterated, unmoved by her protestation.

"What about the war?" Rasha said out of nowhere.

Amin squinted at her. "What does the war have to do with this?"

"Everything, Baba. Despite your good intentions, your aspirations for me, the fact remains that I may not live *long* enough to be married." She stopped for effect. But in truth, the tears she had fought back choked her.

"Rasha, habibti. God forbid!" Her mother said shakily reaching out for her daughter's hand.

"It's a fact, Mama. It *can* happen. My life and Karim's in this country have not been the run-of-the-mill existence of adolescents or adults elsewhere in the world. We've been living through fear and danger. We were deprived periods of happiness you took for granted in your days. And we managed. We respected your wishes and principles, and did as we were told. You can't say we didn't." Rasha paused for breath. "But we can't all go on pretending that destiny is in our hands, that everything is perfect, and that things will go our way. We cannot delude ourselves into thinking that our values and expectations are easily reachable. There are many people who probably at one stage or another pleaded as desperately as you do every day for divine protection, Mama. But they weren't spared, were they? Remember what happened to May?" Her eyes swung to Nuha's. "What prevents me or Karim ending up the same way she did?"

"Rasha, stop it!" Nuha retorted, patently unsettled by a recollection of Karim's girlfriend.

"Why? Because it's a disturbing thought? We sit here arguing whether Luke is the right person for me or not. Has it crossed your mind, or Baba's, that by tomorrow, Luke may never be an issue? It nearly happened, didn't it? He *was* kidnapped, wasn't he? The same could happen to me, couldn't it?"

Amin folded his glasses and stowed them in their case. He closed the ledger, and made to leave.

"Baba," Rasha insisted, following him with her eyes, "All I'm asking for is a taste of true happiness while I have the chance."

"I *will not* enter this discussion," Amin finally murmured, his back to her as he disappeared out the door.

His exit was quick, and catching a glimpse of him as he vanished, Rasha was certain she had seen his eyes redden.

Nuha, feeling at a complete loss, dabbed her eyes with a crumpled-up tissue. Her cheeks suddenly appeared sunken, her face flaccid. Could worry or unhappiness age a person so, overnight? Rasha looked down at her mother's hands, crossed as if in submission in her lap. She reached for one and squeezed it.

"Don't cry, Mama. Things aren't as bad as they seem. Nobody's died, no one's been injured. It's not so terrible that I'm marrying someone Baba doesn't approve of. You don't really disapprove of Luke, do you?"

Nuha tapped Rasha's hand lightly, shaking her head.

"It's not such a calamity that this family won't be able to survive it, is it?"

"But your father . . ." Nuha's voice quavered. "And you'll be so far away . . ."

"Not for a while. I won't be leaving for awhile. We still have time, and I'll fly you over to see me wherever we end up. I don't believe that you'd let Baba stop you from doing so, would you?" Rasha sought her mother's gaze.

A faint smile rose to Nuha's lips. "No," she replied, her expression suggesting that there was no way anyone could step in between her and her daughter.

"I've been thinking it over. Do you want to hear my plan? Well, Luke would have to leave as soon as we've got his papers in order, since the kidnappers have taken his passport. I'll finish the year at AUB then move in with Hana until we're ready to be married. I hope that by then Baba would've, by some miracle, accepted the situation and agreed to it. We've still got another year to go . . ."

"Seven months," Nuha interjected, her eyes growing moist at the prospect of Rasha leaving.

"It's still seven months. At least it's not tomorrow."

Nuha gradually regained her composure. "Are you absolutely sure about this?"

"Without a doubt, Mama."

"And if he makes you unhappy?"

"I'll come running back to you," Rasha said smiling.

"He'd better not." Nuha hugged Rasha tightly. "He'd better not hurt my little girl."

A week flew by as Rasha and Karim made arrangements for Luke's return to Paris. Except for one visit to the hospital for X-rays and a general checkup, Luke was housebound and did not seem to mind. As the day of his departure approached, Rasha called Carol and informed her of what had happened. Luke was all right, she assured her without mentioning two broken ribs and the bruising which was unlikely to disappear before he reached Paris. He was booked and confirmed on a morning flight, and Rasha could say with near-certainty that the situation was calm enough for the airport to remain open.

There were no recriminations on Carol's part. Not that Rasha really expected any. Carol seemed quite sedate at the other end of the phone line, though it was clear to Rasha that she would be awaiting Luke's safe arrival with bated breath. When Rasha apologized for Luke's ordeal, Carol waved it off with, "What do you expect? He never listens to anyone . . . ever."

With their parting looming close, Rasha felt none of the sadness that she had experienced in Paris. Her nerves frayed by the preparations and the determination to keep Luke safe, she could not wait for the day he boarded the plane out of Beirut. It was not easy for her to persuade him that she would follow. Concerned about her safety, he wanted her to leave with him and was adamant that they should marry soon after arriving in Paris. Eventually, she convinced him that she had to tie up loose ends, that it would be more beneficial to both of them if she were to fly out in due course, once she had smoothed matters out with her father. "Can it possibly be so hard for your father to agree to see me?" Luke had asked her, clearly sensing the blow of a rebuff. Rasha had not answered. There was no point.

On the break of a chilly and still Tuesday morning, with the muffled sound of mortars pounding with cruel persistence in the far distance, Hassan parked his taxi at the entrance of Fuad's building, and waited. As Luke, Karim and Rasha piled into his car, they discovered that he had taken on an unexpected passenger, Michael.

"Just to make sure he gets off without a hitch," Michael said with a sly smile.

In total knowing silence, they sat motionless while the experienced driver forged his way through haunted streets. They handed their identity cards wordlessly at roadblocks, Michael flashing his press card with the confidence of a person to whom conflict was old hat. They hit a bottleneck on the airport road as motorists honked and swerved to gain way, and cars stopped wherever they could, like an army of frantic ants, to disgorge their passengers.

Rasha had to say her goodbyes to Luke in full view of the throng, as travellers only were allowed along a covered pathway that led into the airport terminal. Luke held her tightly, and she felt her heart about to burst through her chest. "Just go . . . go safely," she murmured with some urgency. Michael waved a permit which allowed him to escort Luke as far as Passport Control. "For good measure," he said to Rasha.

Fifteen or so minutes passed before Michael re-emerged giving the thumbs up. He dug his hands into his pockets. "He's gone through."

"I'd still like to wait if you don't mind," Rasha said pensively, her heart weighed down with emptiness.

"I'm in no rush." Michael leaned against Hassan's car and lit a cigarette.

A good hour later, the Middle East Airlines plane to Paris thrust its nose up into greyness and disappeared through thick clouds. Arms crossed, eyes following the jet, Rasha let out a breath. With the unmistakable tone of someone at once relieved of a heavy bane, she finally said, "Let's go home."

Home it was. As it had been before Luke's arrival. Like a machine running smoothly on well-oiled cogs but emitting a muffled undefined rumble from within. Everything had changed. Rasha had changed. Suddenly possessed with a sense of purpose, she went about her daily life with the stoicism of a captive who had been assured liberation. However much her freedom was tinged with melancholy.

Her engagement to Luke was in the abstract. There was none of the fanfare that surrounded such an event. In fact, there had been no event at all. There was no ring, no announcement. For Amin's sake, Nuha had advised Rasha not to mention it to family or friends. At least not until her departure date drew closer. Rasha agreed to discretion simply because it did not compromise her or Luke. Their promise was ironclad and she saw no harm in respecting her mother's simple wish to spare herself and Amin unsolicited advice or idle gossip.

When the family gathered at mealtimes, there was no mention of Luke. Amin seemed to have grown convinced that Rasha had gotten over him as if he had been a bout of the flu. She let it go at that, intending sooner or later to broach the subject again. But she no longer received Luke's phone calls in secrecy and readily left the phone to ring until someone else picked it up. Even if it had to be her father. He would then grow momentarily somber and would ignore her for the rest of the day.

The battle was being fought in hushed tones, between her parents, as Nuha strove to make the pending separation an amicable affair and to avoid any rift in the family. Occasionally, Rasha would question her mother about her conversations with Amin, but more often than not she let it pass, hoping that Nuha was making good progress on her behalf. It was neither out of cowardice nor dependence that Rasha stood back. But rather out of the knowledge that so long as she was not allowed to communicate with her father as an equal, she would be eternally stonewalled.

Although Nuha fought fiercely in her daughter's corner, Rasha realized she did so with a heavy heart and some reservation. Her mother had taken the time to absorb the implications of Rasha's relationship with Luke, having grown aware of it the day after—perhaps even the minute—Luke had arrived, that first morning in the kitchen while nonchalantly adding 'tomatoes' to her shopping list. She had made use of that duration to get her mind around Rasha's love for Luke. She had put all her efforts into understanding her only daughter's despair because, reflected in Rasha's eyes, she could see herself as a young woman hopelessly in love. So, rather than be concerned about her father who spared himself any aggravation through outright denial, Rasha's heart went out to her mother who acknowledged Rasha's wish and took it upon herself to respect it—even if it meant giving in to the physical distance that would splay itself between her and her only daughter. It was Nuha's quiet but steadfast support that threatened to pull Rasha's spirits down, leading her to look upon the few months she had left in the bosom of her family with some nostalgia.

Rasha bided her time. Having thanked Youssef for his help and having asked him to convey her deep-felt gratitude to his brother, her relationship with her student resumed as normal. After Luke's release, it was pointless to probe into Ahmed's intervention. Whether or not he had pulled some strings was irrelevant, and Rasha's eagerness to put the whole episode and the associations it entailed behind her stopped her from delving too deeply. With Luke gone, her life revolved once again around her family and the university. She never saw Michael again, nor did she set foot in Fuad's apartment, intentionally avoiding places that reminded her of Luke's stay in Beirut.

Despite their long separation, Rasha felt none of the insecurity she had experienced the first time they were apart. She could no longer question his love for her—his visit to Beirut being the ultimate expression of his sincerity—or hers for him. Their devotion to each other had been tested not only by time but also by tribulation, as his ordeal had forged a solid bond between them. They had met halfway, she reasoned: she, by stepping out of the family mould and he, by acknowledging her fears. They had mutual respect for each other's views and differences.

So it was with unwavering confidence that Rasha set out preparing for her trip with Nuha's help. As June drew closer, Rasha phoned Hana.

"Are you serious? You're marrying him?" Hana whooped with delight.

"Yes, Auntie Hana."

"How wonderful!" Then more cautiously, "Are you absolutely sure?"

Rasha smiled. "Positive."

"What about your father?"

"We're still working on him."

"And your mother?"

"She's right here. She's picking up the other phone."

In a conference call which took the tone of a hen party, the three women squealed, joked, and laughed across the miles that separated them. It was agreed that Rasha would stay with Hana in Paris until her wedding arrangements were underway, at which point Hana may even have to put up Amin (thumbs crossed), Nuha and Karim.

Overjoyed by the prospect of her family meeting up in Paris, Hana broke into tears. Between sobs, she laughed hysterically, calling herself a silly old fool who let her emotions get the better of her. As their conversation drew to a close, Rasha had the feeling that things would go smoothly, that everything was under control and would go according to plan.

It was not to be. While she anticipated wrapping up her life into a neat little parcel before starting a new one with Luke, events blew her expectations right out of the water. On an evening in early June, as the family watched a news broadcast on Israeli air raids in South Lebanon, Amin unexpectedly asked Karim to switch off the TV.

He then removed his glasses and reclined against the sofa, folding the 'abaya around his chest. "Are you going to tell her or shall I?" he finally said to Nuha.

"You tell her," Nuha replied shakily as she reached for a tissue.

Rasha's heart pounded. "Tell me what?"

Amin cleared his throat. "Your mother and I have decided that you should leave for Paris as soon as possible."

Ice coursed through Rasha's veins. Her father sending her off to Paris? It was an all-too-sudden turn of events that made her suspicious.

"But . . . but I don't understand. What's wrong? I mean . . . how come . . . so soon?"

"They've shut down the airport, Rasha." Nuha dabbed her eyes.

"I know, Mama, but it's only because of the air raids. It'll reopen soon. I have until the end of June."

Nuha tilted her head to one side, dubious. "It might not reopen. Not for a while at least. The situation might get worse. There are rumours of another Israeli invasion."

"But that's happened before. It didn't last long."

"This time . . ." Nuha hesitated, "This time, they say, they might go in as far as Beirut."

Rasha's eyes widened. "We've never paid attention to rumours before! They can't possibly invade the capital!"

Amin held out a hand to stop the speculation. "We're not taking any chances."

"Well . . . what about Karim?" she asked, her gaze flitting between him and her parents.

Before her brother could reply, Amin said, "Karim is staying."

Rasha was dumbfounded. "How come?"

"I don't *want* to leave, Rasha." Karim gave her a stern look implying that she should not press the issue, for his sake and hers.

It was all too much. Too soon. Rasha was being handed her wish on a silver platter but could not take it at face value.

Her heart pounded. "What about you?" she croaked, fixing her gaze on her parents.

Palms upturned, Amin replied flatly, "We're staying, naturally."

She was speechless. What was she to do? Leave? Desert her family knowing full well that they would be running into grave danger?

"Rasha," her father pronounced, snapping her out of her introspection.

She raised her head. "Yes, Baba."

"I want you to understand that by doing this, in no way am I going back on my word. I'm *very* disappointed with your choice of a husband. I'm not sending you *to* him . . ." he spoke semantics ". . . I'm simply sending you *away* from here. For your own safety. Paris is the obvious choice with your aunt there to look after you."

Whatever his reasons, his decision was a step further in the direction she desired.

"So I'll be travelling alone?"

"We'll take you to the Port of Jounieh."

From that evening, the days rolled into each other at a horrific speed. Having submitted her month's notice to the university, Rasha packed up her study and bade farewell to her colleagues during a small and subdued gathering in her office. Her departure, like those of others escaping the deterioration of life in Lebanon, was a minor detail in the large scheme of things but one that underscored the aggravated situation in the country. Many had decided to flee and as usual many stayed, bracing themselves for the unspeakable.

While she went through the motions, her finger remained on the pulse. She kept one ear to the ground for developments of the Israeli incursion. She prodded family and friends for their opinions. All in an effort to debunk the rumour that Beirut would be taken. All in a desperate attempt to reassure herself that her parents and Karim were not in certain danger.

But by then the Israelis had taken the South, moved through the Upper-Chouf in Mukhtara, Barouk, Baakline and Ain Zhalta. They were forging ahead and no one could say for certain when they would stop.

A call came through from Luke urging her to get out. He would be waiting for her at Charles-de-Gaulle as soon as he had received details of her flight.

"What about your parents, and Karim?" he asked.

"They're staying, Luke."

"Christ!"

"Luke, what's going to happen?"

"I don't know, sunshine. Your guess is a good as mine. But it doesn't look good."

One question kept cropping up, over and over, with no hope of it ever being answered: how does she brace herself to leave her home knowing that the people she cherishes linger behind at great risk?

On the eve of her departure, once her parents had turned in for the night, Rasha crept into Karim's room. He lay on his back, hands clasped behind his head.

"Are you asleep?"

He propped himself up on an elbow. "No."

She sat silently on the edge of his bed. After a while she said, "You know, Karimo, I never expected to leave like this."

"You'll be fine."

"It's not me I'm worried about. It's you . . . Baba, Mama . . . All of you." Her lip quivered.

"You got what you wanted. Personally, I never thought I'd see the day when Baba would be sending you off to Paris," he sniggered.

"Then why don't I feel good about it?"

Karim tapped her hand. "Once you get there, you'll see, you'll forget all about us."

Tears welled up in her eyes. "Never."

He swung his legs off the bed and held her to him as she shook uncontrollably. "Look out for a job for me in Paris, will you?" he requested in a conciliatory tone of voice.

"Promise me you'll look after them and yourself, Karimo," she murmured.

"I promise."

As the sun rose faithfully on Lebanon that June morning, not a shred of the fledgling light it offered could dispel the darkness in people's hearts. Beirut still slumbered in weariness and foreboding as Rasha and her family climbed into the taxi that would take them to Jounieh. She sat in the back between Karim and her mother while Amin occupied the passenger seat. As the car pulled away, Rasha turned round for a final glimpse of the neighbourhood that had been her home through peacetime and hell.

As they ventured further, evidence of the carnage inflicted in the latest days of air raids and shelling presented itself in stark nakedness. Exhausted fighters manned roadblocks, weapons at the ready for more battles after the brief lull. They looked frightened, in shock.

Under normal circumstances, there would be chatter in the car about plans to meet again, instructions for travel, and verbal commissions to the ones waiting at the other end. But neither Rasha nor her family could bring themselves to speak. Nuha held her daughter's hand tightly, squeezing it now and then when a disturbing thought flashed in her mind. Rasha stared forward, her head lolling from side to side, as the taxi driver failed to circle potholes the size of craters.

At the port of Jounieh they were once again sucked into a whirlwind of human panic and pandemonium. The dread and despair etched on the faces of passengers and well-wishers spoke of a collective misery bringing strangers together in the persecution of war.

This time, there were no tugboats. The resilient civilians had fine-tuned their manner of evacuation, proudly chartering ferries to cross the expanse to Cyprus. Rasha turned her back to the mouth of the sturdy vessel as she embraced her mother who shed her tears uncontrollably, shamelessly. Karim walked up to them and hugged them both, gently moving his mother away under his wing so Rasha could bid her father farewell.

Amin stood erect holding Rasha's suitcase.

"Baba . . ." she said, and could not go on. The words choked her and bitter tears flowed down her cheeks.

He set the suitcase down and held out his arms to her. She tucked her head against his chest and sobbed.

"It's time to go, habibti . . ." his voice broke off mid-sentence.

Rasha picked up her suitcase and took a few steps towards the gangplank. When she turned for the last time, she saw her father with his back to her, bent, head down. Nuha moved to his side and put an arm around him. Karim, alone, followed his sister with his eyes, motioning with a hand for her to move on . . . to move on.

As the ferry pulled away from the pier, Rasha, along with the other passengers, stood by the rails, looking back on the dear ones they were leaving behind against a backdrop of smoke and carnage. Before she lost sight of them, her parents' and Karim's faces reflected a familiar expression. She had seen those same faces in her dream, drawn with sadness and pain as Luke reached out for her hand to take her for a walk.

Too far to speak the last words she had forgotten to convey to them, she repeated them in her mind, in the hope that the wind would carry them like fluttering leaves and deliver them to her beloved family.

I'll be back.